a Look Behind the Mask

a Pride & Prejudice
variation

TIFFANY THOMAS

ACKNOWLEDGMENTS

First, I want to thank the kind people who encouraged me to write this story. In the beginning, I was discouraged by some unkind reviews. There were many who reached out, saddened by the fact that I would not be finishing it. Without their encouragement, this book would never have existed in its entirety.

Second, I want to thank my sister, Michelle. Without her amazing dedication to the English

Finally, this book is dedicated to Phillip, my own Mr. Darcy, without who sees behind my own mask and loves me anyway.

Table of Contents

Prologue

Hertfordshire, September 1803

Elizabeth Bennet skipped down the path from Longbourn, her father's estate house, as she headed out for her morning walk. At thirteen years old, Lizzy knew that her remaining days of skipping, running, and other unladylike behaviors were few in number. Her elder sister, Jane, had recently come out to the local society, and from Lizzy's perspective, it was dreadful.

Fifteen-year-old Jane required fittings for the plethora of dresses that their mother Fanny Bennet insisted were imperative for a daughter as beautiful as Jane. Jane, her mother declared, had a beauty that would lead to a great match if only she would follow all of her mother's edicts regarding appropriate behavior for a gentleman's daughter. Not being the daughter of a gentleman herself was immaterial, in Fanny's mind.

Opportunities to escape Longbourn and its noise were becoming increasingly rare as there had been no children born since Lydia's entrance to the world eight years prior. Longbourn was entailed outside the female line, and an unknown cousin was due to inherit should Thomas Bennet not birth a son. Fanny Bennet's nerves had become increasingly agitated with each girl child she bore, and now it was clear that her childbearing days were over.

While Fanny loved all of her girls, she was quite vocal about her heightened love for Jane and seven-year-old Lydia. Their appearances were like Fanny's had been when she was a girl, so she

1

naturally preferred them to the remaining three girls, whose looks favored their father. Their headstrong and stubborn personalities mirrored their father's as well, much to Fanny's eternal consternation.

Lizzy soon reached the forested path beyond the hedgerows that bordered the small wilderness outside her home. Once she was sure she was out of view of anyone who might happen to peer out the window, she broke into a run. This was freedom.

Several minutes later, Lizzy stopped, panting for breath. As she drank the cool water at the nearby stream, her thoughts again wandered to the morning's events and the chaos she had escaped.

At eight years old, Lydia had discovered that her mother would give her anything she demanded in order to avoid any fuss. As a result, Lydia was becoming spoiled and unmanageable. Unfortunately, Fanny did not see anything wrong with her precious angel's behavior.

That morning, as Jane was fitted for her newest batch of gowns, Lydia insisted upon being attended to as well. Her rambunctious behavior upset the seamstress madame, who threatened to leave and take her bolts of fabric with her. Lizzy managed to slip out the door as her mother wailed for her smelling salts and berated the seamstress for not allowing Lydia to fondle the silks and muslins. Fanny had appeared not to notice that Lydia's hands were encrusted with jam and crumbs from the last of the biscuits, which Cook had reluctantly relinquished to the entitled Lydia before breakfast.

Lizzy grimaced as she recalled how Lydia had waited to eat the treats until Kitty and Mary had risen, shoving them in her mouth and chewing noisily, reveling in the fact that there were none left for her sisters. Kitty had wailed in a fit of temper that was more appropriate for a child of two than of ten, only to be hushed by her mother for upsetting Fanny's nerves so early in the morning. Conversely, Mary maintained a stoic countenance aside from a glimmer of tears behind her glasses. Even at the tender age of twelve, Mary had long ago learned that to betray emotion only increased Lydia's delight at tormenting her sisters.

Lizzy shook her head in consternation as she recollected her father's droll voice echoing above the din—mocking the scene in front of him—and Jane's placid face betraying no hint of disquiet. *How can Jane be so entirely unaffected by such behavior?* Lizzy wondered in frustration. She knew Jane, with her mild temperament, would find a way to excuse the uncouth behavior of both her mother and sister, as she always did.

Stumbling over a tree root, Lizzy jolted from her musings and realized she had reached the border between Longbourn and Netherfield—the neighboring estate—and suddenly halted, unease filling her mind.

Netherfield was owned by Lord _____, who spent most of his time in London. His lordship gave his steward, Mr. Cartwright, carte blanche to run the estate and manage the tenants as he saw fit. Many members of the aristocracy did similarly, but none of them had a steward as wonderful as Mr. Cartwright.

Mr. Cartwright was a favorite of the adults among the four and twenty neighborhood families that dined together. He was well-mannered and charismatic, and he managed Netherfield with fairness and dedication. Indeed, the man was entirely amiable and gentlemanlike. The children loved him because he always had a sweet or two for them in his pocket.

However, Mr. Cartwright was also rather particular and fastidious, as befitted a man of his position. He did not permit neighboring children—regardless of their station to trespass on Netherfield lands. Everybody minded Mr. Cartwright in this matter, including Lizzy.

Retreating slowly, Lizzy turned and scuttled back down the path toward home.

A few hours later, Lizzy approached her home. By the angry shouts echoing across the lawn from the open drawing room window, it was clear that the seamstress was still there. Instead of entering through the front door, Lizzy opted to make use of the servants' entrance in the kitchen.

Upon entering the room, Lizzy noticed Hill and Cook whispering animatedly near the pot over the fire. Hearing the door close, the women startled and fell conspicuously silent. After a few moments, Hill came forward and scolded, "Just look at you, Miss Lizzy! Covered in dirt from head to foot! Mark my words, your mother will be fit to be tied if she sees you in such a state at your age! Quickly, up the stairs and I'll send Sally up with some water."

Lizzy turned toward the staircase and made to climb it. Her foot hesitated on the first step, and she glanced back. She was surprised to notice Hill staring at her, a pensive expression on her face.

"Yes, Hill?" Lizzy asked, "Did you need something from me?"

"Miss Lizzy, where did you walk today?" Hill inquired, seeming to ignore the question.

"Along the stream towards Netherfield. Why?"

Hill hesitated, then ventured, "Miss Lizzy, just be careful around Netherfield's lands. That's all."

Lizzy stared at Hill for a moment, waiting for her to continue. When the woman did not offer further explanation, Lizzy asked, "Why? Is it dangerous?" Lizzy laughed lightly at the mildly ridiculous notion.

Hill hesitated again before replying. "Just—just be careful, Miss Lizzy, that's all I'm saying."

When it became clear Hill would not elaborate, Lizzy nodded and continued up the stairs to freshen herself before her mother noticed her state of disarray.

~∞~∞~∞~

Some weeks later, Lizzy found herself walking the same trail toward Netherfield. As she approached the boundary between Longbourn's tenants and Netherfield's, she paused.

As Lizzy deliberated continuing onward to satisfy her curiosity about Hill's strange warning, something made the decision for her. A faint sobbing reached Lizzy's ears. As she strained to hear where the sound was coming from, she noticed a bonnet blowing across a Netherfield tenant's field, ribbons trailing behind. A few moments later, she saw a girl around Jane's age stumbling fruitlessly after it.

Lizzy didn't hesitate—she rushed down the small hill and raced to intercept the bonnet that swept in her direction. Scooping up the accessory, she slowed her pace but continued toward the girl, intent on returning the bonnet to its owner.

As she grew nearer, Lizzy was startled to recognize Becky, the daughter of one of Netherfield's tenants. Becky was only twelve years old, but she had grown in height and development to appear some years older. Becky's eyes were red with tears.

"Oh, Miss Lizzy," Becky gasped as she approached, "Thank you ever so much." Becky hastily wiped at her eyes with the cuff of her sleeve and grabbed at the bonnet, refusing to meet Lizzy's questioning gaze.

"Becky," asked Lizzy, "are you quite all right?" Her sharp eyes took in Becky's state of dress, which was in disarray. The buttons were misaligned, and there was grass and dirt on the younger girl's hem.

"Yes, Miss Lizzy," Becky answered, eyes cast downward. She grabbed once more at the bonnet; this time, Lizzy allowed her to take it.

"Becky!" boomed a harsh, angry voice. Becky's eyes widened in fear as she turned frantically to look behind her to locate the source of the voice. Lizzy could see that the entire back of Becky's dress was covered with grass and dirt, and she had twigs in her hair.

"Becky, you stupid chit, get back here right now!" The angry voice was drawing closer. Becky's wide eyes met Lizzy's, pleading silently.

"Quick!" Lizzy ordered. "Run toward the trees and hide! I'll distract whoever it is."

"No, Miss Lizzy! You mustn't!" Lizzy didn't think it was possible for Becky to be more frightened, but she was. "It will make things worse, it will. Mr. Cart——." Becky froze mid-sentence.

Lizzy gasped. "Mr. Cartwright? Is that who you are running from? I didn't recognize his voice." Lizzy paused for a moment, considering. "Did he hurt you, Becky?"

Becky began to stammer and backed away, shaking her head emphatically. "No, Miss Lizzy! Please don't ask any questions. Twill only make things worse."

"But Becky," Lizzy insisted, "if someone is hurting you, then maybe I can help. Papa could—"

"No!" Becky said firmly. "Miss Lizzy, you mustn't say anything of what you saw to anyone, especially the gentry. I would be ruined, and my family would be turned from their homes. That's just the way it works at Netherfield."

"I don't understand," Lizzy said.

"Please, Miss Lizzy. Promise me you won't tell anyone about this. Not one word to a single soul."

Lizzy hesitated.

"Promise me!"

Lizzy considered the desperation in Becky's eyes. "Alright, Becky. I promise."

Becky breathed a sigh of relief. Her body tightened in fear again, however, when the murderous voice rang out again. "Becky! Mark my words, girl, if you keep me waiting any longer, things will be much worse for you than they already are!"

Becky looked at Lizzy with desperate eyes, "Run, Miss Lizzy!" she whispered urgently, "Run and hide!"

Lizzy felt a shiver of dread slither up her spine as Becky's terror began to infect her sensibilities. She knew, however, that she should remain and aid the distressed younger girl. She opened her mouth to refuse to leave when Becky suddenly shoved her with surprising force toward Longbourn's fields.

"Go!" Becky ordered emphatically, then turned and ran toward the voice.

Lizzy scrambled back up the slope toward the trees. Once hidden safely on Longbourn's land, she paused, gasping for breath. Turning, she spied Mr. Cartwright mounting a nearby knoll as Becky sped toward him.

"Forgive me, sir!" Becky cried. "The wind carried the bonnet faster than I could run."

Mr. Cartwright's hand lashed out, striking her across the cheek. Becky tumbled to the ground. Lizzy gasped in horror, then covered her mouth with both hands as tears filled her eyes.

Becky's hands cupped her already swelling face. "Please, sir—" she begged.

Lizzy turned away as she heard another loud slap echo across the grounds. Unable to bear what was sure to follow, she fled toward home. Becky rose, unsteady on her feet. She swayed as she walked, which led Mr. Cartwright to grab her by the hair that was falling down around her face. "Quickly, girl!" he ordered.

Lizzy watched mutely, tears streaming down her face. As they disappeared from view, she saw Mr. Cartwright begin pulling Becky's dress down around her shoulders.

Lizzy stood rooted in her place, time passing unnoticed as she kept her eyes on the spot she had last seen Becky and Mr. Cartwright. Being the second oldest of five children and a country girl who enjoyed nature, Lizzy was somewhat aware of the behavior between men and women. However, she had never before seen such brutality, especially towards someone her own age.

After what must have been hours, Lizzy began to feel chilled. She looked around and noticed that the sun was beginning to lower behind Oakham Mount. Realizing the lateness of the hour, Lizzy began to run towards home.

As she ran, Lizzy struggled to process everything she had seen. She knew that tenants were under the power of stewards and masters. She knew her own father was indolent, but she had never known him to be vicious or intentionally cruel. She had thought the same of Mr. Cartwright. It was difficult to reconcile such evil with such a handsome face and pleasant countenance.

Should she tell someone? Lizzy immediately discounted her mother—all Franny would do is gossip to the neighbors, which would ruin Becky and destroy her family. Perhaps Papa? Lizzy recalled her father reclining in his study with a book and port, firmly entrenched in his favorite chair and spectating on his family's lives. If he couldn't stir himself to tend to his own daughters' behaviors, he certainly would not exert himself on the behalf of a common drudge who wasn't even his own tenant.

Lizzy contemplated telling her dear elder sister, but she knew Jane's gentle nature would reject the notion of such wickedness in a man with whom they were acquainted. Jane would insist that it was all a misunderstanding. *Certainly Mr. Cartwright has the appearance of goodness and amiability!* Jane would insist. Next, Lizzy considered Hill. Based on Hill's odd behavior in discussing Netherfield land a few weeks before, the reputable servant most likely already knew—or at least suspected—Mr. Cartwright's true character.

No, Lizzy concluded. *I mustn't tell anyone. And I will never trust a handsome face again until I know what character lies behind it.*

Chapter 1

Hertfordshire, October 1805

Fourteen-year-old Lizzy awoke to her mother's shrieks. She groaned and pulled the pillow over her head. *Why must Mama be so loud this early in the morning?* Lizzy paused. *Wait, why is Mamma awake this early in the morning?*

With her morning walks, Lizzy was often the first to rise in her family on a normal day. The previous night, sixteen-year-old Jane and their parents had attended a local assembly. These occasions usually proceeded long into the early hours of the morning, so Mamma always seized the opportunity to have a lie-in the next day.

Lizzy had remained awake until Jane returned so they could discuss the event. Jane and Lizzy had conversed longer than they normally did so late. Jane, with her beauty, was a popular dance partner and often stood up for every set. Her innate shyness and small dowry had previously failed to elicit a request for a second set from the same man in a single night to say nothing of an offer of marriage—much to the dismay of their mother.

This night, however, had been different. Mr. Cartwright had requested Jane's first and last sets.

"What do you think it means, Jane? Did Mr. Cartwright say anything?" asked Lizzy.

Jane blushed and dipped her head. "He spoke of his security and position as steward. His annual income has recently increased, and he told me of his desire to settle down."

Lizzy became inwardly alarmed. As promised, she had never revealed what had happened between Becky and Mr. Cartwright. Lizzy met Becky a few months after the event, and the anguish in Becky's eyes had strengthened Lizzy's resolve to remain silent. Two weeks later, Lizzy overheard Aunt Phillips telling Mamma that Becky had been sent to live with cousins in Kent due a sprained ankle. Mamma had been with child often enough for Lizzy to understand what Aunt Phillips meant.

Shaking these thoughts from her head, Lizzy had asked Jane how she felt about Mr. Cartwright. Jane hesitated before answering, "Well, he appears to be all that is amiable and kind. He would be a good match."

"But Jane, do you *love* him?" Lizzy persisted.

Jane had not answered, and the two young ladies retired to bed. For Lizzy, sleep refused to appear for many hours

All of these recollections hit Lizzy at once, and she sat up. Discarding her nightclothes on the floor, Lizzy did not even ring for Sally as she quickly donned the morning dress that was easiest to put on. Since she was still not out in society, Lizzy's clothing did not have the level of difficulty that Jane's did.

Lizzy rushed down the stairs, following the sound of her mother's screeches into the breakfast room. Upon opening the door, she discovered Jane and her parents finishing their meal. Mary, Kitty, and Lydia still took their meals in the nursery, but Lizzy was permitted to breakfast and luncheon with her family as she approached her fifteenth birthday.

"Ah, Lizzy," her father lowered his newspaper to look at her as she took her seat. "How was your walk this morning?"

"Good morning, Papa. I have not gone walking yet today. I have only just awakened."

Her father's eyebrows rose over his newspaper in mild surprise. Teasing, he admonished, "Now Lizzy, I understand that you are eager to take your place in society as your sister has, but you still have one more year before you can put on airs and sleep until all hours of the morning!"

Uncharacteristically, Lizzy greeted his banter with silence, causing her father's face to change from amusement to concern. "Well, Lizzy?"

"Oh, who cares about Lizzy right now?!" Mrs. Bennet shrieked. "We need to be focusing on Jane! Jane, you must return upstairs immediately and change into your pink gown. It is the most becoming and will display your figure appealingly for calls."

Lizzy raised an eyebrow inquiringly at Jane. The usual callers their family received the day after an assembly were the Lucases and the Gouldings, who came to gossip about the events that had occurred the night before. Neither family had an eligible son, as the oldest Lucas boy was away on his Grand Tour.

Jane blushed prettily and looked away, silent. Lizzy stared at her, silently willing her sister to explain the situation. There was no need, however, as Mrs. Bennet continued her tirade before Jane could bring herself to meet Lizzy's gaze. "You must be prepare to greet Mr. Cartwright, Jane! Why must you be so passive regarding your future? The man would make an excellent match, considering his recent inheritance."

When Jane maintained her silence, Lizzy turned toward her mother. "What new inheritance, Mamma?"

"Why, Lizzy, haven't you heard a thing I've said all morning? Mr. Cartwright's great uncle has passed away, and he has left his entire fortune to Mr. Cartwright! Three *thousand* pounds a year and a lovely estate in Derbyshire!"

"And how could this affect Jane?" Lizzy asked.

"Oh Lizzy, how could you be so tiresome?" Mrs. Bennet exclaimed incredulously. "You must know that I am thinking of him marrying her! After all, an unmarried man who has come into a fortune must be in want of a wife and heir!"

Lizzy looked to her sister in horror. Jane finally raised her eyes and said quietly, "Mamma, it is by no means certain that Mr. Cartwright is looking for a wife. Even if he were, there is no cause to speculate that I would be his choice."

"Oh Jane, how you agitate my poor nerves!" wailed Mrs. Bennet. "He stood up with you *twice* last night. And now, the man has sent flowers and a note this morning asking to call on you!"

Lizzy felt as though she had fallen into a nightmare. Mr. Cartwright and her gentle Jane, married? Never!

Lizzy looked pleadingly at her father. "Papa, isn't Mr. Cartwright a little old for Jane? After all, Jane is only sixteen," she implored.

Her father opened his mouth to respond, but Mrs. Bennet interrupted before he could begin to speak. "Mr. Cartwright, old?! Who cares about his age when he has such an income and position! Think of the carriages, the dresses, the pin money! A woman may endure a great many things in order to live such a life. Besides, he is only four and thirty, and so handsome, too!"

Lizzy opened her mouth to further object, but before she could begin, the door flew open and Lydia danced into the room, followed closely by a wailing Kitty. Lydia waved a ribbon around, taunting Kitty with it. At ten years old, it was apparent that Lydia would be the tallest of her sisters, having already reached Jane's height. Kitty, on the other hand, was smaller at twelve years of age than any of her sisters had been. After contracting influenza at the age of five, she had always been somewhat small and sickly wisp of a child. Her perennial cough made it difficult for her to eat a full meal or engage in exercise.

"Lydia, give it back!" wailed Kitty in despair.

Lydia pranced around the table. "No, I shan't! You're too ugly to look well in it, and it becomes me much better."

"Mamma, make her give it back!"

"Oh hush, Kitty! You're grating on my nerves. Just let her have it. It does look better on her." Mrs. Bennet cried.

"But I bought it with my own pin money last week!" Kitty cried.

"Oh, never mind the ribbon!" Mrs. Bennet exclaimed in exasperation. "How can I think about ribbons when Jane's suitor is coming to call?"

Lydia stuck her tongue out at Kitty in triumph, causing Kitty to stomp her foot and run sobbing out of the room.

Sensing an opportunity for escape, Mr. Bennet put down his paper and said, "I will be in my study if anyone has need of me."

As he exited the room, Lizzy turned to her mother. "Mamma, surely you can see that Mr. Cartwright is not a good match for Jane?"

"No, I do not see that at all! You are jealous of your sister's fortunate alliance, and I won't stand for it. Come, Jane," Mrs. Bennet demanded. "Let us pick out the perfect gown for you to receive your new beau."

Lizzy watched in despair as Mrs. Bennet ushered Jane out of the room. Grabbing a biscuit off a plate, Lizzy hurried to her father's study. She knocked and entered at his call.

"Well, Lizzy, come to escape the chaos?" intoned Mr. Bennet wryly.

"Papa, you cannot be thinking of allowing Jane to accept Mr. Cartwright!" exclaimed Lizzy.

Her father only chuckled. "Now, Lizzy, not you as well! If Jane is not unwilling and her mother approves, what more can a father do?"

"Papa!"

"No, Lizzy," asserted Mr. Bennet firmly. "I came to my study for some peace, and peace I intend to find. If you are determined to discuss weddings and suitors, then you had better join your mother and Jane. Now please leave me to my quietude."

Lizzy stared helplessly at her father, wordlessly pleading with him to intervene.

"Lizzy, do not make me ask again," he stated.

"Yes, Papa." Lizzy sorrowfully exited the room, closing the door loudly behind her. A muffled thud on the other side indicated the noise had startled him into dropping his book. *Good,* thought Lizzy spitefully.

Her satisfaction lasted only a moment before her thoughts returned to her older sister's situation. How could she protect Jane from Mr. Cartwright?

Inspiration struck. *Of course! Uncle and Aunt Gardiner!*

Just the previous week, the Gardiners had written requesting Jane's presence in London. Aunt Gardiner had just left confinement from the birth of their first child, and they were once again participating in the local society. Uncle Gardiner's business had increased in prominence and prosperity, and their circle had grown to include some minor members of the ton.

Lizzy had begged Jane not to abandon her for London, so Jane had decided to remain at Longbourn. However, in light of the impending danger of Mr. Cartwright's suit, Lizzy would prefer to endure her mother and sisters alone than to allow Jane to fall under Mr. Cartwright's power.

Dashing upstairs, Lizzy flew into Jane's room, intent on sharing her idea with her mother and sister. However, a knock on the front door of the house brought everything to a sudden halt.

"Oh, he's here! He's here!" shrieked Mrs. Bennet. "Make haste, Jane!" Pinching Jane's cheeks and fluffing the girl's skirts, Mrs. Bennet hurried her daughter down the stairs and into the large drawing room.

Lizzy slumped to the floor in despair. What was she to do?

When Lizzy heard Hill announce Mr. Cartwright, she straightened with determination. She would *not* allow Mr. Cartwright to be alone with Jane! If he got the opportunity, he might propose, and Jane was much too kind to turn down a palatable proposal that would please nearly all of her family.

Lizzy entered the drawing room just as Mr. Cartwright proposed a walk in the garden with Jane. Lizzy exclaimed, "A walk sounds wonderful! Since I missed my morning walk today, I will join you!"

Without waiting for an answer, Lizzy put on her boots and coat before anyone had a chance to stop her. So as not to appear rude,

Mr. Cartwright had no option but to allow Lizzy to join them. With a winning smile, he offered his arm to Jane and the little group exited the house.

Lizzy inundated Mr. Cartwright with a stream of conversation, asking all about Netherfield, his new estate, and Derbyshire. After enduring fifteen minutes of unceasing prattle, Mr. Cartwright's patient smile grew strained. He finally said, "Well, Miss Elizabeth! I have enjoyed our conversation, but I'm afraid I must return to Netherfield. I have many pressing duties there in training the new steward before I leave for Derbyshire next month."

He bowed gallantly to Jane. "Miss Bennet, as always, I have greatly enjoyed your company. I leave you with these words: 'My lady fair with golden hair, I leave in sorrow, but shall see thee on the morrow'."

Jane blushed and looked away, a hint of confusion in her expression. Lizzy smothered a laugh at his poor attempt at poetry but did not dare let him see her smile.

"Thank you, Mr. Cartwright," Jane finally said in a quiet voice.

Mr. Cartwright bowed again over Jane's hand and escorted both girls to the front door. Once he had safely deposited the girls at their home, he trudged to the stables to retrieve his horse.

As soon as Lizzy and Jane entered the house, their mother fairly pounced on them. "Well, Jane?" she demanded eagerly. "Are you engaged?"

"No, Mamma, I am not," Jane answered. "However, he said that he would return tomorrow. At least, I believe that is what his poetry intended to say."

Lizzy finally let out the laugh she had been holding in since Mr. Cartwright's recitation of his particularly poor verse.

"Lizzy, you abominable child!" Mrs. Bennet shrieked. "You have ruined all of Jane's chances! Mr. Bennet! Oh, Mr. Bennet!"

Mrs. Bennet rushed to the study, pulling Lizzy and Jane along behind her. She dragged the girls through the door. "Mr. Bennet, we are surely lost, all because of this covetous, foolish, ungrateful miscreant!"

Mr. Bennet snapped his head up in surprise at this clamorous intrusion upon his sanctuary.

"Oh, Mr. Bennet!" Fanny bawled, "We are all in an uproar! You must come and insist that Jane marry Mr. Cartwright!"

Mr. Bennet's eyebrows rose higher than they had at the breakfast table that morning. "I beg your pardon, my dear, but to what are you referring?"

"Of Jane and Mr. Cartwright!" exclaimed the lady.

"Oh? Has he made Jane an offer of marriage, then? It is the general practice that the gentleman ask permission of her father first. Unless, of course, you decided that we should change places, my dear? Perhaps I should put on my dressing gown and call for my salts whilst you manage the books for the estate?"

"Oh, Mr. Bennet!" wailed Mrs. Bennet. "You have no compassion on my nerves!"

"You underestimate me, Mrs. Bennet. I have the highest regard for your nerves, as they have been my constant companions these fifteen years at least," replied Mr. Bennet drolly.

Mrs. Bennet let out a moan. "Mr. Bennet! Must you be so tiresome? Will you or will you not insist on Jane accepting Mr. Cartwright?"

"I will not." At another loud keen from his wife, Mr. Bennet continued: "I will not discuss Jane marrying any man until he has the common decency to discuss it with me first. Only then will it become a topic of conversation in my book room. Now, madam, unless Mr. Cartwright is standing outside the door to ask my permission and has not been frightened off by your caterwauling, please leave me in peace!"

With another wail, Mrs. Bennet rushed from the room, calling imperiously for Hill. Jane gave her father a wry half-smile and followed her mother out the door. Lizzy waited a moment to see if he would speak with her. When he continued to look determinedly down at his book, she quietly left the room.

When she found her mother and Jane in the sitting room moments later, Lizzy took a seat on the chair nearest the fire and—conveniently—farthest away from her mother.

Mrs. Bennet wasted no time before continuing her tirade. "Oh, Jane, I do not know what is to become of us, indeed I do not. Your father will die, and with no heir we will be cast into the hedgerows because Longbourn has been unlawfully entailed away on us."

"Mamma," began Jane, "Father is in excellent health, and there will yet be many opportunities for my sisters and I to meet eligible gentlemen."

Mrs. Bennet did not agree. "With the eldest Lucas boy away, there are very few matches to be had in Meryton! If Mr. Cartwright does not return tomorrow, we are all doomed to homelessness and poverty!"

Lizzy smiled. Mrs. Bennet and Jane had unwittingly provided the perfect segue into her plan.

"Mamma is correct, Jane." Lizzy said. Mrs. Bennet was so surprised by this sudden show of support from her least favorite daughter that she immediately silenced. "There are very few young men in the neighborhood, and certainly none of them are good enough for you!"

Mrs. Bennet began to object. "But Mr. Cartwright—"

"Has only three thousand a year, and Derbyshire is so very far away in the north." Lizzy smoothly continued. "I know I would miss Jane so dearly to have her so distant. Wouldn't you agree, Mamma?"

Mrs. Bennet hesitated, then nodded. "That's true. I don't know what I would do with my dear Jane so far from me."

"Exactly," stated Lizzy. "Mamma, I am concerned that Jane's handsomeness is much too fine for a county like Derbyshire. Her beauty would be wasted there, in so secluded a place."

"Oh, yes, Lizzy!" Exclaimed Mrs. Bennett. "You are absolutely right! Dear Jane's beauty would fade away quickly in the wilds! And

17

Derbyshire is so far north! With all that snow and cold, she will doubtlessly fall ill and perish, and then where would we be?"

Lizzy nodded. "Mamma, I think it would be an appalling tragedy for Jane to marry Mr. Cartwright and leave us for Derbyshire."

Mrs. Bennet was in full agreement by this point. "No, we mustn't allow Mr. Cartwright to propose! Oh, Jane and Lizzy, my clever girls to prevent him from speaking to your father today. I am so glad I had the idea for Lizzy to walk with you. But what shall we do tomorrow? He is certain to return! And with Jane's unparalleled beauty and modest manner—all that is desirable in a bride—he will *have* to propose! Jane, you must not accept him. I absolutely forbid it."

Jane gaped at her mother in astonishment. "But, Mamma! It is most unladylike to refuse an eligible offer of marriage! And Mr. Cartwright is so kind and amiable. I could not bear to bring him pain."

"Then we mustn't allow him to see you. We will claim you have taken ill and are unable to come down."

"Mamma," Lizzy interrupted, "surely you can see the danger in that? He might call for Mr. Jones! Even if he does not, Mr. Cartwright will remain at Netherfield for another month to train the new steward. Jane cannot pretend to be ill for that long without causing great offense, or even giving rise to gossip that she is so ill as to lose all her looks."

Mrs. Bennet looked horrified. "Everyone will be speaking of us! Oh, what shall we do? Jane, you will have to accept Mr. Cartwright. But you cannot accept him or you will die alone in the cold wilds of the north! What can be done? We are surely ruined!"

"Mamma, I have an idea!" Lizzy cried abruptly, as if suddenly struck with a new idea. "What about Uncle and Aunt Gardiner in London? They wrote just last week to say that they are able to go out in society now that Cousin Ellen is old enough for them to leave her at home. Jane has been invited to visit them, and she could attend balls and the theater for the Season."

Mrs. Bennet gazed at Lizzy in astonishment. "Why Lizzy, you

clever girl! That is just the thing! We shall send Jane to my brother Gardiner and his wife immediately!"

Jane looked at Mrs. Bennet in alarm. "Mamma, how can I possibly depart so soon? The Gardiners will have no idea that I am coming!"

"Oh nonsense, girl!" Mrs. Bennet waved her hand in dismissal. "Who better than my own brother to welcome a family member in a time of emergency? No, it is imperative that you decamp tomorrow. I will speak with your father about taking the carriage and horses. It would be no trouble to have them away from the farm for a day or two. Your safety is much more important! Now quickly, Jane; go upstairs and pack your things!"

Mrs. Bennet swept from the room, leaving Jane and Lizzy alone. After a few moments of stunned silence, Lizzy began to laugh.

"Lizzy, what on earth is so funny?" asked Jane, who was nearly in tears.

Lizzy couldn't explain it. She had been so worried about Jane and Mr. Cartwright, and now the problem had been solved! Jane was safe! Lizzy felt lighter than air, and she laughed in relief. "Come, Jane," she said. "Let us go upstairs, and I will help you choose your best dresses to take to London."

~∞~∞~∞~

Early the next morning, Lizzy stepped out of the front door to say farewell to Jane. The girls embraced tearfully, but Lizzy knew that the pain of separation would be eased—on her part—by the knowledge that her sister would be safe.

"You must promise to write to me, Lizzy," Jane insisted. "I will miss our home, and your letters will bring me much comfort."

"Do not worry about us, Jane," Lizzy said. "We will manage. Go and enjoy your time with Aunt and Uncle Gardiner."

"But Mr. Cartwright will come today, expecting to see me. Maybe I should stay after all. I cannot bear to think of his disappointment at my sudden departure."

"Absolutely not, Jane," said Lizzy firmly. "You will not give him another moment's consideration. You do not love him, and he is not the right man for you."

"How can you know?" Jane asked, puzzled.

"I simply know," Lizzy replied. "I know you as well as you know yourself, and I am able to view the situation from the outside. Go enjoy your time with our aunt and uncle. I promise that I will do all in my power to ease any heartbreak he might feel at your leaving."

Only slightly mollified, Jane reluctantly climbed into the coach joining Sally, who would travel as her companion. As Lizzy waved goodbye, she allowed only one small tear to slide down her cheek. She then turned toward the door with a renewed determination to permanently rid her family and Meryton of Mr. Cartwright.

~∞~∞~∞~

Later that morning, while Mrs. Bennet and Lizzy reposed in the drawing room, Hill entered and announced Mr. Cartwright. Mr. Cartwright entered the room and bowed as the ladies stood and curtsied. Rising, he looked around the room.

"Where is Miss Bennet?" he asked in clear puzzlement. He immediately recollected himself and added, "Of course, I am delighted—as always—to encounter such charming ladies this morning! I simply had hoped I might speak with Miss Bennet specifically on a very particular matter."

"Oh, Mr. Cartwright!" exclaimed Mrs. Bennet. "It is the most peculiar thing. My brother Gardiner wrote just yesterday" she prevaricated, "to insist that Jane visit them in London immediately! He has promised outings to the theater and balls every night. Of course, my dearest Jane was not made for the country. With her gifts, she undeniably belongs among the *Ton* for the Season!"

Mr. Cartwright's countenance sparked with anger. He immediately regained control of his expression, the facade of pleasantness slamming back into place so quickly that Mrs. Bennet did take notice. Lizzy did perceive the aberration, however, and studied him more assiduously. While Mrs. Bennet prattled, his fists and jaw clenched tightly, and his eyes darkened with barely concealed rage. Soon the metamorphosis was so apparent that only someone as self-absorbed as Mrs. Bennet could fail to detect the former steward's emotions.

Mrs. Bennet paused for breath, and Mr. Cartwright interrupted in a slightly strangled voice, "Well, I am sorry to have missed Miss Bennet. However, it is now quite clear to me that she prefers town over country and present company. I wish her as much happiness as she deserves." He bowed curtly and quitted the room.

Huffing at his rudeness, Mrs. Bennet turned to Lizzy. "Well, I say good riddance to the man! Imagine a mere steward fancying himself worthy of my eldest daughter! With her beauty, she may even land a titled husband in London this season! And how rude he was, leaving without proper courtesy! I always knew that upstart was no gentleman. How glad I am to have warned Jane away from him and sent her somewhere safe."

Lizzy listened absently to her mother's ramblings. Her thoughts were miles away with Jane, who was safely travelling toward London and away from Mr. Cartwright's evil clutches.

Chapter 2

London, May 1806

Fitzwilliam Darcy was hot.

Leaning against a wall in the overcrowded ballroom, he glowered at the dancers. Once again, Lady M____ had thrown a ball that included more guests than her home could accommodate. The room was poorly lit, stuffy, and smelled as though the attendees had not bathed in weeks. *Knowing some of them, they probably have not*, he thought irritably. Thankfully, this would be the last ball of the season.

A hand suddenly grasped his upper arm, startling him. He jerked away from the jarring grip, mentally bracing to defend himself from yet another conniving mother with a simpering daughter. Instead, he found himself looking into the jovial eyes of his cousin, Major Richard Fitzwilliam.

"Ho, there, Darcy!" Richard cried in feigned dismay. "At ease!"

Darcy offered Richard his most disgruntled look. "I don't know why I allowed you to talk me into this," he grumbled.

"Perhaps because you need to enjoy yourself?" Richard suggested with a smile. "Come, man! There are beautiful women who would barter every dress and bauble they owned for the opportunity to dance with you just once!"

"Not with me," Darcy muttered, "with the master of Pemberley." Since his father's death two years prior, Darcy had abruptly become one of the most eligible bachelors in the *ton*. As the sole proprietor of his estate, rather than the heir apparent—a situation that could conceivably shift— he was an extremely desirable marriage match. Apparently many young ladies would endure a surly husband in exchange for virtually inexhaustible pin money.

Darcy had reentered society after his year of mourning his father had passed, whereupon he was immediately disgusted with the entire coterie. Young ladies were inflicted upon him by their fathers, mothers, and even their brothers. He had narrowly escaped several potentially compromising situations, and many whom he counted as friends could no longer be considered such.

In the last year, Darcy had come to realize that he had a mere two true friends—his cousin Richard and an acquaintance from school, Charles Bingley.

Darcy and Bingley had met in 1801 during Bingley's first year at Eton when he was thirteen years of age. Darcy had always been a naturally quiet and studious boy. He was inclined to keep to himself, even at the age of seventeen. His social status and an early growth spurt had meant that he was mostly left alone by older students, whose main objective seemed to be tormenting the younger students—particularly those born to the trades rather than the peerage.

One day, Darcy had been crossing the campus when he happened upon a group of students. In the middle of the group was a bloodied boy lying beaten on the ground. Above the battered boy stood a scrawny lad with fists raised at the rest of the crowd, his body positioned protectively. "Leave him alone!" the lad demanded, his voice cracking with the changes of puberty.

The older boys laughed, with the largest shoving the lad to the ground next to the first boy. The lad leaped upright and shouted: "I said leave him alone! Or you'll answer to me."

The largest boy sneered, "Bingley, what do you think you're doing? You're half my size, and you aren't even a gentleman. What leads you to believe that you can challenge your betters?"

The lad, Bingley, raised his fists and bellowed, "Betters? What rubbish! My father may be in trade, but he's ten times better than you lot. If the likes of you are examples of gentlemen, then I'm proud to be from trade."

The large boy, currently a marquess and heir to the Duke of _____, dropped his sneer and instead grew angry. He moved menacingly toward the younger boys, and Darcy knew what would happen next. Taking a deep breath, he pushed his way to the center of the crowd. "What's all this?" he demanded.

The young marquess turned to face the newcomer. "Darcy! You're just in time. Help me teach this good-for-nothing tradesman's son a lesson in proper etiquette."

Darcy gazed coolly at the marquess. "Hampton," he said, "I am not entirely certain which of you needs the lesson. As my uncle the earl has frequently instructed me: only a man of inferior breeding and manners mistreats those beneath him. There is no honor in abuse."

Hampton hesitated, taken aback, as he considered the consequences of preserving his pride to the detriment of a connection to the heir to one of the most prosperous and influential estates in Britain. Darcy knew he had succeeded when Hampton glared at and muttered: "Good riddance to the lot of you," then about-faced and stormed away.

The spectators began to disperse, a few of them hanging their heads in shame. One or two patted Darcy on the shoulder, while others groused about missing out on the fun. Darcy waited until the naysayers were gone, then he turned toward Bingley and the other boy, who was still on the ground.

Bingley grinned at Darcy. "Well done, mate!" Squatting down next to the injured boy, Bingley asked, "You all right, Roberts?"

Glancing back up at Darcy, Bingley said, "Roberts and my dad are business partners. Their factories earned so much over the last few years that they decided to send us to school to become gentlemen."

Darcy's eyebrows raised as Bingley's family rose in his estimation. He knew that the cost to bribe the school magistrates into accepting a boy from trade was exorbitant. That Bingley's father and his partner had prospered sufficiently to send two boys to school was impressive indeed.

Crouching down next to Bingley, Darcy asked the still silent boy Roberts, "Are you all right?" Darcy gently rolled the boy over, then hissed in dismay as he surveyed the damage done to Roberts's face. The boy's eyes were swollen shut, his nose was crooked, and blood oozed from his mouth. His arm hung at an awkward angle, and he groaned in pain from the movement.

"Bingley, go and get Headmaster Clarkson" Darcy ordered. "Quickly! Tell him Darcy said it's an emergency." Bingley dashed off toward the building that housed the dean's office.

Nearly ten minutes later, Bingley sprinted back into view. Doubling over, he gasped for breath. "He's… coming… had…. to…. find… doctor."

Some minutes later, the headmaster arrived with Dr. Stephens at a brisk pace. The men increased their speed when they saw Roberts on the ground. Dr. Stephens knelt at the battered boy's side while Headmaster Clarkson looked to Darcy for an explanation.

Darcy quickly summarized the situation, with Bingley's occasional contextual interjections. Headmaster Clarkson's face grew increasingly sterner as he listened to the boys. He did briefly quirk the corner of his mouth upward as Darcy recounted Bingley's courage in standing up to the bullies, alone and outnumbered. Bingley blustered indignantly at the insinuation that he had needed rescuing. At that, both Darcy and the headmaster chuckled lightly.

This shared experience bound Bingley and Darcy together more closely than any familial or social obligation could, and they forged an enduring friendship. Roberts returned home to recover from his injuries, and was eventually sent to Harrow, which his father felt would be more accepting of a boy of his station. By the time the decision was made to permanently remove Roberts from Eton, Bingley and Darcy were such close friends that Bingley chose to remain at the school, regardless of the considerably supercilious student body. Bingley's company and sincere nature supplied a soothing balm to Darcy's cynical heart; Darcy became something of a mentor to Bingley, helping the boy to develop some amount of both political and academic acumen. Bingley never seemed to acquire the older boy's cynicism, for which Darcy was grateful. He did not wish to darken his friend's guileless core.

From a young age, Darcy had been leery of boys who affected an affable and obliging persona. George Wickham—godson to Darcy's father and son of Mr. Wickham, the Pemberley steward—had been such a boy.

Old Mr. Wickham was a good man who had served Pemberley since Darcy's grandfather's time. Old Mr. Wickham and George Darcy—Darcy's father and then master of Pemberley—had cared for Pemberley together since they were in their mid-twenties, when George Darcy's father had died shortly after replacing the former steward with old Mr. Wickham.

Old Mr. Wickham married late in life to a young woman who resented his close relationship with George and Anne Darcy. The steward's bond with his new bride quickly soured. The only bright spot in his marriage was the birth of his son, who was named in honor of the esteemed George Darcy.

George Wickham had been born just a few months after the birth of Fitzwilliam. Mrs. Wickham quickly lost interest in her family after his birth. Realizing there would be no more children, Mr. Wickham devoted himself entirely to his son. He often brought the babe up to the nursery while he worked, as he could not rely on Mrs. Wickham to care for their child.

Consequently, George Wickham and Fitzwilliam Darcy became as close as brothers. When the boys were five years old, however, Mrs. Wickham became obsessed with obtaining a grander life for herself. She thought to develop a relationship with her son in order to forge a connection with the influential Mr. and Mrs. Darcy. George soon learned to become increasingly discontented with the simple life of his father's house when compared with the grandeur of Fitzwilliam's life in Pemberley.

In front of their fathers, George was the ideal playmate for young Master Darcy. When the boys were alone, however, George's secret spiteful propensities emerged, often violently. When time arrived for Master Darcy to leave for Eton, he begged his father not to allow the jealous schemer to join him. George Darcy was confused, but paid for Wickham to attend Harrow instead.

Bingley was everything that George Wickham was not. Where George was full of subtle barbs and feigned compliments, Bingley was unapologetically honest and genial. Darcy had first recognized this lack of pretense when he saw Bingley defending Roberts, which act bypassed the walls Darcy had built around himself.

After Darcy left Eton and went to Cambridge, the two corresponded by letter and visited together every holiday. Eventually, Bingley joined Darcy at Cambridge, while Wickham and Roberts went on to Oxford.

Away from the watchful eyes of his father and godfather, George Wickham became a gambler and a rake. He was careful, however, to keep his escapades from his godfather in the hopes that he would claim an inheritance once the old man finally died.

Much to Wickham's horror (and that of Fitzwilliam), George Darcy's will provided him with a living that he would receive upon taking orders to be a clergyman. Wickham ungratefully accepted three thousand pounds in lieu of his inheritance, and Darcy had not seen his childhood playmate in the year since the reading and execution of the will.

Darcy's thoughts were pulled back to the present as Richard tugged his arm again. "Come on, old man! I see some new debutantes near the refreshments, and I've heard that a few of them have dowries large enough to make up for their looks!"

Darcy cut a look of distaste at his friend. "I am not in any mood to stand up with women who have nothing but flirtation and marriage in their head. Allow them to save their smiles for you; I am in no need of a dowry." With that statement, Darcy turned on his heel and called for his carriage to spirit him away from the hot and over-crowded ballroom.

Early the next morning, Darcy read his correspondence while he breakfasted. His heart warmed when he found a letter from his dear younger sister, Georgiana. He and Richard had been designated as her guardians in his father's will, and it was a duty they executed with gladness. As Darcy was a bachelor and Georgiana too young for society at the tender age of ten, Richard's parents—the Earl and Countess of Matlock—recommended that she remain at Pemberley with her governess during the times he spent the Season in London.

About to open her letter, he paused when he heard a knock at his door. Only two people would disturb him this early in the morning, and one of them was most likely still sleeping off the dance and drink from the night before. As predicted, Bingley soon entered the room wearing his ever-present smile. "Mr. Bingley," pronounced Fortescue, the butler, in a dry voice as he followed a few steps behind Bingley.

"Honestly, Bingley," said Darcy in an amused tone. "You really must give poor Fortescue a chance to announce you *before* you enter the room!"

Bingley's smile widened into a grin. "I know, Darcy, but I simply could not wait to tell you my news!"

Darcy grimaced. "You've met an angel" he intoned flatly at the exact moment Bingley proclaimed: "I've met an angel!"

Bingley gaped at Darcy. "How did you know?" he asked in amazement.

Darcy rolled his eyes and returned to the letter from his sister. "Bingley, every time you interrupt my breakfast with a smile, it's because you've met another angel. Let me guess: blonde hair and blue eyes?"

Bingley sighed and collapsed in a nearby chair. "But this one is different, Darcy! She's unlike any other woman I have ever met." He stared into space for several minutes, then slightly shook his head as if to clear his mind. "What about a frown?" He queried, shifting his gaze back to his vexed companion.

"What?" asked a distracted Darcy, who had already moved on from the conversation.

"You said you know I've met an angel if I interrupt your breakfast with a smile. What if I had a frown instead?"

"Then Miss Bingley or Miss Caroline has overspent her allowance again and written from school to request more money."

Bingley peered at his friend in stunned silence for a moment before bursting into laughter. "That is exactly right, old man!"

He laughed heartily for a few more minutes. Darcy had finished reading his correspondence and continued on to his newspaper by the time Bingley was able to recollect himself. "Darcy, I am ardently sincere. I have never before met such a perfect woman in all my life. Her smile causes me to feel things I've never felt before."

"Now, Bingley, that is rather more information than I want to know," Darcy said archly, without lifting his eyes from his newspaper.

"What? No! Egad, Darcy, that is *not* what I meant at all! I meant— Oh. I see. Mocking me again, are you?"

Darcy smirked. "It is difficult to abstain from provocation when such an easy target occasions to present itself."

Bingley laughed again. "This time is different, Darcy. I don't know how to explain it." An idea occurred to him. "I know! You'll have to meet her! Come with me to a card party tonight."

Darcy looked up at his friend incredulously. "A card party? Bingley, you know that I am no gambler. It would be significantly more productive to engage in conversation."

Bingley rolled his eyes. "Surely you discern the reason we refer to you as an old man? There is nothing more tedious than to accompany the "Master of Pemberley" to an event where he is occupied with nothing more than idle hands and idle conversation. But no matter—you simply *must* come attend and take the measure of this woman personally."

Darcy hesitated before asking, "Where is this card party? Who is hosting?"

"Well, I daresay you have never met them before. They were friends of my late father's from before he sold his business."

"Tradesmen?" Darcy intoned flatly.

Bingley's face flushed slightly, abashed. "Darcy, please remember that *I* come from trade."

"My apologies, Bingley" Darcy responded, instantly contrite. "I'm afraid I had a difficult evening at Lady M____'s ball last night, and I have not quite recovered my temper. If that ball is the standard of high society, then I shudder to think what I would encounter at a mere card party in Cheapside."

Bingley's face reddened even more. "I see," he said stiffly. "I apologize for inserting my lowborn self into your home. May I have Your Eminence's permission to depart, that you may purge your palace of my stench."

Startled, Darcy examined Bingley closely. He could see that he had truly wounded his friend with his words. Setting aside his newspaper, Darcy met Bingley's eyes directly. "I must beg your forgiveness for my thoughtlessness, Bingley. Please accept my apologies for my foul temper. You are the closest friend that I have, and I do not wish to belittle your father or your heritage. I am simply in a foul mood, and you have borne the brunt of it."

Mollified, Bingley took a seat at the table and helped himself to a cherry tart. "I appreciate your apology, old man, and I will heartily forgive you—"

"Thank you, Bingley."

"—*if*," Bingley continued, "you attend the card party with me tonight, with a promise to behave yourself. You will see for yourself that Cheapside is no more vulgar than Grosvenor Square."

Although he spoke in a light tone of voice, the tension around Bingley's eyes warned Darcy that to refuse would be an insult and a grave detriment to their friendship. "Then I shall gladly attend," he said.

Bingley let out a bark of laughter. "I am afraid that 'gladly' may be more than you can muster. I will instead settle for 'politely'."

"Agreed," Darcy accepted. "Now, allow me to finish my breakfast in peace, lest you coerce me into doing anything else."

~∞~∞~∞~

That evening, Darcy's carriage turned onto Gracechurch Street. He was acutely aware of his tardiness, a practice which he typically despised in others. He had not intended to arrive fashionably late (or rudely late, as the case may be), but instead had become involved with matters of estate.

He felt the carriage slow and peered out the window. He beheld a modest yet orderly home with candlelight emanating from the windows. His coachman opened the door and Darcy descended from the carriage, depositing his hat firmly on his head.

Darcy approached the front door, where he was greeted by a maid who received his hat, cane, and cloak. She then directed him to a modest sitting room that was tastefully decorated, wherein several attendees convened at myriad tables to play whist.

At his entrance, the members of the party paused their games and conversation to appraise the newcomer. Darcy cast his gaze about the room, searching for Bingley. *Where is he?* he wondered desperately Finally, he heard a familiar voice behind him exclaim, "Darcy! There you are, old man! I had quite given up on you."

Darcy turned with relief to discover Bingley and a young woman sitting together on a settee, partially separated from the room by the open door. He approached Bingley and said, "My apologies. I was occupied with some business and lost track of the hour."

"Not to worry, old man. I am merely happy to see that you have arrived."

There were a few tense moments as the three looked at one another in silence. Finally, the rest of the party returned to their games and the silence was happily broken. Bingley cleared his throat and glanced significantly at the young woman seated by his side. Startled, Darcy managed, "Will you please do me the honor of introducing me to your friend?"

Relaxing, Bingley said, "With pleasure! Darcy, may I present Miss Jane Bennet of Longbourn in Hertfordshire. Miss Bennett, this is my friend Mr. Fitzwilliam Darcy of Pemberley in Derbyshire."

Miss Bennet performed a delicate bow and ventured "It is a great pleasure to make your acquaintance, Mr. Darcy."

"The pleasure is mine," he replied.

After the introduction, an uneasy wordlessness grew between the three guests. Just before the discomfiture reached an unbearable magnitude, Bingley cleared his throat again and bid Darcy follow him to meet the hosts of the evening. He led the stoic man to a table on the far side of the room, where two fashionably attired couples played whist. Bingley performed the introductions to Mr. and Mrs. Sparrow, along with Mr. and Mrs. Gardiner.

"The Gardiners are Miss Bennet's aunt and uncle," Bingley divulged. "They live a mere three houses down from the Sparrows, and they are often found in one other's company. Mr. Sparrow bought out my father's share of the warehouses."

"Ah, I see," responded Darcy. *What do I say now?* he wondered. *What could I possibly have in common with these people?*

Bingley glanced apprehensively at Darcy, then continued speaking, fueling the conversation with anecdotes from his and Darcy's school days.

At the next lapse in conversation, Mrs. Gardiner spoke. "You are from Derbyshire, Mr. Darcy?" she inquired.

"I am."

"Are you perchance related to the Darcys of Pemberley?" she

continued.

"Yes, I am, he confirmed.

An uncomfortable followed Darcy's assertion. Mrs. Gardiner tried again to engage Darcy in the conversation. "Derbyshire is an exceptionally beautiful county, is it not?"

"It is," Darcy intoned reservedly.

Another lapse in the stilted exchange followed. Unable to further endure the social agony, Bingley broke in, "So glad that you have now become acquainted. Darcy, shall we return to Miss Bennet?"

Darcy nodded mutely. He bowed to the table at large, then accompanied Bingley back to the settee where Miss Bennet awaited their return.

The card room was less crowded and sweltering than the ballroom of the previous evening, but the next several hours were equally excruciating to Darcy He endeavored to attend Bingley and Miss Bennet's conversation, but he found himself unable to feign interest in the inane observations regarding the weather and the delights in town. Frequently, Miss Bennet inquired about Derbyshire and Pemberley. He suspected that the girl was conducting a surreptitious investigation of his income and connections.

When finally the party drew to a close Darcy bowed impeccably yet curtly to his hosts and took his leave. Outside, he waited for Bingley, who had lingered to bid goodnight to Miss Bennet and the Gardiners. After an interminable farewell, Bingley bounded out of the house and down to Darcy's carriage.

"Well," he eagerly asked Darcy, "What do you think of Miss Bennet?"

"She smiles too much," Darcy said flatly.

Bingley's expectant grin faded from his face. "I find her to be perfectly lovely and all that is good and kind."

Darcy snorted. "Bingley, did you not see how she continued to ask me questions about Pemberley? She is clearly a fortune hunter, trying to raise her prospects."

Bingley frowned, considering. "I thought she was being polite and attempting to include you in the conversation."

"You thought incorrectly, then," Darcy stated firmly. "Bingley, I have had much more experience in dealing with women over the years than you have. When they pay particular attention to another man in your presence, they are endeavoring to ensnare as opportune a match as possible." Noting Bingley's dismayed face, he continued less sharply, "Bingley, it was clear to me by her smiles. She smiles too much—she smiled at you, certainly, but she also smiled at me."

Bingley's face twisted with disappointment. "Then you do not believe her affections are sincerely engaged?"

"Most definitely not. Even if they were engaged, however, you are too young to form such attachments. Does she know that you are a mere eighteen years of age and have only just begun at Oxford?"

Bingley shook his head, dejected. Darcy appraised his companion for a few moments, then put his arm around his friend's shoulders.

"Come, Bingley," he coaxed, "Let us retire to Darcy House to drink some port, then tomorrow we shall travel to Pemberley for the remainder of the school break. You will see much more clearly after you are able to clear your head away from these distractions."

Bingley nodded somberly, and the pair climbed into Darcy's carriage.

Chapter 3

Hertfordshire, April 1806

Lizzy jumped as she heard a sound from outside. Racing to the sitting room window, she peered outside.

"Lizzy!" cried her mother. "My nerves cannot take much more of this! Remain seated!"

"Yes, Mamma," Lizzy agreed, though she lingered by the window, trying to catch one last glimpse of the outdoors. It had been three months since the girls had last been together before Jane had fled to London to escape Mr. Cartwright. Jane would return home today, and Lizzy was eager to see her sister again. The older girl's carriage was late, and both Lizzy and Mrs. Bennet were concerned.

"Oh, what could have delayed my dear Jane?" wailed Mrs. Bennet. "What if something dreadful has happened? I am sure that she has been set upon by highwaymen, who have certainly carried her away after a mere glimpse of her fair face. Would that she had been less handsome, for then they might have spared her. What shall become of us if we do not have my beautiful girl to marry well and take care of her mother when her father is dead?"

Lizzy allowed her eyes to roll heavenward, then concealed her exasperation behind a patient smile. "Mamma, remember that there was quite a bit of rain during the night. The more likely explanation for Jane's tardiness is that the roads are difficult due to mud. She will be arriving shortly."

As if she had summoned her sister by magic, Lizzy heard the faint sound of muffled horse hooves outside the house. Jumping to her feet, Lizzy raced toward the front of the house. She burst through the entry door and came to an abrupt halt next to the carriage. She bounced on both feet whilst she waited impatiently for the footman to hand Jane down.

"Oh, it was so good of my brother to send you in his carriage," exclaimed Mrs. Bennet as Jane and Lizzy embraced. "But, of course," she continued haughtily, "What else should he do with the carriage but help his niece return safely home?"

Jane released Lizzy to embrace her mother, kissing her on the cheek. "I am glad to be home, Mamma," she said in a quiet voice.

Lizzy frowned as she examined Jane. Her pale face and red-rimmed eyes hinted that she was not as serene as she had first appeared.

"Come inside, girls," Mrs. Bennet ordered as rain began to fall once again.

Lizzy made to follow Jane up the stairs, but she was delayed by yet another argument between Kitty and Lydia. Once she resolved the question as to whom some scrap of lace belonged, Lizzy made her way upstairs, only to find the door to Jane's room locked.

"Jane?" Lizzy inquired as she knocked softly on the door. "Jane, dear, it's me."

"One moment, Lizzy," came Jane's muffled voice.

It was several moments before the door finally opened a minute amount, revealing a single beautiful blue eye. Jane whispered hoarsely, "Lizzy, I simply need a few minutes of privacy. Please tell Mamma that I will be down soon." Without further explanation, she shut the door. Lizzy managed only to gape at her sister's closed door as she heard the click of the lock securing Jane against any intrusions. Lizzy's older sister had never locked the door against her. After a few moments of astonishment, Lizzy proceeded back down the stairs. She didn't know what to make of her sister's odd behavior, but she was suddenly extremely worried

When Jane eventually joined the group in a worn and faded morning gown, Lizzy's trepidation increased. Before she could say anything, Mrs. Bennet began. "My dear Jane, come and tell me all of the current fashions for sleeves! I am desperate to know all of the latest styles. Your letters spoke of card parties and balls almost every night. I simply must hear each event recounted as well. When can we expect a suitor to come speak to your father?"

Lizzy had not thought it was possible for Jane's face to pale any further, but it turned an awful shade of gray. "There is no such suitor, Mamma," Jane eked out in whisper.

"No suitor? No suitor!" exclaimed an appalled Mrs. Bennet. "Preposterous! Why then did we go to such great expense to send you to London with your aunt and uncle if you were not going to return engaged?"

Unable to bear another minute of Mrs. Bennet's haranguing, Jane stood abruptly. "Please excuse me, Mamma. I fear I have a headache from my travels. I should rest before dinner, so as to recover. No, Lizzy," she said as Lizzy stood to join her, "I will be well enough on my own."

Once again, Lizzy could only stare helplessly as Jane left the room and closed another door on her.

$\sim\infty\sim\infty\sim\infty\sim$

Jane's distant manner persisted for several days. Finally, after an entire miserable week, a determined Lizzy quickly finished her breakfast and excused herself from the table before anyone else had the chance to join her. She climbed the stairs and moved past her bedroom door, marching resolutely to her sister's room instead. She entered and waited quietly on the bed until she heard Jane enter the room.

"Lizzy, I am sorry, but I have—" began Jane.

"No, Jane, this will not do!" interrupted Lizzy. "I cannot endure this any longer. There is something the matter with you. You have been quiet, more so than usual, and you have been avoiding me."

"It is nothing. I am merely fatigued from my travels. I need only to rest and recover." Jane attempted to affect a reassuring smile, but it was obviously forced.

"Jane, it is clearly much more than that." Lizzy asserted, "Have you taken ill? Are you unhappy to be home, Jane? Would you rather have stayed in London?"

"Oh, no!" cried Jane, distressed. "As grateful as I am to my aunt uncle for the time I spent there, I much prefer being at home."

"Did you not enjoy any of it, then?" asked Lizzy, perplexed. "Surely you made some new friends or enjoyed the exhibits and theater, in addition to society."

"It was all very nice," Jane demurred.

The girls sat in silence. They heard the patter of footsteps as their other sisters raced through the hallway. A loud thud reverberated through the house, causing Lizzy to glance toward the door. The concerning noise was soon followed by shrieks of laughter from the hall, so she returned her attention to Jane. To her dismay, she saw Jane's eyes brimming with repressed tears.

"Oh, Jane!" cried Lizzy as she pulled Jane into her arms. Jane's shoulders shook as she sobbed into her delicate hands, leaning into her sister's warmth. Lizzy murmured comforting noises while Jane released all of the wretched heartache she had struggled to contain since returning home.

Once Jane's tears had subsided, Lizzy pulled her handkerchief out of her pocket. Grimacing at the mangled embroidery with which she had tortured the fabric, she began to mop up Jane's tears. She supposed it didn't matter how ugly the handkerchief was, so long as she didn't poke her sister in the eye with it.

"Now, then, Jane," Lizzy said, "tell me what happened."

The tale of her experiences with Mr. Bingley fairly tumbled out of Jane's mouth in a rush, as though it was afraid of being smothered once again. Jane had mentioned Mr. Bingley affectionately in her letters, giving rise to their mother's expectations of an imminent engagement.

"And then he invited his friend to our card party. It was clear the gentleman was exceptionally uncomfortable. He had very fine clothing, much finer than what anyone else was wearing. I believe he also has a house in Governors Street. But he spoke very little and stood listening to Mr. Bingley and me. I tried to engage him in conversation, but he rarely deigned to answer with more than a word or two."

Jane paused for a minute, collecting her thoughts. "Then Mr. Bingley said that Mr. Darcy—his friend—needed to leave, and he would escort him out. He promised to return immediately and said he had something very particular he wished to ask me."

"This sounds rather blissful thus far, Jane. What happened when Mr. Bingley returned to the house?"

"Nothing at all happened, Lizzy! I waited for him until all the other guests had left as well, but he never returned! I asked the butler, and he told me that Mr. Bingley had left with his friend in Mr. Darcy's carriage a few minutes after they stepped out of the house."

Lizzy's mouth fell open. "Jane, are you telling me that is the last time you saw him?"

Jane burst into tears again, burying her face in Lizzy's disfigured handkerchief. She managed to continue through her sobs. "I was certain there had been a misunderstanding of sorts. Perhaps Mr. Darcy had received a message of an urgent nature and he required Mr. Bingley's assistance. The crisis might have been so serious as to prevent any delay, so they would have left without sending word. I remained at home every morning for the remaining three weeks of my visit. Even throughout that final day, I continued to hope that he would arrive with some reasonable explanation for ignoring me so."

Lizzy heard her blood rushing in her ears. "I cannot believe a gentleman would behave so... so... so ungentlemanly!"

The girls lapsed into a dejected silence. Finally, Jane whispered, "I wish I knew what I had done wrong to make him flee."

"There was absolutely nothing that you could have done wrongly!" Lizzy declared hotly. "Jane, you are the kindest, most gentle woman I have ever known. For him to make declarations and then disappear with nary a word is abhorrent behavior! He is the one who has erred, not you."

Jane nodded mutely, but her eyes remained fixed on the bed.

"Jane, you must believe me," pleaded Lizzy.

"It is not that I disbelieve you, Lizzy," Jane said, "Rather, I think you—like I—must not be in possession of all of the facts. After all, Mr. Bingley is such an amiable and tender gentleman. I cannot believe that one who appears so good could have played me so false."

Lizzy frowned. What was she to do now? *If only you had been with me that day to see Mr. Cartwright,* she thought. *You would not have the same opinion of the goodness of men that you do now.*

Lizzy sighed. "Jane, you will never be able to convince me that you did something wrong. You are too good."

Jane brightened slightly, "Perhaps it is still all just a misunder-standing."

"You may think that, Jane, if it gives you comfort." Lizzy stood up. "Now, I believe Mamma shall require our attendance at dinner shortly. Are you well enough to join us?"

"Yes, Lizzy, of course I am. I will soon be as I always was. You'll see."

~∞~∞~∞~

The passing days developed into weeks, and the weeks grew into months. To the entire world, Jane appeared as serene as ever. But Lizzy was more observant than most. There was something in Jane's manner that hinted at her secret heartache.

One particular morning, Mrs. Bennet declared at breakfast that she, Jane, and Lizzy would head into Meryton the next day.

"What for, Mamma?" asked Lizzy.

"Why, for your new gowns, of course!" cried a delighted Mrs. Bennet.

"Why do I need new gowns, Mamma?"

Mrs. Bennet scrutinized her second daughter, eyes narrowed in disbelief. "For your coming out, child! You will be fifteen in a month, at which point you will be out and attending assemblies and balls! Your schoolroom dresses will not be appropriate!"

"I want to come out, Mamma!" cried Lydia.

"Me, too!" seconded Kitty.

Lizzy regarded her mother with horror. "Mamma, I thought that I would not come out this year. After all," she desperately seized on a plausible excuse, "it is more proper for the younger sisters to come out *after* the elder are safely wed."

Lizzy threw an apologetic grimace at her older sister, but only a slight pinkening of her downturned face betrayed that Jane was affected in any way by Lizzy's comment.

"Wait until Jane is married? Why, you silly child!" cried a vexed Mrs. Bennet, "We simply cannot wait. Your father grows older and closer to death every single day!"

"That is typically how time progresses," Mr. Bennet interjected drily.

Mrs. Bennet continued as though her husband had not spoken. "Jane has proven unable to secure an advantageous match in London. You are my second daughter, and as such, must improve our chances at one of you marrying well. The first match made of you girls will set the precedent for all the others. You have no hope of securing your own future this season, but Jane still might. You are not nearly as beautiful and agreeable as Jane. Perhaps the contrast you provide, however, will enable the young men to more fully appreciate your sister's exceedingly valuable qualities."

"Mamma!" gasped Jane in shock. Mr. Bennet's eyebrows rose, and Kitty and Lydia burst into giggles.

"Beauty is only skin deep," intoned Mary piously. She had recently begun reading Fordyce's sermons—among other religious texts—and had taken to spouting moralistic platitudes at every opportunity.

"Exactly right, Mary!" cried their mother. "Jane's beauty will only persist for a brief moment, and Elizabeth's beauty does not penetrate as deeply. We must seize every opportunity we can to find a match for Jane before her beauty fades and your father dies and we are all thrown into the streets."

As her mother lectured, Lizzy slowly sank deeply into her chair. She fought to stifle the tears welling in her eyes. "Excuse me," she murmured then hastily arose and fled the room.

Lizzy raced through the house and erupted out the front door without stopping for her bonnet or boots. She tore down the cobblestone path and into the gardens. She grabbed a fistful of leaves from a hedgerow and threw them at the ground. Finding no satisfaction in the gesture, Lizzy dropped unceremoniously to the ground, pulled her knees to her chest, and hugged them tightly. What she really wanted to do was stomp her feet and yell, but she knew that would only draw the ire of the groundskeeper.

"Lizzy?" Jane's gentle voice came up behind her. She felt Jane's warm, gentle hand on her shoulder, providing a comforting weight that eased her loneliness and anger.

"I'm sorry, Lizzy," Jane soothed.

"You owe me no such apology," Lizzy admonished, "It's Mamma who should apologize."

"It truly is my fault," Jane insisted, "Had I secured Mr. Cartwright or Mr. Bingley, Mamma would feel more secure in our position, and she would not speak so thoughtlessly. It is my selfishness and failure that has disrupted our entire family."

Lizzy leapt to her feet and spun to face her sister, dark eyes flashing. "Jane, you did rightly in avoiding Mr. Cartwright's intention. You do not love him!"

Jane shrugged a shoulder. "Perhaps not, but he is quite handsome and amiable. I am certain that love could have grown in time. I might even have been happy, knowing that I had secured my family's future."

Lizzy sighed heavily. *What do I say to that?* she wondered. *How can I keep my promise to Becky, knowing that Jane continues in such naivety?*

42

Coming to a decision, Lizzy said firmly, "Jane, Mr. Cartwright was *not* a good man."

Jane's eyes widened in reproof. "I know he was not a favorite of yours, Lizzy, but that does not mean—"

"No, Jane," Lizzy interrupted. She fortified herself with a deep breath before continuing, "What I am about to tell you must never be spoken of again. Not even the two of us shall discuss this matter after this moment. Do you agree?"

"Lizzy, what are you talking about?"

"I mean it, Jane. I will not tell you unless you swear that you will never tell another living soul."

"All right, Lizzy," Jane capitulated, "I promise."

Lizzy proceeded to inform Jane of the incident regarding Mr. Cartwright and Becky nearly two years previous. Jane's face grew ashen and her hands began to shake as she listened to the foul recounting. When Lizzy told of Becky leaving home to birth Mr. Cartwright's baby, Jane pressed her hand to her mouth to stifle a sob.

"That's why I encouraged Mamma to send you to London," Lizzy concluded, "I could not bear for you to marry such a monster."

"Oh, Lizzy!" cried Jane, "How could someone with every appearance of goodness hide such evil for so long?"

"I know not," replied Lizzy, "But since that day I have vowed to never judge a man solely by his behavior in company. A handsome face and charming manners matter comparatively little. Mary was correct this morning in her assertion that beauty extends only as deeply as your skin; it does not show what is in your heart."

Jane nodded in agreement. "Then how are we to know?" she asked, "How do we learn whether a man will be a kind husband or a cruel one?"

Lizzy halted the question. She had not yet thought so far into the future as to how she would discover a man's true character; she only knew that she must do so prior to marrying him.

"I am not entirely certain," she said slowly. Her mind grasped for an answer. Was it even possible to take the full measure of a man when a chaperone must observe every moment spent together? How could she observe a man unencumbered by societal expectations if they were never to be alone?

The sound of footsteps crunching over leaves caused both girls to jump. They spun in unison toward the noise and saw their friend Charlotte Lucas walking down the path towards them. Lizzy and Jane locked eyes and nodded to one another. They relaxed and moved to greet their friend.

Charlotte waved as she approached. "Hello, Jane! Hello, Lizzy!" she called. "Your mother said I might find you down here." Charlotte carefully made her way down the last few steps of the garden path, lifting the hem of her oversized dress to avoid tripping on it.

"What a lovely surprise!" cried Lizzy gladly. Although Charlotte was closer in age to Jane, it was Lizzy who had more in common with the oldest daughter of a poor knight. Charlotte and Lizzy were more practical, whereas Jane typically viewed the world with rose-colored lenses. Lizzy saddened at the realization that she had destroyed a part of her sister's blissful perspective

"What are you girls doing out here?" Charlotte asked. She brushed a stray wisp of hair from her face. "I'm not surprised to see you out of doors, Lizzy, but I didn't expect you to accompany her, Jane!"

Jane smiled and replied, "Lizzy and I were discussing how Mamma wants her to get measured for dresses tomorrow. Mamma means for her to come out after she turns fifteen next month."

Charlotte's eyes widened in surprise. "I see," she ventured cautiously, "How momentous."

Lizzy laughed at her friend. "You need not hide your true feelings from me," she teased, "I agree that I am much too young to be gallivanting about with potential husbands!"

Charlotte's face relaxed into a wide smile. "It is not a question of your exceptional maturity. Rather, I am concerned that—thanks to Napoleon—the number of young ladies sitting out at assemblies is already high enough! I think only of the poor girls whose dance cards would assuredly empty to fill yours. The three girls shared an amused moment before Jane asked the question that was on her mind.

"Charlotte," she began, "Lizzy and I have been discussing marriage."

"Why, Jane!" exclaimed Charlotte. "You might have mentioned this sooner! Of course, I'm not surprised to learn that you had such great success in London. You must tell me everything."

"No, no, I am not engaged," Jane hurried to rectify the assumption as a blush spread across her cheeks. "However, Lizzy is coming out, and that has naturally led to discussion as to what constitutes a good match. Lizzy and I are wondering how we can know if a young man will make a good husband."

Charlotte pursed her lips as she considered. "Well," she began slowly, "I have often thought that happiness in marriage is entirely a matter of chance. It is probably best to know as little as possible about the defects of one's partner until after the wedding."

Jane and Lizzy started to laugh, then fell abruptly silent as Charlotte's frown deepened.

"My dear Charlotte," cried Lizzy, "You know you would not behave in such a way regarding your own marriage! How can you be certain of your security or safety?"

Charlotte sighed heavily. "As women, we have very few freedoms in life. We exist always under the regulation of our fathers or our husbands. All I require is a comfortable home of which I will be mistress. The other parts are quite negotiable."

Lizzy looked at her friend in disbelief. "But Charlotte," she implored, "What if he"—her voice lowered to a whisper—"hurts you?"

Charlotte fidgeted anxiously. After a moment, she said, "Some outcomes would be preferable to others. You two can afford to reject unsavory suitors. Those of us who have little but our charms to recommend us may have only one choice to make: an unpleasant husband or an even less agreeable position as a governess or companion. At least as the mistress of a home would be allowed some freedoms."

The three girls stood somberly in the garden, the wind ruffling their skirts about their legs as though whisking away the vestiges of their childhood innocence.

A minute later, Lizzy shook her head and laughed. "Come, girls," she cried, "let us speak of more pleasant things. What colors and styles do you suppose will most become me at the modiste tomorrow?"

~∞~∞~∞~

The next day found Jane, Mrs. Bennet, and Lizzy riding the carriage into town. Lizzy would have much preferred to walk, but after birthing five children, Mrs. Bennet could no longer make the journey into Meryton on foot. As they travelled, Mrs. Bennet spoke of nothing but lace and ribbons.

The women soon entered the modiste and began looking at fashion plates. After a moment, Lizzy was called back behind a curtain to have her measurements taken by two seamstresses.

"Look here, Jane!" called Mrs. Bennet loudly from her occupation with the plates. "Your dresses do not have nearly enough flounces to be in fashion anymore. It is no wonder Mr. Cartwright never offered for you."

Upon hearing Mr. Cartwright's name, the two seamstresses exchanged a glance. When they caught Lizzy peering quizzically at them, they quickly returned their attention to measuring and pinning. Lizzy glanced over the curtain to be sure her mother was still occupied, then whispered, "What do you know about Mr. Cartwright?"

One of the seamstresses looked up fearfully. "We know nothing, Miss Lizzy."

"Nonsense," proclaimed Lizzy too loudly, wincing internally as she realized how much she sounded like her mother. Undeterred, she lowered her voice back to a conspiratorial whisper and continued, "I know that he was not a good man, but it seems everyone else is unaware. Please, what do you know about Mr. Cartwright?"

The first girl remained resolutely silent, but the second seamstress spoke up. "I don't know details, Miss Lizzy, but many of the Netherfield tenants seemed afraid of him. The servants, too."

The first seamstress nodded in agreement, then stated, "My ma always said that a true gentleman treats his lessers the same as he treats his betters."

Lizzy slowly nodded. The girls had given her much to think about, and she began to formulate the beginnings of a plan for the impending months. She resolved to share it with Jane at home that night. Perhaps between the two of them, they had a chance to make a good match with a kind man after all—without having to resort to chance.

Chapter 4

Derbyshire, December 1806

Fitzwilliam Darcy was cold.

At least it's not hot up here, he thought wryly as he looked down on the garden from his position on the balcony. He had been back in Derbyshire for six months, and this was the first event held by any of the landowners during that time.

The hosts were a new family who had taken residence after coming into their inheritance in the last year or so. They were a young couple, without children, and they seemed eager to take their place amongst their neighbors. Their inexperience, however, was unfortunately clear. Although the room held the appropriate number of couples for its size, the heat from the fires rendered the atmosphere more uncomfortable than Lady M____'s crowded ball had been all those months ago.

"There you are, Darcy!" he heard Bingley exclaim. Darcy sighed; his moment of quiet was over.

Bingley called again from the ballroom door. "Darcy, why are you out in the cold? Come inside, man! You've been missed!"

Darcy let out another sigh and relinquished his solitude. He knew that he was missed only by the local country misses who repeatedly pressed Bingley as to the whereabouts of the handsome master of Pemberley. Even here at home, there was no respite for the wealthy.

Darcy entered the ballroom and looked around. Bingley had rejoined their host and entreated the man's wife to grant him the next set. She acquiesced and allowed herself to be escorted to the floor.

Reticent to cross the ballroom and speak to the man to whom he'd only met one other time, Darcy veered toward the punch table instead. He accepted a glass from the servant and drank deeply, then winced as the tepid liquid slid down his throat. Clearly the mistress was unaccustomed to planning events of such magnitude. Any experienced hostess would have been certain to acquire enough ice to cool the refreshments. Perhaps she had neglected to account for the extra warmth of the superfluous fires.

Darcy watched the dancers absentmindedly. He loathed frittering his evenings away at such gatherings. There was very little occasion to engage in more than inane pleasantries with your partner, which struck him as a rather inefficient quest for a proper wife.

He took another sip of his drink and winced again, having already forgotten how warm it was. He motioned to a passing servant who bore away his nearly full cup on an otherwise empty tray. A moment later, he watched in horror as the servant collided with a dancing lady who had turned the wrong way.

Darcy's drink poured down the front of the unfortunate lady's dress. She shrieked and jumped away while she threw her arms into the air. One of her hands came in sharp contact with the beleaguered servant, who slipped on the wet floor and fell directly onto the goblet. The sound of glass shattering was nearly drowned out by said lady's hysterics.

The room seemed frozen in time for a few seconds as the guests turned as one to see the commotion. Darcy—often the first to react in a moment of crisis—rushed to the unmoving servant on the floor. He spared a brief glance for the lady but saw that she was unharmed. *Her maid will never be able to save that dress*, he noted.

Darcy gently rolled the servant onto his back and assessed the damage. While the majority of the glass had been crushed between the floor and the tray, one large shard was embedded in the servant's right forearm. The servant groaned against the increased pain from the movement.

"Easy there, lad," Darcy said placatingly, "Try not to move. We may not have discovered all the damage, and it would be rather troublesome if you ruined the party by spilling more blood on your mistress's floor." Darcy frowned when the young man gave no indication that he had heard Darcy's attempt at humor.

"Cartwright!" Darcy bellowed to his host. "Send a servant for Dr. Porter. Quickly!" Cartwright gave a quick nod and signaled to a footman, who raced to locate the physician. Cartwright then joined Darcy on the floor by the servant.

"Well," said Cartwright with a tight smile. "This is certainly not what I had planned for this evening."

Darcy shot his host a look of commiseration, then refocused his attention on the servant. He opened his mouth to address the wounded man when he was interrupted with a loud shriek, followed by a thud. He looked up to see the lady with the stained dress motionless on the floor, having had a fit of the vapors at the sight of blood.

Darcy raised an eyebrow and suggested to Cartwright in a low voice, "Perhaps it would be prudent of you and your wife to direct your guests to another room until their carriages can be called for."

Cartwright hesitated, then nodded in agreement. He snapped his fingers and his wife scurried over, causing Darcy to raise both of his eyebrows. Cartwright stood to whisper in her ear. While Darcy could not make out the words, Cartwright's tone contrasted sharply with the smile he directed at his guests.

While Mrs. Cartwright directed the guests from the ballroom, Cartwright snapped his fingers again to summon two footmen to join Darcy and the injured servant.

"What is his name?" Darcy asked Cartwright, but the only response he received was silence. Noting Cartwright's baffled expression, Darcy turned to the footmen who had just joined them. "What is this man's name?" he repeated.

"Stevens, sir," answered one of the footmen, who had knelt down next to Darcy and was elevating Stevens's head.

"Alright, Stevens, how do you feel?" Darcy asked the unmoving servant. When no response came, Darcy frowned in concern. "Fetch the housekeeper," he ordered the second footman. The man hesitated and looked at Cartwright, who nodded. The footman dashed away and returned moments later with the wheezing housekeeper.

"Ah, Mrs. Brown!" Darcy exclaimed in surprise. "I was unaware that you had obtained a position here."

"Yes, sir, Mr. Darcy, sir," confirmed Mrs. Brown, glancing warily at Mr. Cartwright.

"Excellent," he responded. Turning to a bewildered Cartwright, Darcy said, "Mrs. Brown is sister to my own housekeeper, Mrs. Reynolds. You will never find a finer pair of women." Mrs. Brown blushed and looked down at Stevens.

"What do you recommend?" Darcy asked Mrs. Brown.

"What?" interjected Cartwright. "Do you honestly mean to consult a mere housekeeper in the care of such an injury? Surely, we should wait for the doctor to arrive. Not only does he have the requisite training, will also be capable of addressing the issue calmly and effectively. You cannot expect a woman to maintain the same level of composure that a man can display."

Any warmth Darcy had previously felt toward his new neighbor instantly evaporated. Ignoring the foolish comments, Darcy repeated his question to the housekeeper.

Mrs. Brown glanced fearfully at Mr. Cartwright, then said, "We should move him as little as possible. Mr. Cartwright is correct; we should wait for the doctor before attempting to remove the glass from his body." At Cartwright's smirk, she faltered, then determinedly continued, "However, we should attempt to clear the area around him and remove any loose glass, as well as place towels around the wound."

Darcy looked at Cartwright, who was glaring slightly at Mrs.

Brown. When the other man failed to act, Darcy admonished, "Cartwright, what are you waiting for, man? Do as she said!"

A derisive sneer marred Cartwright's face for only an instant. Had Darcy not been looking directly at the man, he would have missed the flash of anger and only seen the smooth façade that was set in its place. "Certainly!" he said and sent the second footman back out to collect towel and a broom.

Ten minutes later, Dr. Porter arrived, breathless from his haste. He took one moment to observe the situation, then said, "Well done, Mr. Cartwright. Excellent work in caring for this man."

Darcy waited for Mr. Cartwright to correct the doctor, but no such statement was issued. Instead, Cartwright merely bowed in acknowledgement. Darcy's distaste for the man increased.

Dr. Porter spent several minutes examining the wound and the glass within, then announced, "I will need some men to hold him in place while I remove the glass."

Darcy held the man's injured arm, while the footmen each secured one leg. Mr. Cartwright moved to hold the man's remaining limb only when he noticed the others looking at him expectantly. Once everyone was settled, Dr. Porter quickly yet carefully pulled the glass free.

Stevens arched his back in agony, straining against the hands that restrained him. All had a firm grip on him except Mr. Cartwright, who scrambled backward as soon as Stevens moved.

"Cartwright!" Darcy yelled. Anger briefly contorted Cartwright's face again before he scrambled back into the chaos and secured Stevens's flailing arm. Restrained once more, Stevens ceded his consciousness again.

Dr. Porter frowned, evaluating his patient's status. "It appears the glass missed the proximate major artery, which is very fortunate. However, the shard has sliced one of the muscles. I will need to stitch it closed, but even if it heals without complication, he will be unable to use his arm for many months at least, if ever."

The first footman—who had provided Darcy with Stevens'

name—let out a despairing groan. Dr. Porter removed suture supplies from his medical bag and began to seal the wound.

Darcy stood and turned to Cartwright. "What will you do?" Darcy asked.

Cartwright took a moment to consider. "I suppose I must permit him to remain here tonight. After that, I believe I can afford him a fortnight to heal before we determine whether or not he will regain his capacity. A servant who cannot work cannot be kept."

Darcy bit back a sigh of disappointment. When he first met Cartwright, he had appreciated the man's demeanor and apparent uprightness. What he had seen tonight, however, reminded him too much of his old friend George Wickham: a man with a smooth, pleasing countenance that quickly disappeared whenever he was disconcerted or amid those whom he considered to rank below him.

Darcy knew that Cartwright's actions were no worse than those many other gentlemen would make in the same situation. Indeed, allowing the injured man a fortnight to recuperate in the comfortable manor house itself would be considered generous by most of the peerage, but Darcy knew it would not be sufficient assistance to prevent Stevens from falling into a whirlpool of infirmity, incertitude, and—ultimately—poverty and death. Darcy understood that the latter two conditions were likely to come about sooner than many privileged persons could comprehend.

Dr. Porter completed the stitching and directed the two footmen to carry Stevens to a place where he could rest. Cartwright followed the footmen, and Darcy heard Cartwright direct them to the servants' quarters. Mrs. Brown began to clean the ballroom floor of shattered glass and blood.

"Mrs. Brown," Darcy addressed the stalwart woman, "kindly keep Mrs. Reynolds apprised of any changes in Stevens' condition." At her nod, he continued, "If you or any of your subordinates finds themselves in dire straits, please inform her of the situation."

Mrs. Brown stood from her work and dipped into a somewhat

unstable curtsy. "Thank you, Mr. Darcy. Would that—" She hesitated, then pressed on, "If only all masters were as kind as you, sir."

Darcy nodded his head in acceptance of her gratitude, then left to fetch his coat and find Bingley so they could head home.

As the carriage journeyed toward Pemberley, a light snow began to fall. Bingley extolled Cartwright's apparently masterful management of the difficult situation. Darcy kept his thoughts to himself, not wanting to speak poorly of the man. *After all,* Darcy thought. *Not all of us are at our best during an emergency.*

~∞~∞~∞~

Three weeks later, Darcy and Bingley had ensconced themselves in Darcy's study, poring over the most recent ledgers. Bingley was considering fulfilling his father's wish by purchasing an estate three years after graduating from Oxford as a way to gain entrance into the landed gentry. When Bingley had joined Darcy at Pemberley after the Cheapside debacle and his narrow escape, he began to speak about finding somewhere to settle down when he finished school.

Darcy maintained that Bingley should let an estate before he actually made such a purchase. Before he took even that step, however, Darcy had impressed upon him the importance of knowing *how* to run and maintain an estate. "This is not like simply moving into a new house," Darcy had explained. "The running of an estate is a tremendous responsibility—you hold the wellbeing of many people in your hands."

Bingley determined that he should live at Pemberley with Darcy during each break in order to experience all the work that went into running an estate. Although Darcy frequently returned to London for the Season, he was to forego the visit this year so that Bingley could experience a full year on an estate. He also welcomed the opportunity to evade the conniving mothers of ambitious young ladies.

A knock on the door interrupted Darcy's lecture on some finer points of crop rotation. "Enter," he said, as Bingley made another notation on a pad of paper.

"Sir, might you have a moment?" Darcy looked up in surprise to see Mrs. Reynolds enter the room. Mrs. Reynolds had been working at Pemberley since Darcy was five years old. She managed the entire household with great competence, and it was rare for her to disturb him outside of their regular daily meeting.

"Is everything alright, Mrs. Reynolds?" asked Darcy.

She hesitated, then glanced briefly at Bingley. Darcy's eyes narrowed in concern. "Is it about Georgiana?" His younger sister had begun finishing school earlier that year, and she was home on holiday for a week. When Mrs. Reynolds shook her head, Darcy replied, "If it pertains to household matters, best allow Bingley to hear as well. He will need experience in dealing with such matters once he manages his own estate."

"Ah, you forget!" cried Bingley, "that I have a sister who may tend to such duties!"

Mrs. Reynolds hastily smoothed an expression that had appeared on her face at this assertion. Darcy smiled wryly at Bingley's naivete.

"No, Bingley," he responded, "it is *you* who forgets that your sister will have only just left finishing school when you intend to attain administration of an estate. While Miss Bingley attends one of the more prestigious academies, there are many aspects of managing a country household that differ from tending a house in town. She is, I grant you, a superb city mistress, but there is much more to the duties of a full estate's household custodian than simply keeping the servants on task."

Bingley's face fell slightly, but he quickly regained his cheerful expression. "It is a good thing, then, that you will be joining me for the beginning!"

Darcy smiled indulgently and returned his attention to Mrs. Reynolds. "What household matters require my attention, Mrs. Reynolds?"

"Begging your pardon, sir, but I understand you asked Mrs. Brown to inform me as to any developments in the servant Stevens' recuperation?"

"Yes, I did," Darcy responded. "How fares the young man in question?"

Mrs. Reynolds shook her head sadly. "His healing is going much slower than Dr. Porter would prefer. Unfortunately, with Stevens being in the servants' quarters, he is left alone to tend to his own needs for the majority of the day. The other servants are unable to leave their duties to attend to his care. This allowed a small infection to settle in the wound. But," she hurriedly reassured at Darcy's expression of alarm, "that has all been resolved."

"If everything is resolved, why have you interrupted us?" asked Darcy.

"It appears, sir, that Mr. Cartwright will no longer allow Stevens to reside at the estate, since he cannot work to earn his keep. Further, Mr. Cartwright refuses to pay for the doctor's services, insisting that it was Stevens's own clumsiness that brought about the trouble."

Darcy's lips tightened in anger, and Bingley let out an oath. At Darcy's reproving look, Bingley blushed and muttered an apology for using such language in the woman's presence.

"Of course, sir," she curtsied to Bingley. "You expressed my sentiments precisely."

"Thank you, Mrs. Reynolds, for informing me," said Darcy. "Where is Stevens now?"

"Well, sir," Mrs. Reynolds said hesitantly, "I've put him up in the kitchen right now. You see, Mr. Cartwright demanded suddenly that Stevens depart early this morning. It put quite some strain on his arm to make it from there to the public road, where he collapsed and was found by one of the Pemberley tenants, who brought him here."

Darcy almost uttered an oath himself, and Bingley let out a low whistle. "I say," Bingley declared, "that was not very well done at all."

"One of the most important things you must learn about being master of an estate," said Darcy to Bingley, "is that an accident of birth in no way determines a man's character. Instead, his actions will demonstrate if he is truly a gentleman with honor, or one who merely bears the title like an accessory."

Bingley nodded. "As it was back at school."

"Quite right," said Darcy. He focused his attention again on Mrs. Reynolds. "Please prepare a small chamber in the guest quarters that Stevens may use. Assign a maid to attend him should he require assistance. Settle the bill with Dr. Porter and inform him that I will bear financial responsibility for all future medical services he renders to Stevens arising from the unhappy accident."

Mrs. Reynolds graced her employer with a rare smile. "Very good, sir." She dipped a deeper parting curtsy than was typical and exited the room.

Several loud claps sounded in the room. Darcy turned to see Bingley applauding in a dramatic display of approval. "Darcy, old boy, I've always known that you were a good man, but this was gallantry beyond compare."

Darcy's lips twisted in wry amusement. "Bingley, the master of an estate bears a solemn responsibility. Far too many of the *ton* hold the opinion that their birth and fortune exist to support their excesses."

Darcy paused and stared off into space for a time. "That is part of why I so despise town and fortune hunters. They spend more time looking for ways to elevate themselves as opposed to using what they have to lift others. Too often, they instead use their positions of privilege to flatten others into the dust, that they may ascend to greater heights using the broken bodies of those whom they have defamed."

Bingley nodded thoughtfully, his face uncharacteristically solemn. "Like Miss Bennet."

Darcy confusedly cocked his head. Bingley explained, "The young woman from Cheapside. I thought she would be the making of me, but she merely used me as a stepping stone to rise higher—to you, in this case."

"Precisely," agreed Darcy, "though she was certainly not the first woman to attempt such a maneuver. There was Miss Templeton, Miss Downs, Miss Scott—"

"And Miss Reed!" cried Bingley with a laugh. "I shall never forget your expression when we chanced to hear her say to her mother that, while I had the more congenial personality, she preferred your income over mine, and she did not know which of us two she should endeavor to attract."

Darcy chuckled. "Most members of society—from peerage to trade—continually seek for ways to elevate their position. They make themselves content with "advantageous" marriages to strangers in order to increase their status. You, however, deserve to marry someone who cares for you as a person, not as a person they must tolerate in exchange for pin money."

Bingley looked down sorrowfully. "I appreciate your friendship and advice, Darcy. I would be unable to navigate these treacherous situations by myself."

Darcy tipped his head in acknowledgment. After a moment of silence, he said, "Now, where were we? Ah, yes, looking back to last year's crops..."

Chapter 5

Hertfordshire, November 1807

The upstairs rooms at Longbourn were filled with the sounds of giggling girls. Lizzy and Jane had pulled Mary, who had recently turned fifteen, into their room to try different hairstyles for the upcoming assembly.

The hint of a smile on Mary's lips belied her affected petulance. Scowling at her sisters, she declared sternly, "I will not allow you to ruin my hair!"

Jane and Lizzy looked at one another, then burst into giggles. Lizzy reached to tug at Mary's hairpins again. "Stop!" shouted Mary suddenly, bursting into tears.

Jane and Lizzy froze, thoroughly confused at this uncharacteristic outburst from their younger sister. Jane looked helplessly to Lizzy, who lifted her shoulders helplessly in response.

"Mary, dearest," said Jane in the calm voice one might use with a frightened child, "why are you upset?"

Sniffling, Mary settled onto her bed and buried her face in her hands. "I don't want to come out," she wailed between sobs.

Mrs. Bennet had yet again insisted that another of her daughters come out to their local society at the tender age of fifteen. "After all," she had said authoritatively, "we shall need at least one of you to marry well before your father dies and we are cast out to the hedgerows."

Jane and Lizzy had tried to speak with their father, to persuade him to allow shy Mary to remain at home for another year. He merely teased by declaring that jealousy did not become them, and they should not begrudge Mary stealing away all potential suitors.

"Oh, Mary," said Lizzy. "I know that you are frightened. I was as well. But I swear that Jane and I will accompany and support you through every moment of this event. It shan't be too harrowing; you are already acquainted with nearly all of the guests. The Lucases, Longs, Gouldings shall all attend, and they are our friends."

Mary peeked up from her hands with swollen eyes and blotchy cheeks. "It's not that," she whispered.

Lizzy and Jane exchanged bewildered looks. "If the concern is not fear of the large assembly, what has vexed you so?"

Mary hesitated, then shook her head. "You will think me silly."

"I would never laugh at you," Jane assured her.

"*She* would," stated Mary indignantly, pointing at Lizzy, who was already stifling the smile spurred by Mary's surly tone.

Regaining control of herself, Lizzy fixed her features into an earnest expression and placed her hand over her heart. "I vow to not laugh at you, Mary," she swore solemnly.

Glancing cautiously from one of her sisters to the other, Mary took a deep breath and confessed "I am concerned for the welfare of my soul."

There was a long pause, then Jane said, "I am afraid I don't quite understand, Mary."

Lizzy blurted out, "Do you mean to say that, should you attend this assembly, you are in danger of forsaking heaven?"

Mary rolled her eyes, frustrated. "*No*. Well, not really. You see, I was studying Reverend Fordyce's words again this week. I discovered a passage that refers to the declaration in Proverbs that judges charm to be deceitful and beauty the essence of vanity. Further, Malachi proclaims: 'Cursed be the deceiver.' I do not want to be cursed for being a deceiver by curling my hair and dressing in fine clothing."

Lizzy bit her cheeks and focused on the pain to keep hold of the laughter she had promised to contain. Jane's lips pressed together, restraining a snicker. Fortunately, Mary cradled her face in her hands once more, and their irreverent reaction went unnoticed.

Once Jane regained her composure, she cupped Mary's chin in one hand and gently lifted the younger girl's head. "My dear sister," she said compassionately, "Does this truly trouble you so deeply?"

Mary nodded. "Very well, then," said Jane. "We shall respect your wishes and leave your appearance untouched."

"Well, *I* most certainly shall *not* respect them!" cried Lizzy indignantly. Ignoring Jane's reproachful look, Lizzy said, "Mary, I refer you to Proverbs, where it says that a virtuous woman has a price far above rubies. It states that her clothing is silk and purple. Think also of the Song of Solomon! He describes his love as fair multiple times."

Mary and Jane stared at Lizzy in astonishment. "I had no idea you were such a student of the scriptures," Mary said, puzzled.

Lizzy blushed slightly. "I may have done some research once I noticed that you had endeavored to study Fordyce," she explained.

Jane began to giggle, and a wide smile broke across Mary's face. Lizzy joined their gaiety for a few minutes, laughing heartily.

Once the girls had calmed themselves, Lizzy grew serious. Looking directly into Mary's eyes, she said, "Mary, every member of the clergy who has ever visited Longbourn has spoken in Sunday service about God's love. God is the Creator of all, is He not?"

Mary nodded. Lizzy continued, "Then it behooves us all to remember that He would desire for us to delight in all His creations. That includes ourselves. False pride is unseemly, as is ostentatious embellishment and thinking ourselves above another of God's children. But I believe that there is no deceit or vanity in showing God our appreciation by engaging in efforts that allow us—God's own creations—to blossom."

Mary contemplated this perspective. "This is an interesting interpretation," she mused slowly. "You have given me much to think on. Thank you, Sister."

Lizzy hugged Mary, then she and Jane left their younger sister alone to ponder in her room. Once the door closed, Jane turned to Lizzy and whispered, "Brilliant!"

Lizzy smiled. "It is a conversation I have often wanted to have with Mary, but I have been afraid of her reaction. When she spoke of her fears today, I knew that a door had opened. After watching Becky's tragic experience, I have wanted to help my sisters in every way possible."

Jane embraced her sister. "You have helped, Lizzy. You saved me from Mr. Cartwright, and now you may have saved Mary from herself and whatever man would take advantage of her beliefs."

With that, Jane and Lizzy linked arms and proceeded to their closets to select dresses that might best flatter Mary.

The following evening found Mr. Bennet waiting below-stairs for his wife and daughters. He grumbled to himself and checked his pocket-watch impatiently. The sooner they could leave for the assembly, the sooner they might return home.

Mrs. Bennet descended the stairs first, shrieking at her girls to hurry, lest they miss the strategically vital first set. Jane and Lizzy emerged from Mary's room, then lingered at the top of the stairs. After a pause, Mr. Bennet urged, "Girls, come along now."

"Yes, do hurry!" cried Mrs. Bennet. "We must arrive in plenty of time for the young men to request your sets! It would not do to have my girls seen sitting out. Your potential matches might think that you possess some undesirable quality that has put off the rest of the men. You must be seen to delight all in your company."

Jane and Lizzy shared an indulgent smile, then Lizzy proclaimed, "We do hereby present the lovely Miss Mary Bennet!" They stepped apart and turned to face one another, displaying Mary between the two of them.

"Mary, my child! You do look very well indeed!" declared a pleasantly surprised Mrs. Bennet. And Mary did look well. Her severe braids had been exchanged for soft curls that framed her face becomingly, and her usual brown dress was replaced with a delicate rose gown of Jane's.

Mr. Bennet's face softened slightly, and his eyes misted. As Mary descended the stairs, he swallowed the lump that had suddenly formed in his throat. When his maturing middle daughter reached his position on the ground floor, he kissed the top of her head and said, "You look lovely, my dear. I would be deeply honored to have your first two sets, if you are not too embarrassed to stand up with an old man."

Mary beamed, while Lizzy and Jane looked on with pride.

Mary's smile remained on her face through the two sets with her father and through every other set that night. Jane and Lizzy were able to ensure that Mary did not have to sit down even once at her first assembly. They knew that Mary's success at the assembly would set the tone for all her future interactions in society. While she would never be the famous beauty Jane was—as Mrs. Bennett frequently reminded all of her daughters—Jane and Lizzy hoped that Mary's newly forged self-confidence would prevent her from disappearing entirely back into Fordyce and other religious tracts.

Once at home, the three girls climbed into Jane's bed all together, that they might discuss the evening thoroughly.

"Lizzy?" Mary asked from where her head rested on Lizzy's shoulder.

"What is it, Mary?" Lizzy responded sleepily.

"I had a wonderful time tonight. I do not feel as though I was a deceiver. My outward appearance was different, but I was still myself. I did not project a false guise toward any person this evening."

Lizzy nudged Jane awake. "Jane, did you hear that?"

Jane stirred and blinked her eyes several times in an attempt to focus. "I heard Mary speak, but I am afraid I did not actually understand any of the words she used."

Lizzy rolled her eyes. "Mary said that even though her outward appearance was altered tonight, she was still her same self on the inside."

"Ah," Jane muttered bemusedly.

"Do you not see? This is as we discussed that one day in the garden: One's outward appearance is no reflection of their true inner character. We may be drawn to a handsome face, but there is much more to a person than their beauty, or lack thereof." Lizzy noticed her sisters' confused expressions and elaborated, "As we seek to find proper husbands, we will need to endeavor to ignore their exteriors and give greater consequence to the character of the man underneath."

Jane nodded in understanding. "Mary," she explained, "Lizzy and I have been trying to discover ways to discern whether a man will make for a good husband. We have determined previously that one way to judge this is to observe his treatment of those beneath him."

"And now you have helped us to understand another way," Lizzy continued. "We must vigilantly look beyond their features—whether handsome or ugly—and assess who they are as a person."

"But the Lord said unto Samuel, Look not on his countenance, or on the height of his stature; because I have refused him: for the Lord seeth not as man seeth; for man looketh on the outward appearance, but the Lord looketh on the heart," Mary said. When her sisters merely blinked at her, she elaborated, "From the book of Samuel."

Lizzy began to laugh. "Mary, please don't ever change who you are."

Having thoroughly spent themselves during the happy night, the three girls then fell into a peaceful slumber.

~∞~∞~∞~

Derbyshire, May 1808

Fitzwilliam Darcy put his newspaper down and sighed heavily. The paper was several days out of date, but it had only just arrived at Pemberley that morning. Scanning at the headline again, he scowled in.

"That's quite a fearsome face, old man," observed Bingley as he entered the breakfast room. "Did Georgiana use the front page for her watercolor practice again before you had a chance to read it?" Chuckling, Bingley placed eggs and bacon on his plate from the sideboard before joining Darcy at the table.

Darcy smiled in wry amusement. He clearly remembered how excited Georgiana had been to show him how the watercolor paints smeared and blended with the newspaper ink, creating an illegible—albeit beautiful—mess. Her innocent delight had melted any frustration he may have felt at not being able to read that day's paper.

"She will be thirteen this year," he reminded Bingley. "That seems a little old for such antics. Regardless, she is currently occupied with unpacking her things after her journey from finishing school."

"If the problem does not stem from your young sister, why do you appear as though you have bitten into a candied apple only to find a raw onion inside?" inquired Bingley.

"I am afraid it has more to do with you than it does with me," Darcy said. "I'm surprised you haven't received a missive as of yet." Handing the newspaper to a confused Bingley, Darcy continued: "It appears that unrest persists in the north with the factories. The workers refuse to man the weaving machines. There was some damage to the factories near Yorkshire."

Bingley's expression soured to match Darcy's as he scanned the newspaper. "I admit that I am not entirely surprised. I have endeavored to remain informed of the situation while attending school."

Bingley pondered the issue for a minute, then looked at Darcy with an uncharacteristically somber face. "Even though they have not requested my presence, I believe I should ride north and take my school holidays there until this matter resolves."

Darcy nodded in agreement. He would miss Bingley's presence in his home, but he knew the substantial import of these factories to his friend's income. "If there arises any detail in which I may be of assistance, please send for me immediately," Darcy replied.

Bingley hesitated, then said, "I may be gone for an extended period of time. Pemberley has been a comforting home to me in the eighteen months I have resided here. I would like to return once this mess has been resolved, if you would permit me to do so."

Darcy smiled, "I would greatly appreciate your company." The two men shook hands, and Bingley left to prepare for his journey northward.

While Bingley directed his valet and wrote letters, Darcy ascended the main stairs to check on Georgiana. She had arrived home earlier in the day from finishing school, and he was anxious to spend time with her.

As he approached her chambers in the family wing, he heard a distressed voice echo down the hall from his sister's room. He increased his pace. Darcy was soon in sufficient proximity to hear Georgiana shout: "—and you shall press every single one of these gowns *again* before they are hung! Just look at the creases that remain after your miserable attempts!"

Aghast, Darcy knocked on the door. A maid with reddened eyes opened it and dipped a quick curtsy. "Hello, Maggie," he said gently, smiling at the young woman. "I would like to speak with my sister in private, please."

The girl dipped another curtsy and fairly fled down the hall.

Darcy composed himself with a deep breath before stepping into his sister's room. He surveyed the numerous trunks strewn about the room in various stages of being emptied and sighed. She certainly had no dearth of clothing, though she was just thirteen.

"Brother!" Georgiana exclaimed. She threw herself into his arms, and he swung her about in a circle. She laughed enthusiastically, then suddenly straightened and effected a serene air. "That is," she amended in a formal tone, "How good it is to see you again, Brother," she said in a formal tone, executing a neat curtsy.

"What's this?" cried Darcy in a jovial tone. "Where is my little sister? The school has mistakenly returned a proper young lady in place of her! I must write to the headmistress at once!"

Georgiana let out another peal of laughter that she quickly hid behind her hand.

"Oh, Fitzwilliam," she said, "I am much too old for such silliness. You must endeavor to remember that I am now thirteen years old."

"Yes, you are," Darcy said warmly. "I only wish our parents were able to see you so grown up."

The two siblings looked at one another in a moment of commiseration for shared grief. Then Darcy clapped his hands once and said, "How was your trip from school? I am sorry I was unable to fetch you myself, but I had several responsibilities here at Pemberley that required my personal attention."

Georgiana chattered casually about the drive, the stops, and the scenery. Darcy was concerned to hear her disparage her maid and the coachman several times.

"—I do believe he hit every pothole in the road. It must have been an intentional assault in retribution after I slept over-late at the inn. No person could be so incompetent. And anyway, the delay at the inn was not all Maggie's doing. She barely attempted to rouse me from bed. The maids at school were much more capable of rousing me gently after I demand that they allow me to continue sleeping. That lazy girl—"

"Georgiana!" interrupted Darcy sharply. Her eyes widened at his harsh tone, so he moderated his voice and continued, "It is not Maggie's responsibility to force you out of your bed. It is also not in the coachman's nature to endanger the carriage, horses, and passengers merely to spite a child."

He raised a hand as she opened her mouth to protest. "Because you *are* still a child, Georgiana. You are growing up, certainly, but you are still young. This is clearly evidenced by your treatment of Maggie just now before I entered, as well as your attitude toward those who conveyed you safely home."

Georgiana's mouth dropped open. "But they are only servants!"

she exclaimed, affronted.

"They are *people* first," Darcy corrected sternly. "Their social status does not make them worthy of disrespect."

Georgiana looked confused. "But we have more money than they do. Our grandfather was an earl! Our uncle *is* an earl, and our cousin will be an earl. We own property and belong to a much higher class."

"Those statements are all correct," responded her brother, "but simply being born to wealth and position does not grant you greater intrinsic value than any other person."

"I don't understand," Georgiana whined petulantly.

"That is because I have not been properly diligent in educating you as to the responsibilities inherent in your station. That is a mistake which I shall correct this summer while you are home."

Georgiana pursed her lips, pondering, then said, "I do not see what I have done wrong. I spoke to Maggie in precisely the same way all the other girls at school address their servants. Lady Penelope insists that nobody will respect our positions if even the servants do not fear us, and she is the daughter of a duke!"

Darcy sighed and ran his hands through his hair. "Georgiana, it does not matter what your friends do or say. What matters is what *you* do or say. Contrary to Lady Penelope's inane opinion, I would say that in some ways, a servant is of more value than his master."

"I still do not understand, Fitzwilliam. A servant could never have greater value than his master; I can think of no circumstance under which a servant might amass such a great sum. It is a ridiculous notion."

Darcy sat on the chair by Georgiana's dressing table and motioned for her to sit on her bed. Once settled, he said, "Let's begin with a hypothetical scenario. A wealthy man walks down the streets in London and passes a beggar. He gives the beggar a shilling and goes on his way. After some time, a footman passes that same beggar. The footman also gives the beggar a shilling. Which person gave more: the wealthy man or the footman?"

Georgiana thought for a minute. "Well, they both gave the same amount. But since the wealthy man has more money, it was significantly easier for him to part with his shilling. Therefore, I think the footman gave more."

Darcy smiled in approval. "Exactly, my dear. The footman has much less than the wealthy man, so his contribution was far more valuable. You and I have been born with very much. Our servants have been born with very little. If there is a tenant in need and we send a basket of food, and another tenant also sends a basket of food, what that tenant did was worth more than our contribution because of our great excess."

Nodding her head slowly, Georgiana mused, "I think I begin to understand, Brother. Maggie does much more good than I do, and she has much less with which to do it. She always has a kind word for another servant, or a smile for me when I have had a difficult day."

"Precisely, Georgiana. For a young lady such as yourself, it should not matter if a person is the daughter of a servant, tradesman, or duke; we are all of equal worth. What matters is what we do with what we are given."

Georgiana looked at him, clearly bewildered. "If it is as you say, why do you intend to only marry the daughter of a peer?"

Darcy let out a bark of laughter. "When have I ever said anything like that?"

"I do not recall you ever saying those precise words, I suppose, but all the girls at school have said so."

Darcy barely prevented his eyes from rolling to the ceiling. "The rumors proliferating unchecked about the schoolroom cannot be anything but the absolute truth," he intoned solemnly.

Georgiana gaped at her brother for a moment before saying, "Oh! You are speaking in jest!"

"Of *course* I am jesting, Georgiana! Some gossip is mere embellishment, while the rest is entirely false. I have never once stated that I will only marry the daughter of a peer. I have often, however, spoken of my intent to marry *well*. My definition of marrying well involves significantly more than mere social status."

Understanding flashed across Georgiana's face. "You mean that you endeavor to judge a potential wife by her character, rather than her rank."

"That is correct. Unfortunately, most of the women with whom I am acquainted do not possess the characteristics of a truly accomplished woman. I seek someone to be my partner in life, not an ornament. It would not matter if she is from trade, though I admit that I have yet to encounter a single woman from trade who sees me as more than my income."

"Really?" asked Georgiana, aghast.

"'Tis the truth, Sister. Your cousin Richard has many times extricated me from a scheme wherein some lady or another has contrived to entrap me by compromise. The last time I attended a house party, no fewer than three women sought unsolicited access to my bedchamber."

"How reprehensible! Were all three of these villains from trade?" asked an appalled Georgiana.

Darcy shook his head. "Two of them were, but one of them was the daughter of a penniless baronet."

"My poor brother," Georgiana sighed. "It must be exhausting."

"I have learned to apply exceeding caution," admitted Darcy. "I do not worry about tenants or servants so much; they often behave with greater integrity because they have learned to work hard in life. However, those born to a little privilege and wealth often feel it is their right to obtain as much of it as possible, regardless of whom they must defraud to do so. As such, I tend to assume that any person with social standing will attempt to take advantage of me."

"How is it that you and Mr. Bingley became friends, then?" asked Georgiana. "Is he not in trade?" Darcy grinned. "That, dear sister, is a wonderful story."

The siblings passed the next several hours in warm conversation in which Darcy entertained his sister with stories from his school days. As the dinner hour approached, Darcy stood and rang for Maggie. He was pleased to hear his sister apologizing to her maid for her "inexcusably boorish behavior" as he left the room. He often worried whether he was raising his sister properly, but today's conversation gave him comfort some hope in that regard.

Chapter 6

Yorkshire, May 1809

Charles Bingley checked his pocket watch and sighed heavily. A mere five minutes had elapsed since he last checked the time.

Snapping the watch closed, he began to drum his fingers on the table in front of him. The innkeeper looked over, and Bingley shook his head. Bingley had been letting rooms at this inn for nearly a year, ever since travelling north to deal with the unrest between his factory workers and the local farm-working tenants.

With the of technologies such as stocking frames, many tenant farmers and other lower classes were concerned for their livelihood. Whereas they had once been able to supplement their incomes by weaving and selling blankets, baskets, and other goods by hand, now they were being "invented out of business." Items produced with the new machines could be constructed more quickly and reliably, and therefore could be sold for much less. In addition, many tenants were being forcibly removed from the farms where their families had lived and worked for generations, to make room for factories and workhouses.

This transition led to desperation, and many of the local workers had taken to vandalizing the despised machines at night. The desperation only increased when the government passed the Protection of Stocking Frames, etc. Act in 1788, which significantly increased the fines for damaging such machines.

Over the past year spent in Yorkshire, Bingley had worked tirelessly to build trust between himself and the local workers. Using skills he had learned from Darcy, he was able to demonstrate to both parties that he understood the concerns of each group.

Checking his pocket watch again, Bingley rose from the table. "It appears Mr. Knoxley is late today," he said to the nearby innkeeper. "I must retrieve something from my rooms. If he arrives while I am gone, please see him to the private sitting room and inform him that I will return shortly."

Bingley trudged wearily up the stairs that he had climbed countless times over the last twelve months. Entering his rooms, he retrieved a parcel of papers that contained the contracts he was to discuss with Mr. Knoxley. As he checked his desk for any relevant documents he may have mislaid, Darcy's latest letter caught his eye.

I have missed your company, my friend. With Georgiana at school, you in the North on holidays, and Richard overseas, Pemberley has been quiet—too quiet for even my solitary tastes.

My neighbor, Mr. Cartwright, has had a son. Tragically, Cartwright's young wife perished in childbirth. He has left for Town, leaving the babe in the care of several nursemaids. Georgiana has visited frequently whenever she has been home on holiday, exclaiming each time over his growth.

You will be amazed with Georgiana's growth and progress. She is no longer the spoilt child that you knew, but is instead growing into a fine young woman. My uncle the earl has begun to discuss potential matches for her, but he insists that I must marry first, that she may have a sister to help her navigate the ton after she has come out.

I refuse to be pressured, however. Georgiana and I shall each marry for love and affection, or not at all. She and I have discussed this on multiple occasions. I follow my parents' fine example here. As long as her husband has genuine feelings for her, it will not matter if he is a pauper or a duke.

I am relieved to know that you have not fallen prey to some of the women that you have described in your correspondence with me. If you meet a woman who catches your fancy and you find her to be sincere in her returned affections, then you may receive my warmest felicitations. Please be careful that she genuinely cares for you, however.

This past year spent almost entirely by myself has given me much time for reflection. I begin to wonder if perhaps I have been too quick to judge the young ladies who have endeavored to ensnare my fortune. As Georgiana approaches the age for such discussions, I find myself extremely desirous for her to be properly cared for. Perhaps some meddlesome mothers and desperate daughters search merely for the security wealth brings, as opposed to wealth itself. What are your thoughts on this matter?

Bingley smiled and shook his head. The time spent apart from Darcy had matured them both. He had witnessed personally how many matchmaking mothers that had pursued Darcy and his ten thousand pounds per year, but he was willing to entertain the notion that the women's motives may have been more nuanced than Darcy's previous interpretation.

It's a delicate balance, Bingley thought, *and it is difficult to know which women are trustworthy.*

Suddenly remembering his meeting, Bingley hurried back down the stairs. He slowed his pace, however, when he heard voices emanating from the private sitting room as he approached. Moments before he entered, he realized that one of the voices was that of a familiar young lady, and he stopped to listen.

"Papa, why isn't he here?" she demanded. Bingley's eyes widened. The voice certainly belonged to Miss Knoxley, but he had never before heard her speak in such a hostile tone.

"Patience, pet," Mr. Knoxley replied. "He probably became tired of waiting for us. Your extra preparations caused us to be late."

"I had to look my best, Papa," Miss Knoxley whined. "How else am I to attract a marriage proposal? I cannot act boldly, else he may find me disagreeable and abandon the idea of marrying me entirely."

"If he does not make an offer soon, then perhaps you'll need to take the option from him," her father growled. "We need his fortune to make up what your foolish brother has lost to the gaming tables."

Bingley's mood blackened. He had heard enough. It seemed Darcy may have been correct in his cynical judgement of the women vying for his affection. There were too many young women—often compelled by bankrupt or greedy fathers and brothers—who sought his company merely to improve their fortunes. It was a pity; he had grown fond of the beautiful Miss Knoxley.

Not wanting to be caught eavesdropping, Bingley quietly retreated down the hall and approached the door anew with loud footsteps. He feigned surprise when he greeted Miss Knoxley and accepted their apologies for keeping him waiting.

As he listened to their chatter, he resolved in the future to eavesdrop more frequently on any young lady he fancied. He was grateful it was almost time to return to Oxford, where he would have a respite from the attentions of avaricious women.

~∞~∞~∞~

Hertfordshire, June 1809

"It's not fair!"

Lizzy winced as she heard the screeching voice of thirteen-year-old Lydia. "Why does Kitty get to go to the assembly and not me?"

"Lydia, love," said Mrs. Bennet desperately, "you know that you must be fifteen years old to come out to society."

"They should make an exception, then!" demanded Lydia as she stomped her foot childishly. "I am the tallest *and* the prettiest."

"Yes, you are," said Mrs. Bennet. "Perhaps an exception—"

Lydia's four sisters looked at one another, horrified. "Mamma," said Lizzy hastily, "did I tell you what I heard the other day?"

Mrs. Bennet's attention instantly seized on the hint of new gossip. "What did you hear?" she asked eagerly.

Lizzy thought rapidly. "Charlotte Lucas told me that she received a letter from a cousin in Bath. In it, the cousin said that a local family had allowed one of their daughters to attend an assembly at fourteen."

Jane, Mary, and Kitty stared at Lizzy in astonishment.

"See, I told you!" crowed a triumphant Lydia.

Mrs. Bennet parted her lips to respond, but Lizzy hastened to continue her tale. "You will never guess what happened!"

"Perhaps we should refrain from gossip—" began Mary, but Jane quickly hushed her.

"Go on!" Jane encouraged, finally having caught on to Lizzy's ploy.

"The entire group of guests at the assembly shunned the girl and her family! The gossip lasted for months, and the family had to relocate to Brighton to escape the snubbing."

Mrs. Bennet let out a gasp and swooned on the settee. "Oh no, Lydia, my love!" she wailed. "We cannot allow that to happen to you! You will have to come out at fifteen like all your sisters, lest we be expelled from polite society. We would never recover from such a scandal, and then who would marry you and your sisters? Then when your father dies, we should be left friendless and penniless, starving in the gutter."

Lizzy hid a smile and expelled a quiet sigh of relief as the tension disappeared from the room. Lydia burst into sobs, stomped her feet, and ran from the room. Mrs. Bennet quickly followed, offering Lydia sweets and a new ribbon to make up for the disappointment.

Kitty smiled gratefully at Lizzy, "Thank you, Lizzy! How fortunate that Charlotte told you of her letter!"

The other girls burst into giggles, with Mary failing to cover her smile with a glare at Lizzy. Kitty looked bewildered. Finally, Mary explained, "I don't believe there ever was any such letter, Kitty."

Kitty gasped in shock. "Lizzy! How could you lie to Mamma?"

"Well," replied Lizzy, "we most certainly cannot allow Lydia to come out at the same time as you. She is much too young and indiscrete to attend an assembly."

Mary interjected, "Normally I would condemn such behavior. After all, does not the Lord command 'thou shalt not bear false witness?' Guile of every sort is most abhorrent. However, in a situation such as this, I cannot fault Lizzy for protecting our family's honor."

Jane nodded and said, "We would place our family's reputation at risk were we to allow Lydia to come out at this juncture. As it is, even having Kitty come out while all three of her elder sisters are yet unmarried is still a bit unseemly. There may be some who will regard this as a mark against our reputations."

Kitty's face fell at Jane's words, and her lower lip trembled slightly.

"Oh Kitty, dear," Jane said. "I do not blame you! It is not your fault that men are scarce and we older three have not been able to marry. For that, we must blame Napoleon!"

"Yes," Lizzy agreed with a smile, "how terribly rude of Napoleon to start a war, all so the Bennet sisters are forced to remain unmarried."

Kitty giggled at Lizzy's words, then sobered. "But Lizzy, Jane," she asked, "are you not ashamed to be unwed at eighteen and twenty?"

Jane and Lizzy exchanged significant looks with Mary. "No," Jane said gently, "I am not ashamed. I would much rather remain unmarried and safe than to place myself in the power of a man who would not treat me well."

Although Mary did not know of the details of the situation with Mr. Cartwright, she had heard enough of her sisters' conversations to learn that not all men were as indulgent as their father or Sir William Lucas. She therefore said, "Kitty, once you are married, you are then bound to that person for the entirety of your life, regardless of depraved or malicious behavior. We must therefore guard our charms against the undeserving of the other sex."

Kitty had never before participated in so serious a conversation. With wide eyes, Kitty inquired earnestly, "How do we know if they are undeserving?"

"Well," answered Lizzy, "first, we make certain that they treat their servants and others beneath them with kindness."

"We also endeavor to discount their outward appearance," Mary continued. "A handsome man may hide a vicious nature, while an ugly man may be the essence of goodness and gentility."

Jane concluded by saying, "And we must take our time to discover these things. One assembly and a few morning calls are not sufficient to take a man's true measure."

Looking overwhelmed, Kitty merely nodded as she processed this information. After a few minutes, she asked, "What if I make a mistake?"

Lizzy was quick to reassure her. "That is what you have sisters for! As you become acquainted with more people in society, you will gain experience. In the meantime, follow our lead and come to us for advice."

Kitty smiled softly, "I would enjoy spending more time with my sisters."

Gaily, Jane remarked, "Now that you are coming out, you will be able to do so! Let us begin immediately by choosing the perfect gown for your first assembly tomorrow night!"

The four sisters eagerly hastened to the room Kitty and Mary shared. Their happy laughter drowned out the sounds of Lydia's continuing tantrum and her mother's appeals.

~∞~∞~∞~

Kitty spun around the assembly room, hands grasping those of her father. "How are you enjoying your first assembly?" Mr. Bennet asked her with a loving smile.

"Oh, Papa!" she cried, "I do not know when I have ever had such a wonderful time!"

"I am pleased to see you enjoying yourself, Kitty."

When the music ended, he escorted her back to her sisters and mothers. "Well," he said, clasping his hands together, "now that I have done my duty in dancing with Kitty twice and the rest of you once, I believe I shall retire to the card room."

Mrs. Bennet and her daughters acquiesced, and Mr. Bennet soon disappeared into the crowd.

"Now that you are back, Kitty," said Lizzy, "we want to hear all about your dance with Mr. Fordham."

"Oh, yes!" exclaimed Mrs. Bennet. "Mr. Fordham is such a handsome young man! How fortunate we are that Mr. Jacobson found such a handsome, single curate!"

Kitty blushed. Mr. Fordham had recently come to Meryton as the new curate for the elderly vicar, Mr. Jacobson. His handsome face was frequently discussed during the morning calls of the ladies in the neighborhood.

"He was all that was kind," replied Kitty. "I appreciated his attentiveness; he asked after my interests and seemed to take pleasure in my responses."

All three of her sisters smiled. Thus far, none of them had yet discovered anything the matter with the handsome young man. His servants spoke highly of him, and his kindness was as pleasing as his face.

"I give you leave to like him," Lizzy declared magnanimously. "I daresay you have liked many a stupider person."

After protesting the unfairness of this characterization, Kitty said, "I am absolutely parched. I will fetch a glass of lemonade."

"Allow me to accompany you," said Jane.

"Bring me a glass, too," Mrs. Bennet requested.

The two sisters linked arms and made their way through the crowd to the punch table. Upon selecting two cups, Kitty turned to take them back to her mother. Unfortunately, she did not see Mr. Fordham standing directly behind her, selecting his own refreshment.

"Oh dear!" cried Kitty as she bumped into him. Two full glasses of lemonade dumped down the front of Mr. Fordham's jacket.

Mr. Fordham jumped in alarm, then hissed, "You stupid chit!" as he brushed at his soiled coat. He looked up into Kitty's distraught face, and when he recognized the recipient of his ire, his eyes widened in dismay. "M-Miss Kitty! M-my apologies!" he stammered, "Please forgive—"

Jane, having heard everything, silenced Mr. Fordham with a severe look. She wrapped her arm around her silently weeping sister and said, "Come, Kitty, let us go to the retiring room."

Jane beckoned to Mary and Lizzy, who followed them toward the small room designated for wardrobe malfunctions, repairing hair styles, and any other minor catastrophes that could occur during an assembly. Fortunately, it was empty of everyone except a maid. Lizzy dismissed the girl with a smile and a nod toward the door.

Once they were alone, Kitty dissolved into the sobs she had been holding back. Her sisters gathered around her, stroking her hair and smoothing her back. Jane produced a delicate lace handkerchief Lizzy had embroidered and used it to dry Kitty's tears.

"Come now, Kitty," said Lizzy soothingly. "It cannot be as bad as all that!"

"But it is!" wailed Kitty.

Jane gave Lizzy a pointed look. "Mr. Fordham insulted Kitty with vile speech after she spilled a drink on his jacket," Jane informed them.

"What?" cried Lizzy and Mary in unison, outraged.

"How dare he!" exclaimed Lizzy.

"His actions are definitely not those of a man of God," added Mary in disgust.

"He t-tried to a-p-pologize," stammered Kitty, not unlike Mr. Fordham had done minutes before.

"Yes," said Jane, "but only once he realized it was Kitty, not before."

"Hmm," mused Lizzy, "At least something good has come out of all of this."

"What?" sniffled Kitty as she dried her eyes.

"Two things, actually," Lizzy demurred.

"*What?*" exclaimed her three sisters.

"First, you have helped rid Jane of the horrid handkerchief I made for her, as there can be no rescuing it now," laughed Lizzy.

Kitty giggled softly through her tears.

"And second," Lizzy continued, "you have helped us learn another essential characteristic of a good husband: keeping hold of one's temper in unfortunate and unforeseen circumstances."

Kitty smiled. "At least my embarrassment is good for something!"

"Dearest, you have nothing to be embarrassed about," responded Jane. "It is *he* who should be mortified for his reaction."

With their spirits lifted, the four sisters rejoined the assembly guests, where they caused quite a stir when they uniformly gave Mr. Fordham the cut direct. Thus Kitty's first assembly proved to be the most memorable of them all.

Chapter 7

Derbyshire, May 1810

Fitzwilliam Darcy looked up from his desk at the butler who was knocking on his door. "Yes, Stevens?" he asked.

Stevens, who had regained only half the use of his injured arm, announced, "Mr. Bingley." Stepping back, he allowed Bingley to stride past him and into the room.

"Bingley!" cried Darcy with surprised delight, "You have arrived a full week earlier than your letter stated! What are you doing here?"

Bingley grinned widely. "You know me, old man. With Georgiana at Ramsgate, someone has to ensure you do not waste the summer."

Chuckling, Darcy motioned for Bingley to sit. Once he was settled, Darcy observed, "You look much altered since I last saw you here at Pemberley two years ago. It appears the matrons of Yorkshire have fed you well."

Bingley grimaced. "Yes, well, that has more to do with the daughters of the matrons and my unmarried status. The profound lack of exercise also contributed. I do not believe I have ever in my life gone so long between gallops on horseback."

"Well, then, how would you like to return to the saddle? I had been planning to ride to Ramsgate and surprise Georgiana with a visit for a few days before your return. Obviously, I no longer need to hurry back, as you have already arrived. Would you care to join me?"

"Join you to visit Georgiana? I would be delighted! How she must have grown these three years."

"You shan't even recognize her," Darcy warned. "She may only be fifteen, but she is the exact duplicate of my mother's portrait created upon her marriage to my father at twenty years of age."

Bingley smiled. "She must be beautiful, then. I have always loved that portrait of Mrs. Darcy. You can see her kindness about her eyes."

"Yes, you certainly can," replied Darcy softly.

The two men passed a moment in quiet retrospection when Darcy declared, "We shall go, then! I cannot wait to see Georgiana's reaction when I arrive with you in attendance."

The men left the study and climbed the stairs to the family wing, where Bingley's usual chambers resided. As they ascended, Darcy inquired, "How have you fared? Your last letter was dated nearly six months past, in which you recounted some recent vandalism."

"Yes, that was quite unfortunate for Mr. Knoxley. I attempted multiple times to explain to him that the saboteurs were fearful for their livelihood. His efforts to prosecute the offenders to the severest extent of the law merely fueled their violent desperation. The destruction increased significantly."

"How did it end?" Darcy asked.

"He and his daughter feared for their lives, so they sold me their properties for their market value—which had depreciated markedly amid the growing hostilities—then shipped off to the Americas!" Bingley exclaimed.

Darcy let out a burst of surprised laughter. "You definitely got the better part of that deal!"

"Quite! My three years of holidays there convinced the local populace of my trustworthiness. When I gained ownership over Knoxley's factories, his people eagerly signed the same contracts my own people had signed two years prior. Everyone is working in harmony, and I was able to proceed directly to Pemberley after graduating, rather than travelling there first."

"And you neatly avoided being caught by Knoxley's daughter," said Darcy. Bingley nodded in agreement, and Darcy continued, "I have been considering her situation this past year since you first wrote about her. While I maintain that she is an opportunistic social climber whom you do well to avoid, I pity her for the circumstances that have forced her into such a position."

"I agree," said Bingley. "I refuse to marry anyone with whom I do not share a mutual fondness, but many women in society cannot afford to do likewise."

They reached Bingley's door, and Darcy turned to ask him one last question before heading to his own rooms. "Have you read 'The Vindication of the Rights of Woman' by Mary Wollstonecraft?"

Bingley let out a bark of laughter. "Darcy, you do realize that it's *me* you're asking, right?"

Smiling in amusement, Darcy continued, "My aunt, the wife of my uncle the earl, recommended it as reading material for Georgiana. It was published last year, and I felt it my duty to read it before passing it on to my impressionable sister."

"What did you conclude?" asked Bingley.

"That every woman of society ought to read it," stated Darcy resolutely.

"Really?" Bingley was intrigued. "I have heard that the volume contains some rather radical claims regarding womanhood, and I would have expected you to discard it immediately."

"Yes, well, as I said, I have had much opportunity for solitary rumination this past year. But we should prepare now if we are to depart in the morning. I will explain tomorrow as we ride."

~∞~∞~∞~

The next morning, Bingley and Darcy arose early. They brought along the carriage but chose to ride alongside, allowing their valets the rare privilege of riding inside—rather than atop—the carriage.

Continuing their conversation from the day prior, Darcy said, "In her book, Wollstonecraft wrote very eloquently about the evils of treating women as property to be traded in marriage and kept as ornaments.

Women, she claims, should be as well-educated as men."

"That is not very different from what you have always thought," said Bingley, "You have urged Georgiana to learn mathematics, Latin, and history, in addition to the usual female education."

"Yes," agreed Darcy, "but until recently, I had never considered the great disservice society gives to most other women. A person is shaped by their experiences and their knowledge. Many women are brought up believing that their only value lies in how advantageously they manage to wed. With no opportunities to learn otherwise, how can they be faulted for any resultant behavior they demonstrate? It is all they are taught to do."

When Bingley nodded that he understood, Darcy pressed on. "Wollstonecraft deems the lack of rights and opportunities for women to be akin to slavery, which is an abhorrent practice. I believe that she may have observed correctly. The women in our society enjoy fewer freedoms than men; this cannot be denied by any reasonable person. Her arguments moved me to compassion for the opposite sex."

This speech stunned Bingley into silence for a short time. "Bravo, old man," he finally said. "I have always told you that women could not be as bad as all that. I say that you have taken far too long to reach this conclusion."

"Well," answered Darcy wryly, "with the innumerable designs on my bachelorhood that I have endured, could I be held to blame?"

Bingley laughed, and the men continued to discuss the impediments to women's mobility in society for the remainder of the journey.

~∞~∞~∞~

Darcy and Bingley arrived in Ramsgate as evening bloomed over the town. The streets were empty, and they made good time to the house that Darcy had let for his sister. Darcy knocked on the door, which was opened by a surprised maid. Her expression gave Darcy an idea, and he smiled.

"Do not announce us," he entreated as he stepped into the house, "I wish to surprise my sister. Where is she?"

"In the drawing room," the girl said, "but, Sir—"

Darcy paid no heed to the young maid's objection as he walked briskly down the hall, eager to see the look on Georgiana's face. When he opened the door, he froze.

Georgiana sat entwined in the intimate embrace of a young man. The scoundrel's cravat was askew, and the shoulder of her gown had slipped down her arm, exposing a scandalous amount of his young sister's decolletage.

"What is this?" thundered Darcy. The couple broke apart, gaping at him. "Wickham!" Darcy roared at the blackguard.

"Brother!" Georgiana cried delightedly as she stood and flung herself into his arms. "You have arrived just in time! We are leaving for Gretna Green tomorrow to be married! But with you in attendance as my guardian, we can wed here with your permission instead!"

George Wickham rose from the couch. He straightened his clothing and extended his hand, smirking. "Well, Darcy, it appears we are to be brothers!"

"Not bloody likely," growled Darcy.

Georgiana gasped and looked up at her brother. "Fitzwilliam, what do you mean?"

"I shall *never* give my consent for Georgiana to marry the likes of you, Wickham," Darcy declared.

Wickham's grin grew wider. "You have no choice, Darcy. She is quite ruined otherwise. I have seen to that."

Georgiana's face grew pale. "George, darling, what are you saying?"

"You do realize," interjected Darcy, "that Georgiana's dowry cannot be released until she is of age, and then only with the approval of her guardians?"

Wickham's face twisted in anger. "You lie!" he spat.

"I speak only the truth," said Darcy. "Although, if you truly love my sister, then you should not mind working to support your family for the next six years."

"George won't mind," said Georgiana, "He loves me for myself, not my fortune."

"Shut your mouth, you stupid chit," snarled Wickham. Georgiana's wide eyes stood out on her pale face. She burst into tears and ran out of the room. Darcy shook with rage and the desperate need to punish the fraudster, but before he could cross the room, Darcy's friend intervened.

"Now that was well done," Bingley drawled, draping himself across a nearby chair and peering at Wickham. The pure rage in Bingley's eyes belied his laissez-faire demeanor.

"What do you mean?" Wickham demanded, spinning to face Bingley.

"Tsk, tsk," Bingley mocked. "You lost your temper in front of Georgiana. You have betrayed yourself with your words. Had you restrained your temper and instead made love to her with your words, she may have convinced her brother to provide for you both until her dowry was released. But I daresay she will have nothing to do with you now."

Darcy gaped at Bingley in amazement. Since when had his friend gained the ability to take charge of such a tense situation? *Yorkshire*, thought Darcy.

Turning back to Wickham, Darcy coldly said, "Leave my house. Now."

"B-but," stammered Wickham, "your sister is already ruined!"

Darcy wrapped his hand around Wickham's throat and slammed him against the wall. "You *dared* to defile her!" he roared.

"N-n-no," rasped Wickham as he struggled for breath, supported only by Darcy's hand and the barest contact between the toe of his right boot and the floor. "J-j-just a kiss. But the g-g-gossip rags have the story of our elopement already p-p-printed for tomorrow."

Bingley laid a hand on Darcy's shoulder. "Better let him go before you kill him," he said mildly. "Not that I would object, but the last thing Georgiana needs is the magistrate showing up to collect a body."

The reminder of his sister was the only thing that enabled Darcy to release his hold on Wickham. The faux beau collapsed to the floor, gasping for breath, hands at his throat. Bingley crouched next to him. "You *will* leave," he intoned evenly, "and you will never breathe a word of this again." The dangerous tone of Bingley's calm assertion managed to inspire more fear in Wickham's desiccated heart than even Darcy's deafening outrage had.

Wickham nodded mutely, unable to force words past the swelling of his throat. He staggered to his feet and clumsily stumbled out the door.

Darcy looked helplessly at Bingley, despair in his eyes. "What do I do now?" he asked hoarsely.

"First, you comfort your sister. Make certain that Georgiana is well," said Bingley. "Meanwhile, I will see what I can do about the gossip."

Darcy nodded dumbly, which Bingley took for agreement. Donning his hat, Bingley cut an appraising look at his broken friend. Resolve filled him, and he exited the home to assess the extent of damage.

A maid quietly entered the sitting room where Darcy stood, numb and immobile. He turned to look at her with blank eyes, and she dipped a quick curtsy. "Begging your pardon, sir," she ventured hesitantly, "but Mrs. Younge just ran out the back door with her things."

Darcy nodded, and she continued, "Miss Stewart has gone upstairs to your sister. I tried to tell her that the house was not admitting callers, but she pushed her way around me and went up."

Darcy began to nod again, then froze. "Who is upstairs with Georgiana?"

"Miss Stewart," the maid said.

Darcy repeated the name blankly and asked, "Who might that be?"

"Her father is a local tradesman, sir," the maid said, "She has called on Georgiana several times. They practice the piano-forte together."

Darcy closed his eyes and groaned. Just what he needed in the middle of this mess: a tradesman's daughter discovering his sister's ruin. *What will it cost me to keep her silent?* he wondered. *Hopefully, the payment will be remitted in pounds and not in a wedding license.*

After thanking the maid, Darcy slowly climbed the stairs. He knew he should be thinking about what to say or do, but he was incapable of generating anything worthwhile. His mind felt as though he had drunk an entire decanter of brandy.

Hearing his sister's sobs from down the hallway, Darcy winced. *What was it Bingley said? Right—comfort Georgiana.*

He knocked gently on the door to his sister's room. "Georgiana?" he called softly.

The door opened to reveal a young woman in fashionable dress of about twenty-five years. She looked him up and down, then declared, "You had better not be George Wickham. If you are, then I shall set the footmen on you."

Darcy's eyes widened in surprise. *Perhaps this won't be as bad as I expected,* he thought hopefully. He removed his hat and bowed. "Fitzwilliam Darcy, at your service."

The flames in the girl's eyes faded into relief. She curtsied and introduced herself, "Miss Samantha Stewart. Delighted to make your acquaintance." Then she chuckled slightly. "Of all the absurdities, introducing ourselves formally at a time like this. Well, at least society's rules for etiquette and decorum are good for something. They apparently give us something to focus on when we would rather not think about a dreadful situation."

She shook her head and opened the door wider. "I am extremely glad that you are here, sir," she said. "I have been unable to understand much of what has happened, other than Georgiana has repeatedly sobbed that George Wickham has ruined her."

Darcy's heart twisted on hearing those words. He entered the room and found Georgiana sobbing into her pillow on the bed.

He gently sat next to her. "Dearest," he soothed, rubbing his hand on her back. Georgiana only sobbed harder. Darcy looked imploringly to Miss Stewart, who shrugged. He continued rubbing his sister's back.

After a few minutes, Darcy tried again. "Georgiana, please look at me," he pleaded.

She shook her head and forced her face deeper into her pillow.

"Rubbish," said Miss Stewart firmly. She walked over to the bed and sat down as well. Darcy looked at her in alarm, and she laughed. "Mr. Darcy, I promise that claiming a compromise because we sat on the same bed in your sister's room is the *last* thing on my mind."

Darcy blushed, vaguely remembering his words to Bingley about not judging women so harshly. "My apologies, madam," he mumbled.

She waved her hand dismissively. Turning to his sister, she said, "Now Georgiana, that is quite enough. I cannot understand a word of what you have said, nor can your brother, I daresay. Be a good girl and sit up so we can help resolve this matter."

Georgiana obeyed, but she kept her eyes focused on her trembling hands.

"Very good," Miss Stewart approved. "Now, Georgiana, can you please explain why you believe you are ruined? Without crying, dear," she added as Georgiana's blue eyes filled with tears again.

In halting breaths, Georgiana explained that she had chanced to encounter George Wickham at the beach in Ramsgate. Mrs. Younge had assured her that there was no danger in allowing an old family friend to call. The two were often left alone, although Georgiana made certain that a door always remained open. She found herself drawn in by the man's flattering words and charming company. She imagined herself to be in love with the man. Earlier that very day, Wickham had confessed his love. He convinced Georgiana to elope to Gretna Green, and the kiss Darcy witnessed was in celebration of her acceptance.

Darcy let out a quiet sigh of relief, as did Miss Stewart. They exchanged brief smiles, and Darcy asked, "Georgiana, why would you agree to an elopement?"

"George told me that you would never allow us to marry," she said quietly. "He said that he could not bear to be apart from me for the unknowable length of time that it would take to convince you to approve. I knew you would not have any objection to his station, since he truly loved me, but George said that you were under the impression that he loved another and would think he wanted me only for my dowry."

At these last words, Georgiana remembered the hurtful things Wickham had said and her heart broke anew. Bursting into tears again, she collapsed into her brother's arms. "What must you think of me?" she sobbed into his coat.

Darcy immediately wrapped his arms around his distraught sister and pulled her close. "I think you are a wonderful girl," he assured her. Georgiana stilled in his arms. He continued, "You were betrayed by your companion and by a man much older than you who has fooled many a person in his lifetime, including our own father."

Georgiana looked up at him, her eyes hopeful. "You aren't upset with me?"

"I am more upset with myself," Darcy admitted. "Had I enlightened you to the deceitful nature of one whom you once called a friend, you would have not been taken in. Even so, had I chosen a better companion than Mrs. Younge, you might have been protected. I have failed in my duty to you as your brother and your guardian."

Miss Stewart shook her head emphatically. "I disagree, Mr. Darcy," she stated firmly. "The guilt lies solely with those who deceive. Your sister cannot be faulted either, as she is still young and unsuspecting of those who prey on the innocent. This is not a detriment to her character, however. To trust freely is a beautiful trait, and she is actually better educated than many young ladies her age. That is why I chose to befriend her; I appreciated her company much more than the vapid misses who congregate at Ramsgate every summer."

Darcy gave her a grateful smile as Georgiana beamed. Then the younger girl's face crumpled as she wailed, "I am still ruined! I kissed a man, and we are not engaged."

Miss Stewart sighed despondently. "Unfortunately, my dear, you may be correct. You are not ruined in the literal sense, but I came to your home when I did because I heard one of your maids telling mine that you intended to elope."

Gratitude filled Darcy for this unselfish woman who clearly valued friendship over potential taint by association. "Thank you," he said, "from the depths of my soul, I thank you for your kindness to my sister. I don't know how we shall ever repay you." Though he now trusted her honor, he still watched her closely for any reaction to the word 'repay'.

Miss Stewart gave Darcy a scornful look. "No repayment is necessary," she declared haughtily, "I merely ask that you allow Georgiana and I to correspond after you leave Ramsgate."

"Of course," Darcy said, thoroughly impressed.

Miss Stewart hugged Georgiana tightly. "Now that the issue of repayment is settled," she glared at Darcy, "we unfortunately do need to discuss where to go from here."

"I will have to marry him, won't I?" asked Georgiana sadly, "Even though he does not truly care for me."

"Absolutely not," said Darcy firmly, "I will not allow you to be shackled to such a scoundrel."

"But what will I do? Where will I go?" Georgiana's fearful voice tore at Darcy's heart. "I cannot return home ruined, and no one will want to marry me now."

"I will marry you, Georgiana, if you will have me."

Three heads turned to see Bingley standing in the doorway. He removed his hat and crossed the room to kneel at Georgiana's feet.

"I will marry you," he repeated solemnly, "Will you marry me?"

"Bingley," Darcy warned, "perhaps we should discuss this in private first."

"No, we should not," stated Bingley, keeping his gaze on Georgiana's face. He took the girl's small hand in his. "I do not love you the way a man ought to love a woman when he marries her," he remarked, "But I do love you as the sister of my dearest friend."

Turning his face to look at Darcy, Bingley continued: "Darcy, more than a decade ago, you saved my life—perhaps literally—in standing with me to protect my friend. Allow me to now do the same."

Everyone was silent. Darcy looked at Georgiana, then back at his friend. "This is not what I wanted for you—for either of you," he added, taking Georgiana's other hand in his.

"I cannot guarantee that we will have a grand passion," Bingley said to Georgiana, "But what I can promise you is that I will always treat you with kindness and respect."

Darcy opened his mouth to speak, but Miss Stewart voiced her thoughts first.

"Mr. Bingley, is it?" At Bingley's nod, she continued, "What I am about to ask may seem indelicate, but Georgiana's wellbeing is too important for me to worry about being ladylike." She fixed Bingley with a stern look and said, "She is still a child. A young woman, certainly—particularly in appearance—but still a child. Do you intend to wed and bed a child, or will you consider waiting until she is ready for that step in her life?"

Darcy's jaw dropped open in shock, then he shuddered. He fervently wished that Miss Stewart had never painted that image in his mind, but he was simultaneously grateful for the foresight and tenacity she had displayed in positing the question.

Bingley considered the question, which had not occurred to him until that moment. After a brief introspection, he responded: "I will wait. I would want both of us to come to know one another as partners before taking that step, which will only occur when she wishes it, and not a moment sooner," he added firmly.

Miss Stewart nodded her approval, and Darcy released the breath he had instinctively held. "Bingley," he said hoarsely, "I cannot begin to express what this means to me."

Bingley looked directly into Darcy's eyes. "I swear to you that I will care for Georgiana," he vowed.

Darcy looked at Georgiana, who had listened silently to the exchange. "What do you say, my dear sister?" asked Darcy, "Would you prefer to marry Bingley, or should we discuss other possibilities?"

Miss Stewart nodded approvingly at Darcy. "I had not thought you would consider her feelings on the matter," she admitted.

"In the past, I might not have," Darcy acknowledged, "But I must confess: Wollstonecraft makes a compelling argument."

Miss Stewart let out a surprised bark of laughter, then covered her mouth with a delicate hand. "She is probably the reason I have not yet found a husband," she declared mirthfully. Sobering, she looked down at Georgiana. "What do you think, child?" she asked fondly.

Georgiana bit her lip, then looked at Bingley. "Yes, Mr. Bingley," she said clearly, "I will marry you. I thank you for the honor."

Bingley smiled gently at her. Silence reigned for a minute, then was interrupted by the gurgling of someone's stomach. The four companions burst into laughter at the unexpected disruption.

"Perhaps we should eat," Darcy suggested with a smile.

The rest agreed and passed the evening in a pleasant manner.

Chapter 8

Hertfordshire, April 1811

"Well, my dear," said Mr. Bennet at the breakfast table. "I have news for you. It appears my cousin, Mr. Collins, who has the power to turn you out of this house upon my demise, has passed away himself."

His wife and all five of his daughters stared at him in shock.

"Oh, what luck!" exclaimed Mrs. Bennet. "Now that he is dead and gone, we are all saved! Dear Jane will of course inherit! We must away to London immediately!"

"Whatever for?" inquired her husband.

"We must shop for new dresses! My beautiful Jane will have need of a wardrobe befitting her station as the heiress of Longbourn!"

"Before you make any purchases," replied Mr. Bennet, "I must inform you that Jane will *not* inherit Longbourn." When Mrs. Bennet opened her mouth to object, he raised a hand to silence her before continuing. "The estate will pass to a man whom I have never met. Mr. Collins—what a miserly man that was—married later in life and fathered a son, a Mr. William Collins. This younger Mr. Collins is now the heir to Longbourn."

Mrs. Bennet wailed mournfully. "Oh, we are still lost! To have your estate taken away from your daughters to be given to a mere child!"

"I would be very much surprised if he were a child," Mr. Bennet said wryly, "as he has just taken orders and has been granted a living in Kent."

Looking sharply at her husband, Mrs. Bennet delicately asked, "Does he go to Kent with his wife?"

"He has no wife."

Mrs. Bennet emitted a discordant squeal reminiscent of the noise Lydia made whenever she was excited. "Oh, my dear Mr. Bennet! You must invite him here at once!"

The Misses Bennet looked at their mother quizzically. "Why would we want to do that?" snorted Lydia derisively.

"Why, so he might marry one of you, of course!" cried Mrs. Bennet.

"Lah, what a grand joke!" cried Lydia. "I wonder if he should choose me? I should like above all things—to marry before my sisters that they may give way to me."

Mrs. Bennet smiled fondly at her daughter. "You are almost fifteen and ready to come out, my dear. And since you are the liveliest, he may decide he likes you the best."

Three of Lydia's older sisters exchanged exasperated looks while Lizzy rolled her eyes heavenward.

Mr. Bennet stood to leave the room, and Mrs. Bennet demanded that before the day's end he should issue an invitation to their "dear cousin Collins." Mr. Bennet waved sardonically at her in agreement and dismissal before heading to his bookroom for the day.

"We must head to Meryton at once!" declared Mrs. Bennet as the door closed behind her husband. "Each of you must have a new dress! We must display you to your best advantage."

After completing breakfast, Jane, Lizzy, Mary, and Kitty gathered in Jane's bedroom to discuss the younger Mr. Collins. They knew very little about him, other than his father had a falling out with their own father many years ago.

"Is he amiable?" wondered Jane.

"He may be amiable, or he may be a scoundrel," said Lizzy, "or somewhere in between the two. We will have no means of knowing until he arrives."

The girls waited in rigid anticipation for a full week until a letter finally arrived from Mr. Collins. Mr. Bennet's daughters produced such a disturbance about the letter that Mr. Bennet opened it immediately, rather than allowing it to languish on his desk for days, as was his usual custom.

"Well?" demanded Kitty eagerly.

Her father slowly folded the letter and replaced it on the breakfast table, a glimmer of amusement in his eyes. "It appears you will meet Mr. Collins in a fortnight," he informed the girls.

At this pronouncement, Mrs. Bennet immediately called for Hill that they might discuss how to best prepare the house, which chambers should be used to host their illustrious guest, and what menu he might prefer on his first day in the house.

"May I read the letter?" Lizzy inquired. Mr. Bennet wordlessly handed it over, then retreated to his study in search of solitude. The girls gathered around Lizzy while she read the letter aloud.

"Hunsford, near Westerham, Kent, 15th April.

"Dear Sir,—

"The disagreement subsisting between yourself and my late honored father always gave me much uneasiness, and since I have had the misfortune to lose him, I have frequently wished to heal the breach; but for some time I was kept back by my own doubts, fearing lest it might seem disrespectful to his memory for me to be on good terms with anyone with whom it had always pleased him to be at variance

My mind, however, is now made up on the subject, for having received ordination at Easter, I have been so fortunate as to be distinguished by the patronage of the Right Honorable Lady Catherine de Bourgh, widow of Sir Lewis de Bourgh, whose bounty and beneficence has preferred me to the valuable rectory of this parish, where it shall be my earnest endeavor to demean myself with grateful respect towards her ladyship, and be ever ready to perform those rites and ceremonies which are instituted by the Church of England.

As a clergyman, moreover, I feel it my duty to promote and establish the blessing of peace in all families within the reach of my influence; and on these grounds I flatter myself that my present overtures are highly commendable, and that the circumstance of my being next in the entail of Longbourn estate will be kindly overlooked on your side, and not lead you to reject the offered olive branch.

I cannot be otherwise than concerned at being the means of injuring your amiable daughters, and beg leave to apologize for it, as well as to assure you of my readiness to make them every possible amends—but of this hereafter.

If you should have no objection to receive me into your house, I propose myself the satisfaction of waiting on you and your family, Monday, May 18th, by four o'clock, and shall probably trespass on your hospitality till the Saturday se'ennight following, which I can do without any inconvenience, as Lady Catherine is far from objecting to my occasional absence on a Sunday, provided that some other clergyman is engaged to do the duty of the day.

I remain, dear sir, with respectful compliments to your lady and daughters, your well-wisher and friend,

"William Collins"

Upon its completion, there was silence. "He seems to be a rather... odd sort of fellow, wouldn't you say?" commented Kitty.

Jane fixed her sister with a stern look. "Perhaps his manner of expression is different from those to which we are accustomed."

"It behooves us all," said Mary, "to reserve judgment until we have met him for ourselves and can determine his character."

"La, I have no need to meet him," declared Lydia, flipping her braid over her shoulder. "That letter gives me enough information to decide that I will *never* marry Mr. Collins."

~∞~∞~∞~

A fortnight later, Mr. Collins arrived in his rented gig at the precise minute his letter had said to expect him. Coming down from the gig, he greeted his cousins.

"I am very pleased to meet you all!" he said, mopping his brow. "I say, the windows here at Longbourn remind me very much of the windows at Rosings!"

"Rosings?" inquired Mrs. Bennet suspiciously as they entered the house. "What sort of place is Rosings?"

"My dear Mrs. Bennet!" he cried in shock. "Rosings is the beautiful estate of my new patroness, Lady Catherine de Bourgh!" Mr. Collins then spent a tedious several minutes extolling the virtues of his noble lady and her estate.

When he finally paused to draw breath, Mrs. Bennet interrupted. "And what can you tell us of your living?" she inquired with a sly smile.

"There is a grand residence—though not nearly as fine as Rosings, of course—that abuts her estate. Lady Catherine especially involved herself with the repairs and furnishings to prepare it for my arrival. It lacks only a mistress to make it complete," he finished with a significant look at his fair cousins.

Mrs. Bennet smiled in satisfaction. Mary, however, looked at him with a small frown on her face. "What about the people you serve?" she asked.

"Ah, yes! Lady Catherine and her daughter—"

"No, I mean, what about the tenants? The servants? The tradesmen?" pressed Mary.

Mr. Collins looked at her with a blank face. His mouth moved several times, but no words pushed past his lips. Finally he said, "Well, as I have not been there long, I have not had a chance to become acquainted with them all."

Mary nodded and replied, "That is quite understandable. I trust, however, that upon your return, you will immediately begin to visit those who live in your domain?"

Mr. Collins nodded fervently. "What an inspired idea, Cousin Mary! I certainly shall!"

Lizzy and Jane looked at Mary curiously. Mr. Collins went upstairs to refresh himself from the journey after Mrs. Bennet finished quizzing him on his favorite dishes. When she bustled out to speak with the cook about the menu, Mary's sisters turned their full attention toward her.

"Mary, what did you mean by questioning him so?" demanded Lizzy.

Mary looked calmly at her sisters. "I was inquiring to see if he would easily be led to do what is right, or if he would insist on putting Lady Catherine at the front."

"And what—pray tell—do such questions portend?" Jane asked.

"Why, to see if he would make for a good husband," Mary answered.

Lydia burst into laughter, and Kitty tried hard not to follow suit.

"Lydia," Lizzy corrected sharply, "you may be excused to the schoolroom. Once you are out in society, then you may participate in these conversations. Until then, they are not fit for your ears."

Though Lydia opened her mouth to protest, a firm nod from Jane warned the young girl that resistance would be futile. Letting out a loud huff, she flounced from the room, closing the door forcefully behind her.

"Why on earth would you want to marry Mr. Collins?" Kitty cried in confusion. "He is ridiculous!"

Mary gave Kitty a hard look. "While it is true that he is not the most clever of men, he does not appear to be vicious. His lack of sophistication would make it difficult to hide a duplicitous nature."

Lizzy nodded thoughtfully. "I see now why you asked your question. You wanted to see if he would be willing to be led by a strong wife."

Jane pursed her lips. "Mary, dear, could you be truly happy with such an arrangement?"

Mary nodded thoughtfully. "I believe so. I have given this a great deal of consideration ever since we saw the letter he wrote to my father. As you know, I have always felt a great predilection toward living a markedly religious life. Had I been born a man, I would have taken orders with alacrity. As a woman, the closest I may come to such a life is to marry a man of the cloth. Mr. Collins has the additional benefit of inheriting our family home."

Lizzy still looked troubled. "But what about love, Mary?"

Smiling gently at her sister, Mary replied, "I'm not romantic, you know. I never was. I require only that I be treated well by my husband

and that he provides us with a comfortable home. I have not yet set myself solely on this course, however. I would not want to align myself with someone like Mr. Fordham, for example."

"Lord, no!" Kitty burst out loudly. The sudden sound helped to ease the serious mood that had enveloped the sisters, and the tension in their brows waned.

"Well, then," Jane finally said. "If this is your wish, Mary, then we will help you discover if Mr. Collins is worthy of your hand."

"Indeed!" cried Lizzy. "I will not allow him to marry any of my dear sisters—not even Lydia—if he is hiding a deceitful nature!"

~∞~∞~∞~

Over the following weeks, Mary's sisters undertook to test Mr. Collins in a series of campaigns that would have been worthy of the British army itself. First, Kitty spilled a glass of water on Mr. Collins one evening at dinner, much to her mother's horror. Mr. Collins, however, merely smiled at her and teased, "Quite alright, my dear cousin. I daresay my shirt wanted washing regardless. You appear to have spared the maid some effort."

Jane had much time to spend with Mr. Collins, as Mrs. Bennet was forever leaving the two of them together in an attempt to matchmake. This allowed Jane to inquire about Mr. Collins's family history, which she then shared with Mary, Lizzy, and Kitty. It was to their sorrow that they learned how the elder Mr. Collins had been a miserly man who was nearly impossible to please. "His father was so cruel, and yet the son has shown himself to be kind. This demonstrates a goodness of character at his core."

Lizzy undertook the responsibility of discovering what the servants thought of Mr. Collins. In this, Charlotte Lucas was of use. Charlotte simply asked her servants what the Longbourn servants had said about the man. All reports were favorable, indicating that Mr. Collins was frequently apologetic when he caused extra work, and that he never attempted to misbehave around pretty young maids.

For her part, Mary spent many hours in doctrinal discourse with Mr. Collins in an attempt to see if their views about the Almighty would be compatible. She was pleased to find that their perspectives seemed to be in alignment on nearly every point. Oftentimes he would parrot an edict of Lady Catherine, which Mary would counter with scripture. Every time, he altered his opinion to accommodate scripture.

Her consistent praise of his understanding gave him a sense of confidence that he had never before felt. Having lacked the approval of every important figure in his life, the kind attentions of a lovely young woman had a much-desired effect. As the days passed, Mr. Collins spent less and less time quoting Lady Catherine. After a fortnight complete, he began to go an entire day without once mentioning her name.

On the eve of this momentous day, the four elder Bennet sisters gathered in Mary's room to discuss Mr. Collins. Time was pressing, as he was due to return to Hunsford and his parsonage in less than a sennight. All reports were highly favorable, and the girls were inclined to allow Mary to accept his addresses, should he offer them.

The next morning, Jane and Lizzy intimated several times that Mary would make a superb wife to some fortunate clergyman, due to her love of the scriptures and her practical nature. These comments were all Mr. Collins needed to override his concern for approaching a younger sister when the elder sisters were still unwed.

After a brief discussion with Mr. Bennet, Mr. Collins entered the sitting room and asked to speak with his dear Cousin Mary in private. Mrs. Bennet, who had still fixed in her mind that Mr. Collins was for Jane, sat with her mouth agape for several seconds. Taking pity on their bewildered mother, Lizzy and Jane guided her from the room, along with Kitty and Lydia.

While Mrs. Bennet repeated, "I do not understand," Lydia pressed her ear to the door, much to the dismay of her elder sisters. Some five minutes later, an ebullient Mr. Collins opened the door and—

alongside a beaming Mary—announced their betrothal.

As it was May and life on Longbourn would be busy during the planting and harvesting seasons, a wedding date was scheduled for December. This would also allow Mary's aunt and uncle Gardiner to attend, as they usually visited for Christmas. Mr. Gardiner's work schedule did not easily allow him to travel otherwise.

With a joyful heart, Mr. Collins returned to Kent, eager to share news of his betrothed with Lady Catherine, and the ladies began to make wedding preparations.

Chapter 9

Hertfordshire, July 1811

Lizzy covered her ears against the shrill sounds emanating from the sitting room. Lydia was currently being fitted for the clothes she needed for her come out. She had recently turned fifteen and was to attend her first assembly. Her happiness was apparent by the squeals of joy that were echoed by her mother.

Jane smiled kindly at Lizzy over the linens they were making for Mary to take with her upon her marriage to Mr. Collins later that year. "She is still young, and she has been waiting for this day for quite a long time."

"She's no younger than any of us were when we came out," grumbled Lizzy.

"Yes, well, you were upset to not get more walking dresses!" laughed Mary.

The four elder Bennet girls were working together on the linens Mary would take with her upon her marriage to Mr. Collins later that year. Since there were many months yet, the girls were able to take their time and make each item as close to perfect as possible.

Kitty looked up from a bedsheet and said, "It will be different to have Lydia attend an assembly with us. I hope she comports herself with more decorum than she does at home."

Lizzy let out a laugh and replied, "I doubt it."

"Lizzy, that is unkind!" cried Jane.

"But also true," Lizzy retorted.

Jane let out a sigh, but she could not argue with her sister on this point. In truth, all four of Lydia's elder sisters were concerned about Lydia coming out into society. While she was of age, her behavior in company did not exhibit the maturity one would hope for a girl of her years.

Changing the subject, Kitty said, "I wonder if Colonel Forster and Captain Denny will be there."

"I'm sure they will be," Lizzy said. "They promised when we saw them in Meryton that they will have returned from London by then."

Colonel Forster and Captain Denny had come to Meryton a fortnight prior in search of locations for their regiment to quarter for the winter. Though the troops would not arrive for some months, the officers had several different towns to scout before then. They had taken a room at the local inn for a month complete in order to branch out to neighboring communities.

Colonel Forster was a smart young colonel—as Mrs. Bennet described him—and had shown some small amount of attention toward Miss Harriet Long.

Finally, the sounds from the sitting room quieted, and the Bennet girls thought it safe to rejoin their mother and youngest sister. As they filed into the room, their eyes widened in astonishment at the sheer amount of ribbons, lace, and fabrics scattered throughout.

"Mamma," gasped Jane in dismay, "how much have you purchased?"

"It is not really that much," Mrs. Bennet said airily. "My dear Lydia needs the very best for her first assembly!"

"But the expense!" said Mary with a frown.

"Oh, hang the expense!" cried Mrs. Bennet without concern. "This is my last child to come out, so a bit of extravagance is warranted!"

The older girls gave exchanged concerned looks while an oblivious Mrs. Bennet prattled on about the flounces and accessories for each of the fabrics that were in the room. It was into this circumstance that Mr. Bennet entered the room.

"Mrs. Bennet!" he exclaimed in alarm when he viewed the rather large pile of frippery. "I trust you have sufficient funds to cover these purchases?"

His wife's eyes widened in slight alarm. "Well, sir," she said hesitantly, "since this is the last child to need a wardrobe for their coming out, I may have spent a bit more than usual."

Mr. Bennet gave her a long look, then said, "I told you last time you overspent your allowance that the excess would come from the next quarter's pin money. Looking at all of these piles, I imagine you have made enough purchases to deplete the following quarter's pin money as well. The orders will either need to be cancelled, or you will have to make do with no allowance until January."

Mrs. Bennet gasped in shock and indignation, while her elder daughters raised their eyebrows in surprise. "Mr. Bennet," she said in dismay, "think of the gossip!"

"You should have thought of the gossip before exceeding your income," he told her sternly.

Mrs. Bennet turned towards her youngest. "Lydia, dear—" she began, but before she could continue, Lydia let out a loud wail.

"No! No, no, no!" she screamed, stomping her foot. "Mamma, you promised I could have these gowns and be the most beautiful girl at the assembly! How else shall I be the first of my sisters married?"

Lizzy let out a laugh as her other sisters watched with wide eyes. "Lydia, you are barely out, and Mary is already engaged! How can you expect to be married before her?"

"You'll see! I *will* be married first! Mamma, you *promised!*" Lydia punctuated her tantrum with another stomp of her foot.

Mr. Bennet chuckled at his wife's dilemma, finding amusement in her choice between herself and her favorite daughter.

Mrs. Bennet looked between her husband, her daughter, and back at her husband. Finally, she said, "I supposed I can make do without pin money until January."

Lydia let out a squeal of delight, while Mrs. Bennet's other daughters lowered their heads in disappointment.

Lydia's exultations continued for the remainder of the week until it was time for the assembly. They crowded into the carriage, which was now a very tight fit with five girls and two parents. Lydia insisted on taking more than her share of the space to prevent her new gown from creasing.

After a difficult ride, the sisters poured from the carriage in relief. They entered the building and were immediately greeted by Sir William Lucas.

"Ah, the Bennets!" the man cried. "How delighted I am to see you! I see Miss Lydia is with us tonight. I must tell you, Miss Lydia, that tonight's decorations remind me greatly of Saint James's court."

Lydia interrupted and asked, "Where is Maria?" before dashing off without pausing for an answer. Her friend—the younger Miss Lucas—had come out only two months before.

Lizzy began to apologize for her sister's poor manners, but the affable Sir William merely waved his hand and chuckled. "Not to worry, Miss Elizabeth," he said with a wink. "I know my Maria was just as eager for her first assembly as well. And who could blame them when such delights are to be had?"

Smiling in gratitude, Lizzy and her remaining sisters continued into the ballroom. Upon entering, they were approached by two young men in crisp red uniforms.

"Good evening, ladies," Colonel Forster greeted them with a bow.

Captain Denny echoed with his own greetings. "I trust you have all come to dance?" he asked.

At their nods, Colonel Forster asked each young lady for a dance. Captain Denny solicited Kitty's hand for the first set, which set her to blush. As the music began, he escorted her to the floor, while the Colonel sought out Miss Harriet for the first dance.

Lizzy looked around in disappointment. While she enjoyed dancing, there were so few men available with whom to partner, even at the public assemblies. Her father was escorting Lydia to the floor, who beamed with excitement. She turned to her sisters, "Would any of you care to stand up with me?" she asked with a grin.

"I will, Lizzy!" volunteered Kitty. The two headed to the dance floor while Jane and Mary stood at the side, watching them with pleasure.

Although standing up with a sister did not bring the same enjoyment as standing up with a young man, Lizzy still enjoyed dancing. It was as close to running as she could get while comporting herself properly in the presence of her friends and family. The exertion also lent a sparkle to her eye and a flush to her cheek that was most becoming.

Several sets later, Lizzy left the dance floor, having stood up with all of her sisters but one. "Where is Lydia?" she asked her elder sister, searching around the room.

Jane frowned. "She was just over there," she said, motioning to a refreshment table near the hallway door. "She had finished dancing with Colonel Forster, and he was escorting her to get some punch."

Lizzy shrugged. "I'm certain she'll appear on the floor for the next set. Since this is her first assembly, I do not believe she would want to miss a single dance!"

The next dance began, and Mary joined them. "Have you seen Lydia?" she asked in a low voice. When the girls shook their heads, Mary frowned in concern. "I just saw Miss Harriet in tears in the retiring room. Colonel Forster had been paying her some particular attention, but he has ignored her since their first dance together, in favor of speaking with Lydia in between sets."

Lizzy raised her eyebrows in astonishment. "Well, that is not the mark of a good suitor, to pay attention to another young lady instead of the one he appears to prefer."

Jane nodded in agreement. "Some young men attempt to increase a woman's love by inspiring jealousy. It is disappointing if Colonel Forster is using such tactics. Poor Lydia would not understand that he is not truly interested in her."

The conversation halted as Kitty rushed toward them. "Lizzy, where is Papa?" she asked in an urgent whisper.

"He is standing with Sir William, Mamma, and Lady Lucas," answered Jane. "Is something the matter?"

Kitty opened her mouth to respond, but she was interrupted by a piercing shriek from across the room.

"Too late," Kitty groaned, covering her face with her hands.

Mrs. Long had opened the door to the hallway, where she found Lydia and Colonel Forster in the midst of a kiss. The shock of her discovery caused Mrs. Long to emit the aforementioned disruptive outburst before falling to the floor in a swoon. Miss Harriet—Mrs. Long's niece—burst into tears at the sight of her beau with another young lady.

"Mamma, you must congratulate me!" cried an oblivious Lydia, her arms twined around a now struggling Colonel Forster. "I am to be married!"

Colonel Forster finally broke free of Lydia's embrace. Horrified, he cast a desperate eye from Lydia to Miss Harriet. He opened his mouth as though to speak, but no sound emerged. Finally, his shoulders slumped, and he turned to an uncharacteristically grim Mr. Bennet.

"May I speak with you in private?" the colonel asked Lydia's father solemnly.

"Yes, I think we should," Mr. Bennet replied. "I will expect you to call early tomorrow morning."

Colonel Forster nodded dejectedly. He looked once more at Miss Harriet, who turned her back on him. Thoroughly dispirited, he left the assembly, followed closely by Captain Denny.

For a few moments, silence held court in the crowded ballroom. Soon, however, a few guests murmured to their neighbors, and it did not take long for the gossip to stampede about unfettered. An ebullient Mrs. Bennet loudly congratulated her "cleverest daughter" while Mr. Jones helped revive Mrs. Long.

Lizzy and her sisters quietly gathered their wraps and exited the manor to wait for their carriage. An unusually taciturn Mr. Bennet ushered his wife and youngest child out the door after them, and they all waited outside. Lizzy struggled to contain her temper in face of her mother's raptures over another daughter's engagement.

"Silence!" barked Mr. Bennet at his wife. She froze, her eyes wide in astonishment.

"La, Papa," cried a gay Lydia, "I would have thought you would be happy for me!"

"Happy for you?" he roared. "You have ensnared a man who was making love to another, and you have brought great shame to your family!"

Lydia tossed her head indifferently. "He doesn't care three straws for Harriet Long! Else why would he have spent the evening with me?"

Mr. Bennet shook his head in disgust. "Believe what you will, if it gives you comfort. But if I hear one more word depart your lips tonight, I will deny your young man when he comes tomorrow."

Lydia gasped in horror. "You wouldn't!"

"I would," he said firmly. "And furthermore, I will deny you any wedding clothes. Do not test me tonight. Not one more word."

Lydia clamped her mouth closed and glared mutinously at him until the carriage finally arrived and bore them home.

Once back at Longbourn, Lydia was banished to the nursery, much to her displeasure. Her father's threats, however, ensured she kept her temper. The four remaining Bennet girls gathered in Jane's room to discuss the events of the night.

"I keep hoping it was a bad dream," Lizzy bemoaned.

"Unfortunately not," responded Mary.

"I don't know how I can show my face to Mrs. Long again," Jane said.

"We will be much talked of," replied Mary.

The three looked to Kitty, who was sitting quietly against the wall.

"I fear this is all my fault," she whispered. "I am to blame."

"You are not to blame!" cried Lizzy, "Why would you even think that?"

"Because I saw Lydia leave with Colonel Forster," said Kitty. "I considered stopping her, but I was afraid it would call attention. That is when I hurried to find Papa, but I could not discover where he was in time to prevent it. I should have accompanied her instead. I am to blame."

Jane wrapped her arm around Kitty's shoulders. "This is not your fault, dear Kitty."

"No indeed," agreed Mary. "The blame lies with Lydia."

"And with Colonel Forster," added Lizzy. "I do not believe he intended for things to go as far as they did, but he should not have been paying his attentions to Lydia when it was clear that he was interested in Harriet Long."

Mary nodded. "It is a form of deceit."

"And now they will be married," Jane said sadly. "Poor Harriet."

"Perhaps we should call on her tomorrow," Lizzy suggested.

"Are you certain?" Kitty asked anxiously. "We do not know her very well. She has only been visiting Mrs. Long for a few months."

"It is the Christian thing to do," Mary stated firmly.

Eventually all four sisters agreed, and they each retired to their rooms to fall into an uneasy sleep.

Colonel Forster appeared at the house before the family had finished their breakfast. Mr. Bennet immediately invited him into the bookroom for a conversation. As soon as the doors had shut on the two men, Lydia began discussing the new clothes she would need to order as a married woman.

Lizzy could no longer remain silent. "You foolish girl!" she cried.

"Elizabeth Bennet!" shrieked her mother. "You should not speak to your sister in such a way!"

"La, she is just jealous that she must give way to me. I have caught a husband, and I am the youngest of them all," Lydia airily responded with a dismissive toss of her head.

"I do not particularly like your way of getting husbands," Mary stated.

Lizzy opened her mouth to again speak to Lydia, but she was stopped by Jane's hand on her arm.

"It will do no good, Lizzy," Jane whispered to her. "Lydia will simply need to learn this from experience."

Resigned, Lizzy sat down again. She was unable to settle her emotions, however. After a moment, she excused herself from the table to prepare for their call on the Longs. Lydia and Mrs. Bennet would remain at home to receive callers, but the other Bennet girls joined Lizzy and the four began their walk towards the Longs' residence.

Once arriving at their home, Lizzy knocked. The housekeeper opened the door. "The family is not at home to callers today, ladies," the woman said apologetically.

Lizzy bowed her head in sorrow; she had suspected this would be the reaction to their visit. Jane stepped forward.

"I have written a note," she said, to the surprise of her sisters. "Would you be so good as to give it to Miss Harriet for me?"

The housekeeper took the paper, bobbed a curtsy, and closed the door.

"What did you write?" asked Kitty curiously as they began to walk back down the lane toward Longbourn.

"I told Harriet that I was very sorry for how her evening ended. I assured her that we knew nothing about the circumstances, and we were all quite shocked by our sister's behavior."

The girls heard a shout behind them. "Wait!"

They turned as one to see Harriet Long rushing down the lane to meet them. Her red-rimmed eyes and pale face confirmed the difficulties she had experienced the previous night. Upon reaching them, she threw her arms around Jane. "Thank you for your note, Jane," she whispered.

Jane returned the embrace. Lizzy said, "Truly, Harriet, we are so sorry for Lydia's actions."

Harriet released Jane and hugged Lizzy. "I admit, it has been an extremely disappointing state of affairs."

"There is one benefit, however," Mary said.

Harriet turned to her, astounded, "What possible benefit could you mean?"

"You were able to see Colonel Forster's true nature before being wed to him. If his attentions were so easily turned in one night, then marriage to him would not have been agreeable," Mary answered.

Harriet nodded thoughtfully. "That is true. I did not like how he was spending time with Lydia, but then looking at me on occasion throughout the assembly."

"He was attempting to increase your fondness through jealousy," said Lizzy. "A habit that would make for a very poor husband indeed."

"That still cannot ease all of the pain," interjected Jane.

"But it does help," Harriet said. "I had not thought of it in that light. I am so grateful you came to see me this morning."

The girls all embraced once more before returning to their respective homes.

Upon arriving home, the four elder Bennet girls were greeted by an ecstatic Lydia and a somber Colonel Forster. After listening to Lydia's chatter for several minutes, Colonel Forster excused himself, stating that he was required in London immediately to inform his superiors of his upcoming wedding. He would be gone for the entire three weeks that were required for calling the banns.

No one was sorry to see him go, not even his intended bride. She was more eager to begin making calls with her mother to inform all their neighbors of her new status as an engaged woman. Lizzy rolled her eyes when she heard this and whispered to Jane that she would be surprised if there was a single servant in all the neighborhood who did not belong to it that had not heard the news by the end of the day before.

The next three weeks were difficult ones at Longbourn. Mr. Bennet held fast that he would not purchase any wedding clothes, as Lydia had received a sufficient number of new gowns for her coming-out that had not yet been sewn, let alone worn. He did, however, allow for a new gown to be made for the day of the wedding.

On the day before the wedding, Colonel Forster returned to Hertfordshire and immediately called on Longbourn. While absent, he had written to Lydia but once. Fortunately, he corresponded frequently with Captain Denny, who in turn paid a few calls to Longbourn and was able to share any news with the Bennet family.

Colonel Forster entered the sitting room and was greeted by the Bennet family and an enthusiastic Lydia. She chattered for some minutes about everything that had passed over the last few weeks. Her betrothed eventually interrupted with a loud clearing of his throat. She froze, silent, as he said, "Allow me to introduce my friend, Colonel Fitzwilliam."

All eyes turned to the doorway where another red-coated officer stood, previously unobserved. His features were not handsome, in person and address he was must truly the gentleman. He executed a sharp bow and seemed sincerely delighted to make everyone's acquaintance. Seating himself between Kitty and Jane, he initiated a conversation about his travel from London.

"Forster and I have been friends since we were together at the Battle of Raismes last year," he explained. "Since then, we had been assigned to the same units until our recent promotions as colonels, being reassigned from the Regulars to train soldiers in the militia. When Forster arrived in London to inform our superiors of his engagement, I naturally requested leave that I might stand up with him at the wedding."

Accepting the tea offered to him by Mrs. Bennet, he continued, "Forster has saved my life more times than I can count."

At this, he was interrupted by his friend, "Ah, but not nearly as many times as Fitzwilliam has saved mine!"

Lydia sighed adoringly at such obvious bravery, and Colonel Forster graced her with a smile. He looked more at ease than he had ever appeared in the Bennet household. He seemed to have accepted that he was to marry a silly wife not of his choosing.

Lizzy leaned over to whisper at Mary, "It appears the colonel's attachments to poor Harriet were not as fixed as they appeared."

Mary frowned, "Yes, but I hope they remain on Lydia, or she will not have a happy marriage."

After a long visit and an invigorating walk outdoors, the two gentlemen made their farewells. Mrs. Bennet's invitation to stay for dinner was regretfully declined, as they had much to do in preparation for the wedding the next day.

This reminder sent Mrs. Bennet into a flurry of activity that did not cease until the early morning hours, when the bride-to-be fell asleep at the table. At that, Mr. Bennet declared they must all have some sleep before the wedding, else they would be liable to sleep through it.

A short few hours later—too short, in Lizzy's estimation—Mr. Bennet escorted his youngest and least-deserving daughter down the aisle of Longbourn chapel. Much to her elder sisters' relief, the wedding was attended by all four-and-twenty families with whom they regularly dined, including Harriet Long and her family.

The vows were said, the register was signed, and the happy couple returned to Longbourn for the wedding breakfast. When it finally came time for Colonel and Mrs. Forster to leave for their wedding trip, Mrs. Bennet was the only one whose farewells were genuine in their sorrow and tears. "Write to me, my dear," she begged her daughter.

"Oh, I shall," said Lydia carelessly, "when I find the time. We married women don't have much time for such things. My sisters may write to me, however, as I'm sure they will have nothing better to do."

Her four elder sisters rolled their eyes, which did not go unnoticed by Colonel Forster. "Well, my dear, shall we depart?" he asked as he ushered her into the carriage.

He turned and gave a smart bow of farewell to his new family. "We shall see you again when I return with the regiment in November to quarter here at Meryton. Until then, I bid a fond farewell to my new parents and sisters." Another bow, and Colonel and Mrs. Forster were gone.

Chapter 10

Derbyshire, September 1811

Fitzwilliam Darcy urged his horse into a trot as he left the tenant farm. He had met with the Smith family about the state of their roof, which had begun to leak a few days before. The building would need to be repaired quickly before the imminent heavy snows of the north made any such work impossible.

Approaching Pemberley, he directed his steward to make the necessary preparations—all at the expense of the manor house, of course. It was an estate owner's obligation to care for the natural wear of a tenant's property and home.

Darcy entered his home and asked Stewart where he could find his sister. He was directed to the large sitting room, where Georgiana sat doing needlework. He crossed over to her quietly, and she jumped when she noticed his shadow slip across her stitching.

"William, you gave me a fright!" she laughed.

"Someone has to keep you on your toes," he said in return.

She stood and gave him a quick embrace. "How are the Smiths doing?" she asked.

"Their daughters will probably need a few more dresses soon," he responded, "They appear to have grown several inches over the past few months."

"I will see what I have in the workbasket," she said, "And where is Bingley? Did he not accompany you on your rounds today?"

Darcy shook his head. "Your husband said something about a surprise

117

for you and disappeared toward Lambton at first light." At Georgiana's surprised look, he added, "He does dote on you, you know."

She smiled shyly. It had been a rather difficult year since the three of them had left Ramsgate. Bingley had purchased a special license, and he and Georgiana had been married from the chapel at Pemberley, where she had been christened as a babe. Since then, she had continued in her rooms in the family wing and he in his as they grew accustomed to their new life. Apart from the servants addressing her as Mrs. Bingley, their routine was very much the same as it had been when Bingley lived with them before his journey to the north.

Eight months after the wedding, chaos descended on Pemberley in the form of Mrs. Hurst and her sister Miss Bingley. As sisters only one year apart in age, they had completed their time at finishing school and were to take up residence with their brother.

Mrs. Hurst—Miss Bingley-as-was—had in fact outgrown her finishing school the year before. Due to his and Georgiana's sudden wedding, however, Bingley had written to keep Miss Bingley at the school for an extra year while Miss Caroline finished her last year. Miss Bingley had no desire to remain in a place she had outgrown, however. Instead, she wrote to her brother to request permission to join a schoolmate at her home in Surrey for the summer. It was there that she met Mr. Hurst, and they quickly fell in love—he with her dowry of twenty thousand pounds and she with his status as a landed gentleman.

The younger Miss Bingley then finished her year of school and went to reside with her sister and new brother in Surrey. Unfortunately, Mrs. Hurst's dowry had not been sufficient to absolve all of her husband's debts. They were forced to retrench, choosing to let their estate and instead join Bingley.

The sudden influx of people at Pemberley nearly forced Georgiana back into the shell of a person she had been immediately after the debacle at Ramsgate. However, with the patient love of her brother and tender kindness of her husband, she developed an inner strength that allowed her to retain her position as mistress of her brother's home, despite the presence of two sisters-in-law who sought to impose their will on their young new sister.

Darcy was proud of the strong young woman his sister was becoming. After Ramsgate, he feared she would crawl into herself and never return whole again. However, Bingley's cheerful presence and gentle solicitude helped her blossom into an intelligent, self-assured young woman.

She was still young, however; he and Bingley spoke on occasion about the nature of their marital relationship. Bingley was desirous to wait until his wife was seventeen—the age at which she was going to come out to the ton's society and be presented to the queen—to begin a romantic courtship. Bingley had spoken with Georgiana about the idea, and she had agreed that it would be best for her. Although she was confident, her heart was still rather bruised from Wickham's betrayal.

"Where has your mind gone?"

Georgiana's voice cut through Darcy's musings. He realized with a start that he had been staring at her for several minutes without hearing a word she had said. "My apologies, my dear sister," he said tenderly. "I was simply contemplating what an incredible young woman you have grown into. I wish our parents could see you."

She blushed with pride and looked down at her needlework. Her brother—while the best of men—was still very guarded and rarely spoke about his feelings. This bit of praise from him was quite astonishing. She returned her gaze to his face and smiled brightly at him. "Well, that is what comes from being in the married state. Now we need only to get you to the altar!"

Darcy's horrified expression caused her to break into peals of laughter.

"What, pray tell, is so amusing?" came a somewhat snide voice behind them.

Caroline Bingley entered the sitting room, having just changed for dinner. Her sister, Mrs. Hurst, accompanied her, and the two were followed closely by Mr. Hurst, who was never late for a meal at Pemberley.

Georgiana and Darcy gave one another a knowing look, then Georgiana said with an air of reserve, "Fitzwilliam was merely telling me that my husband had gone to town in search of a surprise for me. I was expressing my delight at such kindness."

"Yes, my brother is the most thoughtful of husbands," Caroline agreed. "If only I could find such a man," she added, batting her eyes at Darcy, who became suddenly preoccupied with something out the window.

When her hint went unnoticed—for she could not imagine herself rebuffed—Miss Bingley walked over to join him at the window. "Such a lovely view," she simpered. "I have always said since we came here that I would be content to stay at Pemberley and never leave."

Darcy sighed inwardly. He had made great efforts to overcome his tendency to label every unmarried miss a social climber, but Miss Bingley's cloying attentions made it extremely difficult to not revert back to the broad application of such stereotypes.

Fortunately for Darcy, he was spared constructing a response when the door opened, and Bingley entered the room. His smile was exceedingly broad—more so than usual—and he greeted Georgiana with a kiss on her hand. "My dear wife," he exclaimed, "I have the most wonderful surprise for you!"

Georgiana laughed at his endearing antics. "I am all anticipation, sir."

Bingley let out a long, loud wolf whistle that caused Darcy to raise his eyebrows. The door opened again, and in stepped Colonel Fitzwilliam.

"Richard!" cried Georgiana, truly delighted. She leapt to her feet and embraced her cousin. He lifted her up and twirled her around, causing Mrs. Hurst and Miss Bingley to gasp at the display.

"Put her down, you big oaf," reproached Darcy genially. He crossed the room and embraced his cousin. "She is a married woman now, after all."

Richard's smile dimmed slightly at this reminder. He had been on the continent when the debacle at Ramsgate had occurred. The letter of explanation that Darcy sent inspired in him a rage beyond anything he had ever felt, surpassing even his hatred of Napoleon. He had been unable to return to England for the majority of Georgiana's first year of marriage, and they had only seen one another but once before his duties of training militia men began.

"She may be a grown married woman by now," he said, gently placing the young girl back on her feet, "but she's still my little cousin," he added with a wink and a tweak of her nose.

A loud sniff from the window marred the celebratory atmosphere. Miss Bingley stood with her nose pressed nearly to the ceiling, regarding the scene before her with no small measure of condescension and condemnation.

Bingley laughed, clapping Richard on the back. "Where are my manners? Richard, may I introduce my sisters to you?"

Miss Bingley paled slightly at Bingley's wording; making the request to Richard meant the newcomer enjoyed a higher position in society than she.

"Certainly, my dear cousin-in-law," said the colonel.

"Colonel Fitzwilliam, allow me to present my sister Mrs. Hurst and her husband, as well as my sister Miss Bingley. Sisters and brother, this is Colonel Richard Fitzwilliam, son of the Earl of Matlock and cousin to Darcy and Georgiana."

Miss Bingley immediately attempted to rectify her mistake by dipping into a low curtsey. "It is an honor to meet you, sir. Any family of our dear Georgiana's is most welcome."

Richard looked bewilderedly at Miss Bingley's phrasing, which made her appear as the mistress of the house. Georgiana simply rolled her eyes at him, then smiled and said, "Yes, Richard, you are welcome any time to the *Darcy* home."

Miss Bingley blushed slightly in confusion and remained silent. Georgiana turned to her brother and said, "Fitzwilliam, did you know that Richard was planning to visit?"

Darcy shook his head. "I am just as surprised as you are, my dear."

Bingley beamed and Richard laughed. "I wrote directly to Bingley as soon as I knew I would have a few weeks leave. I wanted to surprise both of my cousins!"

"We did not suspect a thing, did we, Brother?" exclaimed Georgiana.

"I had not the slightest inkling," he confirmed.

At that moment, Stewart entered the room. "Dinner is ready," he announced.

Georgiana looked around the room. "We will not have formal seating tonight," she declared, "I would like to stay with my cousin the entire evening!"

Richard laughed again and offered her his arm. Bingley offered his arm to Caroline, and the Hursts brought up the rear, with Darcy following on his own behind them.

The dinner table was full of laughter and cheer. Even Miss Bingley relaxed some of her airs to actually emit a giggle at a story Richard shared wherein he had let a small rabbit into the tent of a fellow soldier in the middle of the night. "You should have seen the look on Forster's face," he said, wiping tears of laughter from his eyes. "There he was in his nightshirt, searching frantically for his rifle, all the while screaming that we were under attack from the French."

The table burst into laughter again. "You are fortunate he took so long to find his gun, else he may have actually shot you!" said Darcy in between gasps.

Richard grinned. Then he sobered, and said, "Speaking of Forster, I had the great fortune of standing up with him at his wedding about a fortnight ago. Poor man. He had been courting a young lady, only to be compromised by another young lady at an assembly! Fortunately, his feelings were easily transferred from one girl to the other. A more silly girl I've never seen in my life. She had just barely come out—only fifteen years old! She was completely mad for a uniform. Well, all's well that ends well, I say."

Darcy grimaced and Georgiana blushed slightly, remembering her own foolish action just a year prior at the same age. An awkward pause filled the room for a moment. Bingley finally ended the silence by asking Richard, "So, what have you been doing since your return from the continent?"

Relieved, Richard answered, "With this latest promotion and my father's influence, I have been asked to train several militia regiments that are stationed throughout the realm. Forster had been in Hertfordshire looking for places for his officers to quarter for the winter. I plan to take my regiment to join his down there." He let out a regretful sigh, "After being here, however, it will be difficult to leave you all again."

"When do you have to leave?" asked Georgiana.

"I am afraid, poppet, that I can only stay a sennight, and then I must away to Hertfordshire. Had I not already made this commitment, I would be tempted to turn in my resignation and take up the estate that my uncle left for me in his will two years ago."

"What is being done with the estate while you are serving?" asked Darcy.

"My brother, the viscount, is caring for it. He knew I felt a duty for service quite intensely, so he graciously agreed to have his steward oversee it, along with his other properties," Richard explained. "I have one more year of service, and then I will be free to take over the management."

"Managing an estate can be difficult," said Bingley. "I have been amazed watching Darcy and what he deals with on a daily basis. I only hope to be half as good when I take my own estate."

"Take your own estate? What do you mean, Charles?" asked Caroline sharply.

"My plan has always been to learn from Darcy for a while, then let my own estate. Once I have had the practice, I will then make a purchase," he said patiently, although he had repeated this conversation with Caroline multiple times since she took up residency at Pemberley.

"Say, I have a brilliant idea!" cried Richard. "I will be quartering in Hertfordshire with Forster outside a town called Meryton. Forster's new wife is from a family that owns an estate there. Near their estate is another empty estate called Netherfield. What say you to letting Netherfield while I am stationed nearby? That way we will be able to be in one another's company over this next year."

"What a wonderful idea!" exclaimed Georgiana with enthusiasm. "Oh, Charles, may we?"

"Of course, my darling," replied Bingley, lifting her hand and giving it a gentle kiss.

Darcy interrupted, "Before you decide on this Netherfield, Bingley, we should probably make a few inquiries about the condition of the house, the quality of the families in the neighborhood, and other considerations."

Bingley laughed. "What would I do without you, Darcy? If we let this house, you must join me! I would be lost without your guidance. Although I think I may have heard of this place before. The name Meryton sounds familiar, but I cannot think of why."

Darcy smiled but said, "Nonsense, Bingley. You may be a bit impetuous, but you are quite capable of running an estate now after having seen me do it these several years. However, I believe I will take you up on your invitation, as I would like to remain near my sister and cousin."

"It is settled, then!" said Bingley with a grin.

"*After* we make those inquiries, Bingley!"

The discussion continued as the ladies retired to the music room while the men drank their port. A servant quickly fetched Darcy's steward, who confirmed that Netherfield was one of the many estates about which Bingley had already made inquiries about over the last six months. Bingley knew that Darcy was uncomfortable with Miss

Bingley in the house, and he was eager to give his friend some space.

Bingley had used the time Caroline was occupied with impressing Darcy to do some research into estates. Netherfield had been his favorite, but he had previously dismissed the place because he had not wanted to take Georgiana so far from her brother. Richard settling for a year in Meryton would allow Georgiana to continue to have the support of her family.

When the gentlemen rejoined the ladies, they shared the good news—to Netherfield they would all go.

Chapter 11

Hertfordshire, October 1811

"Mr. Bennet! Mr. Bennet!" cried his lady as she rushed into the house. She had just been in Meryton to visit her sister Phillips and was eager to impart the news she had received.

"What is it, my dear?" he asked as he exited his bookroom to see what all the fuss was. "Have the pigs gotten into the garden again?"

"What? No! It is something wonderful! Netherfield Park has been let at last!" Mrs. Bennet collapsed into a settee in the sitting room, shoulders heaving with gasps as she caught her breath.

"Has it?" he inquired.

"Yes, my dear! To a gentleman from the North! A man with a large fortune! Oh, what a fine thing for our girls!" she exclaimed.

The four Bennet sisters joined their parents in the sitting room, having heard the entire conversation from up the stairs.

"For our girls?" Mr. Bennet asked, winking at Lizzy. "How can it affect them?"

"Why, you must know that I am thinking of him marrying one of them! He will prefer Jane, of course, as she is the handsomest. Oh, but Kitty is the most lively now that dear Lydia is Mrs. Forster."

Jane blushed slightly as Lizzy smirked at her. Kitty laughed at the idea of her being the next to marry.

"Mr. Bennet, you must call on him! I insist," Mrs. Bennet declared.

"I do not believe I will have the time," said Mr. Bennet with another sly wink to his daughters. "I will be much occupied with preparations on the estate for the winter."

"Oh Mr. Bennet!" wailed his wife. "How can you be so cruel? What will become of us when you are dead if all your daughters end up as old maids?"

Mary laughed. "Mamma, please remember that I am now engaged to Mr. Collins. When Papa does pass away—which I hope will be many years from now—I will be prepared to care for my mother and for any of my sisters who are in need."

Mrs. Bennet paused and blinked at her middle daughter. "Why that is right! I had quite forgotten about you, Mary. But your other sisters will still need husbands! What would our neighbors think if I could only manage to have two of my five girls safely married?"

Lizzy bit the inside of her cheek to keep from laughing at her mother. Far from being offended at having been forgotten, Mary chose to derive amusement from the situation.

"Perhaps the new tenant of Netherfield will bring a large party," suggested Jane in an attempt to please her mother.

"It would not matter if twenty such men should come," sniffed Mrs. Bennet in indignation, "If your father will not visit them."

"Depend upon it, my dear, when there are twenty, I shall visit them all," declared her husband as he quit the sitting room in favor of the quiet solitude of his bookroom.

Over the next several days, Mrs. Bennet continued to bemoan the unfairness of having such a husband that did not care whether his daughters died as old maids. Her daughters took as many opportunities as possible to escape her musings by going for long walks and visiting Meryton.

One day, Kitty returned home from Meryton with news. "I have just heard the most wonderful thing about Mr. Bingham, the new tenant at Netherfield!" she crowed.

"Oh, I am sick to death of hearing about this man!" cried Mrs. Bennet. "What did you say his name was again?"

"Mr. Bingham, I believe," Kitty said. "Although it was rather difficult to understand my aunt, as she has had a sore throat as of late."

"Ah yes," Mrs. Bennet nodded wisely. "It is from too many chocolates."

"More likely from too much gossip," Lizzy whispered to Mary, who stifled a giggle and looked at her sister in mock reproach.

"Mr. Bingham—I never want to hear his name again!" cried their mother, returning to the topic at hand.

"Well, I am very sorry to hear that," said Mr. Bennet as he closed his newspaper. "Had I known as much, I should never have called on him."

"What?" cried the lady. "You have called on Mr. Bingham!"

"I called on the new tenant of Netherfield yesterday morning," he said with a private smile. "I am afraid we cannot escape the acquaintance now."

"And you said not a single word! You sly man. What a good joke!" said Mrs. Bennet in delight, jumping to her feet and giving her husband a hug in a rare show of affection.

"You shall all meet Netherfield's new tenant and all who reside there tomorrow at the assembly," he informed them.

"I hope he comes eager to dance," said Lizzy.

"We shall see," said Mary.

The young ladies spent the remainder of the day begging their father for as much information as could be had about Netherfield's new tenant. The onset of rain that lasted into the next evening prevented them from going calling on their neighbors, so their father was the only source of information. To their frustration, Mr. Bennet claimed to not know who this Mr. Bingham was, but said that the new tenant of Netherfield was a kind young man. This was the only answer they received, in spite of their constant badgering.

In their frustration, the girls turned their attentions towards their clothing for the assembly. As they could not go into Meryton to the milliner's shop for new fripperies to make over their dresses, they had to settle for the bits of ribbon and lace that they had on hand. Although their futures were secure with Lydia married and Mary engaged, they were eager to make a good impression on their new neighbor. It was not often that a single man in possession of a large fortune came into their part of the country, and—according to Mrs. Bennet—he would surely be in want of a wife.

Jane, Lizzy, and Kitty were not wild to be married, per se, but they also recognized that with their small dowries, they had little but their charms to recommend them. They each wanted to marry someone with whom they were in love (or at least of whom they were rather fond), but they also wanted that person to reciprocate those feelings. With so many ladies and so few gentlemen in Hertfordshire thanks to Napoleon, they knew they must make the most of these opportunities to eclipse the other girls who would attend the assembly.

With these thoughts in mind, the hours passed swiftly until the carriage was called to take them to the assembly.

~∞~∞~∞~

Fitzwilliam Darcy looked up as Caroline Bingley sashayed into the drawing room. He had been reading aloud a book to his sister as she made a few repairs to a gown.

"Is there any better way to spend an afternoon than by reading?" Miss Bingley asked as she sat down.

"I do enjoy listening to my brother read to me," agreed Georgiana as she tied off a stitch.

"There is nothing like a good book to pass the time away. How I wish my brother had a more extensive library. The one here at Netherfield is quite empty," Miss Bingley sighed.

"It is a situation that I will quickly rectify," Georgiana assured her sister.

"Neglect of a library is unpardonable in this day and age," Miss Bingley declared. "After all, books are a wonderful way of improving one's mind."

"Yes, and their ability to improve one's mind and to be enjoyable is greatly dependent on one's ability to find a quiet time to do the reading," Darcy commented in a dry voice.

Georgiana shot her brother a warning look, even as Miss Bingley tittered, "Quite right, Mr. Darcy! Those who do not enjoy reading often distract—by means of idle conversation—those who would rather spend the day with a book. It is quite vexing!"

Georgiana looked a bit surprised at the absence of irony in Miss Bingley's comment. Rather than respond, she chose to change the subject of conversation. "I hope, Brother, that you will not be vexed with our entertainment for tomorrow evening. One of our new neighbors, a Sir William Lucas, informed Charles that there is to be a public assembly. He is the Master of Ceremonies and assured my husband that we are all invited. Of course, Charles immediately agreed on behalf of the entire Netherfield party."

Miss Bingley immediately made her opinion known. "I cannot believe my brother accepted! Surely it is bad enough that we have been relegated to such an uncivilized place. We cannot be expected to mix with the locals as well, and at a *public* assembly?"

Georgiana raised her eyebrows at this comment. "I am grateful my husband accepted the invitation. One thing that you will learn, Miss Bingley, is that a landowner is responsible for fostering good relationships amongst his neighbors at *all* levels of society. A public assembly is the perfect way for us to establish ourselves as one of the leading families in the neighborhood, even if we do only stay for the year of leasing."

Chastened, Miss Bingley turned to Mr. Darcy. "Sir, I know you must feel the same as I about being forced to mingle amongst strangers. Should you choose to remain at home, I will stay behind as well to keep you company."

Darcy looked towards his sister in alarm. "Quite the contrary, Miss Bingley. I agree with my sister's opinion of the matter and will support her and Charles. Additionally, my cousin Colonel Fitzwilliam quite frequently enjoyed attending public assemblies at Matlock while in his youth with my aunt and uncle. He will be delighted to attend. With so many friends present, it will not be a hardship for me."

Defeated, Miss Bingley said, "Well then, we are all in agreement; we shall go to the assembly tomorrow. I only hope I can find something suitable to wear."

"This is what I am wearing," said Georgiana, gesturing to the gown she was mending. "I have only to finish repairing the slight damage that occurred during our travels here."

"You are mending your own dress?" gasped Miss Bingley in horror. "Why is your maid not doing the task?"

"She already has much to do with unpacking and getting us settled. I offered to do this," Georgiana answered calmly. "I do not mind."

Miss Bingley could not have looked more horrified. Torn between her disdain for common work and her obligation to not openly insult her brother's wife, she merely opened and closed her mouth.

Darcy felt it necessary to contribute to the conversation. "I have raised my sister to recognize servants for their value. Their time is worth just as much as ours. If Georgiana wants to mend her own dress, she should be able to do so without anyone in Society looking down on her."

"I quite agree," said Miss Bingley weakly.

"It is too easy, if one is not careful, to assign characteristics and attributes based on someone's station," said Georgiana. "My brother has taught me to not assume that every servant is worthless or that every peer is without fault. Some members of our station, for example, would feel it beneath them to befriend the son of tradesman and would label his sisters as grasping social climbers," she added with a pointed look at Miss Bingley.

"I begin to understand you," said a chastened Miss Bingley.

Fortunately, the lady was spared from further humiliation when the door opened to admit Bingley and Colonel Fitzwilliam. "What are you all doing in here when it is such a beautiful day?" cried Bingley. "Come, my dear, and let us go for a walk before supper." He extended his hand to his wife.

Georgiana agreed, having just that moment finished the last part of her dress. "Allow me to return this dress to my room and fetch my hat and gloves."

Colonel Fitzwilliam turned to Darcy. "Would you like to go for a ride?" he invited. "There are several trails that I have been eager to explore."

"Perhaps tomorrow morning," Darcy answered. "I have quite a lot of correspondence that I cannot postpone any longer."

The Colonel sighed. "I should join you, then, and learn from you as well if I am to take up my estate after this assignment."

"When do you report to the barracks?" Darcy asked.

"I head to London in a fortnight to escort my officers here to make camp. At that point I will continuously reside with them rather than reposing in luxury here at Netherfield," Colonel Fitzwilliam sighed again.

"Will you be able to tolerate that after having become soft while on leave?" teased Darcy.

The colonel pretended to be affronted. "Soft? I'll have you know I could best you at a saber duel with my eyes blindfolded!" he cried in mock anger.

The two men left for the library to tend to their correspondence, continuing their friendly banter the entire way.

Once shut safely in the library on their own, Darcy let out a sigh of relief. Colonel Fitzwilliam laughed, "Finally able to relax?"

"Quite," said Darcy. "I have learned over the years, I hope, to no longer quickly judge people. However, in Miss Bingley's case, I do not think it is too much to say that she is a fortune hunter of the worst kind. We could not be more dissimilar, but that does not matter to her."

Fitzwilliam clapped his cousin on the back. "I have been impressed by the changes you've made in recent years. You are no longer the disdainful lad you were five years ago. Even then, though, you were never that bad. You *were* chased by multiple women who only cared for your pocketbook. It would have been foolish of you to not be wary."

Darcy shook his head. "There were several times when I was quite abominable. I still relapse when I am ill at ease; I am quick to judge and speak dismissively, rather than try to see another's perspective of the matter at hand."

"You will have plenty of opportunities to practice at the assembly tomorrow night," Fitzwilliam assured him with a smile. "There are several very pretty ladies who will be in attendance, I am sure. I met many of them personally when I attended Forster's wedding."

"Just be careful to not fall for a pretty face and nothing else," Darcy cautioned, "I imagine that in a society such as this, there are many desperate women."

"Darcy, you hypocrite!" cried Fitzwilliam. "First you speak of how much you have improved, then you immediately warn me to be on my guard! Which is it, man?"

"It is both!" insisted Darcy emphatically. "Simply because I no longer lump all persons of the same class together does not mean I cannot be cautious. Once people hear of my income or your income, they immediately thrust their daughters and sisters forward. This *is understandable*," he emphasized as Fitzwilliam opened his mouth to object. "But it is wise to accompany sympathy with some skepticism."

Fitzwilliam sighed. "I understand what you are trying to say," he allowed. "However, you have a tendency to phrase these sentiments in the worst possible way, so as to give rise to the worst possible interpretation. You may need to practice avoiding that, too, at the assembly. Otherwise you are likely to give offense to the entire neighborhood."

"I will have to rely on you to prevent me making an oaf of myself," Darcy replied. "Now, I really must see to this correspondence."

~∞~∞~∞~

The evening of the assembly finally arrived. The Netherfield party's carriages left quite later than they had intended. Miss Bingley's toilette

133

took much longer than she had anticipated, and—she claimed—it was all due to the incompetence of her maid.

"No matter the reason!" cried Bingley impatiently. "The first dances have likely already begun. Our arrival time is rapidly approaching rudeness, rather than an hour that is merely fashionable."

"These people would not know fashion from outdated," sneered Miss Bingley.

When her statement was ignored, she interpreted the silence as accord. She began to feel all the satisfaction of one who misleads themselves in such a manner, and the remainder of the carriage ride passed in relative peace.

Upon arrival, they removed their hats, cloaks, and gloves, and their presence was announced: "Mr. Bingley, Mrs. Bingley, Mr. Darcy, Colonel Fitzwilliam, Mr. Hurst, Mrs. Hurst, and Miss Bingley."

Chapter 12

Meryton, October 1811

Upon arriving at the Meryton assembly, Jane and her three sisters exited the carriage, followed by their parents. When they entered the room, they were immediately struck by the unusually large number of guests.

"I think everyone in Hertfordshire must be here," whispered Kitty in awe.

She was mostly correct. Upon hearing about the promised attendance of the illustrious guests who inhabited Netherfield, many people who typically chose to avoid public assemblies decided instead to eschew their usual habits in the hopes of a possible introduction.

The Bennets made their way through the crowd and greeted Sir William. After many lengthy pleasantries that exceeded the short amount of time since they had last seen one another, they moved amongst the crush of people toward a table near a window.

"Put your things here, girls," said their mother, "and I will watch them so as to lay claim to this table for when you are overheated."

"Mamma, it's October," laughed Kitty.

"Just you wait," her mother warned, "and you will see. Whensoever there are so many couples, the room inevitably grows unbearably hot before the end of the first dance."

Lizzy and Jane looked at each other.

"I should like to find Charlotte," said Lizzy.

"I will go with you," said Jane.

The two women moved through the multitude, holding hands so as not to allow themselves to separate. Thankfully, the musicians began at that moment to warm up, and those with partners for the first dance made their way to the floor in preparation for the first set. This allowed for more room in which to maneuver, and the two sisters quickly found their friend.

"Hello!" cried Charlotte in excitement, "You'll never guess! Mr. Jones asked me to stand up with him for the first set!"

"Mr. Jones?" asked Lizzy in confusion. "Why ever would that excite you? The man is sixty years old if he has lived a day."

Charlotte laughed, "No, I mean his son! Have you not met him before? He is an apothecary—like his father—but he has his own practice, which is closer to London. He is visiting his father for several months, and he has called at my house twice since I was introduced to him in Meryton this week."

"The rains have kept us indoors for several days," said Lizzy glumly. "I have not even been allowed to go out for my daily walks."

"That is wonderful news," Jane told her friend. "Do you like him?"

"I believe I do," said Charlotte, beaming. "He seems to be a very hard worker, and he frequently came to my home when we were children. You may not remember, as he is a good deal older than the two of you. He left for London and has not returned to visit since his marriage."

"His marriage?" exclaimed a surprised Lizzy.

"Well, his first marriage, I should say," Charlotte clarified. "His wife died in childbirth two years after they were wed. She left behind a sickly baby girl born premature, who is now six years of age. Mr. Jones brought her here for the winter because the air near London aggravates her lungs."

"Are you ready to become a mother at the same time as you become a wife?" asked Jane.

Charlotte nodded her head. "I do have seven younger siblings," she pointed out. "In many ways, I am like a mother already!"

Jane and Lizzy laughed with her, then congratulated her on her good fortune. Mr. Jones came shortly after to claim Charlotte for the set. He was not handsome, but he possessed a kindly face. He bowed politely to the Misses Bennet and expressed his great happiness in finally meeting "dear Miss Lucas's closest friends." As the couple walked toward the dancing, Jane and Lizzy shared a delighted smile.

"Oh, I do hope he turns out to be a good man!" said Lizzy with great feeling. "I could not bear to imagine Charlotte in a challenging marriage."

"Should we make the efforts to discover whether he might be good for her, as we did with Mary?" Jane asked.

Elizabeth pondered for a few minutes. "I think so, provided we do not test him too much. We must make allowance for differences of temperament, after all. Mary had the desire to marry for fond regard, and she was willing to help Mr. Collins make changes only if he proved easily led by a wife. Charlotte does not seem to have such requirements. As long as he is a kind man, it should be alright."

As she finished, the first set came to an end. The music stopped and the room split into myriad personal conversations. The younger Mr. Jones escorted Charlotte back to her friends, where he solicited each of them for the third and fourth sets—he was promised to Maria Lucas for the second—before turning back to Charlotte and requesting the last set. She accepted with obvious pleasure, and Mr. Jones left to fetch Maria.

Suddenly, the doors opened, and all conversation ceased. Each guest turned toward the entrance, with some craning their necks to gain a clearer view of the doorway. Such a late ingress to the assembly promised to be the product of either an emergency or a shockingly rude party. The late arrivals as they were announced: "Mr. Bingley, Mrs. Bingley, Mr. Darcy, Colonel Fitzwilliam, Mr. Hurst, Mrs. Hurst, and Miss Bingley."

Jane gasped and grabbed her sister's hand with fingers that seemed suddenly to be carved from ice. "Oh, Lizzy," whispered Jane. "It's him."

Turning to face her sister, Lizzy gasped herself at Jane's white face. "Who?" she asked urgently, desperate to know who had affected her sister so.

"Mr. Bingley. He's the one... the one who left me in London," Jane whispered. Her blue eyes filled with tears.

Lizzy quickly moved to shield Jane from view, but the gesture proved unnecessary, as all eyes were still fixed on the Netherfield guests.

"Are you well, Jane?" Lizzy asked. "Allow me to ask Papa to fetch the carriage for you. We can say that you came down with a sudden headache due to the crowd and the heat."

Shaking her head slightly in declination, Jane withdrew a delicate handkerchief to dab her eyes, then she pinched her cheeks. Reaffixing her customary serene smile to her face, she appeared once again as though nothing was the matter.

"No, I am well," said Jane.

"Very well," said Lizzy, "but do tell me if you change your mind. You will have to be introduced to him at some point. Do you think you are able to bear it?"

"I will be well, Lizzy," said Jane affirmed quietly.

The two girls clasped hands and slowly wound through the crowded room to their table, where their mother was beckoning for them insistently. "What do you think, girls?" she cried in dismay. "There is no Mr. Bingham at all, and Mr. Bingley is married!"

Kitty and Mary joined them. "It appears I did not completely understand my aunt Phillips after all," said Kitty ruefully.

A mirthless laugh escaped Lizzy's lips, but she quickly covered her mouth. Kitty and Mary peered at her questioningly, but there was no time to speak. Sir William was already headed their way with Mr. Bingley and his party.

Lizzy felt her older sister stiffen, and she grabbed Jane's hand to steady her. As the Netherfield party approached, the eldest Bennet girls were able to discern the precise moment that Mr. Bingley saw

Jane. He looked at her, blinked a few times in rapid succession, and turned a brilliant shade of red. As it was too late to redirect Sir William with causing an incident, the party stopped directly in front of Mrs. Bennet.

Before Sir William could speak, Jane curtsied and addressed the newcomers, an act which surprised Lizzy greatly. "Mr. Bingley, Mr. Darcy," she greeted them in a strong, clear voice, dipping a curtsy. "How good to see you again."

Mr. Darcy looked at her in confusion. Mr. Bingley bowed and glanced at his motionless friend, then ventured uncertainly, "Miss Bennet. I had not thought... That is, I did... It has been many years since you last graced us with your company at that card party in Cheapside."

A light of recognition came on in Darcy's face, though this expression was soon mitigated by a flash of what appeared to be guilt. He bowed deeply. "Miss Bennet," he said, "it is a true honor to see you again."

Mrs. Bennet, Sir William, and the rest of the party stared at them in silent uncertainty for a few moments. Then Mr. Bingley said, "Allow me to present the rest of my party. These are my sisters: Miss Bingley and Mrs. Hurst, along with her husband Mr. Hurst. Then here is Colonel Fitzwilliam—"

Here Fitzwilliam interrupted. "Delighted to make your acquaintance once again, ladies." At Bingley's confused expression, he clarified, "We met at my friend Forster's wedding. He is now married to their sister."

"Erm, yes, well, this is Mr. Darcy, who has already met Miss Bennet some years ago. Lastly, I would like to introduce Darcy's sister—Georgiana—who is also my wife." He took her hand and gently drew her forward.

Jane inhaled sharply. For once, Lizzy was grateful for her mother's forward nature as she interjected herself and presented her remaining daughters. Bows and curtsies were exchanged. Mrs. Bennet's voice masked any awkward silences—rather than inciting such—which was a novel experience for anyone acquainted with the Bennet family.

"…what a great shame it is that we had no idea of you already knowing Jane! But that is no matter, we are all friends now. How good it is to have a family finally take Netherfield. It is clear that you are a man desirous of companions, Mr. Bingley, as shown by the large party you have brought. What do you say of our assembly, hm? We dine with four-and-twenty families, you know, and such relationships always make for the best gatherings. My girls do enjoy a good dance, all except Mary, but as she is engaged to the heir of Longbourn, it is of no matter…"

As Mrs. Bennet continued to prattle ceaselessly, Lizzy could feel Jane's tension ease, and she sent a silent prayer of thanks heavenward for her mother's social insouciance. Jane tried very hard to not look at Mrs. Bingley, but she could not help glancing over at her on occasion. Similarly, Mr. Darcy and Mr. Bingley kept looking at each other and at Jane.

Finally, Sir William interjected himself. "Capital, capital! So good to see everyone enjoying themselves. Mr. Bingley, we had best continue on, lots of introductions to make, you know!"

At that, Mr. Bingley and his party bowed and curtsied to the Bennet ladies. Once they were gone, Mrs. Bennet spun around to face Jane. "Jane!" she demanded in a shrill voice. "You did not tell me you had met such wealthy and handsome gentlemen when you were in town! Why did you return home still unmarried? With your beauty, you could have caught any one of them!"

Jane blushed, but courageously said, "Mamma, I do not think any of those gentlemen would have been a good match for me."

"Not a good match! Why, girl, what are you saying? Do you know that the taller one has ten thousand a year?" shrieked Mrs. Bennet.

"Mamma," Lizzy admonished in a harsh whisper, "lower your voice. It is many years in the past, and Mr. Bingley is married now to Mr. Darcy's sister."

"There are still two unmarried gentlemen in that group!" cried Mrs. Bennet, heedless of Lizzy's direction. "Jane, you will have Mr. Darcy. With your beauty and me to guide you, you should catch him easily this time. Kitty, you shall have Colonel Fitzwilliam. Your liveliness will fit well with his red coat."

"And who shall be for me, Mamma?" Lizzy asked in fatalistic amusement.

"None, because you are a wild, ungrateful girl!" declared Mrs. Bennet vehemently.

Lizzy bit her lip to keep from laughing. She turned to Jane. "Jane, would you care to stand up with me? Even with Mr. Bingley's party, there are still not enough gentlemen, and this dance allows you to stay with your partner."

Jane acquiesced, and the two stood at the bottom of the dance. Once the music had begun, Lizzy whispered, "Oh, Jane, how brave you are!"

Her sister blushed. "I don't know what came over me. When I first saw him, it was as if I had been transported back in time. I felt every moment of sorrow and anguish as strongly as I had that day. When I recognized his friend, however, and then he introduced his wife… well, I am unsure as to how I may describe it. Something came over me. I was suddenly able to see the entire situation clearly. I did nothing wrong, nothing to deserve him leaving abruptly after making his intentions so plain. I have nothing of which I ought to be embarrassed. If anyone is to leave or be ashamed, it should be him."

Lizzy smiled at her sister, duly impressed. "Bravo, Jane! I declare, that is the most unforgiving speech I have ever heard you make!"

Blushing again, Jane replied, "These five years since I last saw Mr. Bingley have altered my perspective on so many things. I am no longer the young girl that he made love to. Whatever made him leave, it is clear that it was more important to him than I was. I do not want a husband like that. In many ways, I am grateful he left when he did. It prevented me from marrying a man who would not have made me a good husband."

With that statement, the dance ended. They politely applauded, then Lizzy grabbed her sister in a violent hug. "My dear Jane, I am so proud of you," she whispered.

Unbeknownst to them, Georgiana had been standing behind them the majority of the dance, dancing with her cousin Colonel Fitzwilliam. She had wondered at the strange looks her husband and brother had shared during the introductions, but she had not yet had the opportunity to ask about them. When she saw the sisters stand up to dance, she had seized Fitzwilliam's hand and pulled him to the floor without so much as a by-your-leave.

The two cousins shamelessly eavesdropped for the entire set. Fitzwilliam had reddened with indignation, and Georgiana was pale in sorrow on behalf of the eldest Bennet daughter. "It is all my fault," she whispered as tears of shame gathered in her eyes. "Had I not erred with Wickham, Charles would have been free to marry this woman."

Fitzwilliam looked at her in surprised. "This is certainly no fault of yours!" he declared hotly. At her shushing, he lowered his voice and continued, "Did you not hear? Jane met your husband *five* years ago. You were but eleven years old. Whatever happened to make him leave her occurred long before your misadventure in Ramsgate."

Georgiana brightened slightly. "That is true," she conceded, "but if he had not married me to save my reputation, he would have been free when he met her again tonight. I still feel as though I have separated a great love."

Fitzwilliam shook his head. "My dear," he said gently, "you have grown into a wonderful and kind woman. Part of your gentle nature, however, leads you to assume a burden which is not yours to bear. True, you should not have consorted with Wickham. But that is the extent of your error. Wickham is guilty for what I shall delicately refer to as 'dishonesty', and Bingley is guilty of leaving Miss Bennet in such a manner. There is nothing you can do to change the past. All you can do is move forward with what you have."

Georgiana nodded, but her face still held doubt. Fitzwilliam squeezed her hand that rested on his arm and conducted her to where Bingley and Darcy stood engaged in what seemed to be a rather heated conversation. "Talk to your husband," he encouraged. "Let him have a day or two, and if he does not approach you to initiate the conversation before then, broach the subject yourself. You have been married for 18 months now, and you talk about everything, even if you do not share everything yet." Georgiana blushed at his reference to the marriage bed, but she nodded again, this time with confidence.

"You are right," she agreed. "I cannot change the past, nor can I hold myself responsible for events of which I had no knowledge. I am not blameless, but that does not mean I deserve to shoulder all of the blame."

When Darcy and Bingley noticed the pair's approach, they abruptly halted their tense discussion. After a moment of uneasy silence, Bingley said with forced cheerfulness, "My dear Georgiana, would you honor me with the next set?" She agreed, and the two joined the dance floor.

Darcy looked on as he mulled over the interrupted conversation, ignoring Fitzwilliam.

"Did you see her face?" Bingley had demanded. "You cannot say now that she was unmoved by our connection."

Darcy blanched. "Bingley, I can see that now. What I did was inexcusable. I have thought back on that day several times, always with abhorrence. In that moment, I truly did not believe her heart to be touched by you. I genuinely thought that I was saving you from a match of unequal affections. Now—five years later—I see the damage I caused."

Bingley had paced back and forth on a tight invisible line in front of Darcy, who ignored the beckoning waves of Miss Bingley from across the room. "It is my fault as well. I had made her promises, assurances of my return, and yet I disappeared without even a word. I am a duplicitous cad. I assured myself that, as her feelings for me were mere affectations, she would move on to another wealthy man.

It is very obvious that she did not. I allowed myself to be led by you, and I let your observations of a small portion of a single evening override the multiple encounters I had experienced with her that spoke to the contrary."

Letting out a sigh of frustration, Bingley stopped pacing. "There is obviously nothing I can do to mend the situation. I am, after all, married. I doubt that Miss Bennet would receive me even if I were unwed. Regardless, I am a much different person than I was five years ago, and I imagine that she is as well. She does appear to carry herself differently, at least. But it is no matter; I cannot change it. What I can do, however, is make reparations the best I can."

"How do you propose to do that?" Darcy had asked, aghast.

This was the question that had hung—unanswered—between them when Georgiana and Fitzwilliam arrived.

Darcy despised himself for orchestrating the rejection, which he now knew had been unwarranted. As his eyes moved around the room, he asked himself the same question: *how can I make this right?*

Chapter 13

The remaining time of the Meryton Assembly was torturous for multiple parties. Lizzy was desperate to speak with Jane, but she could not do so until they had privacy. Georgiana simply wanted the solitude of her room where she could contemplate the revelations that had occurred that evening. Miss Bingley and Mrs. Hurst were bored, and Colonel Fitzwilliam felt as though he would be shredded by the bindings of friendship and blood that anchored him to divergent forces.

Darcy and Bingley noticed Lizzy's repeated glances made in their direction, and they felt certain that they were being talked about, though not as prizes to be snared in a contest among fortune hunters. In fact, they were entirely correct. Lizzy made it known to her various acquaintances that the gentlemen had not behaved kindly to Jane in the past. No details were made known beyond that, and Jane was mortified when she discovered what Lizzy had done. Lizzy remained firm, however, that their general acquaintance should be warned against the newcomers.

When finally the assembly reached its conclusion, both the Longbourn and Netherfield carriages conveyed silent passengers to their respective estates. Each occupant had much to consider.

Upon arrival at Longbourn, Lizzy rushed inside to prepare for bed. Once she had completed her toilette, she entered Jane's room. Mary and Kitty soon followed; though they were not aware of the history between Jane and Mr. Bingley, they were certainly aware that Lizzy had been the cause of the tense atmosphere at the assembly.

"Lizzy, how could you tell others about what happened between Mr. Bingley and myself?" Jane demanded, hurt and exposed.

"I shared no specifics, Jane," Lizzy defended. "I merely said that he was unkind to you once when you were in London."

"But why would you do such a thing?"

"I do not believe them to be trustworthy," said Lizzy firmly, "and our general acquaintance deserves to be informed before they accepted any of them into their homes."

"What did happen?" Kitty interjected.

Jane emitted an unladylike huff, surprising her sisters. "When I was fifteen and in London, Mr. Bingley paid his attentions to me. He introduced me to Mr. Darcy one night, and I never saw either of them again until this evening."

"It was not as harmless as that," insisted Lizzy. "You forget, Jane, that I saw you when you returned from London. He paid his attentions to you and then left without a word immediately after requesting to speak to you about a particular subject. He broke your heart."

"Which has since been repaired!" cried Jane in exasperation. "Lizzy, what happened was *five* years ago."

"If you are so untouched, then why did you react so strongly when they appeared?" questioned Lizzy.

"Because I had not anticipated the meeting! For but a few brief moments I felt all of those feelings of hurt and abandonment and betrayal anew. After the initial shock wore off, however, I realized that those emotions no longer live in my heart. Yes, he hurt me in the past, but he does not continue to hurt me," explained Jane.

"But if you truly loved him—" began Lizzy.

Jane threw her hands up in the air in frustration. "I do not know that I loved him, Lizzy! I was only fifteen years old. *Fifteen.* That is the same age as Lydia is right now. I felt strong feelings for him, yes. He was kind and amiable. But I did not know much about him or his character. In many ways, he did me a service by leaving when he did."

Mary interrupted at this point. "Lizzy, I know you tried to help

Jane and protect our neighbors this evening, but you also acted out of prejudice and spite. As Jane pointed out, these events occurred five years ago. We have *all* changed much in five years."

Lizzy sighed in resignation. "I see your point, Jane, Mary. It may not have been the most rational course of action. However, I cannot change what I said and did this evening. I do apologize, Jane, for sharing your confidences."

Jane smiled at her sister. "I accept your apologies, Lizzy, and I appreciate your dedication in securing my happiness. I *am* happy. I would much rather remain unwed than to have married a man with so little firmness of purpose."

"I am also glad you did not marry him," Kitty chimed in. "Poor Colonel Fitzwilliam, to have such disagreeable family members."

The girls fell silent for a few minutes as they contemplated how differently their lives might have turned out had different choices been made all those years ago.

Finally Lizzy said, "Very well, I will make an effort to be pleasant toward the gentlemen in future."

"I am eager to get to know his wife," added Kitty. "From what little I saw, she appeared to be very kind. She had a lovely smile."

"She also appeared to be rather young," Mary pointed out.

"I am less eager to know his sisters," Lizzy said with a wry grin. "They were better pleased with themselves than anything they saw at the assembly."

"Perhaps they were uncomfortable in company?" suggested Jane.

Her three sisters looked at one another, then they began to laugh.

"Oh Jane," said Lizzy in between giggles, "Would that I were as good as you."

"They most certainly were uncomfortable in *our* company," observed Mary.

"Well, maybe they will improve upon further acquaintance," said Jane.

"It is possible," said Lizzy doubtfully, "but I believe we have more important things to speak of than the Netherfield party."

Her three sisters looked at her in confusion.

"What things?" asked Kitty.

"Not what—whom. Mr. Jones!" exclaimed Lizzy.

"Why is our apothecary more important than the Netherfield occupants?" Kitty asked.

"Not our Mr. Jones, but his son," said Jane. "He appears to be courting Charlotte Lucas."

"What do we know about him?" inquired Mary.

"He has been married before," Lizzy began. "His wife passed away in childbirth, and he was left alone to raise a sickly daughter, who is now six years old. She does not breathe very well in the winter near London, so they have come here for the cold months to see if her health improves."

"What does that have to do with us?" questioned Kitty.

"We simply cannot allow our dear Charlotte to be united with a man who will treat her poorly!" Lizzy stated firmly. "Just as we did with Mr. Collins, we must discover if the younger Mr. Jones is a good match for our friend."

"What do you have in mind?" asked Mary.

"Nothing too elaborate," Jane warned.

"No, not at all. I simply want to see what the servants have to say about his character. We already know the elder Mr. Jones to be a kind man. It is difficult to think he would raise his son to be anything else, but it is always good to be sure," said Lizzy.

"I can try flirting with him," said Kitty, "and see if he responds."

"Only if Charlotte is aware of the reason," Jane cautioned. "Otherwise, she may believe you are in earnest, which would wound her."

Kitty assured them that she would not act without having first sought Charlotte's approval. With this course of action settled, the girls bid each other goodnight, unaware that conversations of a similar nature were being conducted at Netherfield.

Upon their return to Netherfield after the assembly, the ladies all retired to their rooms. Georgiana eagerly sought the privacy of her chambers to reflect on all that had happened that evening. Mr. Hurst followed his wife and Miss Bingley up the stairs.

The remaining gentlemen retired to the billiards room. Colonel Fitzwilliam eyed Bingley and Darcy as they waited for a servant to bring refreshments and then depart the room. Once alone, Colonel Fitzwilliam unleashed the pent-up fury he had allowed ever since he had overheard the discussion between the eldest Misses Bennet while dancing.

"Would one of you care to explain the complete and utter *idiocy* the two of you have displayed?"

Startled, Darcy and Bingley eyed the infuriated man. "To what do you refer, Cousin?" Darcy asked cautiously.

"To what do I ref—? No, this will not do. I am not uninformed of the behavior the two of you exhibited five years ago. The sheer and utter gall of making love to a lady, Bingley, and then abandoning her after promising to return for a proposal—"

"A *what?*" exclaimed Darcy.

Bingley looked down at the floor, his face an unusual shade of purple. "I may have told Miss Bennet that I would return after escorting you out in order to 'discuss a particular matter'," he muttered in shame.

"You did not tell me that!" Darcy accused furiously.

Bingley raised his head to give Darcy a hard look. "Would it have made a difference?"

"Yes, Bingley!" Darcy said defensively, "Your honor was engaged!"

"Whether or not I had been so explicit in that particular conversation with Miss Bennet, my honor had *already* been engaged by the marked attentions I had been paying to her for weeks previous. You *knew* that!" Bingley retorted.

Darcy opened his mouth to respond.

"Enough!" shouted Fitzwilliam. Darcy and Bingley stopped short, both having forgotten that he was in the room.

"It appears to me that both of you are to blame," Fitzwilliam said harshly. "I have spent time with the Bennet family. While it is true that their youngest sister is a flibbertigibbet and their mother is coarse, the remaining daughters are themselves above reproach."

Chastened, Bingley and Darcy fell silent. Fitzwilliam continued berating his cousin and his cousin-by-marriage. For a full quarter of an hour, he gave them a dressing down that neither man had experienced in their lifetime, not even as trouble-making lads in school.

Neither Darcy nor Bingley interrupted. For the first time, both men were confronted unavoidably with the hypocrisy and shameful behavior they both had exhibited. Once his tirade had finished, Fitzwilliam put down his empty glass. As he made to leave the room, he turned and gave them both one last hard look. "One thing more: Georgiana is as familiar with the situation as I am, as she had the misfortune of being on the dance floor with me to overhear the two elder Bennet sisters discussing your history. I have counseled her to give you a day or two for contemplation, Bingley. If you do not discuss the situation with her, she will approach you. If she has to initiate the conversation, I can guarantee that it will be much less pleasant for you. Women do not take kindly to being lied to, even by omission."

On that note, Fitzwilliam exited the room, shutting the door firmly behind him.

Bingley jumped at the harsh noise of the slamming door. After a few minutes of silent reflection, he said: "He's right, you know."

"Pardon?" asked Darcy. He had been so caught up in his own thoughts of self-castigation that he had failed to take notice of Bingley's words.

"Fitzwilliam is entirely correct," Bingley repeated, "We deserve every single thing he said to us, and possibly worse. I behaved so dishonorably that I cannot look upon my behavior without abhorrence. I paid court to a genuine young woman and left without a fair-thee-well."

Darcy shook his head. "Bingley, it is more my fault than yours. I was an arrogant, jaded young man who took the worst that society had to offer and placed it on the shoulders of an innocent young woman who did nothing more than try to ease my discomfort in an unfamiliar setting. I looked only for the worst in her, which caused me to misread her every word and action."

"But I was the one who allowed myself to be easily led," Bingley argued. "You had spent only a few hours in her company, whereas I had spent weeks learning her character. You had no evidence other than your own suppositions, and I paid more heed to your baseless opinions than to my own experience."

Darcy was silent for a few minutes, then said, "I think, Bingley, that we are both to blame. We both behaved abominably. Our behavior was no better than Wickham's in treating someone else's feelings with complete disregard."

Bingley nodded soberly. "We need to make amends. I know we cannot change things, and I daresay that even were I in a position to do so, Miss Bennet would not have me."

Darcy looked at Bingley sharply. "Kindly remember that you are married to *my sister.*"

Bingley looked at him in shock. "Of course I remember! By amends, I mean to say that we should start with an apology. After that, I am not certain what the best course of action is. I do not think we are in any condition to make that kind of decision tonight, anyway."

"We are tired," Darcy admitted.

"And drunk," Bingley said, gesturing to the now empty decanter that had been full when the conversation began.

"We should retire and speak again on the matter tomorrow," Darcy said.

"Agreed," said Bingley. He hesitated, then said, "I do plan to discuss the matter with Georgiana as well. We are married, and as much as I believe in making reparations for past sins, she is my first priority. I will not take any action without her input and guidance."

Darcy nodded his approval. He downed the last swallow from his glass, and the two headed to bed.

Chapter 14

The occupants of Longbourn awoke late the morning after the assembly to a bright, sunny day. The peaceful skies reflected the newfound peace in Jane's heart. Although her experience with Bingley had occurred years in the past, she had not fully recognized the weight she had carried from the experience. The closure provided by the brief interaction of the previous evening had set her free. Her shoulders felt lighter from the unseen burden that had weighed down her spirit.

As the Bennets ate their breakfast—which should almost be considered lunch due to the late hour of the day—a servant entered bearing the recently arrived post. Mr. Bennet sorted through the mail and handed his wife a letter. Recognizing the handwriting of her beloved youngest daughter, Mrs. Bennet began to read eagerly.

"My dear Mr. Bennet!" she cried with excitement. "Lydia is coming home!"

Her family stared at her in shock. "Why is she coming home?" asked Kitty warily. She had quite enjoyed her younger sister's absence, as she was no longer overshadowed by Lydia's exuberant nature.

"Is Forster sending her back?" Mr. Bennet asked sardonically. "If so, I am afraid that I will not accept any returns. She has already been purchased and used."

"Oh, Mr. Bennet!" exclaimed his lady, "How can you be so tiresome? No, Mrs. Forster and her husband will be returning to Meryton in less than a fortnight with the regiment to settle here for the winter. What fun we shall have! I long to see my dear Lydia. It has been so quiet without her lively presence."

Lizzy and Mary let out small sighs of relief, then smiled at one another. There had existed the very real possibility that Lydia was being returned to her father in shame due to misbehavior. Any concern they felt had evaporated with the news that her husband was to accompany her.

"I expect our little town will be quite changed with the influx of so many officers and members of the militia," remarked Mary as she spread some jam on a slice of toast.

"Yes!" said Kitty enthusiastically. "I will no longer have to stand up with my sisters at assemblies! Perhaps Colonel Forster will even hold a ball."

"Is that the thanks I get for all the dances we've shared?" cried Lizzy in mock indignation. "What an ungrateful sister I have!"

"Oh, Lizzy," sighed Kitty as she rolled her eyes at her sister. "You know I adore dancing with you. However, it is much more exciting when I do not have to remember whether I am dancing the steps for the lady's part or the gentleman's!"

"I once was fond of a redcoat myself, once," Mrs. Bennet sighed in remembrance. "I cried for two days together when Colonel Miller's regiment went away. I thought I should have broken my heart."

Jane smiled fondly at her mother. "I look forward to making many new acquaintances."

Mrs. Bennet shook her head, her thoughts returning to the present. "Girls, we must head into Meryton immediately after breakfast. We cannot allow the officers to see you without new lace and ribbons to freshen your gowns."

"I believe that is my cue to leave," said Mr. Bennet.

His daughters laughed as he briskly strode from the room, anxious to avoid any tedious conversation that included how his women adorned themselves.

Mrs. Bennet began to discuss the necessary colors and lengths of ribbons they were to purchase, but she was interrupted by a loud clap of thunder.

"What on earth?" she cried in bewilderment.

Lizzy looked confused. "It was sunny not an hour ago when I returned from my morning walk. There was nary a cloud in the sky!"

All faces turned toward the windows, and Kitty drew back the curtains. The once-bright skies had darkened with rain clouds and lightning lit up the sky.

"I imagine we will have to postpone our shopping," said Mrs. Bennet in disappointment.

"No matter, Mamma," said Kitty kindly. "It will give us time to go through our closets to determine exactly what purchases we shall need to make."

Mrs. Bennet brightened at this. "Indeed, my love, what a clever idea! Come, we will begin with you."

She led the way out of the breakfast room with Kitty following closely behind. Once the doors closed, Lizzy turned to Jane. "How are you doing this morning, Jane, dear?"

"I am quite well, Lizzy," said Jane with a slightly confused expression. "Is there a reason I shouldn't be?"

"I merely wanted to assure myself that you were still alright following Mr. Bingley's attendance at the assembly last night," Lizzy admitted.

"Lizzy," Mary admonished. "You should do Jane the courtesy of believing her when she stated that she is quite recovered from the heartache that occurred *five years ago.*"

"Yes, thank you, Mary," Jane said. She turned to Lizzy impatiently, "Elizabeth Bennet, as I stated last night, I am completely recovered. Mr. Bingley and I may meet as indifferent acquaintances, for that is all we are. He is a married man, and I am no longer the naïve girl I was all those years ago."

Chastened, Lizzy nodded. Before she could respond, Hill entered the room. "Miss Lizzy, Miss Jane, your father has requested your

155

presence in his bookroom."

Jane and Lizzy looked at one another curiously. "I wonder what that could be about," Lizzy said.

"We shall never know if we do not go to him," laughed Jane.

The three ladies stood.

"Not you, Miss Mary," said Hill.

Mary smiled kindly at Hill and said, "Thank you, Hill, but I was not going to go to my father. I will join Mamma and Kitty upstairs while they look through gowns. I know Kitty enjoys such things, but sometimes Mamma can be a bit tiresome. Hopefully my presence will help temper the multitude of purchases she wishes to make."

With that, Mary went above stairs, while Jane and Lizzy followed Hill down the corridor and into their father's study.

"Do you have need of us, sir?" asked Jane.

"Ah yes, do come in, girls." Mr. Bennet beckoned his daughters into the room and closed the door, indicating for them to sit.

"I have just received a letter this morning from your uncle Gardiner. He writes to inform me that his wife is once again in the family way. Unfortunately, this time she is more ill than usual and has been ordered to remain in her bed until she has felt the quickening, which should be in a month or so. He writes to inquire if one of you would be able to visit them in Gracechurch Street to help manage the household and your young cousins. Whichever of you is to go will need to leave tomorrow, and will not return until they come for Mary's wedding at Christmas."

Jane and Lizzy exchanged looks. "Which one of us do you think should go, Papa?" asked Lizzy.

"It matters not to me," Mr. Bennet with a sardonic tone, "As either way, the amount of sensible conversation I may have will be cut in half for the duration." He softened this pronouncement with a wink.

At one point Mr. Bennet had considered himself the father of two—if not three—of the silliest girls to be found in all of England.

Over the past few years, however, he had witnessed the changes in Mary and Kitty with pride, though he also felt no small degree of shame at having neglected them. Lydia, he knew, would always be silly, but her behavior and propriety were no longer his concern. Kitty and Mary no longer caused him embarrassment, and he found that he quite enjoyed the presence of each of his daughters.

Jane looked at Lizzy and said, "I believe I should be the one to go. After all, I have more patience for the tending of younger children than you do. Furthermore, you hate London in the winter."

Lizzy laughed, "That is all true, Jane, but you had to go to London the last time our aunt was ill. Are you sure you are willing to take my turn?"

"I am quite certain, Lizzy. There is nothing for me in Meryton at the present time, even with the new tenants at Netherfield and the militia about to arrive." Jane gave her sister a meaningful look.

"I do confess that I would much prefer to remain in Longbourn for the upcoming months," Lizzy admitted. "As you said, I do hate London in the wintertime. As it is the Season, it is considered the fashionable time to be there, but I do not enjoy being confined to my aunt's house when the weather precludes walks in the park to divert the children."

"Then it is settled," said Mr. Bennet. "I will write to my brother Gardiner immediately, although I believe you may arrive before my note does, Jane."

The girls excused themselves and went upstairs to begin Jane's preparations for her journey. As she began packing a trunk, Jane noticed Lizzy giving her a strange stare.

"Lizzy," warned Jane.

"What?" Lizzy asked in affected innocence.

"I know what you are thinking, Lizzy. You are thinking that I am using this opportunity as a way to escape Mr. Bingley's presence."

Lizzy blushed slightly at being caught out. "I admit, the thought did cross my mind."

Jane sighed and faced her sister with her hands on her hips. "I will not repeat myself again, Lizzy. I have no feelings for Mr. Bingley. I wish him all the best, and I hope he is happy. My heart is not touched by him any longer. Truly, Lizzy, you must believe me. Although," she sighed, "I do wish that you had not told our neighbors about what happened. It will appear to everyone that I have left to escape his presence."

Lizzy lowered her head in shame. "I am very sorry, Jane," she said quietly, "It was thoughtlessly done. I will do what I can to quell any gossip I may hear."

Jane expressed her gratitude, and the two girls returned their focus to Jane's preparations for London.

The Netherfield party also arose later the day after the assembly than was their custom. The only person to enjoy a full night's rest was Mr. Hurst. Mrs. Hurst was disturbed by her husband's snoring, even in her separate chambers. Miss Bingley's sleep was filled with dreadful dreams of never being allowed to return to London. Colonel Fitzwilliam passed the night in restless concern for Georgiana, who in turn spent a sleepless night considering what she would say to her husband. Darcy and Bingley had imbibed sufficient drink to leave them with terrible headaches the next morning.

When the conscious members of the party gathered in the breakfast room, Fitzwilliam smirked at the green-tinged expressions of pain on the other men's faces. "It serves them right," he whispered to Georgiana as she took her seat next to him.

"I quite agree," she replied, smiling slightly as her husband paled when offered a plate of bacon by the footman.

The two cousins kept up a steady stream of polite banter as they filled their plates. Miss Bingley and Mrs. Hurst had chosen to take breakfast in their beds, while Mr. Hurst was sleeping off the drink from the previous day. *Or he has already begun the current day's alcohol consumption—it is difficult to tell,* thought Georgiana.

Over the last 18 months since she had married Bingley and relocated with him to Pemberley, she had come to know Miss Bingley and the Hursts better than she ever would have cared to. She was grateful to Charles, however, for saving her reputation that awful day in Ramsgate, so she bore their company without complaint. Their presence brought him joy, and although she found them annoying, they also caused her no real harm.

When a footman arrived to inform Bingley that there would be no one else from the household to join them at breakfast, the atmosphere lightened slightly. They had all been in one another's company for a very long time, but the cloying presence of Miss Bingley often elevated the tension in whichever room she occupied.

"So, gentlemen, what is the plan for today?" Georgiana asked her brother, husband, and cousin.

"I have quite a bit of business that will keep me in my study for most of the day," said Darcy quickly. "I believe Bingley was going to accompany me so he can continue learning."

"I do believe I will join you," Fitzwilliam said.

"Er, yes, that would be fine," said Darcy with a strained smile.

"When you have some time to spare from your business, Brother," said Georgiana as she daintily wiped her mouth with her napkin, "I would appreciate a few minutes of your time. I have something particular I wish to discuss with you."

At those familiar words, Bingley turned slightly red. Darcy swallowed nervously, then said, "I would be happy to meet with you this afternoon. Perhaps over tea?"

"Excellent," she said, standing. "I shall inform the housekeeper that you and I will have tea in my private sitting room. Charles," she added, turning to her husband, "I understand that you wish to have a conversation with me as well. Would you prefer to speak tonight or tomorrow?"

Fitzwilliam hid a smirk as Bingley paled and tugged at his cravat.

159

"I think tonight after we all retire would be best." *Best to get it over with*, he thought privately.

"Wonderful. I look forward to it. Now, if you gentlemen will excuse me, I have some business of my own to attend to."

As Georgiana left the room, she finally allowed herself a smile. *Oh, the looks on their faces!* she thought. *They looked as though I had informed them they were required to spend the day with Caroline and her friends!*

The previous evening, Georgiana had spent many hours examining her life. She was extremely grateful for the comfortable situation she enjoyed. She had her reputation, a loving brother, and an understanding husband. Any ills in her life were simply minor nuisances, like dealing with Caroline. Nonetheless, she felt as though she had been merely going through the motions since Ramsgate. For the first time in eighteen months, she was awake and wanted to take charge of her life.

First, she wanted to issue an invitation to Longbourn to request the Bennet sisters' presence for tea in two days. They seemed to be genuine girls—if their discussion from the previous evening was any indication—and she was in desperate want of sincere friendship. Their history with her brother and husband was immaterial. *But we must have a frank conversation about that, away from the prying eyes of their parents and friends. I would not want to provide fodder for gossip. Before we can become friends, we must clear the air.*

This afternoon, though, she needed to discuss matters with her brother. Although she had seen him be kind to tenants and servants, he had an abominable sort of pride that often caused offence. He was an odd mix of selfless and selfish at the same time. Raised with good morals but little oversight, he was left to determine how to apply those principles solely by his own judgment. As could be predicted, Darcy had not learned to remove his pride and conceit from his personal interactions. It had never directly affected her, so she had allowed him to continue to be who he was, especially as he was more father than brother to her.

Georgiana reached her private sitting room and dipped her pen into the ink. Her pen hovered over the paper, however, as she considered that she needed to speak with her husband.

She winced slightly as she used the word. Even though it had been so long, she still was not accustomed to that term. They lived in separate rooms, and he was like a brother to her. While that had been sufficient while she was recovering her heart from Ramsgate and Wickham, she now needed to move forward with her life. *After all, it would be nice to have children someday, if nothing else, she mused.* She appreciated his patience with her; she was still young. Nevertheless, if they were to have progress in their relationship, she needed to be the one to instigate it.

While Georgiana wrote her invitation to the Bennet girls, Fitzwilliam ushered Bingley and Darcy into the room.

"Is it to be another flogging, then?" asked Bingley miserably as soon as the door closed.

Fitzwilliam laughed, "And if it were?"

"Then we would take it like men," said Darcy firmly, "It is no more than we deserve."

"It is less than I deserve," said Bingley.

Fitzwilliam shook his head. "Remember, lads, that one action does not define you. Yes, you made a foolish choice that had far-reaching consequences on persons other than yourselves. But you also have made many, many good decisions over your lifetimes."

Bingley looked a bit cheerier at this comment, but Darcy shook his head. "There were none so consequential as this, whether good or bad."

"You are not the first man to have misinterpreted a woman's intentions, and I doubt you shall be the last," reassured Fitzwilliam. "If you want to continue to blame yourself, though, I will not stop you, as you do deserve the guilt. But no matter, that is not why I wanted to join you today. I truly meant what I said in the breakfast room: I will be resigning my commission and taking control over my estate at the end of training these officers, and I need to learn the business. Who better to learn from than the Master of Pemberley and his protégé?"

"I know why Darcy needed to teach me," said Bingley, settling into a chair, "but you are not from trade. Why do you not know how to manage an estate?"

"As a younger son of an earl—and with the elder son having now fathered three sons—there was little point in teaching me much administration as a youth," explained Fitzwilliam, "The estate that I am to control is in reality the property of a great uncle on my mother's side. In a fit of pique against his wastrel son, the uncle changed his will and left the entire estate to me without informing anyone other than his solicitor. It was quite a shock when the will was read last year, upon his death."

"Now I begin to understand," said Bingley. "I had often wondered why you chose a life in the militia. I figured you had a strong sense of patriotic duty and were merely waiting until that had been satisfied."

"That is why I chose to be a soldier instead of taking orders or studying the law," Fitzwilliam confirmed, "But had I been raised knowing about the estate, I may have found other ways to serve my country that are not so hard on the body."

"Well, Darcy is the best person to learn from," Bingley said, "I have appreciated being able to shadow him these several years. So many landowners keep their sons with them from a young age to teach them all they know. I had no such luxury with my tradesman father, and I have learned more from observation than I could have from direct instruction. Even now, I only feel comfortable enough to lease an estate."

"I had wondered why you lived so long at Pemberley," said Fitzwilliam. "To be quite honest, I was concerned when Darcy wrote that your sisters were joining you at Pemberley. I thought you may have grown accustomed to a parasitical life and were bleeding Darcy dry."

Darcy let loose a great burst of laughter. "Bingley, take advantage of me? Never!"

"Those who are being taken advantage of are rarely the first to recognize it. Or even the second or third," Fitzwilliam pointed out. "In fact, they are often the last to realize that their companions are mere leeches, if they recognize it at all."

"I understand and appreciate your concern, Cousin," Darcy said, "But it is quite unnecessary. At least once a month, Bingley offers to set up a house for Miss Bingley and the Hursts. He has even offered to leave himself, but I want him and Georgiana to be together, and I will not abandon her to her sisters-in-law until she is ready to face them herself."

Bingley nodded. "I wrote a few letters of inquiry for houses in town. When Darcy found out, he was rather upset. He reminded me that any money I am able to save now goes toward dowries for my future daughters and increases the quality of estate I can purchase."

Fitzwilliam was taken aback. "Begging your pardon, but I was under the impression that your father left you a sizable fortune that should have been more than adequate to make the purchase."

Bingley looked a bit embarrassed. "Well, yes, he did. However, the difficulties in the North caused me to liquidate and expend some of those assets in order to purchase the business of a man who was relocating to the Americas with his daughter. Those funds are now tied up; while the investment is proving fruitful, there is not enough capital at the moment."

"There would be if he would take Georgiana's dowry," interrupted Darcy.

"*Darcy,*" Bingley hissed.

"He is her guardian as well," Darcy said defensively. Turning to Fitzwilliam, he continued, "When Bingley first offered to marry Georgiana in Ramsgate, I was relieved. I would have gladly given up her dowry in order to keep her safe. Bingley, I knew, could be trusted to treat her with kindness and respect."

Here Darcy paused to pour himself a brandy. Fitzwilliam raised his brows; it was a bit early in the day to indulge so. *Then again, it has been a rather difficult twenty-four hours for the man,* he reminded himself.

After downing the entire glass, Darcy continued, "When it came time to draw up the settlements, Bingley refused to sign unless Georgiana's dowry was tied up in a trust."

"I was *not* going to be accused of being a fortune hunter," said Bingley hotly. "I don't care what society thinks, but Georgina had just barely escaped from a rake of the worst kind. Her self-esteem had been shattered. I knew that one day we would want to have a real marriage, not just in name only. To that end, I wanted to be able to show her that she was worth more than her dowry."

"So Bingley has not used any of her dowry?" asked Fitzwilliam incredulously.

"Not even a penny of the interest," Darcy informed him, "The principal was put into the banks, and the interest has been marked for Georgiana's sole use. Bingley cannot touch a shilling of any of it, and it was all his idea."

Bingley blushed in embarrassment as Fitzwilliam gave him a long appraising look. The colonel then stood and sketched his cousin-in-law a deep bow. "You have my most sincere apologies, Bingley."

"For what?" asked a confused Bingley.

"For thinking you a bit of a cad."

Darcy moved to protest at this, but Fitzwilliam silenced him with a wave of his hand. "I have always known you to be a true friend to Darcy—your actions when you first met at school demonstrated your integrity well enough. But I assumed that your offer to marry Georgiana was—in part—motivated by her dowry. So again, sir, you have my sincerest apologies."

"Of course, of course," Bingley muttered with an embarrassed wave of his hand.

After a moment of tense silence, Fitzwilliam clasped his hands together and asked, "So, gentlemen, what do you have in store for me for my first lesson in estate management?" The awkwardness eased as they all chuckled, then they bent over the estate ledgers to commence Fitzwilliam's education.

Chapter 15

Jane sighed in relief as the carriage left Longbourn. She had not lied to Lizzy—she truly did not care for Bingley—but neither did she wish to stay and bear the firestorm of gossip that Lizzy had ignited.

As the sisters had said their goodbyes at the carriage that morning, Lizzy's eyes had filled with tears. "I am so sorry, Jane," she had whispered in her ear during their farewell embrace.

Jane had reassured her sister that she bore her no ill will. This, again, was not a lie. Jane knew her sister was only looking out for Jane's best interests, just as she had done so many years previous with Mr. Cartwright. Would that Lizzy had been as circumspect in this situation as she had five years prior. For all her strengths, Lizzy's fatal flaw was that she protected her loved ones a little too fiercely.

I shall need to write to Charlotte when we next stop to rest and warn her that Lizzy plans to interfere, thought Jane. Pulling out her reticule, she retrieved a small piece of paper and quill with a miniature bottle of ink. Penning a quick note to Charlotte, she addressed the envelope to be sent to Lucas Lodge. With luck, Charlotte would receive it before the next assembly. *Mr. Jones appears to still be the same good person he was when he was growing up. I wish Charlotte success.*

Jane returned the items to their place and again closed her eyes. She had little desire to dwell on what she was leaving behind in Meryton. Instead, she turned her thoughts toward the upcoming weeks at the Gardiners' home. Ostensibly she was there to help manage the household, but experience had taught her that the majority of her time would be spent entertaining her young cousins.

Jane began a mental list of activities she could do to keep them occupied whilst their mother retired to her bed until she could feel her unborn babe stir within her womb. The weather would not be ideal, as they would be nearing the colder seasons, but she could still convey the children to the local park for exercise and fresh air. She had many new games she could teach them, now that the elder two of her cousins were able to read.

The gentle movement of the carriage eventually drove these thoughts from Jane's mind, and she drifted into a deep sleep from which she did not awaken until the next stop. Then, once she had posted her letter to Charlotte and reboarded the carriage, she again slept until she arrived well-rested at Gracechurch Street, where her loving family welcomed her with open arms.

Lizzy wiped tears from her eyes as she watched Jane's carriage drive toward London. Once again, she was sending her sister away because of the actions of a man. It was difficult to personally witness the dearth of freedoms the members of her sex were able to enjoy.

Kitty greeted her at the door. "How is Jane?" she asked kindly.

"As well as can be expected," replied Lizzy. "Oh, how I wish Mr. Bingley and his friends had stayed away from Hertfordshire."

Mary joined them and, upon hearing Lizzy's last statement, raised her eyebrows. "You must admit, Lizzy, that you had no small part in Jane's decision to leave."

Lizzy bowed her head. "I know," she whispered. "I should not have said what I did about Mr. Bingley and our Jane. I was so angry that my tongue ran away with me."

"'But the tongue can no man tame; it is an unruly evil, full of deadly poison'," Mary intoned solemnly. When Kitty looked at her in confusion, she added, "James, chapter three."

"Oh, that I had kept my mouth shut!" cried Lizzy in frustration.

"Never mind that," said Mary primly, "for all we can do now is attempt to repair any damage."

The girls entered the sitting room, where their mother was speaking with Hill about the preparations necessary to welcome Lydia back. "—and we will need to wash the linens for her bedroom."

"Mamma," said Kitty, interrupting, "is Lydia to stay with us for the duration of their visit?"

"Where else would my dear daughter stay than at the home of her mother?" demanded Mrs. Bennet.

"I believe, my dear," said Mr. Bennet as he entered the room, "that Lydia will reside with her husband, where she belongs."

"My darling Lydia, living in a tent? Certainly not!" Mrs. Bennet exclaimed.

"She must become accustomed to it at some time," he responded mildly. "This was the choice she made in wedding a man in uniform."

"But how could she have known?" wailed his wife.

"Had she taken the time to do things properly and not rushed to be wed, then she would have discovered it. This is a situation entirely of her own making." replied her husband firmly, thus ending the conversation.

Mrs. Bennet sulked on the settee until Kitty—assuming Jane's role as peacemaker—said, "Mamma, you can still host dinners here for Lydia."

"Why yes, Kitty, what a wonderful idea! Hill! Come back! We must discuss dinner parties for Mrs. Forster!" Mrs. Bennet rushed from the room in search of the beleaguered housekeeper. Mr. Bennet gave Kitty a mildly amused look, then returned to his bookroom.

The girls were then interrupted by the arrival of a note from Netherfield.

"It is from Mrs. Bingley!" exclaimed Lizzy in surprise. "I wonder what she could want from us."

"You shall never know unless you open it," answered Mary, a bit snippily. "What does it say?"

"We Bennet sisters have all been invited to Netherfield for tea the day after tomorrow," Lizzy read aloud.

Kitty clapped her hands in glee. "Oh, I do so want to know the ladies better! The lace on Mrs. Hurst's dress—"

"No lace!" cried her two remaining sisters with laughter.

Kitty affected a mock pout, which merely served to encourage her sisters in their teasing. Wiping mirthful tears from her eyes, Lizzy said, "Shall we accept, then?"

"Yes!" demanded Kitty. "You must accept the invitation immediately!"

As Lizzy went in search of pen and parchment, Mary said, "I am afraid that—for my part—I must decline the invitation. Mr. Collins is to visit us the following day, and I must ensure everything is in readiness."

Kitty looked at Mary with confusion. "I did not know he was to come. Does Mamma know? I would have thought she would have begun preparations by now."

Mary had the grace to look embarrassed. "I have not yet informed my mother of his visit. I wished to have peace for as long as possible before hearing her effusions about my engagement to the heir of Longbourn."

Lizzy laughed at this, having returned from her search. "I do not blame you, Mary," she said as she wrote her acceptance to Mrs. Bingley. Upon completion, she sent the note with a maid to give to the Netherfield footman who awaited a response in the kitchen. The departing maid nearly collided with Hill, who entered the room to announce another visitor.

"Miss Lucas and Miss Maria Lucas."

The girls turned to the door as Charlotte Lucas entered the room.

"Charlotte!" Lizzy exclaimed with joy as she crossed the room to embrace her friend. "You sly thing, you never once hinted that you were receiving the attentions of a gentleman!"

A broad smile spread across Charlotte's plain features, the pleasant expression rendering her almost pretty. "I dared not speak of it until I was certain," she said, "but the attentions he paid me at last night's assembly demonstrated his intentions, even though he has not yet spoken with my father."

"We are very happy for you, Charlotte," said Mary. "It seems like a comfortable situation."

"But you will be a mother as soon as you are a bride!" cried Kitty.

"That is what I said!" cried Maria.

"Penelope is such a dear, sweet girl," Charlotte explained, "and there is no assurance that I will be able to bear a child of my own. Such difficulties do happen, though no one knows why. My future is very secure, and I am happy to be mother to such a beautiful child."

Maria and Kitty looked dubious, but they nodded at her words. Mary also nodded, in full accord with Charlotte's sentiments. "I understand your feelings exactly."

"But Charlotte, how can you know he will treat you well?" asked Lizzy. "He will be taking you so far away."

"Of course, there is no way of knowing to a full degree of certainty that he will continue to be kind, but I feel confident in my assessment of his character," her friend replied. "I have watched him interact lovingly with his daughter when he believes no one else is around. The way he speaks of his father, his patients, and even his late wife shows that he is a man capable of deep and tender feelings. It is not a love match, but there is a strong affection and respect between us."

Lizzy nodded slowly. "I asked Hill this morning if the servants had anything to say about him. She said no one has spoken an ill word of him."

Charlotte smiled. "I appreciate you looking out for me, but I am going to request that you do not attempt to discover anything more."

"Why not?" Lizzy asked in surprise.

"Because I know you. You probably want to have one of your sisters flirt with him to see if he will stray. Perhaps you wish to see how he will react in a bad situation, the way you did with Mr. Collins," Charlotte paused, then continued, "I also received a letter from Jane this morning, informing me of some of your intent." Leaning forward, Charlotte looked Lizzy directly in the eyes. "Please, Lizzy, do not do any more. I am thankful for your efforts on my behalf, but I will not allow you to jeopardize this for me."

"What do you mean, Charlotte?" cried Lizzy.

Mary sat down next to Lizzy. "I think what Charlotte is trying to say, Lizzy, is that sometimes you are a little too zealous in your attempts to discover if a man is genuine." When Lizzy opened her mouth to protest, Mary raised a hand. "Your greatest strength is your love for your family and friends. That strength, however, can be a detriment when used without caution."

"Such as the rumors you began about Jane and Mr. Bingley," Charlotte added pointedly.

Kitty groaned. "What are the rumors saying?"

"Thankfully, it is all against Mr. Bingley, but people are saying that the reason Jane remains unwed is that she has been pining for him all this time. There is even talk of a broken engagement, and one person hinted at a foiled elopement," Charlotte said with concern.

Lizzy's eyes filled with tears. "An elopement?" she asked in a broken whisper. "That could destroy Jane's reputation."

"Thankfully, the person who raised the subject was immediately silenced by many of the matrons in Meryton. They have all known Jane since she was a babe, and they know her nature. They are, however, earnestly discussing her broken heart," Maria chimed in.

"Which would be devastating for her to hear," said Mary, "especially as she would feel uncomfortable denying such claims. For all her beauty, Jane does hate to be at the center of speculation."

Lizzy fought back tears as the conversation continued around her. *How could things go so terribly wrong?* she wondered.

After a few minutes, the Lucas girls made their farewells. They patted Lizzy's shoulder understandingly before they departed. Lizzy felt numb, unable to move or think. Finally, Mary took her hand and gently urged her to go upstairs. Mutely, Lizzy made her way to her bedroom, where she collapsed onto the bed and sobbed into her pillow.

Lizzy's greatest desire had only ever been to protect her sisters. She wanted them to make good matches with kind men who would not mistreat them or betray them. *Where did I go so wrong?* Lizzy cried.

The majority of the day passed with Lizzy's emotions swinging wildly between self-castigation and indignation that her loved ones did not appreciate her efforts. Eventually, self-castigation won the battle. *'Til this moment, I have never known myself,* she thought. *How humiliating is this discovery! Yet, how just a humiliation!*

When the dinner bell rang, she sent word down that she still suffered a headache. She requested that a tray be sent up. When a knock sounded against the door some ten minutes later, she gave permission for the servant to enter without bothering to lift her face from her pillow. "Please place the tray on the chair."

"Lizzy?" Mary's gentle voice broke through Lizzy's mournful thoughts, and she sat up to see her sister standing in the doorway. "Are you quite alright, dear?"

Lizzy opened her voice to answer, but she instead resumed weeping. Mary crossed the room, sat on the bed, and embraced her sister.

"What a fool I have been," Lizzy cried into her sister's arms.

"You are *not* a fool," said Mary sharply. "You are a mite overzealous, perhaps, but never a fool. If anything, you are the wisest of us all; you have kept us safe. In that quest you may have done more than is necessary, but it is better to overdo than underdo in matters of protection."

Lizzy's tears waned slightly. "I feared I had lost you all."

"'He that covereth his sins shall not prosper: but whoso confesseth and forsaketh them shall have mercy'," Mary replied. "Proverbs," she added at Lizzy's confused look.

"You are saying that I am forgiven, because I recognize what I have done and will work to improve," interpreted Lizzy.

"Precisely. You have not been malicious or selfish. Every action has been conducted with love. You need to continue to be yourself, but perhaps a touch less fanatically," said Mary.

"I shall," promised Lizzy.

"Now, then, let us go down to dinner," Mary suggested. Arm in arm, the girls descended the stairs to join their family.

~∞~∞~∞~

"A note from Longbourn, Mrs. Bingley," said a footman as he bowed to Georgiana, extending a tray with a note.

Georgiana took the envelope from the tray, attempting to conceal her excitement from the servant. "Thank you, Fawcett, that will be all," she said as she laid it on the small table next to her.

Once he had left the room, Georgiana eagerly tore open the missive. Colonel Fitzwilliam laughed at her antics. "You would not be excited to see the ladies of Longbourn, would you?" he teased.

"Oh hush, you," she said with a smile. Scanning the note, her smile widened. "My invitation to tea has been accepted. It appears the eldest Miss Bennet has left for London this morning, however." At this, her smile dimmed. "I hope she did not leave because of Charles."

"That may have played a part," Fitzwilliam admitted with a frown.

"Well, two of the sisters have agreed to come, which means they do not despise me," said Georgiana with a rueful grin.

"Is there not a fourth sister?" Fitzwilliam asked.

"Yes, the middle sister," she answered, reading the note again. "I believe her name is Mary. She is engaged, and her fiancé is scheduled to arrive the day after the tea, so she will be preoccupied with ensuring all is in readiness for his visit."

"Ah, yes, now I remember," Fitzwilliam said. "She is engaged to the heir of the estate—a certain Mr. Collins, if memory serves me."

"Mr. Collins," mused Georgiana. "The name sounds familiar, but I cannot quite place it. Perhaps I have met someone with a similar name in the past."

"Well, you will have plenty to discuss with the Misses Bennet who will be coming for tea. I quite look forward to meeting them again."

"Fitzwilliam, you will not be joining us for tea," Georgiana told her cousin sternly.

"What! I am wounded!" cried the colonel, putting one hand dramatically over his heart and feigning a swoon.

"Be serious!" she laughed. "I wish to have a serious conversation with these ladies about Charles. If we are to be friends, we will need to clear the air. Your presence—or that of any of the gentlemen—will only impede conversation."

"Very well," sighed Fitzwilliam. "I will find something to keep myself occupied."

"And my husband and brother," she demanded.

"As you wish, my dear cousin," he said with a kiss on her hand. "And now, it is time for me to take my afternoon ride before the dinner bell is rung. Please excuse me."

Bowing deeply in false mockery, Colonel Fitzwilliam left the parlor, leaving behind a laughing Georgiana. Once he had gone, her smile faded as her mind turned to the upcoming tea. She was eagerly anticipating making new friends, but she felt anxious about the conversation she must have with them before they could become intimates. *At least the one who Charles hurt the most will not be present. That may help ease the discomfort,* she thought. *Either way, it will all be over in a few days.*

Checking the time, she realized she still had much to do before dinner. She picked up the note from Longbourn and hurried from the room, eager to begin making preparations for the tea.

Chapter 16

The days leading up to the highly anticipated event passed swiftly for the inhabitants of both Longbourn and Netherfield. Georgiana diligently avoided the company of her brother and husband, having at last decided to conduct her conversation with the Bennets before speaking to the gentlemen. She feigned her courses and an ensuing megrim to avoid any encounters with her cousin, so he could not insist she speak to her husband on the matter of Jane Bennet.

As the hour approached, Lizzy and Kitty called for their carriage. Mrs. Bennet began to insist they go on horseback, as it looked like rain, but Lizzy stood firm in her refusal.

"I would rather walk the three miles than arrive on horseback," she told her mother.

"Walk three miles? In all that dirt? You would not be fit to be seen!" cried the lady. Grumbling, Lizzy acquiesced, and the girls departed via carriage with no small amount of relief.

As the carriage took them to Netherfield, Georgiana stood anxiously in the parlor. She had chosen that room specifically for the view of the drive. Although she had gained quite a lot of confidence since her marriage, at heart she was still the shy girl she had always been. Making new friends had never come easy for her, but she was determined to make the attempt.

Finally, the carriage arrived, and both Bennet sisters disembarked. Georgiana sat down and smoothed her dress, then smoothed it again anxiously.

Lizzy and Kitty were admitted at the front door. While a footman took their cloaks and bonnets, they looked around admiringly at the décor. It had been several years since Netherfield had been inhabited, and even then, the furnishings had been rather drab. Now, however, the carpets and draperies bespoke the classic elegance of the mistress. It boded well for their visit. *If she had filled Netherfield with ornate bric-a-brac and decorated in the Egyptian style, then we could not be friends!* thought Lizzy in amusement, following the footman down the hall.

"Miss Bennet and Miss Catherine," the footman announced.

"Mrs. Bingley," murmured Kitty and Lizzy in unison as they curtsied.

Georgianna curtsied in response, then cleared her throat before speaking, "I am delighted to have you visit. Please, sit." She beckoned the girls to sit on the settee near her.

After a few moments of awkward silence, Lizzy said, "This is a lovely room."

"Yes, it is," smiled Georgiana. *Why can I not think of anything to say? Stupid girl, loosen your tongue!* "My sisters-in-law were very helpful in sharing their opinions about the furnishings." *Not that I took any heed of their poor taste.*

Lizzy noticed the unique phrasing and smiled to herself. A few more seconds passed in silence.

"Tea!" exclaimed Georgiana. Kitty and Lizzy jumped slightly, and Georgiana blushed. "I mean, allow me to ring for tea." She stood and pulled the bell.

A maid quickly entered, bobbing a curtsy. "We would like some tea," Georgiana requested. The maid bobbed another curtsy and left without a word.

A few more minutes passed in silence, which persisted while the housekeeper brought in the tea service. Georgiana broke the silence only to ask Lizzy and Kitty how they took their tea. She poured the tea, making sure to cater to their requests, and served each girl a teacup and saucer.

The following silence was punctuated by the sips of tea as the ladies kept their eyes trained firmly on their saucers. Lizzy and Kitty were waiting for their hostess to begin the conversation, whereas all of Georgiana's carefully rehearsed small talk had disappeared from her brain.

"Oh, for heaven's sake!" Georgiana blurted out, unable to bear the silence any longer. Seeing the startled faces of her guests, she continued, "I cannot think of anything to say that would work for new acquaintances."

Lizzy looked at her curiously. "Why not say what you want to say instead?"

Georgiana looked at her gratefully. "I am not entirely unaware of the history my husband has with your sister. I do not know all the details, but I understand he paid his attentions to her once, several years ago, and that he did not behave in a gentlemanlike manner." At Lizzy's raised eyebrows, she rushed on, "My marriage to Charles occurred due to a rather uncomfortable situation in which he did the honorable thing. It was not a love match, but nor was it arranged by my brother."

Biting her tongue to quell her curiosity, Lizzy nodded.

"I know, however, that your sister cared for him very much, and he felt the same for her. I know my brother is not without blame, either. At that time, our father had recently passed, and he was in a contrary mood for a few years, with Charles blinding following his lead."

Kitty's mouth was slightly agape at this flood of knowledge, and Lizzy discreetly elbowed her to close it.

"I know that nothing can change the past or the present circumstances. I can, however, heartily apologize for any role my marriage may have played in your sister's current departure from Longbourn and any sorrow she may feel. Also, while it is not my place to apologize for my husband and brother—as I was only eleven years old when the situation occurred—I still wish to offer my sincerest apologies for their shameful actions," Georgiana concluded in a rush.

The room was quiet for a few minutes. Georgiana focused on sipping her tea to quench her parched throat. Kitty was at a loss for words and tried to cover a nervous giggle with a cough.

Lizzy opened her mouth several times to speak, only to close it again when nothing came out. Finally, she said carefully, "My dear Mrs. Bingley, I am grateful beyond words for your forthright candor. Please be assured that Jane's travels to London are not a sign of a broken heart. Our aunt Gardiner has been confined to her bed, and Jane goes to help tend the children and run the household."

Seeing Georgiana's embarrassment, she continued, "I cannot deny that my sister was much hurt by their behavior. However, given her reticent nature and your husband's apparent inability—at the time— to stand firm in his resolve, it seems as though it has all turned out for the best. She bears you no ill will in the slightest."

Here Kitty interrupted, "Indeed not! Shortly before she left, she shared her disappointment with me in not being able to further her acquaintance with you, as she expressed a desire to know you better after seeing you at the assembly."

Georgiana's shoulders straightened as the weight of her trepidation lifted. "I, too, have desired a further acquaintance with her and all of you." She faltered, then pressed forward, "I have not had many friends over the last few years."

Lizzy reached out and grasped Georgiana's hand, "I would like to be your friend," she said earnestly, "We all need friends in whom we can trust."

Georgiana squeezed her hand in return, overcome with emotion at the kindness from the Bennet sisters.

"Now then," said Lizzy, sitting back and picking up her tea once more, "if we are to be friends, we must learn everything about one another!"

After a moment of stunned silence, Georgiana burst into laughter. "Very well, but you must share first!"

The ladies passed several hours becoming better acquainted, their conversation regularly punctuated with bursts of giggles. Lizzy and Kitty shared their childhood adventures with Georgiana, who was fascinated to hear about life with many siblings. In return, Georgiana told of her quiet life at Pemberley and her discomfort at finishing school. Ramsgate was never mentioned, however. *That will be shared at a later date, when I have more assurance of their discretion,* Georgiana told herself.

Their cheer was only interrupted when Georgiana saw a carriage arrive bearing Mrs. Hurst and Miss Bingley. "Oh, Lord, look at the time!" exclaimed Georgiana, interrupting Lizzy in the middle of a story about when the pig had gotten into the gardens.

At first, Lizzy was slightly hurt that her new friend seemed desirous of ending what she had felt was an enjoyable visit. Then she followed her hostess's gaze to the scene beyond the window. Remembering the other women's hubris and snobbery at the assembly, she nodded at a confused Kitty. "Quite right!" Lizzy said hastily, pulling her sister to her feet. "The day has certainly gotten away from us. Come along, Kitty."

"I am so terribly sorry," Georgiana said in embarrassment. "I did not mean to interrupt, I simply—"

"Really, Mrs. Bingley," Lizzy broke in, nodding at the window, "I understand *entirely.*"

Georgiana smiled with relief, then said, "Please, call me Georgiana."

"And we are Lizzy and Kitty," Lizzy tugged a bewildered Kitty toward the door.

The Bennets met Mrs. Hurst and Miss Bingley in the entrance hall. Curtsies were exchanged as footmen and maids retrieved and collected cloaks and bonnets.

"I did not know you expected visitors today, Georgiana dear," said Miss Bingley in a saccharine tone. "We would never have left you by yourself to entertain company otherwise."

Kitty stifled a gasp at the implied criticism, and Lizzy gave Miss

Bingley a sharp look, "We had quite an enjoyable visit, dear Georgiana," Lizzy said.

Miss Bingley's eyes widened slightly at Lizzy's casual use of Georgiana's name. She opened her mouth, but she was silenced by Georgiana's response.

"Thank you, Lizzy, for coming, and you as well, Kitty," replied Georgiana with a warm smile at the two of them. "I will return the call in a few days. I look forward to renewing my acquaintance with the others of your family."

"We would be delighted!" exclaimed Kitty gaily, oblivious to the tension pervading the room. Lizzy hid a smile. For all of Kitty's maturations over the years, she occasionally showed signs of the girl she had once been.

Curtsies were exchanged once more, and the Bennet girls exited the manor and climbed into their awaiting transport. Once the Bennet carriage had disappeared from view, Georgiana returned to the parlor, closely followed by Miss Bingley and Mrs. Hurst.

"Georgiana, dear," began Miss Bingley in a cloying voice, "perhaps you are unaware of the Bennet family's true situation in life. While we were in the rather small village of Meryton this afternoon, we inquired after them."

"Why would you do that?" Georgiana asked, calmly picking up her embroidery hoop.

Mrs. Hurst blinked in surprise. "We must ensure that we surround ourselves with good society, of course. It would not do to keep company with those who are beneath us."

"Mr. Bennet is a gentleman, is he not? Whereas your father was from trade," Georgiana pointed out.

"Yes, but their mother and her family are not of good breeding. Her father was a solicitor, and her brother is in trade and lives in Cheapside," Miss Bingley impatiently explained.

"But marriage raises a woman's status, does it not? Otherwise, Mrs. Hurst could not be considered a gentlewoman, or so I believe."

Georgiana blinked innocently.

Mrs. Hurst blushed, but Miss Bingley continued on, "My dear Georgiana, surely you must see that the Bennets are simply grasping for whatever scrap of respectability and fortune they can purloin! Their estate is entailed away from the female line, and their dowries are small. Additionally, their uncle must be coarse indeed, if he is dwelling in Cheapside."

"Upon my word!" exclaimed Georgiana. "It would not matter if they had uncles enough to fill *all* of Cheapside! It would not render the Misses Bennet one jot less agreeable. No," she said firmly as her sisters-by-marriage made to protest, "I will not be dissuaded. I enjoyed their company very much, and I plan to continue the acquaintance. Now, if you will excuse me, it is time to dress for dinner."

With her final statement ringing in the air, Georgiana marched from the parlor and up the stairs to her bedroom. Once there, she rang for her maid. As her maid helped her change clothes, Georgiana said, "Sarah, please inform my husband's valet that I have something I need to discuss with Charles in private after we retire."

"Yes, Miss Da— I mean, Mrs. Bingley," her maid stammered in surprise. Georgiana gave her a fond smile. Sarah had been her lady's maid since she went to finishing school. She was the only person in the world, other than her brother and her husband, who knew the truth about Ramsgate and the celibate state of her marriage. Sarah was more than a servant—she was a trusted confidant. As such, she found this request that Bingley join Georgiana in her rooms to be unprecedented and surprising.

"Thank you, Sarah. I merely have some things to discuss with him that I do not want anyone to overhear," she explained as Sarah finished pinning up the last few strands of hair into her coiffure.

Sarah bobbed a curtsied and departed. Georgiana took a few deep breaths, then left her room and knocked on her brother's bedroom door.

Darcy's valet answered, a stern look on his face. "My master is not to—" He halted suddenly when he recognized the person in front of him. "My apologies, Mrs. Bingley. I did not expect you," he stammered.

Georgiana smiled, "Do not fret; I am not Miss Bingley," she teased, and he blushed.

"Georgiana, come in and leave the poor man be," an amused Darcy called from where he was buttoning his shirtsleeves deeper into the room. "To what do I owe the pleasure of your company?"

"You may change your mind about 'pleasure' when I tell you that I would like to discuss the Bennets," answered Georgiana as she entered the room.

The smile faded from Darcy's face. "Ah, yes, Fitzwilliam mentioned you would want to speak with me about them."

Georgiana related the conversation she had shared with the two Misses Bennet. As she spoke, his face grew progressively grim. "I sincerely regret any distress that Miss Bennet felt by my actions," he said fervently. "I was unaware that Bingley had made such assurances to her, and that her heart was engaged, or I would have advised him differently."

"You would have allowed him to court her and propose?" Georgiana asked in astonishment.

"Certainly not," Darcy said firmly. "Bingley was only eighteen years old at the time, and he had several years left at Oxford. I do not regret counseling him against *any* woman during those years. What I do regret, however, was labeling her a fortune hunter and absconding with him without even a farewell."

"You were of a more cynical nature at that time," Georgiana admitted.

"Yes, well, Father had recently passed, I had the burdens of Pemberley and you, and since I was master instead of heir, my value had suddenly increased tremendously. I was in no humor to give consequence to any young woman searching for an increase or slighted by other men and still unwed."

"Brother, that is harsh," chided Georgiana.

Darcy hung his head. "You are correct, Sister. Although I have made efforts to not give way to pride, it does not come easily for me. I have much to learn, and much for which to make amends."

"You will be relieved to learn, then, that while Miss Bennet was heartbroken when Charles left her, she has quite recovered. Further, I have determined that her sisters are all that is gracious, and I intend to befriend them," Georgiana informed him.

The worry lines in Darcy's face eased somewhat. "I am grateful for it. I still feel the need to atone, however."

"Then be kind," she said.

"Be kind? That is all?" Darcy asked incredulously.

"You may owe a formal verbal apology when you are better acquainted," she admitted, "But for now, the best thing you can do is to offer them your respect and your friendship. They will then understand that you do not view them in a negative light, and that your actions from years ago were not of a personal nature."

"I will do my best," he told her. She smiled at him. Just then, Darcy's valet entered the room again, having left to give them privacy for their conversation. "It is time for you to go down to dinner, sir," he informed his master.

"Thank you, Carson," Darcy said, and he offered Georgiana his arm.

When they reached the sitting room, they saw all of the other occupants of Netherfield had already gathered together, even Miss Bingley. "There you are!" the lady pronounced in a loud voice. "How we despaired of you!"

Darcy rolled his eyes slightly at Georgiana. She grinned at him, then turned to her sister-in-law. "My apologies, Caroline, but my brother and I were having an important conversation."

"And what, pray tell, was so important that you were late for dinner?" Miss Bingley asked in a coy voice.

"A private matter," Darcy answered shortly.

"A private matter! But we are all family, are we not? Surely, we should have no secrets from each other, being as close as we are!" cried Miss Bingley, crossing the room to Darcy.

"Then it would have been pointless to speak in private!" Fitzwilliam said in a loudly cheerful voice. "We must allow siblings to have their own secrets," he said, winking at Miss Bingley when she opened her mouth to protest.

"Quite right!" Bingley added. He gave his sister a sharp look. "May I remind you, Caroline, that there are certain things you would prefer I discuss with you in private rather than in front of guests or even family?"

Caroline blushed and murmured her assent. The butler spared them any further discord when he chose that moment to enter and announce dinner. Charles collected Georgiana, then extended his other arm to his sister. She glanced at Darcy, then took her brother's arm in annoyance when Darcy's remained stubbornly at his side. They were followed by the Hursts, who were in turn followed by Darcy.

Dinner was unexceptional: Miss Bingley carried the conversation by disparaging the unacceptably limited wares she had discovered at the shops in Meryton. Darcy listened absentmindedly, his unfocused gaze betraying that his thoughts were elsewhere. Bingley kept giving Georgiana furtive glances, which she took to mean that his valet had passed along her request. Mrs. Hurst periodically made statements in accordance with her sister's, and Mr. Hurst was heavily involved in his food.

"Superb meal, as always," Mr. Hurst grunted in appreciation to Georgiana once the last course was completed.

Georgiana signaled to the ladies to retire to the piano room. Colonel Fitzwilliam jumped to his feet and pulled her aside. "You spoke to your brother?" he asked in a whisper.

"Yes," she confirmed, "and it appears he is much repentant for what happened. Lizzy and Kitty assured me at our tea today that they bear no ill will toward anyone, and neither does their sister."

Fitzwilliam nodded, then bowed as she and the other ladies made their way toward the music room, where Georgiana and Miss Bingley took turns at the pianoforte.

The men were not long at their port, and shortly after they joined the women, Bingley performed an exaggerated yawn. "I do believe I will retire early tonight," he said, looking everywhere but at his wife.

"I believe I will as well," Darcy said hastily, and Fitzwilliam echoed the sentiment. With Bingley and Georgiana quitting the room, neither man wanted to stay with the remaining members of the party. Without allowing anyone the opportunity to protest, Bingley hurried out the door, followed immediately by Darcy and Fitzwilliam. After a few minutes, Georgiana also excused herself early. She reached the top of the stairs to discover her husband waiting for her.

"I will join you shortly," he informed her solemnly.

She nodded, suddenly nervous, and went to her room. Sarah helped her put on a plain nightgown with a modest dressing gown secured over the top. It occurred to Georgiana that her husband might have an altogether different understanding as to what she wanted to discuss.

Oh dear, she thought to herself. *This might not go at all well.*

About ten minutes later, a knock sounded at the door that separated her room from the master's suite. It had never been locked, but neither had they ever opened it. Georgiana dismissed Sarah, and she called for Bingley to enter.

When he emerged, Bingley was also dressed for the night, and he had a worried expression on his face. "My dear—" he began hesitantly but found himself unable to speak further.

Georgiana gave a nervous giggle, then said, "Do not be alarmed, Charles. I only wish to discuss Jane Bennet with you."

Bingley started, then stared at her in astonishment. It was clear that it was not the topic of conversation that he had anticipated. "I beg your pardon?" he said in a strangled voice.

At his expression, Georgiana could not help but to let out a hardy laugh. "Oh, Charles, you should see your face!"

Bingley blushed and then began to laugh himself. Once they had settled, she bade him sit on the settee next to her chair.

"You have been extremely patient with me," she said, "and I cannot begin to express my gratitude for everything that you have done for me."

Bingley waved his hand as though to dismiss her thanks. "It was the right thing to do."

"It was the *generous* thing to do," she insisted, "Not many men would agree to marry a young woman who was potentially compromised, refuse to touch her dowry, allow her to remain with her brother, actively work to elevate her confidence, and leave the marriage unconsummated." She blushed fiercely at this last assertion.

Bingley shook his head. "Your brother saved my life when we were boys. It was the least I could do for him. And for Jane Bennet."

"For Miss Bennet?" Georgiana asked in confusion. Whatever she had expected him to say, it had not been that.

"I always regretted leaving her the way that I did. I was ashamed to tell your brother that I had committed myself at such a young age, so I simply left. It was easier to betray a lady's trust than to disappoint my greatest friend. I carried that burden for years, knowing that I had engaged a young woman's affections and then abandoned her. I meant to return, but the Luddite business up north prevented me. By the time it was resolved, I knew she must be married, with her beauty and grace. Too much time had passed. I still felt the guilt, however. When we came to Ramsgate and discovered the situation Wickham had put you in, I knew that I could make the right decision this time. I felt as though saving one woman could make up for deserting another."

Georgiana nodded slowly. "I have always wondered why you offered me your hand. I knew you felt you owed my brother, but I believed there was more to it than that." She hesitated but pressed on. "Do—do you regret it?"

He thought for a minute, then answered: "Yes."

Her heart sank, but she pressed on, despite the fiery claws she now felt shredding her insides: "Because... Because... We could change it, you know."

Bingley looked up, startled. "What do you mean?"

"Our marriage—it could be annulled. Then you would be free to marry according to your heart's desire." She found the words so difficult to force past her lips that by the end of this suggestion, her final word was little more than a whispered squeak. Georgiana held her breath—dreading and craving his response—with tears burning behind her eyes.

"Annulled? No! Never!" he cried, aghast.

"But you said you regret marrying me," she whispered, refusing to meet his eyes.

Bingley crossed the room and knelt at her chair, lifting his hand to caress her cheek. "Georgiana, look at me," he said, moving his hand to cup her chin and lift her face. He waited until she raised her teary blue eyes to meet his sober green ones. "You misunderstand, darling. I regret my previous poor behavior. I regret mistreating a good and gentle lady. However, I do not regret escaping a commitment I made at eighteen before I had enough experience to know my own mind. And I do not regret marrying you. That is the one thing in this life that I could never regret. And I shall never apologize for joining my life with that of the kindest, cleverest, and fairest lady I have ever had the happy chance to know."

She burst into tears and threw her arms around his neck, nearly knocking him backward onto the floor. He eased carefully from his knees to sit more comfortably on the rug and settled her into his lap, where he cradled her protectively against his chest. All of the worry she had felt melted away as he patted her back and smoothed her hair. After several minutes, her tears subsided, and she searched for a handkerchief. Dabbing her eyes as she looked up into his face, she said, "I needed to be sure. I do not want you to resent me."

He smiled kindly at her. "Georgiana, sweetheart, you are my wife. I made a vow in a church before God and man that I will comfort and honor you until death parts us. I take that seriously. On that day, I put all thoughts of Jane Bennet in the past. I have striven to correct the childish behaviors that caused me to make promises I could not—or would not—keep."

Georgiana's eyes filled with tears. "At Ramsgate, I thought I was in love. These last eighteen months have shown me that I was wrong. 'Love is not love that bends with the remover to remove, but it looks on tempests and is never shaken.' My regard for you is beginning to turn to that, I believe."

"As is mine," he said. He hesitated, then ventured, "Georgiana, I do not believe you are yet ready to consummate our marriage, are you?"

She blushed furiously, dropped her eyes to her lap, and shook her head. Then she said hesitantly, "But Charles, if you want to—"

"No!" he interrupted forcefully. She recoiled in hurt and shame, nearly tumbling to the ground. Bingley wrapped one arm around her back, steadying her before pulling her back into his embrace. Grasping her hand and clasping it to his heart, he said in a softer voice, "Georgiana, I will not be ready until you are. I have never taken an unwilling woman, and I will not begin with my wife."

Astonished, Georgiana twisted suddenly, that she might turn her head to look him fully in the face. He smiled ruefully. "I know these are not the kinds of conversations one has with a maiden, but we are also married, and it is important that we discuss them, regardless of the potential for discomfiture. I had planned to wait until you were eighteen to broach the subject, as that is when you would otherwise have come out into Society and been ready to make decisions about marriage."

Gently stroking his thumb across the back of her hand, he said, "This conversation may have come a bit earlier than I had planned, but circumstances necessitated it. If it is alright with you, I would like to begin to court you."

Georgiana blinked up at him in surprise. "But we are already married."

He laughed softly and gave her a tender smile. "Yes, we are, and we are very fond of one another because we have known one another so long. We have a friendship. I would like for us to have more than that with one another. I would like for our affections to be more engaged. Had we engaged in a proper courtship, I could have wooed you and we could have grown to love one another before we said our vows. Though we are already wed, I would like to court you now and cultivate a romantic bond between us." He drew her hand to his lips and gently kissed her palm. "Would that be all right?"

Georgiana nodded silently, unable to speak.

"Very well, then," he gifted her with a smile before smoothly standing up—with her still cradled in his arms—and placing her gently on her feet. "I will leave you now. Sweet dreams, my dear," he said before he kissed her cheek and returned to his room.

Georgiana raised her fingertips to touch the spot on her cheek where the feel of his kiss still lingered. She stood there, gazing at her husband's door for what seemed like hours, until the noise of the footmen in the hallway securing the house for the night startled her from her repose and into her bed. That night, she drifted on a sea of light, embraced by dreams of happiness and love.

Chapter 17

Jane Bennet smiled as she watched her young cousins run with their kite. They had come to Hyde Park as a special outing for the day in order to give Mrs. Gardiner some peaceful time to rest. The few days she had spent at the Gardiner's home in Gracechurch Street had already proven to be of great value to Mrs. Gardiner. With Jane minding the children and running the household, the expectant mother was able to get sufficient rest to join her family for dinner each day.

At first, the children were shy around their cousin; it had been some time since Jane had visited London. Her gentle nature quickly won them over, however, and she was rewarding their good behavior with a day at Hyde Park, accompanied by their somewhat elderly nurse.

"Jonathan, please do not go so near the lake!" she called as the nine-year-old boy ran gleefully ahead of his seven-year-old brother Timothy. Three-year-old Lucy stayed close to Nurse as the elderly woman carefully navigated the path.

"Miss Bennet?" a voice called incredulously. Jane turned and saw a vaguely familiar man approaching her, removing his hat.

"Yes?" she responded curiously. As the man grew closer, she let out a small gasp. "Mr. Cartwright!"

"I am pleased you remember me," said the handsome man, sketching a precise bow. "I have not seen you in, what, seven years now?"

"Why, yes, I believe so," Jane murmured, uneasy. Although she had not witnessed Cartwright's abuse of a young tenant's daughter so many years ago, her soul still stung from the scars it had received upon hearing of the evil deed.

Casting her gaze about, Jane sought Nurse and the children, but they had continued further along the path. "It is certainly a surprise to see you," she said hastily, "but I must return to the children."

"Are they your children?" Mr. Cartwright asked bluntly.

Jane shook her head, "They are my young cousins. I am in town to help mind them while their mother is ill."

"Ah, yes, the Gardiners, right? Are they still on Gracechurch Street?" he inquired.

Jane hesitated. How had he remembered that after all these years? She could no longer see the children or the Nurse, and there was no one else on their part of the path. She dipped a curtsy and said, "If you will excuse me, sir, I must catch up with the children. They will be needing me"

As she turned to leave, he reached out and grabbed her arm. "Not so hastily, *Miss* Bennet," he hissed, "We have had no time to properly reacquaint ourselves."

Jane felt fear rising up in her. "Please," she whispered, "let me go." Her plea only provoked an evil grin to form on his face, and she felt her heart stutter, then race. "Please," she begged, tears forming in her eyes.

Mr. Cartwright chuckled, tightening his grip on her arm. "We never were able to have that private conversation all those years ago. Fortunately, I am again in search of a wife, and now need a mother for my son. You have only grown more beautiful with time," he leered, raking his gaze down her figure.

When he lifted a finger to stroke her cheek, angry determination rose in Jane's breast. "I said, sir, to please unhand me," she demanded as she tried to wrench her arm from his bruising grip.

Mr. Cartwright's face turned ugly, and he pulled her closer. She stomped on his foot, and he raised his other hand above his head, preparing to strike.

"Oy! What's going on there? Unhand the lady at once!"

Jane and Mr. Cartwright turned—the movement wrenching Jane's arm painfully—to see a well-dressed man rushing down the path toward them.

"I say there, let the lady go!" the man demanded again, steel tempering his tone.

Mr. Cartwright reluctantly loosened his grip, and Jane tore her arm from his grasp. Rubbing the spot that had already grown puffy and would surely bruise severely, she glared at him.

"This is not finished, *Miss* Bennet," he sneered, then turned on his heel and hurried off away from the stranger.

The mystery rescuer finally reached her. "Are you all right, miss?" he asked breathlessly. "My apologies for waiting so long to intervene. I was not entirely certain of the situation at first."

"I am fine now, sir. Thank you," she said.

"Shall I call for a constable?" he asked in concern. "Or perhaps a physician? He seemed to have a tight grip on your arm."

"No, no constable or doctor," she said quickly. "I would not like the attention. In any case, he is gone now."

"The children!" she cried, looking around frantically for her charges and their nurse. Finding no sign of them, she turned and hurried down the path in the direction she had last seen them. She turned her head to bid a grateful adieu to her rescuer but found that—to her surprise—he was right behind her.

"Pardon the intrusion," he said, "but I would not be able to consider myself a gentleman if I left you alone after what just occurred. I will accompany you to your children, then see you home safely."

Jane glanced at him in surprise but managed to keep her quick pace. "That is very good of you, sir. Another time, I would assure you that we are quite safe, but today I will gratefully accept your escort." They rounded a turn in the path, and she sighed in relief to see Nurse minding all three children.

"There you are, Miss Bennet!" cried Nurse. "We were about to turn back for you." As Jane and her defender approached, the older woman's smile reformed into a concerned frown. She fixed her sharp gaze on the conspicuous red mark on Jane's arm. "But what is this, Miss Bennet? Are you well?" Nurse turned and narrowed her eyes suspiciously at the unknown man behind her master's niece.

"I am quite well, thank you, Nurse," Jane hastened to assure the woman, while surreptitiously tugging her sleeve down to cover the evidence of Mr. Cartwright's abuse. "This is—well, I am afraid we have not yet been properly introduced, but he rescued me from a man who was importuning me."

Nurse's expression softened slightly, though lips remained tightly drawn. "I thank you for your help, Mr.—?"

The man smiled, and Jane noticed for the first time how very handsome he was. "As there is no one here to do the appropriate introductions, I believe we shall simply have to introduce ourselves. I am Lord Oakley, eldest son of the Earl of Matlock." He gave a courtly bow.

Jane's wits deserted her momentarily. Thankfully, Nurse—who had seen many years and even more surprising things on this earth— had not lost her wits at the presence of a member of the Peerage. "This is Miss Bennet. Her father's estate is Longbourn in Hertford- shire. And I am called Nurse, your Lordship," she added, bobbing a curtsy.

Lord Oakley's smile widened slightly. "A pleasure to meet you, Miss Bennet, Nurse," he said, giving each of them a deep bow.

Offering his arm to Miss Bennet, he said to Nurse, "Miss Bennet had an unfortunate encounter with a man who—regardless of his gentlemanly attire—was decidedly *not* behaving in a gentlemanlike manner." He sniffed disdainfully.

When Jane hesitated in taking his arm, he looked at her. "Miss Bennet, as promised, I will escort you and your companions to your home in safety."

Jane smiled at him. "I am grateful for the offer, your Lordship, truly."

"Then what seems to be the problem?" he asked.

"I find myself facing a minor conundrum. You see, I promised my young cousins that we would spend the entire day at Hyde Park as a reward for their good behavior. I would not like to renege on my promise, but neither do I wish to return home unaccompanied. I am afraid Mr. Cartwright knows where my aunt and uncle live."

Lord Oakley raised an eyebrow. "I see. Well," he said, crouching down to look at Jonathan and Timothy in their eyes, "A lady must always keep her word. As should a gentleman, if he has any honor. Do you boys agree?"

They both nodded solemnly.

"There is no helping it, Miss Bennet. The only way for both of us to keep our promises is if I stay with you the remainder of the day here at Hyde Park, then escort you and the children home at the end."

Jane's eyes widened. "But sir!" she protested, "I could not ask that of you!"

"Nonsense, you have not asked anything of me," he said airily, waving his hand. "I made a promise, and I intend to keep it. As I have no fixed engagements today and had planned to spend much of it here at the park anyway, enjoying the uncommonly fine weather, it is no trouble to me. Besides," he added with a charming smile, "I do believe your company will be much more enjoyable than my own."

Nurse looked at Jane and said, "You know your aunt was counting on a full day of quiet rest."

"Then that settles the matter," Lord Oakley declared. "You simply must stay here, and I insist on remaining until you are home safely." He affected a forlorn demeanor. "However, if my company is so abominable to you, I shall be happy to remain on the bench over there in case I am needed."

Jane stifled a giggle behind her hand. "It seems I have no choice," she said. "If you are to remain, and I am to remain, then I believe I would prefer we remain together. Your company does not seem too terrible a thing to endure."

The Viscount let out a burst of surprised laughter. "I say, Miss Bennet, I appreciate your wit, even if it is employed at my expense."

A bubble of warmth grew in Jane's chest. In Meryton, she was the beautiful one and Lizzy was the witty one. She rather enjoyed being appreciated for her more substantive qualities. It seemed that this man saw past her looks, at least at the start.

They spent the next several hours together at the park. To Jane's surprise, the Viscount not only remained with them, but he joined the boys in their fun of kite-flying and chase. He taught them Blind Man's Bluff and insisted they pick some wildflowers to give to the ladies. The boys gave theirs to Jane and little Lucy, while the Viscount presented his with a flourish to Nurse, who blushingly accepted them.

When the sun began to lower in the sky, Jane regretfully recalled the children to her, informing them that it was time to head for home. Lord Oakley again offered Jane his arm, and this time she accepted. The three adults and three children began the walk to the Park's entrance.

"Where are we headed?" the Viscount asked Jane.

"Gracechurch Street," was her quiet reply. She had no illusions that she would retain his company and favor after he discovered how near to Cheapside her uncle's home was built.

"Ah, excellent neighborhood," he declared with aplomb. At Jane's look of disbelief, he continued: "My cousin has a good friend in trade whose family used to have a house in the area. I also have school chums whose families reside nearby. It is not Grosvenor's Square, but neither is it the East End!"

They walked in silence for some minutes. Jane's mind was awhirl with all that had occurred that day. As they approached her uncle's house, she realized with sorrow that her acquaintance with the gentleman was nearing its end. *I should have liked to see him again,* she thought glumly.

The party climbed the front steps, and Nurse ushered the children inside. As Jane turned to thank Lord Oakley for his company and escort, he took her by surprise with a question. "Would it be too much of an imposition to call on you in a few days, that I might assure myself of your safety and recovery?" he asked.

Jane could only stare at him, blinking. The confident smile on his face began to falter. "Of course, if that would be too intrusive—"

"No!" Jane blurted out unthinkingly. At his startled countenance, she composed herself and said, "I mean to say: No, of course that would not be an imposition or an intrusion. I would be delighted to see you again, your Lordship. I simply would not wish to inconvenience you more than I already have."

Lord Oakley's smile returned to his face. "Nonsense, dear lady, nothing would please me more than to know that you are safe from the vile blaggard who dared to importune you. In fact," he said after a pause, "I would like to inform your uncle of the situation myself."

Jane looked at him in surprise. "If you do not mind waiting, I will see if he is home." She opened the door and beckoned a maid. At her affirmative response, Jane returned her attention to the viscount. "He is at home, sir, if you would like to speak with him."

"I would indeed," he said. Jane led him down the hall and into the parlor, where Nurse and the children were sharing the events of the day with their father and pale mother.

From his place in a chair beside the settee on which his wife rested, Mr. Gardiner smiled warmly at his niece. His face froze momentarily when he noticed the stranger behind her, but he recovered himself quickly and crossed the room to where Jane stood.

"Jane, it is good to see you," he greeted her with a shade of question in his tone.

"Mr. Gardiner, his Lordship Viscount Oakley has requested an introduction to you. Lord Oakley, this is my uncle, Mr. Edward Gardiner."

The gentlemen exchanged bows, and only the brief furrow on Mr. Gardiner's brow betrayed his confusion. "Welcome to my home, your Lordship," he said.

"Mr. Gardiner, would it be too much trouble to request a private audience with yourself?" the viscount requested.

This time, Mr. Gardiner's surprise was enough to raise both eyebrows. "Certainly," he said. "There is time before we are called to dinner. Please, come with me to my bookroom." Lord Oakley followed Mr. Gardiner from the room, and Jane crossed over to her aunt before collapsing in the chair her uncle had recently vacated.

"Jane, what on earth—?" asked Mrs. Gardiner in astonishment.

Jane began to laugh as the stress of the day caught up with her. Her mild hysteria only inspired confusion in her aunt, who waited patiently for the girl to calm herself. Once she was able to speak, Jane related the entirety of the day's events, including her encounter with Mr. Cartwright.

At the end of her recitation, Mrs. Gardiner said, "My goodness! Who would have thought a simple excursion to Hyde Park would result in the eldest son of an earl in my home!" She sobered and asked, "But Jane, dear, are you quite all right? Your meeting with Mr. Cartwright sounds more than just unpleasant; it in fact seems to have been rather dangerous."

Jane sighed, "If I did not know of his black history, I believe I would feel less disturbed by these events. Knowing his vicious nature, however, I cannot help but worry that worse is yet to come."

Mrs. Gardiner's concerned expression sharpened. "What do you mean by 'his vicious nature'?"

Jane took a deep breath and considered for a moment. Lizzy had told her in confidence, and that was only due to Jane's history with Mr. Cartwright. It would not do to betray that confidence. On the other hand, Mr. Cartwright posed a very real danger to Jane, and therefore to the children she had in her charge. Finally, she settled on saying, "Mr. Cartwright is the former steward of Netherfield. He inherited some property in Derbyshire and is a landowner there, now. He once thought himself in love with me, when I was but fifteen years old. After he left Netherfield, a close friend shared with me a firsthand account in which he misused a young tenant girl in unspeakable ways. He is *not* a good man."

Jane's aunt looked at her in astonishment. "Upon my word, Jane!" she exclaimed. "This is very serious news indeed." She looked troubled. "Did you share any of this with the viscount?"

"Certainly not!" Jane exclaimed. "He did, however, witness Mr. Cartwright treating me roughly." Jane had forgotten about the pain in light of the enjoyment of her company. She pushed back sleeve and both women gasped at the dark bruise that had already formed what was clearly a man's handprint.

"Good God!" a man's voice cried out in anger.

The two women looked up to see Lord Oakley staring at Jane's arm in horror. Embarrassed, Jane hastily pulled her sleeve back over the bruise. Behind the viscount stood Mr. Gardiner, a violent storm of emotion darkening his face.

"Jane, you are henceforth forbidden to leave this house without my escort or the presence of at least two footmen," Mr. Gardiner ordered gravely.

"Of course, Uncle," Jane said obediently. She had little desire to meet Mr. Cartwright alone again. "I would also like to tell the servants that I am not at home to Mr. Cartwright."

"Do you think he will dare to call on you?" gasped Mrs. Gardiner, covering her mouth.

"He told me that he was not finished with me, and he remembered your names and that you live on Gracechurch Street," Jane informed her.

Mr. Gardiner's face darkened further. "I will hire two more footmen tomorrow," he said firmly "For tonight, I will remain awake and watchful myself."

"If you don't mind, sir," interjected Lord Oakley, "I would send over two of my footmen tonight. They can stay for as long as Miss Bennet resides here, or until you find men you can trust with her safety. It would not be wise to hire strangers, as they could be bought with coin."

Jane looked at Lord Oakley in astonishment. *What can he mean, doing so much?*

Sighing, Mr. Gardiner said, "I do not like it, but I do not see how I can object. The added protection would do much to ease my mind."

The viscount bowed then looked directly into Jane's eyes, "Then I will depart immediately so as to not delay their arrival. I will see you all again in a few days when I call to check on Miss Bennet's welfare."

Jane blushed but made herself hold his gaze. The moment was broken by an amused cough from Mrs. Gardiner. Jane blushed further, but the viscount merely bowed and took his leave.

Once alone with her aunt and uncle, Jane was subjected to all manner of questions. Jane answered them as best as she could. The interrogation only ended when the housekeeper entered to say that all was in readiness for their evening meal.

"Well, Jane," said Mr. Gardiner as he led his niece and wife into the dining room, "As your mother always says: We knew you could not be so beautiful for nothing. What a handsome son-in-law this viscount will make for my sister."

Jane blushed deeply, but she was unable to hide her pleasure at her uncle's words. "He is a very kind man," she demurred.

"A kind man who is a Peer," her aunt pointed out.

"And who has asked permission to call on our niece," Mr. Gardiner reminded his wife. "Would you like that, Jane?"

Jane blushed even further. "I would be happy to become better acquainted with him," she said cautiously, "but I also wish to know him further before any sort of commitment is made."

Mr. Gardiner nodded his approval. "I will put out some inquiries about Lord Oakley in the morning," he said.

The remainder of the evening passed in quiet contemplation of the day's events. *I could never have anticipated such a happy outcome from another London visit*, Jane thought with pleasure. *Let us hope he proves to be as genuine as he seems.*

Chapter 18

As their carriage took them home from Netherfield and their first tea with Mrs. Bingley—*Georgiana,* Lizzy reminded herself—Kitty let out an excited squeal.

"Oh, Lizzy!" she exclaimed. "Have you ever met such a wonderful lady?"

Lizzy laughed at her sister. "I think Jane might still rank above her in that competition; but yes, Georgiana is a lovely young woman."

"Young woman?" Kitty said in confusion, "But she is married!"

"Yes, but did you notice how she said she was only eleven when her brother met Jane? That was five years ago; she is only sixteen years old," Lizzy patiently explained.

"She is younger than I am!" exclaimed Kitty. "How is she married already?"

"That is a very good question," Lizzy mused, "She did not tell us specifically, but she did tell us that it was not a love match. My first inclination was that her brother arranged it, but she said that was not the case, either."

"Perhaps it was an accidental compromise of some sort?" Kitty suggested.

"That is a possibility. Gossip can be quite cruel," Lizzy considered. Then she groaned, "I still cannot believe I told our neighbors about Bingley and Jane. What on earth came over me?"

"You love Jane and were angry on her behalf," answered Kitty. "To be honest, I had the same feelings as you."

Lizzy gave Kitty a grateful smile, but said ruefully, "I am afraid that I am not always in control of my temper when it comes to my sisters and their hearts. My good opinion, once lost, is lost forever, I daresay."

Kitty laughed. "You know that is not true. You have the capacity for forgiveness, if you so choose. I do think, though, that you willfully assume that every man is capable of great wickedness until he proves otherwise."

"You may be right," Lizzy admitted. *But I have seen such wickedness firsthand,* she thought, *and I would not wish it on anyone. I may have failed Becky, but I will not fail anyone else in this.*

"Either way, Lizzy, we know you love us, and we love you as well," Kitty said seriously.

"It could be a great scandal if you did not!" exclaimed Lizzy in jest, sending both girls into peals of laughter that continued until the carriage arrived at Longbourn.

Once inside, Lizzy and Kitty found Mary in the drawing room, discussing the upcoming meals with Hill. "Remember, Mr. Collins is particularly fond of boiled potatoes, so I would like to have that dish served at least twice while he is here."

Hill nodded, bobbed a curtsy, and departed toward the kitchens.

"Why is Mamma not planning the meals?" Kitty asked her sister.

Mary smiled, "I asked Mamma if I could make the preparations for Mr. Collins, as a way for me to prepare to be his wife and future mistress of Longbourn. She was more than happy to turn her duties over to me."

"Where is she now?" Lizzy asked.

"In her rooms, writing a letter to Lydia," Mary answered. "She is ensuring all is in readiness for the militia to quarter at Meryton for the winter."

"Lord, don't remind me," groaned Lizzy as she collapsed into a chair near the fire. "I love Lydia, but I confess that I have enjoyed the peace at Longbourn since she married."

"You are not the only one," admitted Mary.

Kitty, who had always been closest to Lydia, said, "I miss the way she was when we were girls."

Mary gave her sister a hug while Lizzy nodded sympathetically. At that moment, Mrs. Phillips was announced, and she bustled into the room.

"Girls!" she exclaimed before sitting down. "You will not believe the news in Meryton. I came as soon as I heard. How could I not have known that Bingley was such a scoundrel to jilt our poor Jane?"

Lizzy let out an unladylike groan and put her head in her hands.

Mrs. Bennet, who had come out of her room when she heard her sister was announced, heard this declaration when she entered the room.

"You must be mistaken, my dear sister!" she cried. "If Jane had captured the notice of such a wealthy suitor, I would have known of it! Besides, my dear Jane would never be jilted; she is far too beautiful."

"But I heard it from Mrs. Long, who heard it from Mrs. Goulding, who said that she was informed by Lady Lucas, who heard it directly from Lizzy!" protested Mrs. Phillips.

Mrs. Bennet turned angrily to her daughter. "Elizabeth!" she shrieked, "Have you no compassion on my poor nerves? Why would you tell such a falsehood about your own sister?"

Lizzy paled slightly as she searched about in her mind for an answer. "I believe there may have been a misunderstanding," she said finally, looking at her sisters in desperation.

"Indeed, Mamma!" Mary said in support. "We all know Lizzy would never tell a falsehood about Jane."

"Perhaps someone misspoke?" suggested Kitty innocently.

"Then why would Lady Lucas say that you said such a thing?" demanded Mrs. Phillips.

Lizzy froze. *What do I say? Jane does not wish people to know the truth of this matter. But I do not wish to tell a falsehood, either. How can I fix this mess?* Lizzy looked helplessly at Mary, then seized upon an idea.

"It is all my fault, Mamma," cried Lizzy. Kitty and Mary gaped at her. Ignoring their reactions, she continued, "I believe Lady Lucas may have misunderstood something I said. It is true that Jane met Mr. Bingley in London a few times, but he never requested permission to court her, let alone marry her! You may remember that this was around the same time that Mr. Cartwright was paying Jane his attentions. I said in jest that it was hard to tell if Jane jilted him or he jilted Jane. Lady Lucas must have heard the end of what I said about Mr. Cartwright and thought I was speaking of Mr. Bingley."

Mrs. Bennet's face cleared, and Mrs. Phillips nodded wisely.

"There," declared Mrs. Bennet with satisfaction. "I knew no one could have jilted my Jane! Especially not an amiable man like Mr. Bingley. What an excellent man, to settle at Netherfield and invite two single gentlemen of large fortune to visit him."

Lizzy studiously ignored Mary's hard gaze.

"Well, then, Sister," said Mrs. Phillips, "I must be on my way!"

"I will join you," Mrs. Bennet replied, "and perhaps along the way we can call upon Lady Lucas to inform her of the mistake."

"Remember that it was my own fault, Mamma," reminded Lizzy. "Lady Lucas cannot be blamed for the misunderstanding if I was foolish enough to speak so loudly at the assembly."

"Who could blame poor Lady Lucas?" cried Mrs. Phillips. "She would never spread such insidious rumors. She is merely concerned for the wellbeing of our dear Jane."

Mrs. Bennet nodded her agreement. "We will be certain to assure her that she holds no fault for Lizzy's ill-spoken jest about her sister." She spoke in a loud whisper to her sister, "Lizzy has always been allowed to run on in a wild way at home."

Mrs. Phillips nodded in understanding and sent Lizzy a pitying look. The two matrons donned their cloaks, called for the carriage, and departed towards Meryton.

As soon as they were out of earshot, Mary and Kitty turned their attention towards Lizzy. "Very well done, Lizzy," Mary said approvingly.

Tension eased out of Lizzy's posture. "I know that it was a falsehood, but I could think of no other way to take the focus off Jane and Mr. Bingley."

"What you did was very brave, Lizzy," said Kitty.

"'Lying lips are abomination to the Lord: but those who act faithfully are his delight'," said Mary. At Lizzy's stricken look, she continued, "That is from Proverbs 12. A lie is a sin; however, you acted faithfully. By sharing the truth, you created an impossible situation. You resolved that situation by taking blame and placing it upon yourself. You were a faithful sister and a faithful friend to change the gossip so that it focused on you for doing wrong. You have done right in bringing this little punishment back to rest on yourself, rather than on those who did no wrong."

"And it was the truth, mostly," Kitty allowed. "Mr. Bingley never actually courted Jane officially. He never came to Papa or Uncle Gardiner for permission."

"And Jane *did* run away from Mr. Cartwright!" Mary said with a smile. "Truly, Lizzy, you dealt faithfully today. You righted a wrong, and you did so by shouldering the responsibility of the rumors."

Lizzy sighed in relief. "Thank you, sisters. I knew I could not leave things as they were. The mistake was mine, and so should the remedy be."

The sisters shared a hug, then returned to helping Mary prepare for Mr. Collins's visit on the morrow.

~∞~∞~∞~

Jane Bennet's head raised from its bowed position over her book when she heard footsteps travelling down the hall toward the Gardiners' sitting room.

"Lord Oakley," the maid announced, and the viscount entered the room.

Jane and Mrs. Gardiner stood, offering curtsies, and the viscount bowed in return. Mrs. Gardiner invited him to sit and rang for tea.

"How have you been, Miss Bennet?" the viscount inquired.

"Very well, sir," said Jane with a slight blush.

"I must admit, I have experienced a great deal of anxiety over you these past days," said the viscount with a piercing gaze.

Jane's blush deepened, and she found herself unable to respond. Mrs. Gardiner, thankfully, did not experience such difficulties.

"Jane has been quite safe. I must thank you again, your Lordship, for the two footmen you provided. They have relieved much of our worries."

"I understand Mr. Cartwright has not made an attempt to visit?" he inquired.

"No, your Lordship," Mrs. Gardiner answered.

"Please, call me Oakley," requested the viscount.

Mrs. Gardiner's eyebrows raised in surprise. "That is most generous of you, sir."

Oakley fixed his gaze on Jane as he replied, "Nonsense. I have a feeling we are all going to be very close friends."

Astonished, Jane snapped her gaze back up to meet the viscount's face. The naked yearning she found there caused her to blush deeply from the tips of her ears and down her neck. She let out a soft gasp.

"Mrs. Gardiner, would it be too much trouble to ask for a private audience with Miss Bennet?" the viscount requested.

Mrs. Gardiner hesitated, looking at Jane. At Jane's slight nod, Mrs. Gardiner stood. "I will leave the door ajar. You may have five minutes, but no more, sir."

Mrs. Gardiner vacated the room, leaving the door open as promised.

Oakley stood and walked over to Jane. He sat next to her on the couch. "Miss Bennet, I know this may seem sudden, but I would be honored if you would enter into a courtship with me."

Jane started, and discovered that it was, in fact, possible for her blush to deepen. "Why me?" she asked, "We know nothing of one another."

He smiled softly,. "That is precisely why." At her bewilderment, he elaborated "The fact that you know nothing about me, when my life has been the subject of gossip for the past two years, is part of what draws me to you. Your lack of artifice, your kindness toward your young cousins, and the clear absence of social-climbing in your behavior are what make you a rare jewel amid the coals and gravel of London Society."

"I am afraid I still do not understand, sir," Jane said, hearing the bitterness in his tone at his last words.

He sighed and stood, pacing a few steps in front of the couch. "Five years ago, my father—who is an earl—arranged my marriage to the daughter of a duke."

At Jane's wide eyes and gasp of surprise, he nodded grimly. "It was not a marriage that either of us desired, but neither did we have the ability to fight our parents. It was a—difficult marriage," he said carefully.

"She did not care for me, but I thought she was resigned to the match. She fell with child and our first son was born before we had been wed for a year. She gave birth to another son the following year, and our third son was born in the third year. The majority of our marriage, she was with child. Each confinement was worse than the previous had been. Each time, she became angry and hateful, then tearful, then sullen. After each birth, as soon as she recovered, she demanded another child. She wanted a daughter so badly. I could not deny her; it was the only thing she ever asked of me. The last birth, however, was difficult for her physically. She took ill with fever and died a fortnight after he was born."

Jane covered her mouth in horror as her eyes filled with tears.

Oakley smiled grimly and said, "Our marriage was considered a huge success by society. I, however, found it dark and lonely." Pausing, he smiled softly and said, "The one thing about that marriage that made it bearable were my sons. Each one was shining light in the blackness that shrouded the house." His voice broke, eyes filling with

206

tears.

Jane stood and walked over to where he paced, gently laying a hand on his arm. She was surprised by her boldness, but desperately yearned to comfort him. He placed his hand over hers and continued speaking.

"I came out of mourning last year. My father has been urging me to remarry, but I have consistently refused him. I have an heir; what need have I for another loveless match filled with scorn and indifference? Then I met you at the park. At first, I was drawn to your beauty. I have never met a woman your equal." He raised her hand and kissed it gently.

"It was your concern for your cousins that induced me to stay, however. In spite of the horror you had just experienced, your only thought was for their safety. I contributed it to a mother's feelings, but then Nurse called you 'Miss' and you introduced the children as your cousins. I watched as you interacted with them, and I knew that I wanted the same love you showed them for my own boys."

"So, you are asking to court me as a mother for your children?" Jane asked, hurt.

"No, my dear Miss Bennet; you misunderstand me. I also wanted that same love for *myself*. The last five years have been terribly lonely and painful for me. Until I met you, I had resigned myself to an eternity of loneliness, with only my sons to ease the solitude. But that one day at Hyde Park showed me that all of my days could be filled with the same happiness I witnessed you sharing with your cousins."

Jane hesitated, then ventured, "Why ask for a courtship, then?"

Oakley laughed. "For *you*, my dear. I have experienced enough to know what I want, but as you said yourself, you barely know me. I do not wish to have a repeat of my first marriage, two strangers joining together for life. No, no, I wish for you to know me and feel as happy in my company as I feel in yours."

"How can you be so certain that you will be happy in my company? Suppose I hide a dark, terrible secret?" Jane teased as her heart lightened.

Oakley threw back his head and laughed. "Miss Bennet—"

"*Jane*," she corrected.

His smile widened. "Jane," he seemed to caress her name, "I learned everything I need to know of your character from the day we spent at the park. I was able to witness your reactions at Hyde Park to a terrifying situation. Even after your alarming experience with that blackguard," his lips tightened at this mention of Mr. Cartwright, "your greatest desire was to keep your promise to your young cousins, though it meant remaining in a place where you had been so recently maltreated. I know that no number of society events could give me as full an illustration of your integrity of character."

Jane nodded in understanding. "Yes, your Lordship—"

"Oakley," he insisted.

"Very well. Yes, *Oakley*; you may ask my uncle for permission to court me."

~∞~∞~∞~

While Jane enjoyed the attentions of her new suitor, Mary was enjoying the attentions of her fiancé, who had at last arrived at Longbourn.

"My dear Mary," he said warmly, when he presented himself to the drawing room after refreshing himself in his rooms, "I am beyond happy to once again be in your presence." He bowed over her hand, placing a wet kiss upon it.

Mary smiled at him fondly and replied, "William, please join me over at the fire, that we may speak of all that has happened since you were last at Longbourn. You have written to me, but I find I much prefer hearing you speak of your experiences."

Grateful that Mary had arranged things so Mr. Collins was only speaking to her as opposed to the room in general, Lizzy turned to Kitty and engaged her in a discussion about the preparations they were to make for Georgiana's call the next day.

The private conversations continued for a quarter of an hour, with

Mr. Collins detailing every incident that involved each member of his parish over the previous months. Mary was very pleased to find that Mr. Collins had not reverted particularly much to his former habits, even after being in the company of Lady Catherine so frequently. While he still spoke highly of her ladyship, he tempered his conversation with reports regarding his efforts amongst the tenants and other members of his congregation. In general, Mary was more convinced than ever of the rightness of her choice.

Their conversation was interrupted when Mrs. Bennet entered the room. "Oh, Mr. Collins!" she exclaimed, "I had not known you had arrived! Mary, why did you not inform me at once?" she demanded.

"My apologies, Mamma," Mary said innocently. "I did not wish to disturb your rest. You have been greatly occupied with planning my wedding and preparing for Lydia's visit; your nerves must be in need of any respite we can grant them."

"My, yes!" cried her mother, "I have been working tirelessly day and night to ensure that everything is perfect for my daughters! How thoughtful of you, Mary, to think of me in that way. No one knows what I suffer. But then again, I never complain."

Lizzy rolled her eyes towards Kitty, who stifled a giggle. Attempting to change the subject before Mrs. Bennet could continue to expound upon her nerves, Lizzy said, "Mamma, I was about to go for a walk in the garden to select some roses for Georgiana's visit tomorrow."

"Oh yes, my dear! We must make everything perfect for Mrs. Bingley! Kitty, you had better go, too. You have a much better eye for flower arranging than your sister. Mary, Mr. Collins, you may as well join them and take a turn about the garden before dinner."

The four young people obediently rose and went outside. As they walked through the flowers, Mr. Collins asked, "Did I hear correctly that a Mrs. Bingley will be visiting tomorrow?"

"Yes, Georgiana Bingley. Her husband has let Netherfield Park, and they are there with her brother, Mr. Darcy, and her cousin Colonel Fitzwilliam. Mr. Bingley's sisters are also in residence, along with a husband for one of them," Kitty explained.

"Upon my word!" Mr. Collins said excitedly. "My dear cousins, do you know what an honor it is for you to be in the company of such distinguished persons?"

"Do you know them?" Lizzy asked curiously.

"Well, no, I have never met them," he said somewhat sheepishly. "However, I have heard much about them from my noble patroness. Mrs. Bingley, you see, is the niece of Lady Catherine! Mr. Darcy and Colonel Fitzwilliam are her nephews of course," he said triumphantly.

"What an astonishing connection!" exclaimed Lizzy. "I can certainly see how there might be some family resemblance between Lady Catherine and Mr. Darcy," she said slyly.

Mr. Collins stared at her blankly, and Mary hissed, "*Lizzy.*"

"Have you met Lady Catherine?" Mr. Collins asked in confusion.

"Er, no, Mr. Collins," said Mary. "Lizzy was just making a jest, but it was not a very funny one."

Mr. Collins's expression cleared, and he gave Lizzy a haughty look. "The family relations of Lady Catherine and the Earl of Matlock should not be the subject of humor," he said stiffly.

"My apologies, Mr. Collins," said Lizzy in contrition while Kitty stifled a laugh.

"All is forgiven, my dear cousin!" Mr. Collins said, cheerful once again. "I look forward to making Mrs. Bingley's acquaintance when she calls tomorrow," he added brightly.

Lizzy looked at him in surprise, and Kitty gave Mary a beseeching look.

"You forget, my dear," said Mary hastily, "That we have calls of our own to make tomorrow!"

"Have we?" Mr. Collins asked confusedly.

"Why, yes, of course," Lizzy affirmed, "Surely you should call on our neighbors every time you come to Longbourn. After all, not only are you to marry a local gentlewoman, but you will be the master of the estate one day. You will need to establish relationships with all of the local families."

"I see," Mr. Collins said a bit dejectedly.

Lizzy, feeling sorry for Mr. Collins, added, "But I do not see why you cannot make her acquaintance when she arrives, then leave for your own calls shortly after the introduction."

Mary smiled gratefully at Lizzy as Mr. Collins brightened. "You do not think it would be rude to be introduced and then immediately depart?"

"Certainly not," said Kitty, following Lizzy's lead. "Mrs. Bingley is the daughter of a gentleman. She will understand the duties of the heir of an estate."

Mr. Collins puffed his chest out. "That is true. How fortunate I am to have such wise women in my family!"

The girls smiled at one another. *For all his flaws,* thought Lizzy, *he truly does have a good heart. I am glad for Mary; they both will be very happy together.*

"Shall we go inside and arrange the flowers?" asked Kitty, her arms full of blooms.

That conversation set the tone for the rest of Mr. Collins's interactions with the Bennet family members that day and into the next. Mary continued to engage Mr. Collins in substantive conversation, all the while nurturing his fledgling confidence.

~∞~∞~∞~

At last, the Bingley carriage was seen pulling into the drive at Longbourn. She entered the house and was announced at the sitting room. Bows and curtsies were exchanged, and Lizzy introduced Mr. Collins to Mrs. Bingley. After indulging a few minutes of his raptures, Mary reminded her fiancé of the calls they were to make. He was graciously excused by Georgiana, and the two betrothed began the walk into Meryton for their visits.

Lizzy, Georgiana, and Kitty sat quietly for a minute, then Lizzy began to laugh. "We cannot have a repeat of our last visit!" she exclaimed, and the other two girls joined her in laughter.

"I was so nervous at that tea," admitted Georgiana.

"I was, too," Kitty said. "We were unsure of what to expect."

"I just did not want you to hate me," Georgiana responded.

"Who could ever hate you?" cried Lizzy. "You are all that is good and kind!"

Georgiana blushed at the compliment. "I think you are describing yourself," she said.

Lizzy laughed again and said, "Very well, we shall all three of us be all that is good and kind!"

Georgiana laughed, then peered around the room. "Is your mother not joining us for the visit?" she asked.

Kitty blushed faintly. "She may have been under the impression that she was engaged with our Aunt Phillips this morning."

"Kitty!" Georgiana said in mild shock.

"Yes, well, I wanted to get to know you better without having to watch our words," Kitty said defensively.

"I can hardly chastise you; I am guilty of doing the same with Caroline and Louisa the other day," Georgiana confessed.

The girls began again to laugh heartily. "I must say, I was surprised to meet Mr. Collins," Georgiana admitted when the giggles subsided.

"Why is that?" Lizzy asked, taking a sip of tea.

"I should say that I was surprised to learn my aunt chose him. In the past, she has chosen men of the cloth who are—for lack of a more fitting term—sycophants," Georgiana answered bluntly.

Lizzy and Kitty smiled at each other. "Mr. Collins was such a man at first," Lizzy confided. "However, the kind attentions and encouraging words he receives from Mary have done much to bolster his confidence in himself and to focus his attention on serving the entirety of his flock, rather than his patroness exclusively."

Georgiana smiled, "I am glad to hear it. Mary will need that confidence when she moves to Hunsford. My aunt can be quite demanding."

"How often do you visit?" inquired Lizzy.

"I have not seen her since before my marriage," was the reply. "She was disappointed that I made a match with someone in trade and has refused to speak with me since. I do correspond with my cousin Anne, however."

"What is she like?" Kitty asked curiously.

They spent the next half hour listening to Georgiana describe her cousin Anne and the difficulties with her health. "It is unlikely that she will be able to bear a child," Georgiana said in a hushed voice, "So she will need to marry someone who already has a babe that can inherit Rosings. Otherwise, it reverts back to the deBourgh line."

Lizzy made to inquire further, but they were interrupted by the return of Mrs. Bennet, who immediately monopolized the conversation with an account of all the gossip from Meryton. These tales no longer involved Jane, much to Lizzy's relief.

At length, the time came for Georgiana to depart. She made Kitty promise to call on her the next day. Lizzy had a prior commitment to spend time with Charlotte, but she vowed to call another time. The visit ended with each girl satisfied with the bond of friendship that was forming between them.

Chapter 19

The next morning, Kitty awoke early to prepare for her visit to Netherfield. While Kitty breakfasted, Lizzy returned from her morning rambles.

"You are awake early this morning, Kitty," Lizzy said in surprise. "Are you feeling well?'

"Oh yes," Kitty assured her. "I simply am somewhat nervous about my visit to Netherfield."

"Do you think Georgiana will eat you?" Lizzy teased, helping herself to a slice of toast with strawberry preserves.

Kitty laughed, "No, but Miss Bingley might!"

The two shared a smile, then Kitty elaborated, "Within our circle of four and twenty families, we are known and respected. However, outside of our circle of acquaintances, we are naught but poor country misses, with little but our charms to recommend us. I would not wish to appear at disadvantage to our new acquaintances."

Lizzy gave Kitty a comforting smile and said, "Kitty, wherever you are known, you will be respected for your behavior and manners. You have nothing for which to be embarrassed or ashamed."

"I simply do not want to make a fool of myself. What if I spill the tea or am asked what accomplishments I have developed?"

"With the tea, you simply laugh at yourself," Lizzy told her firmly. "No one is perfect, and I daresay Miss Bingley has spilled tea herself on occasion. In regard to relating your accomplishments, you may assure them of your excellent proficiency in indulging dull acquaintances throughout the entirety of an assembly without betraying to

214

such persons any hint that you have actually fallen asleep, or some other such jest."

"I have not your confidence, nor your wit, to turn my failings into strengths," Kitty said ruefully.

"Confidence takes practice, Kitty," Lizzy responded. "The queer thing about confidence is that you need only pretend that you are confident to appear so. Conversely, the more you worry, the less confidence you will feel. Do not borrow trouble; if you fret over the possibility of spilling your tea, your nerves will cause it to happen. Or worse yet, you will lose control of your tongue and turn into Mamma."

Kitty burst into laughter. "Lizzy, that is unkind!" she chastised.

Lizzy had the grace to look embarrassed, but she pressed on. "Kitty, you are a wonderful young woman with much to offer by way of friendship. Do not allow anyone to make you feel otherwise."

Lizzy gave her sister a hug, then added, "I believe the carriage is waiting for you outside. You had best hurry."

Kitty gave a squeak and darted from the room. Lizzy giggled, then walked leisurely to the parlor to wait for Charlotte. She had just settled onto a chaise lounge when the door opened, and a maid announced Charlotte's presence.

Charlotte crossed the room and sat down next to Lizzy. "Oh Lizzy," she cried in excitement, "I have the most wonderful news!"

"What is it?" Lizzy asked, suspecting she could already guess the answer.

"Mr. Jones has asked me to marry him! And I accepted him! I am engaged!"

"Congratulations, Charlotte!" Lizzy exclaimed, "I am so happy for you!"

"Thank you, Lizzy," Charlotte said graciously. "He asked me just last night!" Her eyes misted joyfully at the treasured memory. "He had come to dine at Lucas Lodge, along with his daughter. After we finished eating, I took her to the nursery to spend some time with my younger siblings. Before I could rejoin the group, he sought me out. He said he had wanted to wait for a more opportune moment, but when he saw how gently I treated his daughter, he could not delay another minute."

Lizzy's smile widened as Charlotte continued to recount the scene. *It sounds as if he really is a good man*, Lizzy thought privately. *I am so happy for her; she is marrying for more than just a comfortable home, which she once believed was the best she could hope to derive from a marriage.*

"When will you be married?" Lizzy asked, ringing for tea. When the maid immediately stepped into the room bearing a tray with the beverage, Lizzy requested that she bring some cake as well, in celebration.

"They will begin calling the banns this Sunday," Charlotte answered. "The wedding will be in a month."

The two friends continued discussing wedding details—only pausing briefly when the cake arrived—until Mrs. Bennet joined them. Upon hearing the news, Mrs. Bennet graciously bid her congratulations.

"I will speak with your mother and set a date for a special dinner to be held in your honor within the next fortnight," Mrs. Bennet informed Charlotte.

Charlotte, who at her age had witnessed many such dinners dedicated to her friends, was overcome with gratitude. "Thank you, Mrs. Bennet," she said with heartfelt appreciation. "I would be delighted to be the recipient of such a kindness."

The women continued their talk of wedding plans until a knock sounded at the parlor door. Hill entered, carrying a note. "This just arrived from Netherfield, ma'am," she said, handing it to Mrs. Bennet.

"I wonder what it could be about," Lizzy said worriedly. "Kitty should already be at Netherfield visiting Georgiana. I hope nothing has occurred to prevent her safe arrival."

DEAR MAMMA,

I find myself somewhat unwell this afternoon. Upon arriving at Netherfield, I slipped on the wet staircase where a maid had spilled a bucket of soapy water. My kind friends will not hear of my coming home until Mr. Jones has examined my ankle, which is somewhat swollen. Excepting the acute pain I feel whenever it is moved, there is not much the matter with me.

Yours, etc.

"What great fortune!" exclaimed Mrs. Bennet gleefully.

Lizzy gaped openly at her mother. "How can a swollen ankle be called great fortune, Mamma?"

"Why, if her ankle is indeed injured, there can be no possibility of her returning to Longbourn for at least a fortnight, or else risk damaging it further. She will have to remain at Netherfield, where she will have the company of two marriageable men!"

Irked by her mother's lack of concern, Lizzy determined to go to Kitty as soon as possible to ascertain her true condition for herself. Lizzy could not help but feel sorry for poor Kitty, who had been quite nervous about spilling tea on herself. *Instead, it was she who was spilled,* she thought wryly.

Lizzy sought her father and found him in his bookroom, reading from the latest addition to his library.

"Ah, Lizzy," he said as she entered, "I just read the most amusing anecdote! Here, allow me to read it to you."

Knowing well her father's penchant for surliness if he were not allowed to share a witticism with her, Lizzy sat impatiently and listened to him read aloud. After laughing at all the appropriate moments, she was finally able to ask her question. "Papa, may I have the carriage? Kitty has injured her ankle at Netherfield, and I would like to go to discover her situation."

Mr. Bennet's eyebrows raised at the news of his youngest-but-one's clumsiness. "I daresay she should have eaten the cake at the tea before she made a cake of the visit herself!" Lizzy did not join in his laughter.

Once his guffaws subsided, he shook his head and said, "I'm

afraid, Lizzy, that I have already put the horses to work in the fields. They will not be available until tomorrow. You will have to delay to your visit to your clumsy sister. I daresay she will be cared for well enough."

Lizzy struggled to hide her frustration. "I understand, Papa. I am concerned more for her embarrassment than her ankle. I shall walk to Netherfield; it is but three miles."

Mr. Bennet shook his head, unusually stern. "I'm sorry, Lizzy, but it is too late in the day for you to make the walk. I know you to be an excellent walker, but there would not be enough time to reach Netherfield, even for you."

Lizzy sighed but acquiesced.

Dinner was unusually quiet that night. Mr. Collins and Mrs. Bennet carried the majority of the conversation, which revolved around the visits they had separately paid that day and the calls they still needed to make. This bland exchange was tempered only by Mary's occasional comments, which managed to insinuate some sense into the discussion.

Mr. Bennet offered the occasional sardonic comment, but since Lizzy was preoccupied with thoughts of Kitty and her assumed distress, his remarks did not elicit the usual response. Consequently, he finished his dinner with alacrity and retired to his bookroom before the end of the meal.

Lizzy passed a restless night, spending more time wishing for sleep than participating in the act of sleep itself. She arose with the dawn and took a vigorous walk around her favorite paths, hoping to pass the time until it was late enough in the morning to be considered acceptable to make a call.

Upon returning to the house, she was met with a note from Netherfield. Fear filled her as she spied feminine handwriting that was not Kitty's. She tore open the letter immediately and read the missive from Georgiana.

LIZZY—

Do not be alarmed upon receiving this letter. I write to invite you to call upon Netherfield to see how Kitty is faring. She is currently asleep; Mr. Jones came last night to look at her ankle, which was swollen. He has determined that it is a bad sprain, and she is not to be moved for two weeks. He gave her some laudanum for the pain, which is why I have taken the initiative to write. You are welcome to reside at Longbourn to care for her, as she is somewhat distressed by the situation. Please bring clothing and other necessities for her and for yourself, should you choose to stay. I anticipate your call as early as you desire, as I am sure you are quite anxious to see your sister.

Yours,

Georgiana

Lizzy sighed with relief to know that the news was no worse than she had feared. Grateful for Georgiana's kindness and friendship, she immediately went upstairs to pack two valises, one for herself and the other for Kitty. She informed her father of the situation and was unsurprised to hear him grumble that with her gone, he would not hear two words of sense spoken together for the entire fortnight. She kissed his cheek, then boarded the carriage to go to her sister.

As the carriage turned to enter the drive to Netherfield, the carriage lurched to a sudden halt. Lizzy could hear the coachman urging the horses forward with no success. The carriage shuddered a few times, and Lizzy braced herself to keep from falling off the bench. Finally, all movement ceased, and a knock sounded at the carriage door.

"My apologies, Miss Lizzy, but the rain puddles concealed a rather deep rut, and I am afraid the carriage is stuck," the coachman informed her.

"No matter!" she replied cheerfully, "I can easily walk up the drive."

"Allow me to carry the valises, Miss Bennet," he offered, reaching for the luggage.

"Oh, no need!" she said, waving him off, "You have more important matters to attend to at present, and I imagine Kitty would like her own belongings as soon as possible."

"Yes, miss."

Lizzy descended from the carriage, holding a valise in each hand. She rounded the corners of the winding drive, enjoying the gradual revelation of the Netherfield house. As she approached the lawn, she spied a gentleman come from the other side of the building.

"Miss Bennet!" he exclaimed. As she drew nearer, she was slightly dismayed to discover that it was Mr. Darcy.

"Hello, Mr. Darcy," she said, attempting a shallow curtsy while holding the valises. Struggling not to fall over, she continued, "I am come to inquire after my sister."

"On foot?" he asked incredulously. *And disdainfully,* she thought.

She turned around to see that her carriage was not able to be seen from this part of the house. With a sly smile, she turned around and said archly, "As you see."

Mr. Darcy continued to stare, dumbfounded, and Lizzy grew uncomfortable under his scrutiny. "Would you be so good as to take me to her?"

The gentleman blinked twice. "Of course," he said hastily, "If you would follow me."

He walked briskly to the front of the house, and she struggled to keep pace with his long stride while also managing the additional weight and bulk of the valises. *He might have offered to carry one! What a condescending, supercilious man! How can he be related to Georgiana?* Lizzy stewed silently.

When they reached the front door, it was opened by the butler. Noticing Lizzy's burden, he directed two passing footmen to collect the bags from her. She grateful handed them over, marking Darcy's obviously affected expression of surprise, as though he were seeing the bags for the first time. *That man has no great sense of courtesy,* she thought. *And he is a poor actor besides. Why feign such a reaction? Merely to avoid helping me with the valises?* She silently added "lazy" to her mental record of his flaws.

Georgiana fairly skipped down the hall. "The housekeeper sent a maid to inform me you had arrived, Lizzy," she said. "I wanted to greet you myself before you ensconced yourself in Kitty's rooms to tend to her. I do plan to visit with you both this afternoon, after she has had a rest."

Lizzy thanked Georgiana with sincere appreciation and followed the maid up the stairs. Before she was out of earshot, she heard Mr. Darcy say with surprise, "You use one another's Christian names?"

Insufferable man! she huffed quietly before fixing a smile on her face for the maid who had led her to Kitty's room.

As Lizzy settled in next to her sleeping sister, Georgiana explained to her brother that she had indeed given the Misses Bennet permission to use her given name, and she had received the same permission from them.

"I had not realized you had become so close," he said, "Nor that you had invited them for a house party," he added with a wry smile.

"A house party? Honestly, Brother, you can be quite vexing!" she said in mock consternation.

"How does Miss Catherine fair?" he asked.

Georgiana's expression dimmed. "Her poor ankle looks to be very painful. I am relieved Mr. Jones was able to arrive so quickly and provide laudanum for her relief."

"Was the laudanum truly necessary?" he asked.

She nodded. "I know how Fitzwilliam feels about laudanum and its addictive properties. Indeed, Kitty herself was loathe to take it, but she would not have been able to sleep otherwise. She was barely able to bear the pain when fully awake. I have never before seen an ankle so bruised, nor so swollen."

Darcy opened his mouth to respond, but a nauseatingly saccharine voice preempted his remark. "Was that Miss Eliza I saw coming up the stairs? What on earth is she doing, calling so early in the day?"

Miss Bingley descended, wearing a dress that was more suited for dinner than for morning. Her sister, Mrs. Hurst, followed closely behind. Without waiting for a response, she continued, "I daresay she must have tramped across the most repugnant route to be found in the entire countryside! Did you see her hem, Louisa? Six inches deep in mud!"

"It proves an affection for her sister that is very pleasing," Georgiana said as she quirked an eyebrow at her husband's sister. "I wish I had enjoyed the devotion of such a sister. Alas, I have only a brother on whom I can depend."

Miss Bingley and Mrs. Hurst rushed to assure Georgiana of their affection and faithfulness. Darcy, attempting to rescue his sister, interrupted. "Georgiana, speaking of siblings, there is something that I must discuss with you privately. If you will please excuse us, ladies."

He bowed to the sisters and took Georgiana's arm to steer her out of the entry before any of the three ladies could protest.

"William!" Georgiana scolded, though her indignation was marred by her laughter.

"It is the truth," he defended, "You know that I abhor deceit of any sort."

"Very well," she capitulated, "What is it you wish to discuss?"

"How long will the Bennet sisters remain with us?" he asked.

"Mr. Jones said that Kitty cannot be moved for two weeks. After a few days, she may be carried down to join us for visits, but the jostling of a carriage would prove to be too damaging sooner," she answered.

"Mrs. Bennet will be in raptures," he said in an annoyed tone. At her sharp glance, he sighed. "My apologies. I simply did not expect Miss Elizabeth's arrival and acted quite the fool. I am only vexed with myself."

Georgiana looked at him curiously and asked, "What happened?"

I saw her eyes, Darcy thought. He cleared his throat, then answered, "I was returning from the stables after checking on my horse. When I came around the house, she was standing there, without a carriage, as though she had materialized in that exact spot just moments before. It took me so off guard that I simply stared at her. It was only after I led her to the house that I noticed she carried valises. It was most ungentlemanly of me, which is the opposite impression I want to give."

Georgiana laughed softly. "How could you not have noticed the valises?" she gibed.

He looked away, sheepish. *I was distracted by other parts of her. He shook his head. Where are these thoughts coming from? We have hardly spoken two words together! I know nothing about her; only the fire burning in her eyes when she saw me at the Assembly.*

"She must think me the worst of men," he said miserably.

"Why does it matter?" she asked him.

"I do not know. I simply know that I cannot bear that she is alive in the world and thinking ill of me."

Georgiana was struck by an epiphany. *Could he be attracted to her?* She smiled to herself. *The next two weeks will prove to be very interesting, indeed!*

"William, you need not worry," she assured him. "Lizzy has a very forgiving nature. I am certain if you apologize, she will not hold your behavior against you."

If anything, Darcy looked even more uncomfortable. "Apologies do not come naturally to me," he admitted. *I would only make a greater fool of myself.*

Georgiana rolled her eyes at him. "Apologies do not come very easily to *anyone*, Brother, unless they take the trouble to *practice*."

"I will do my best," Darcy promised miserably. *After all, she cannot hate me any more than she already does, given my hand in Bingley's previous ill treatment of her sister. And my sister is correct: there is much for which I must apologize.*

Brother and sister remained lost in thought for several moments, the silence punctuated only by the sounds of footsteps outside the door and the voice of Miss Bingley asking a nearby servant if he had noticed where her "dear sister Georgiana" had gone.

Georgiana sighed, then pinned her brother with another substantial look. "William, you have two weeks to correct things with the

Bennets. I suggest you use them wisely."

With that final word, she left him to his thoughts.

Chapter 20

Lizzy heard Kitty begin to stir and put her book down without marking her place. It was a treasured favorite of hers, and she had nearly completed it for the fifth time as Kitty slept the day away.

Kitty looked at her sister groggily, "You lied to me," she whispered hoarsely.

"I beg your pardon?" Lizzy responded in confusion. She offered Kitty a sip of water.

Kitty cleared her throat. "You lied to me," she repeated in a more normal voice. "You said if I had positive thoughts, I would not spill the tea. That does not appear to be the case."

Lizzy burst into unladylike laughter, the tension easing from her body. "If you are able to tease, then perhaps you are not truly injured and simply wish to remain at Netherfield to catch a husband. Mayhap you share more characteristics with our mother and Lydia than previously revealed?"

Kitty's eyes widened in horror, and Lizzy laughed even harder. The sisterly moment was interrupted a moment later by a knock at the door.

"Come in," Lizzy called.

Georgiana entered the room. "I thought I heard laughter," she said, looking unsure, "and I wanted to join the fun."

Lizzy smiled at the younger girl and gestured for her to take Lizzy's place in the chair. Moving to the bed, Lizzy said, "A friend is always welcome when one is confined to their bed."

"What are you reading?" Georgiana asked, spying Lizzy's book on the small table near the chair.

"Gulliver's Travels," Lizzy replied. "Have you read it?"

Georgiana blushed, "I am afraid I prefer a good romance novel to a book that will cause me to think too deeply."

Kitty smiled at her. "My sister Lydia and I feel the same way. Lizzy, however, prefers to read books and novels that will broaden her mind."

The three young women spent the next hour comparing the books they had read, as well as their feelings about them. Lizzy quickly saw that Georgiana was sincere in her statement that she preferred to read simple novels, many of which Lizzy had never read. As Kitty and Georgiana became engrossed in their discussion over Mrs. Radcliffe's latest novel, Lizzy's mind wandered to her copy of *Gulliver's Travels*.

"Georgiana," Lizzy said when there was a pause in the younger girls' conversation, "Might I visit your library? I was unable to bring many books with me, and I fear that I have already exhausted my supply."

Georgiana laughed. "You may borrow any book you choose," she said.

~∞~∞~∞~

The next day found Lizzy perusing the library bookshelves after her early morning walk. She had dined with Kitty the previous night and had yet to encounter any of the Netherfield party that day. Finding the selection of books to be rather sparse, she finally settled on one that she judged to have the potential to be at least somewhat interesting. She settled herself onto an overstuffed chair to read the first few pages.

After a few minutes, the library door opened, and Mr. Darcy entered the room. *What could he be doing in here?* Lizzy thought in frustration at this intrusion on her solitude.

Darcy was equally surprised to find Lizzy in the library. He was even more surprised at the book she had apparently chosen to read:

a series of discourses on the importance of mathematics. It was a volume he had purchased a few weeks prior and had read on their journey to Netherfield.

Could she have known that I visit the library in the mornings after my ride? He mused suspiciously. *That would explain her choice in reading material.* He remembered his recent determination to have more faith in the virtues of the single women he encountered, and he cut off that avenue of conjecture. *Remember, you owe her an apology.*

Unable to find the words, however, he picked up a book and sat on another chair, determined to give the impression he was reading so he could consider the correct words with which to voice his regrets. Unfortunately, he had chosen a novel by Mrs. Radcliffe. *Georgiana*, he groaned internally, *If I am fortunate, Miss Bennet will not take notice of my choice.*

Fortune was not with him, however.

Mr. Darcy reads romance novels? Lizzy thought in surprise. *I had not expected it of him. Perhaps he reads all the books his sister desires before allowing her to read them. Could he really censor her so?*

Their private thoughts continued in this manner for a quarter of an hour, until Miss Bingley entered the room. She affected surprised at encountering Mr. Darcy, but her astonishment turned genuine upon spying Lizzy also in the room.

She crossed the room and ran her fingers along the shelves. "I am ashamed my brother has such a small library!" she cried in feigned dismay. "There is nothing more enjoyable than passing an afternoon by reading."

She chose a book and sat on a settee near the fireplace. However, Miss Bingley's attention was rather more engaged in watching Mr. Darcy's progress through his book than in reading her own; and she was perpetually making some enquiry or looking at his page. She could not win him, to any conversation, however; he merely answered her question, and read on.

At length, quite exhausted by the attempt to be amused with her own book, which she had only chosen because it was the second volume of his, she gave a great yawn, tossed aside her book, and cast her eyes round the room in quest for some amusement.

She got up and walked about the room. Her figure was elegant, and she walked well; but Darcy—at whom it was all aimed— inflexibly studious. In desperation, she resolved on one effort more, and, turning to Elizabeth, said:

"Miss Eliza Bennet, let me persuade you to join me and take a turn about the room. I assure you it is very refreshing after sitting so long in one attitude."

Elizabeth was surprised but agreed to the request immediately. Miss Bingley succeeded no less in the real object of her civility; Mr. Darcy looked up. He was as much awake to the novelty of attention in that quarter as Elizabeth herself could be, and unconsciously closed his book. He was directly invited to join their party, but he declined it, observing that he could imagine but two motives for their choosing to walk up and down the room together, either of which his joining them would disrupt.

"What could he mean?" Miss Bingley mused aloud to her walking companion. She declared herself dying to know what could be his meaning, and asked Elizabeth whether she could at all understand him.

"Not at all," was her answer; "but depend upon it, he means to be severe on us, and our surest way of disappointing him will be to ask nothing about it."

Miss Bingley, however, was incapable of disappointing Mr. Darcy in anything, and persevered therefore in requiring an explanation of his two motives.

"I have not the smallest objection to explaining them," said he, as soon as she allowed him to speak. "You either choose this method of passing the morning because you are in each other's confidence, and have secret affairs to discuss, or because you are conscious that your figures appear to the greatest advantage in walking; if the first, I would be completely in your way, and if the second, I can admire you much better as I sit by the fire."

"Oh! Shocking!" cried Miss Bingley. "I never heard anything so abominable. How shall we punish him for such a speech?"

"Nothing so easy, if you have but the inclination," said Elizabeth. "We can all plague and punish one another. Tease him—laugh at him. Intimate as you are, you must know how it is to be done."

"But upon my honor, I do not. I do assure you that my intimacy has not yet taught me that. Tease calmness of manner and presence of mind?! No, no; I feel he may defy us there. And as to laughter, we will not expose ourselves, if you please, by attempting to laugh without a subject. Mr. Darcy may hug himself."

"Mr. Darcy is not to be laughed at!" cried Elizabeth. Dismayed, "That is an uncommon advantage for him to possess—and uncommon I hope it will continue, for it would be a great loss to me to have many such acquaintances. I dearly love a laugh."

"Miss Bingley," said he, "has given me more credit than is due. The wisest and the best of men—nay, the wisest and best of their actions—may be rendered ridiculous by a person whose first object in life is a joke."

"Certainly," replied Elizabeth. "There are such people, but I hope I am not one of them. I hope I never ridicule what is wise and good. Follies and nonsense, whims and inconsistencies, do divert me—I own—and I laugh at them whenever I can. But these, I suppose, are precisely what you are without."

"Perhaps that is not possible for anyone. But it has been the study of my life to avoid those weaknesses which often expose a strong understanding to ridicule."

"Such as vanity and pride."

"Yes, vanity is a weakness indeed. But pride—where there is a real superiority of mind, pride will be always under good regulation."

Elizabeth turned away to hide a smile. *What conceit!* she thought, satisfied to find Mr. Darcy exactly as she imagined him.

"Your examination of Mr. Darcy is over, I presume," said Miss Bingley, "and pray what is the result?"

"I am perfectly convinced by it that Mr. Darcy has no defect. He owns it himself without disguise."

"No," said Darcy, "I have made no such pretension. I have faults enough, but they are not, I hope, of understanding. My temper I dare not vouch for. It is, I believe, too little yielding—certainly too little for the convenience of the world. I cannot forget the follies and vices of others so soon as I ought, nor their offenses against myself. My feelings are not puffed about with every attempt to move them. My temper would perhaps be called resentful. My good opinion—once lost—is lost forever."

"That is a failing indeed!" cried Elizabeth. "Implacable resentment is a shade in a character. But you have chosen your fault well. I really cannot laugh at it. You are safe from me."

"There is, I believe, in every disposition a tendency to some particular evil—a natural defect, which not even the best education can overcome."

"And your defect is to hate everybody."

"And yours," he replied with a smile, "is willfully to misunderstand them."

Miss Bingley frowned throughout the conversation. "Come!" she exclaimed, interrupting their banter, "it is almost time to go down to dinner."

Lizzy looked at the clock, startled by the time. "My goodness!" she cried in dismay, standing hastily, "I have quite forgotten Kitty and Georgiana!" Picking up her book, she quickly curtsied and hurried from the room.

"Elizabeth Bennet," said Miss Bingley, when the door was closed on her, "is one of those young ladies who seek to recommend themselves to the other sex by undervaluing their own; and with many men, I dare say, it succeeds. But, in my opinion, it is a paltry device, a very mean art."

"Undoubtedly," replied Darcy, "there is a meanness in all the arts which ladies sometimes condescend to employ for captivation. Whatever bears affinity to cunning is despicable."

Miss Bingley was not so entirely satisfied with this reply as to continue the subject. There was no need, however, as Mr. Darcy immediately excused himself to dress for dinner. He was quite put-out that an entire day had passed without the opportunity to tender his apologies to Miss Bennet. *No matter*, he reassured himself, *as she will be here for a fortnight complete*.

The opportunity to offer those regrets was repeatedly delayed, however. With Kitty's ankle too painful to be moved, Lizzy took advantage of the opportunity to avoid the Bingley sisters and the Netherfield men by remaining in Kitty's rooms. Georgiana was a frequent visitor, and she and Kitty had struck up a friendship rooted in gaiety and frivolities. The two were frequently found giggling together over romance novels, gossip, and ribbons. At first, Lizzy was surprised at their seeming immaturity, but she reminded herself of their young ages, despite Georgiana's marital status.

After a week of little exercise, however, Lizzy was driven into the garden early one morning to escape her self-imposed confinement. With another week at Netherfield looming before her, she desperately yearned to escape outdoors.

Lizzy walked quickly down the path and towards the forested area at the back of the lawn. Once out of sight of the house, she broke into a run. It had been several years since she had moved quicker than a brisk gait, but it had also been years since she had gone so long without exercise.

Once the exertion had cleared the last of the agitation from her body, she slowed to a walk, allowing her breathing to slow along with her pace. When she broke through the trees into a clearing near a brook, however, she stopped abruptly. "Mr. Darcy!" she exclaimed.

Darcy turned, shocked at the intrusion. He had been out for his morning ride. Frustrating at his failure to contrive an opportunity to apologize to Miss Bennet had spurred him to run his mount faster and farther than usual. Not one to mistreat a horse, Darcy had stopped at the brook, where he dismounted to allow the animal time to recover and get a drink of water.

For the first time, Darcy was struck by Miss Bennet's singular beauty. *She must be part fae*, he thought incredulously as he took in her heightened color, loose curls, and damp gown. He stared, fascinated by her dangerously alluring state of dishevelment.

Several seconds passed in silence. Disconcerted by his unwavering gaze, Lizzy shifted uneasily and felt a few wisps of hair fall from her pinned coiffure. *What must he think of me?* she thought in consternation as she considered how she must look, wild from her run.

As she began to lift her hands to hair, she suddenly stopped. She fought the urge to fidget and repair the damage to her appearance. *I will not allow his disapproval to intimidate me*, she decided. She straightened her shoulders and lifted her chin.

"You are by yourself?" Darcy blurted out.

"As you see," she said coolly, echoing her words from her arrival at Netherfield.

Darcy mentally cursed himself for his foolishness. "Allow me to escort you back to Netherfield," he offered, reaching for his horse's reins.

Lizzy made to protest but realized she would need to return now anyway. Kitty would soon leave her bedroom for the parlor for the first time since she had come to Netherfield, and Lizzy wished to be present in case the Bingley sisters decided to join them. Lizzy and Kitty had fortunately been able to avoid their company thus far—for the most part.

"Thank you," she responded, and his shoulders relaxed slightly.

The two walked in silence for several minutes, Darcy's horse following docilely behind them, occasionally nipping at tall grass along the path.

Speak, man! Darcy ordered himself furiously. *You have been waiting for a chance to have a private conversation with her. Now that your chance has come, you are silent. Open your mouth!*

"I am sorry," Darcy said abruptly.

Lizzy startled out of her private musings. "I beg your pardon?" she responded blankly.

"I —I am sorry," he stammered, "I owe you—and your family—my apologies."

"Whatever for?" Lizzy asked curiously. *Let us see which action he thinks merits an apology*, she thought, amused.

Darcy took a deep breath, gathering his courage, "For encouraging Bingley to leave your elder sister."

After a few moments of silence, Lizzy asked, "Why did you?"

"At the time, Bingley was only eighteen years of age. He still had a few years of school left. I felt he was too young for such an attachment, and I was unaware until a few weeks ago that he had engaged his honor with a promise to return to her." He took another breath, then continued, "I was also in a foul mood. My father had recently passed, and I had only just exited my mourning. There had been several attempts already at compromise, and I became cynical and jaded. I passed judgment on your sister after only a few hours, which was grievously wrong of me."

Lizzy stopped walking, unsure what to make of this unexpected divergence from the man's typical haughty conduct. Darcy halted his advancement as well and waited nervously as she considered his words.

Finally, she resumed walking and Darcy, leading his horse, followed. Lizzy said slowly, "I admit, my anger toward yourself and Mr. Bingley five years ago was quite fierce. My sister was heartbroken at Mr. Bingley's abandonment. She is of a very sensitive nature. However, with the benefit of hindsight, I can see why you made the recommendation you did. Mr. Bingley did not have the maturity or constancy to be in a serious relationship, and I believe my sister was fortunate to escape an imprudent match."

Darcy opened his mouth to interject, but she held up her hand to stop him. "Your disparagement of my sister was unwarranted. However, I can see why you may have had those feelings, however incorrect. In short, Mr. Darcy, you have my forgiveness."

A weight lifted off Darcy's shoulders. "Thank you, Miss Bennet," he said feelingly.

The two continued in silence, but this time, the silence was peaceful as opposed to awkward. Upon reaching the house, he bowed, and she responded with a curtsy.

"Thank you for walking with me," he began.

"Oh Mr. Darcy!" a shrill voice exclaimed as they entered the front door. "We have been wondering where you disappeared to!"

Miss Bingley came bustling down the corridor. Upon seeing Lizzy, she stopped and looked between the two of them curiously.

"Miss Eliza, I believe your sister is looking for you," the lady said.

"Thank you, Miss Bingley," Lizzy said, meeting Darcy's eyes with a twinkle in her own. When she ascended the stairs, Miss Bingley turned towards Darcy.

"I can guess the subject of your reverie," she said.

"I should imagine not," he returned.

"You are considering how insupportable it would be to pass many mornings in this manner—in such society; and indeed, I am quite of your opinion. I was never more annoyed! The insipidity, and yet the noise—the nothingness, and yet the self-importance of all those people! What would I give to hear your strictures on them!"

"Your conjecture is totally wrong, I assure you. My mind was more agreeably engaged. I have been meditating on the very great pleasure which a pair of fine eyes in the face of a pretty woman can bestow."

Miss Bingley immediately fixed her eyes on his face and queried as to what lady had the credit of inspiring such reflections.

Mr. Darcy replied succinctly, "Miss Elizabeth Bennet." He then bowed and ascended the same stairs Miss Bennet had climbed moments prior, leaving an injured Miss Bingley behind him.

Chapter 21

Kitty was ecstatic about finally leaving her bedchamber, having been confined for an entire week. Although she had enjoyed the company of Georgiana and Lizzy, she had grown bored of the same four walls. The day before, under Mr. Jones's guidance, she had been moved to the chair near her bedchamber window without much pain. That success induced Mr. Jones to grant his approval for her to be moved to a room below for some of the day.

"If your ankle begins to increase in swelling or pain, you must immediately elevate it," he cautioned her. "Do not attempt to put any weight on it, and I would recommend using a footstool or settee to keep the joint elevated while downstairs."

Kitty assured him that she would follow all of his edicts. After extricating Lizzy's and Georgiana's promises to take care of Kitty and not allow her to attempt to walk, Mr. Jones left. He promised to call the day after her sojourn below stairs to see how the endeavor affected her ankle.

Amid this furor, Lizzy's distraction over Darcy's apologies—and their subsequent conversation—went unnoticed by Kitty.

"Lizzy, why must you dawdle?" Kitty demanded impatiently as she bounced on the bed.

Lizzy shook her head and smiled at her sister. "Perhaps if you would quit interrupting me, I would be able to prepare more quickly," she teased.

Finally, Lizzy's ablutions were completed, and she rang for a maid to fetch a few manservants to carry Kitty down the stairs. To their surprise, the next knock on the door heralded Georgiana with Colonel Fitzwilliam.

"My cousin has offered to carry Kitty down the stairs," Georgiana informed them. "His time in the military has given him a surety of foot that many manservants do not have, therefore he is more likely to prevent further injury."

Kitty thanked him graciously, and the entire party proceeded down the hallway before descending the stairs. Colonel Fitzwilliam cautiously carried Kitty down each step, taking care to not jostle her ankle. When they at last reached the parlor, they were greeted by a light applause from Bingley, his sisters, and Darcy.

"We are very glad to have you join us, Miss Catherine," Bingley told her. "My dear wife has been eager to enjoy your companionship in another room."

He crossed to Georgiana and kissed her hand lovingly. She blushed and smiled at him, then turned her attention to the newcomers. Miss Bingley and Mrs. Hurst engaged in a whispered conversation on the settee they were sharing, while Mr. Hurst dozed on a sofa. Mr. Darcy sat at the writing desk, and Miss Bingley stood from the settee that she might join him.

"What do you do so secretly, sir?" she asked him coyly.

"It is no secret; I am writing to my cousin," he replied without looking up from the letter.

"Please give the cranky old man my regards," said Colonel Fitzwilliam cheerfully. At Kitty's surprised look, he added, "My elder brother by several years has always been a bit formal."

"This letter is not to the viscount," Darcy responded.

"You are writing to Anne?" Georgiana asked in surprise.

"Yes, to discuss our visit to Rosings in the spring," Mr. Darcy responded.

"Lady Catherine's daughter?" inquired Kitty, much to Lizzy's relief. She was still somewhat discomposed over her *tete-a-tete* with Darcy earlier in the day and did not feel equipped to speak to him with equanimity.

Mr. Darcy looked up from his paper and eyed Kitty, who blushed under his scrutiny. "You are acquainted with my aunt?"

Georgiana laughed and answered for her friend, "Their sister Mary is engaged to Mr. Collins. Do you not remember?" she added when she saw his confusion. "The new rector at the Hunsford parish."

Darcy raised his eyebrows slightly, and Colonel Fitzwilliam chuckled slightly. "He is a difficult man to forget," the colonel remarked. "Hunsford is quite a distance; how did your sister come to meet him?"

"He is the heir to our father's estate," Lizzy answered, finally finding her tongue.

"What a terrible thing an entail is!" cried Miss Bingley, somewhat disdainfully. "Charles, when you purchase your estate, you must not allow it to be entailed."

Darcy shook his head in disagreement. "While entailing an estate away from the female line is a somewhat archaic notion," he said, "An entail does protect an inheritance from being gambled away or sold off by a dissolute or indolent master."

Miss Bingley immediately agreed with his opinion, which caused him to smile slightly.

"Is there an entail on Rosings?" Kitty asked curiously.

"Not entirely," said Colonel Fitzwilliam. "Anne's oldest son will inherit, or if she only has daughters, the first of her daughters who bears a son will. If there are no male descendants in Anne's line, then the estate will devolve to the de Bourgh cousins."

"But Anne is too sickly to bear a child!" exclaimed Georgiana, then blushed as the single females in the group delicately averted their eyes.

"I believe she could adopt a child," Mr. Darcy told her kindly, "Although she must be married for that child to inherit."

"That seems to be an odd sort of way to inherit," Lizzy remarked.

"Sir Lewis's father had some unique notions about birth and education," Colonel Fitzwilliam informed her.

"What sort of place is Rosings?" Kitty inquired, and she and Colonel Fitzwilliam spent the better part of an hour discussing the property.

As the two conversed, Mrs. Hurst listened and Miss Bingley asked Georgiana more about Anne de Bourgh: "Is she very accomplished?"

"It is amazing to me," interjected Bingley, "How young ladies can have patience to be so very accomplished as they all are."

"All young ladies accomplished! My dear Charles, what do you mean?" Miss Bingley declared in astonishment.

"Yes, all of them, I think. They all paint tables, cover screens, and net purses. I scarcely know anyone who cannot do all this, and I am sure I never heard a young lady spoken of for the first time, without being informed that she was very accomplished."

"Your list of the common extent of accomplishments," said Darcy, "has too much truth. The word is applied to many a woman who deserves it no otherwise than by netting a purse or covering a screen. But I am very far from agreeing with you in your estimation of ladies in general. I cannot boast of knowing more than half-a-dozen, in the whole range of my acquaintance, that are really accomplished."

"Nor I, I am sure," said Miss Bingley.

"Then," observed Lizzy, "you must comprehend a great deal in your idea of an accomplished woman."

"Yes, I do comprehend a great deal in it," he responded.

"Oh! Certainly," cried Miss Bingley, "no one can be really esteemed accomplished who does not greatly surpass what is usually met with. A woman must have a thorough knowledge of music, singing, drawing, dancing, and the modern languages, to deserve the word; and besides all this, she must possess a certain something in her air and manner of walking, the tone of her voice, her address and expressions, or the word will be but half-deserved."

"All this she must possess," added Darcy, "and to all this she must yet add something more substantial, in the improvement of her mind by extensive reading," and his eyes flicked towards the book Lizzy held in her lap.

Lizzy laughingly said, "I am no longer surprised at your knowing only six accomplished women. I rather wonder now at your knowing any."

"Are you so severe upon your own sex as to doubt the possibility of all this?" Mr. Darcy asked with severity, though she thought she spied a twinkle in his eye.

"I never saw such a woman. I never saw such capacity, and taste, and application, and elegance, as you describe united," Lizzy retorted, softening her reply with a smile.

Miss Bingley cried out against the injustice of her implied doubt. "Perhaps not in *your* circle, Miss Eliza," she said condescendingly, "but I assure you, there are many in *our* circle who match that description."

"I see," Lizzy replied with a smile at the contradiction of the lady's words with her previous assertion. "Perhaps you could tell me, Mr. Darcy, which books a truly accomplished woman should be reading?"

This sparked a lively discussion between Lizzy and the gentleman. Lizzy was surprised to discover that they had read many of the same books, and with the same feelings.

Soon growing tired of listening to a conversation in which she could play no part—as she was not a great reader—Miss Bingley attempted to turn the subject. Before she could do so successfully, however, the housekeeper entered with a letter for Georgiana.

Georgiana looked at the envelope, puzzled, and said, "It is from Oakley. I wonder why he could be writing to me."

All eyes were on her, and she blushed slightly at being the focus of so much attention. "Would you mind very much if I read my letter now? I confess I am intrigued; usually he corresponds with my brother or his. I cannot remember the last time he wrote to me directly."

After receiving assurances that no one would take offense, she opened the letter and read it. "Charles," she said, breaking the silence that had fallen she read, "my cousin writes to beg an invitation to join us here at Netherfield in a fortnight. Would that be acceptable?"

Miss Bingley gasped slightly. "Of *course* Charles would be happy to invite a viscount to his estate!"

Georgiana looked uncomfortable at this appropriation of the duties she and Charles held. Mr. Bingley said in an uncharacteristically stern voice, "Georgiana, as *mistress* of this house, you are welcome to invite anyone you desire, especially a family member."

Colonel Fitzwilliam whispered something to Kitty, who burst into giggles. Noticing Georgiana's hurt expression, he repeated in a louder voice: "You may regret that if she decides to invite our aunt, Lady Catherine."

Darcy rolled his eyes and shook his head, and Georgiana smiled in relief. "Thank you, Charles," the young lady said, turning to her husband, "I will write him immediately and extend the invitation."

"Will he be bringing his sons?" asked the Colonel.

"Bring children to a house party?" Miss Bingley interjected incredulously. "Surely someone of his position has sufficient staff to tend to them."

"Certainly, he does," Colonel Fitzwilliam said in a mild tone and with a steely gaze, "but he prefers to keep his children with him, no matter where he travels."

"He is a devoted father, then," Kitty said appreciatively.

"As was our mother," said the colonel, smiling fondly at Kitty.

"My aunt was all that is good and kind," added Darcy, "and she ensured her children were always with her, no matter where she took up residence."

Colonel Fitzwilliam again whispered to Kitty, who nodded solemnly. She saw Lizzy's discerning gaze upon her and the colonel, and she gave her elder sister an innocent smile.

Kitty and I will need to have a conversation this evening, Lizzy thought with some concern. She looked around the room and saw Darcy looking at Kitty and Colonel as well, his brow furrowed. She bristled at the possibility that he might again be taking issue with one of her sisters bonding with a man in his circle. Sensing her eyes on him, he turned his gaze toward her. Their eyes locked and held for several moments before Miss Bingley's shrill voice washed over them. Bingley's sister was at that moment lecturing Georgiana as to the proper preparations for hosting a viscount.

"Thank you, Caroline," Bingley interrupted firmly, "but as my wife is the granddaughter of an earl, I trust she was raised with an education that included how to be mistress of a house party that includes members of the Peerage."

"Indeed," Darcy added, "I spared no expense on her education. Though she may have lowered in status by marrying Bingley—no offense, my friend—she is quite capable of hosting her cousin, having been much in his company since she was a child."

Georgiana's countenance, which had dimmed under Miss Bingley's onslaught of advice, brightened, and she bestowed a heartfelt smile on her husband for his unanticipated defense. In the past, he had often allowed her to handle his sisters. *I think I will enjoy this aspect of courting*, she thought.

Miss Bingley's face reddened, and she began to whisper furiously to her sister, not stopping her quiet diatribe until the party was called to dress for dinner.

~∞~∞~∞~

The next few days at Netherfield followed a similar pattern. Lizzy would awaken early in the morning and go for a walk. She would always encounter Mr. Darcy on some path, and the two would converse as he escorted her for the remainder of her exercise. After refreshing herself, Lizzy would assist Kitty in making preparations to join the party downstairs.

Colonel Fitzwilliam insisted on carrying Kitty down to the parlor each morning, where he gently set her on one chair of a matching set before he took the other. The two would converse privately, but openly. Lizzy attempted to speak with Kitty about these *tete-a-tetes*, but Kitty insisted they were merely speaking about trivialities, such as the Colonel's plans for the regiment when they came to Meryton in a fortnight.

Miss Bingley continuously contrived to gain Mr. Darcy's attentions, with the help of Mrs. Hurst. Mr. Hurst would frequently go hunting, or he would doze on a couch. Lizzy would read or engage in conversation with Mr. Bingley, who was often left without his wife while she made preparations for the viscount's arrival. When Georgiana was present, however, Bingley devoted his entire focus to her amusement and comfort.

The routine was only interrupted on the day that Mrs. Bennet called to check on the wellbeing of her daughter. Had she found Kitty in any apparent danger of her ankle not healing, Mrs. Bennet would have been very miserable; but being satisfied on seeing her that her injury was not alarming, she had no wish of her recovering immediately, as her restoration to health would probably remove her from Netherfield.

She would not listen, therefore, to her daughter's proposal of being carried home; neither did the apothecary, who arrived about the same time, think it at all advisable. "No," declared Mr. Jones, "she still must wait several more days. The jostling of the carriage before all swelling has receded could cause permanent injury."

Georgiana invited the matron to tea in the sitting room. Bingley greeted them with hopes that Mrs. Bennet had not found Kitty worse than she expected.

"Indeed I have, sir," was her answer. "Her ankle is a great deal too swollen to be moved. Mr. Jones says we must not think of moving her. We must trespass a little longer on your kindness."

"Removed!" cried Bingley. "It must not be thought of. My wife, I am sure, will not hear of her removal."

"You may depend upon it, Madam," said Miss Bingley, with cold civility, "that Miss Catherine will receive every possible attention while she remains with us."

"Indeed," Georgiana said with a dark look at Miss Bingley, "as *mistress* of this house, I will do all in my power to keep Miss Catherine comfortable."

Mrs. Bennet was profuse in her acknowledgments.

"I am sure," she added, "if it was not for such good friends, I do not know what would become of her, for she is in a great deal of pain, indeed, and suffers a vast deal, though with the greatest patience in the world, which is always the way with her, for she has, without exception, the sweetest temper I have ever met with. I often tell my other girls they are nothing to her."

"You have a sweet room here, Mr. Bingley," the lady continued without pausing for breath, "and a charming prospect over the gravel walk. I do not know a place in the country that is equal to Netherfield. You will not think of quitting it in a hurry, I hope, though you have but a short lease."

"Whatever I do is done in a hurry," replied he; "and therefore if I should resolve to quit Netherfield, I should probably be off in five minutes. At present, however, I consider myself as quite fixed here."

"That is exactly what I should have supposed of you," said Elizabeth with a smile.

"You begin to comprehend me, do you?" cried he, turning towards her.

"Oh! Yes—I understand you perfectly," she said, winking at Georgiana.

"I wish I might take this for a compliment; but to be so easily seen through I am afraid is pitiful."

"That is as it happens. It does not follow that a deep, intricate character is more or less estimable than such a one as yours."

"Lizzy," cried her mother, "remember where you are, and do not run on in the wild manner that you are suffered to do at home."

"I did not know before," continued Bingley immediately, "that you were a studier of character. It must be an amusing study."

"Yes, but intricate characters are the most amusing. They have at least that advantage," Lizzy responded.

"The country," said Darcy, "can in general supply but a few subjects for such a study. In a country neighborhood you move in a very confined and unvarying society."

Lizzy smiled at his rejoinder, remembering he had said something similar that morning on their walk. "But people themselves alter so much, that there is something new to be observed in them forever."

"Yes, indeed," cried Mrs. Bennet, offended by his manner of mentioning a country neighborhood. "I assure you there is quite as much of that going on in the country as in town."

Everybody was surprised, and Darcy, after looking at her for a moment, turned silently away. Mrs. Bennet, who fancied she had gained a complete victory over him, continued her triumph. Lizzy blushed at Darcy's incivility toward her mother and at her mother's lack of decorum.

"I cannot see that London has any great advantage over the country, for my part, except the shops and public places. The country is a vast deal pleasanter, is it not, Mr. Bingley?"

"When I am in the country," he replied, "I never wish to leave it; and when I am in town it is pretty much the same. They have each their advantages, and I can be equally happy in either."

"Aye—that is because you have the right disposition. But that gentleman," looking at Darcy, "seemed to think the country was nothing at all."

"Indeed, Mamma, you are mistaken," Elizabeth interjected, noting Georgiana's pale face. "You quite mistook Mr. Darcy. He only meant that there was not such a variety of people to be met with in the country as in the town, which you must acknowledge to be true."

"Certainly, my dear, nobody said there were; but as to not meeting with many people in this neighborhood, I believe there are few neighborhoods larger. I know we dine with four-and-twenty families."

Nothing but concern for Elizabeth could enable Bingley to keep his countenance. His sister was less delicate and directed her eyes towards Mr. Darcy with a very expressive smile. Elizabeth, for the sake of saying something that might turn her mother's thoughts, now asked her if Charlotte Lucas had been at Longbourn since her coming away.

"Yes, she called yesterday with her father. What an agreeable man Sir William is, Mr. Bingley, is not he? So much the man of fashion! So genteel and easy! He has always something to say to everybody. That is my idea of good breeding; and those persons who fancy themselves very important, and never open their mouths, quite mistake the matter."

"Did Charlotte's fiancé attend as well?"

"No, she would go home. I fancy she was wanted about the mince-pies. For my part, Mr. Bingley, I always keep servants that can do their own work; my daughters are brought up very differently. But everybody is to judge for themselves, and the Lucases are a very good sort of girls, I assure you. It is a pity they are not handsome! Not that I think Charlotte so very plain—but then she is our particular friend."

"She seems a very pleasant young woman," Georgiana added.

"Oh! dear, yes; but you must own she is very plain. Lady Lucas herself has often said so, and envied me Jane's beauty. I do not like to boast of my own child, but to be sure, Jane—one does not often see anybody better looking. It is what everybody says. I do not trust my own partiality. When she was only fifteen, there was a man here at Netherfield so much in love with her and wanted to make her an offer. He was only a steward, however, and about to move far north. She went to London, though not before he wrote some verses on her, and very pretty they were."

"And so ended his affection," said Elizabeth quickly in an effort to change the subject. "There has been many a one, I fancy, overcome in the same way. I wonder who first discovered the efficacy of poetry in driving away love!"

"I have been used to consider poetry as the food of love," said Darcy.

"Of a fine, stout, healthy love it may. Everything nourishes what is strong already. But if it be only a slight, thin sort of inclination, I am convinced that one good sonnet will starve it entirely away," Lizzy remarked, smilingly winningly at Darcy.

Darcy could only smile in return; and the general pause which ensued made Elizabeth tremble lest her mother should be exposing herself again. She longed to speak but could think of nothing to say; and after a short silence, Mrs. Bennet began repeating her thanks to Mr. Bingley for his kindness to Kitty with an apology for troubling him also with Lizzy.

Mr. Bingley and his wife were both unaffectedly civil in their answers, and Mr. Bingley forced his younger sister to be civil also and say what the occasion required. She performed her part indeed without much graciousness, but Mrs. Bennet was satisfied, and soon afterwards ordered her carriage.

Lizzy breathed a sigh of relief at her mother's departure, and the household resumed what had become its accustomed routine before Mrs. Bennet's intrusion.

So the days passed until Mr. Jones arrived and deemed Kitty well enough to return to Longbourn. It was determined that she would leave the next morning. The night before their departure passed uneventfully, and soon the entire party of Netherfield bid farewell to their guests.

As the carriage drove from sight, Miss Bingley sighed in relief. "What a pleasure it is to have one's house to oneself."

"Really?" Bingley said, intrigued. "Is that a hint that I should set you up with a house in town and a companion?"

"Charles!" she protested as the rest of the group hid their amusement.

"Come," Georgiana said, ushering everyone inside, "we have much to do before Oakley and the militia arrive."

Chapter 22

Jane leaned back against the luxurious velvet that lined the private carriage Oakley had insisted she take to return to Hertfordshire. *There are definitely benefits to marrying into wealth*, she thought privately. This mode of transportation was much preferred to the mail coach with naught but a surly maid and cramped passengers for companionship.

As the carriage approached Longbourn, she thought back on all that occurred over her last few weeks in London. She was being courted, and by a viscount, no less! Her emotions ranged from happiness at the stability, nervousness about telling her mother, and a bit of smug pride at finally returning from a Season and *not* being required to endure her mother's laments over her single state.

The night after Jane accepted Oakley's courtship, she could not sleep. Jane had many concerns: *Will he treat me well? Am I merely a mother figure? Could I grow to love him? Am I prepared to enter a social sphere so above my own?*

Those nerves had granted her a new empathy for her mother. *How Mamma must have suffered all these years with five daughters, a neighborhood with very few single men, an entailed estate, and no heir or money saved.* They truly would have been at the mercy of a man none of them knew until last year.

Fortunately for Jane, her concerns had been eased somewhat in the days following the initiation of the courtship, as her uncle received responses to the inquiries he had made about Oakley. Oakley did not spend time at gambling hells or prostitute dens. The rumors alleged that he gave up his last mistress upon wedding his first wife, being a firm believer that the vows of matrimony were made before God Himself.

If Jane suffered any more reservations after reading those reports, they were swept away by the efforts Lord Oakley made to introduce her to his family. His father had been very reserved, suffering from disappointment over Jane's lack of dowry and social status. Once he was able to observe her beauty and gentle nature himself, however, his stern demeanor eased somewhat.

Oakley's mother, Lady Matlock, had been welcoming and gracious. She had seen firsthand the suffering her son experienced at the hands of his first wife, and she was delighted that he had at last found a match that appeared to be all that was good and kind.

Jane was surprised to discover that Oakley's three sons had come to London with him, as she had anticipated someone of his rank would keep his children in the country. The boys were somewhat shy at first, but Jane's gentle smile and soothing voice quickly brought out their unique and individual personalities.

Even more relieving to Jane was how well Oakley interacted with his children. They were completely at ease with their father, with no signs of fear that so often are present in a child who has been disciplined severely by an adult. He also knew much about their likes and dislikes, and playtime was a clear continuation of a campaign with toy soldiers that they had obviously been waging for quite a while.

A soft smile crossed Jane's face at the memory of Oakley—a viscount and heir to an earldom—crawling about on the floor with his three boys, moving toy soldiers about. The familiar manner and complete ease with which he engaged his children did even more to further his suit with Jane than had his rescue from Mr. Cartwright.

Jane frowned slightly as her thoughts turned to the former steward. He had tried calling twice at Gracechurch Street; both times a burly footman had informed him that Jane was not at home to him. After that, it appeared he had given up and moved on easier prey. Jane hoped that perhaps the circumstances would compel him to think on his behavior and change his ways.

The carriage turned onto the drive to Longbourn, and the change in pavement startled Jane from her thoughts. She looked out the carriage window to see Lizzy, Kitty, and Mary fairly tripping out of the house in their haste to welcome her home. A smile quickly replaced her frown, and she moved to the edge of the bench in anticipation of exiting the carriage to embrace her sisters.

Almost before Jane had completed her descent from the carriage, Lizzy flew into her sister's arms, hugging her tightly. Mary and Kitty soon followed, exclaiming how delighted they were to see their eldest sister and inquiring after her health and her journey. Laughing, Jane said, "Allow me to at least enter the home before you pepper me with questions!"

The three girls joined Jane's laughter and accompanied her into the house. They allowed her respite as they followed her up the stairs into her bedroom.

The moment the door was closed, however, Lizzy whirled to her eldest sister and demanded, "Jane, you have hardly written since you went away! Was our aunt really so ill that you could not take the time to send a proper letter?"

Jane blushed, and Lizzy's eyes widened. "Jane," she gasped, "Should we attribute your neglect of us to a *suitor?*"

Kitty's jaw dropped as Mary's eyes widened. "But you never said a word!" cried Kitty.

Jane's blush deepened. "So much has happened, and I could not contain it all in a letter. I had to tell you in person."

Mary looked suspiciously at Lizzy. "How did you know there was a suitor?" she asked.

Lizzy raised her eyebrows and said, "Did none of you notice how fine the carriage was that brought Jane home? Uncle Gardiner's business is successful, but not enough to afford a chaise and four. The only other likely explanation was that Jane had acquired a suitor of some fortune."

Kitty's mouth fell open once again and Mary turned her gaze to Jane.

"Well, Jane?" Mary demanded in an uncharacteristically impatient tone, "What have you to say?"

"Alright, but you must promise not to tell Mamma until he comes to speak with Papa," Jane said hesitantly.

Her sisters swore themselves to secrecy and Jane half-whispered, "He is a viscount."

Kitty let out a loud squeal, quickly hushed by her sisters.

"I can see Mamma now," Lizzy declared gaily. *"My Jane could not be so beautiful for nothing!"*

"How did you meet him? How did he ask you to court? Is he handsome?" Kitty blurted out.

"You'll never find out unless you mind your tongue and allow her to speak!" Lizzy chided with a broad smile.

The girls fell into giggles, but quickly silenced themselves in order to hear Jane's account. Jane spent the next half hour relating the series of events that led to her encounter with the Viscount and their subsequent meetings. She glossed over the parts about Mr. Cartwright and simply explained that a former suitor would not leave her alone. At Lizzy's sharp glance, she shook her head subtly. She would explain everything in detail later when it was just the two of them.

Finally, their curiosity sated, Lizzy asked, "When shall we meet this paragon of manhood?"

Jane blushed and replied, "He will come in less than a fortnight. He is—coincidentally—cousin to some of the residents at Netherfield and will therefore reside there for the duration of his stay."

Lizzy's eyebrows rose, "Jane, is he the brother of Colonel Fitzwilliam? The heir who has several sons already?"

At Jane's nod, Lizzy continued, "Are you prepared to be a mother as soon as you are a wife?"

Jane nodded. "I have spent much time in thought over the last weeks in an attempt to answer that question for myself. I believe so.

The boys are very well-behaved, and their father has a wonderfully close relationship with them. He takes an active interest in their education, as well as their character."

"Do you love him, Jane?" Lizzy asked, her eyes fixed on her elder sister's face.

Jane hesitated. "Love him? No, I do not believe so. I confess I like him. I greatly esteem him, and I believe that love can and will grow."

"Then why did you accept?" Lizzy cried in disbelief.

"Because it is by no means certain that another offer of marriage will ever be made. No, Lizzy," Jane held up her hand as Lizzy opened her mouth to object. "I am rapidly becoming an old maid. I have no dowry, and I would like to be settled. I am confident in Viscount Oakley's character, and I believe I have a better chance at happiness with him than any other man I have thus far met."

Lizzy was silent for a few minutes, then nodded in acquiescence. "Then I am happy for you, Jane."

"It is only a courtship, Lizzy," Jane pointed out gently. "I am still coming to know him."

Lizzy nodded pensively. The four sisters continued in conversation until they were called down to dinner. After the conclusion of their meal, they spent the remainder of the day in the parlor with their mother and Mr. Collins, who had been spending much of his time with the local rector. Mary had encouraged that relationship, as the man was known throughout Meryton for his kind words of wisdom and gentle style of preaching.

After the girls bade one another good night, Lizzy followed Jane into her bedroom. "Now, Jane," she said firmly, "what have you not told me?"

Jane related the entirety of her encounter with Mr. Cartwright, and Lizzy's face grew increasingly grim as the tale continued. "Fortunately," Jane concluded, "I am well protected."

"I begin to see why you accepted Lord Oakley," Lizzy replied. "When compared to the fickleness of Mr. Bingley and the cruelty of

Mr. Cartwright, it is easy to judge which is the best man."

"I had not considered it that way," Jane said thoughtfully, "but I believe you are correct."

The girls sat silently for a few minutes, then Lizzy mused, "I wonder if Mr. Darcy is acquainted with Mr. Cartwright. After all, they both own estates in Derbyshire."

"Derbyshire is a large county," Jane pointed out.

"And Mr. Darcy is not likely to socialize much with his neighbors!" Lizzy said, laughing. "Mr. Darcy also seems to be a good sort of man; I cannot imagine him in close confidence with a scoundrel."

Jane looked surprised. "I thought you did not like Mr. Darcy?"

"I believe he improves on further acquaintance." Lizzy told Jane of her walks with Mr. Darcy and the apology he had offered for his behavior.

Jane nodded in acceptance. "This certainly does allow a different perspective on Mr. Bingley's abandonment. To be so young, the both of them, struggling to make their way through society. I had not realized how young Mr. Bingley was at that time." Jane was quiet for a moment, then said, "I begin to see that although I enjoyed Mr. Bingley's company very much—especially compared to Mr. Cartwright, whom I had just escaped—I did not know him well at all. Heavens, I did not even know that he had not yet completed his schooling!"

After a few more minutes spent in discussion of the matter, Lizzy said, "Perhaps we had best retire for the night. After all, Lydia comes tomorrow, and we will need to be well-rested to deal with her."

"Oh, Lord," Jane loosed a groan identical to the ones uttered frequently by Kitty.

Laughing, Lizzy returned to her rooms, and the two girls quickly fell asleep.

~∞~∞~∞~

Late the next morning, the four sisters were sitting in the parlor with their mother when Lydia was announced.

"Mrs. Forster," Hill declared as Lydia swept into the room, smartly dressed in the latest fashion.

"My dearest sisters!" Lydia exclaimed, sweeping around the room and embracing each one. "And my dearest Mamma!"

Mary and Lizzy exchanged surprised looks when Lydia included them in this effusive greeting; it was uncommon for Lydia to show so much affection to the two of them. Kitty was accustomed to it, as was Jane, for she was the kindest and more likely to share something that Lydia wanted.

Lydia took her seat and declared, "I say, I have never been so happy to see Longbourn again! And here you are, all the same as when I left! I daresay not much changes when you are unmarried, but there have been a great many changes in my life since I went away with my dear Forster!"

It was not to be supposed that time would give Lydia that embarrassment from which she had been so wholly free at first. Her ease and good spirits increased. She longed to see Mrs. Phillips, the Lucases, and all their other neighbors, and to hear herself called "Mrs. Forster" by each of them. In this, she was encouraged by Mrs. Bennet. The two began to make plans for the calls they would make.

Lydia giggled as she told her mother, "We overtook William Goulding in his curricle, so I was determined he should know I had returned with my husband, and so I let down the side-glass next to him, and took off my glove, and let my hand just rest upon the window frame, so that he might see the ring, and then I bowed and smiled like anything."

Lizzy and Mary again exchanged looks during this exchange; it was clear that Lydia was indeed her same self. *Although that may be for the best,* Lizzy thought privately, *for if she were much altered, I would be concerned as to the nature of the treatment she received from her husband.*

Once Lydia and Mrs. Bennet had finished making the plans for their calls, Lydia turned to her sisters and exclaimed, "Oh, let us walk into Meryton! The entire militia has arrived with us, and there are so many officers! I can introduce you to each one, and I dare say I shall get husbands for you before the winter is over."

"I thank you for my share of the favor," said Elizabeth; "but I do not particularly like your way of getting husbands."

Lydia stared blankly at her sister for a minute, then said, "La, Lizzy, how droll you are!"

Her enthusiasm for introducing her elder sisters to the officers inspired their mother to encourage all the girls to walk to Meryton with their youngest sister. Sighing in resignation, the girls changed their shoes, put on their bonnets, and headed toward Meryton. Lizzy, who had taken slightly more time than the others to prepare for the excursion, caught up to the group in time to hear Lydia say to her eldest sister, "Ah! Jane, I take your place now, and you must go lower, because I am a married woman."

Mary, Lizzy, and Jane walked together, doing their best to ignore Lydia's effusions to Kitty as she recounted everything she had done during their time apart. For all of Kitty's improvements over the years, with Lydia's return, she was as giddy as a child. The two youngest giggled and gossiped all the way into Meryton.

"Denny!" shouted Lydia, waving her arm as they entered the village.

A young man in regimentals turned at the sound of his name. He and his friends, all dressed in red save one, approached the Bennet sisters. "Mrs. Forster," said the one who answered to Denny, bowing in greeting.

"Sisters, these officers are part of my husband's regiment," Lydia said, pointing to each one as she said their names. "Denny, Saunderson, Pratt, Carter, and... Oh, I don't know you..."

Lydia faltered upon pointing at the only member of the group who was not in uniform.

"Ah, allow me to introduce my friend, Mr. Wickham," Denny said. "Wickham has just signed on to join our regiment. We are on our way now to collect his uniform."

Greetings were exchanged all around, and the group fell into easy conversation. The introduction was followed up on Wickham's side by a happy readiness of conversation—a readiness that managed simultaneously to be perfectly correct and unassuming; his appearance was greatly in his favor he had all the best part of beauty, a fine countenance, a good figure, and a very pleasing address.

The whole party were still standing and talking together very agreeably, when the sound of horses drew their notice, and Darcy and Bingley were seen riding down the street. On distinguishing the ladies of the group, the two gentlemen came directly toward them, and began the usual civilities. Bingley was the principal spokesman, and he greeted all of the women warmly, including Jane.

"We were just on our way to town to fetch a few things Mrs. Bingley requires for our guest," Bingley explained.

Mr. Darcy corroborated Mr. Bingley's words with a bow, and had just determined not to fix his eyes on Elizabeth, when they were suddenly arrested by the sight of the Mr. Wickham.

Elizabeth happened to see the countenance of both as the two men looked at one other, and was all astonishment at the effect of the meeting. Both changed color; one looked white, the other red. Mr. Wickham, after a few moments, touched his hat—a salutation which Mr. Darcy only just deigned to return. What could be the meaning of it? It was impossible to imagine; it was impossible not to long to know.

At Mr. Darcy's sudden low hiss upon seeing Wickham, Bingley turned to see what had discomposed his friend. Upon spying Wickham, Bingley's face went red with rage. He gave a curt bow to the ladies, cast another murderous look at Wickham, then rode away with Darcy following close behind.

Lizzy glanced frequently toward Wickham throughout the remainder of the group's stroll, curiosity brimming inside of her. She had never before seen Mr. Bingley upset, not even when a footman had tripped and spilled a plate of scalding soup on his lap at dinner at Netherfield. She wondered at the possible history between the men that could inspire such a reaction.

The officers escorted the young ladies to the door of Mr. Phillip's house, and then made their parting bows. In spite of Lydia's pressing entreaties that they should come in—and even in spite of Mrs. Phillips' throwing up the parlor window and loudly seconding the invitation—the men remained out of doors. They did accept the invitation to a card party the following evening, however.

After an uneventful visit with Mrs. Phillips, the Bennet girls began to walk home. Along the way, Elizabeth related to Jane and Mary what she had seen pass between the three gentlemen; but though Jane would have defended either or both, had they appeared to be in the wrong, she could no more explain such behavior than could her sister.

"Perhaps we shall learn more upon further acquaintance," Mary suggested, and all agreed it was a good idea.

Chapter 23

Once out of sight from Meryton, Bingley urged his horse into a gallop, with Darcy close behind. They road their horses hard all the way to Netherfield. Practically leaping from his horse, Bingley shoved the reins into the hands of a startled groom. He tore up the steps into Netherfield, Darcy right on his heels.

"Fawcett, where is Mrs. Bingley?" Bingley demanded in a harsh voice.

Fawcett struggled to keep his usual imperturbable mien in face of Bingley's aberrant rage. "I believe you will find Mrs. Bingley in her private sitting room," he said, after the moment he required to regain his equanimity.

Bingley and Darcy both rushed up the stairs to Georgiana's room. Without pausing even to knock, they threw the door open.

"Georgiana, pack your things," Darcy barked, "We must leave Netherfield immediately."

Georgiana looked up from her letters in astonishment. "Brother, Charles, what is going on? Is everyone alright?" Her face paled slightly. "Is it Anne?"

"What? Anne? No, Anne is fine," Darcy stammered, thrown by the question. "Everyone is well. It is just that we must leave at once."

"But, why?" Georgiana asked, brows knit in confusion.

Bingley and Darcy looked at one another, silently debating the extent to which they should enlighten her. The debate was cut abruptly short when Georgiana stood, placed her hands on her hips, and firmly stated, "I am a grown, married woman. I believe the mistress of this house is owed an explanation as to why she must abandon her home and friends on a moment's notice."

Darcy's face remained stern, but Bingley's softened. He crossed the room and, taking her by the shoulders, eased his wife back into her chair. He knelt at her feet, grasped her hands, and looked into her eyes as he said gently, "Georgiana, Mr. Wickham is in Meryton."

Whatever Georgiana had been expecting, it was not that. Her eyes widened, her breathing increased in pace, and her face went so pale, Darcy thought she would faint. Her brother glared at her husband, who stared defiantly back. "She deserved to know," Bingley insisted.

Georgiana closed her eyes and drew a few deep breaths. The color returned slightly to her cheeks, and she asked, "What is he doing here?"

"We don't know," Bingley said bluntly. "We were riding into town to fetch the last of the things you needed to prepare for Oakley's arrival, and we saw him in the street, speaking with the Bennets."

"And you just *left* them with him?" Georgiana asked, her voice pitched high.

"They were also in the company of several members of the militia," Darcy explained. "We could not very well cause a scene in the middle of the road."

"No, I suppose not," she murmured.

Darcy opened his mouth to again demand that she begin to pack, but she held up her hand for silence that she might contemplate the repercussions of Wickham's appearance. After several minutes, with both gentlemen shifting impatiently, she said in a quiet voice, "I will not be leaving Netherfield."

"What?" her brother and her husband exclaimed.

"I said, I will not leave. I have done nothing wrong, and I have no need to flee," she repeated firmly. Raising her chin, she continued, "This is *my* home. I am well-protected by you two and my cousins. I will not abandon my friends to deal alone with a scoundrel. Additionally, Oakley is most likely already on his way here, and I will not allow the likes of such a man as Wickham to ruin my felicity."

Bingley looked at her closely. "Are you certain, my dear?" he asked in a gentle voice.

"Georgiana, I strongly urge you to consider—" Darcy began.

"No!" she cried, nearly toppling her husband from his position on the floor near her chair when she shot to her feet, fists clenched tightly at her sides. "I *have* considered this. I have done little over the past year but think about how I would face him were we to encounter one another. I am touched by no feelings for him beyond pity and disdain. I do, however, hold dear the feelings I have developed for my friends and neighbors."

"If you are certain, then I will support you, dearest," Bingley said, standing and lifting a hand to caress her face gently.

Georgiana blushed slightly at this intimacy, and Darcy's mouth fell open slightly. Closing it, he cleared his throat and said, "Well, if this is the course you are determined to take—"

"It is," she assured him.

Darcy nodded and said, "Then I will, of course, remain with you. With Fitzwilliam and Oakley here as well, you will be quite safe."

"Oh, I am not worried about my safety," she said, "but I am worried about the welfare of the Bennet girls. They are such lovely women, and Wickham has great charm."

Both gentlemen nodded in agreement, then Bingley replied, "They are your friends, dearest, and you know them best. What would you suggest we do?"

"Allow me to think on it for a few days," Georgiana said. "They are smart enough girls that a few days will not make a long-term difference. Plus, with Oakley coming, I have much to do."

"Very well," Darcy said. "We will leave you to your preparations, and I will find Fitzwilliam to inform him of the situation. If Wickham was indeed near several men in regimentals, perhaps he will have purchased a commission. If he has, then we have much more power over him to prevent him causing harm."

With that decided, Darcy bowed to Georgiana and left to find their cousin. Bingley lingered a moment longer, placing a kiss on Georgiana's cheek. "I am proud of your courage," he whispered tenderly, then left the room after his friend, leaving Georgiana with the feel of his lips against her cheek that lingered for a long time afterward.

~∞~∞~∞~

At Longbourn the next evening—as no objection was made to the young people's engagement with their aunt—the coach conveyed the four single Bennet girls at a suitable hour to Meryton. The girls had the pleasure of hearing, as they entered the drawing room, that Mr. Wickham had accepted their aunt's invitation, and was then in the house.

The officers of the ——shire were in general a very creditable, gentlemanlike set, and the best of them were of the present party; but Mr. Wickham was as far beyond them all in person, countenance, air, and walk, as they were superior to the broad-faced, stuffy uncle Phillips.

Mr. Wickham was the happy man toward whom almost every female eye was turned, and Lizzy was the happy woman by whom he finally seated himself. The agreeable manner in which he immediately fell into conversation—though it was only on the subject of it being a wet night—made her feel that the commonest, dullest, most threadbare topic might be rendered interesting by the skill of the speaker.

While many of the guests sat down to play at whist, Mr. Wickham took a seat at an open table where Lizzy also sat. He appeared eager to speak with her, and she was very willing to hear him, though what she chiefly wished to hear she could not hope to be told—the history of his acquaintance with Mr. Darcy. She dared not even mention that gentleman. Her curiosity, however, was unexpectedly relieved. Mr. Wickham began the subject himself. He enquired how far Netherfield was from Meryton; and, after receiving her answer, asked in a hesitating

261

manner how long Mr. Darcy had been staying there.

"About a month," said Lizzy; and then, unwilling to let the subject drop, added, "He is a man of very large property in Derbyshire, I understand."

"Yes," replied Mr. Wickham, "his estate there is a noble one. A clear ten thousand per annum. You could not have met with a person more capable of giving you certain information on that head than myself, for I have been connected with his family in a particular manner from my infancy."

Lizzy could not but look surprised.

"You may well be surprised, Miss Bennet, at such an assertion, after seeing, as you probably might, the very cold manner of our meeting yesterday. Are you much acquainted with Mr. Darcy?"

"Not very well acquainted," she replied, hoping he would provide information if she assumed a lack of knowledge. "He appears to be a man of strong convictions, however," she added.

"I have no right to give my opinion," said Wickham, "as to his being agreeable or otherwise. I am not qualified to form one. I have known him too long and too well to be a fair judge. It is impossible for me to be impartial. I wonder," he said, changing the topic slightly, "whether he is likely be much in this country much longer."

"I do not at all know; but I heard nothing of his going away when I was at Netherfield. I hope your plans in favor of the ——shire will not be affected by his being in the neighborhood."

"Oh! No—it is not for me to be driven away by Mr. Darcy. If he wishes to avoid seeing me, he must go. We are not on friendly terms, and it always gives me pain to meet him, but I have no reason for avoiding him but what I might proclaim before all the world, a sense of very great ill-usage, and most painful regrets at his being what he is. His father, Miss Bennet, the late Mr. Darcy, was one of the best men that ever breathed, and the truest friend I ever had; and I can never be in company with this Mr. Darcy without being grieved to the soul by a thousand tender recollections. His behavior to myself has been scandalous; but I verily believe I could forgive him anything and everything, rather than his disappointing the hopes and disgracing the memory of his father."

Lizzy found the interest of the subject increase and listened with all her heart; but the delicacy of it prevented further enquiry.

Mr. Wickham began to speak on more general topics, Meryton, the neighborhood, the society, appearing highly pleased with all that he had yet seen, and speaking of the latter with gentle but very intelligible gallantry.

"It was the prospect of constant society, and good society," he added, "which was my chief inducement to enter the ——shire. I knew it to be a most respectable, agreeable corps, and my friend Denny tempted me further by his account of their present quarters, and the very great attentions and excellent acquaintances Meryton had procured them. Society, I own, is necessary to me. I have been a disappointed man, and my spirits will not bear solitude. I must have employment and society. A military life is not what I was intended for, but circumstances have now made it eligible. The church ought to have been my profession—I was brought up for the church, and I should at this time have been in possession of a most valuable living, had it pleased the gentleman we were speaking of just now."

"Indeed!"

"Yes—the late Mr. Darcy bequeathed me the next presentation of the best living in his gift. He was my godfather, and excessively attached to me. I cannot do justice to his kindness. He meant to provide for me amply, and he thought he had done it; but when the living fell, it was given elsewhere."

"Good heavens!" cried Lizzy; "but how could that be? How could his will be disregarded? Why did you not seek legal redress?"

"There was just such an informality in the terms of the bequest as to give me no hope from law. A man of honor could not have doubted the intention, but Mr. Darcy chose to doubt it—or to treat it as a merely conditional recommendation, and to assert that I had forfeited all claim to it by extravagance, imprudence—in short anything or nothing. Certain it is, that the living became vacant two years ago, exactly as I was of an age to hold it, and that it was given to another man; and no less certain is it, that I cannot accuse myself of having really done anything to deserve to lose it. I have a warm, unguarded temper, and I may have spoken my opinion of him, and to him, too freely. I can recall nothing worse. But the fact is, that we are very different sort of men, and that he hates me."

"This is quite shocking! He deserves to be publicly disgraced. I had always thought him a man of strong moral character."

"Some time or other he will be—but it shall not be by me. Till I can forget his father, I can never defy or expose him."

Lizzy noted the slight contradiction of this statement, as Mr. Wickham was in fact exposing Mr. Darcy to herself, but she was eager to hear more of Mr. Wickham's opinion on the subject. "How could he act in such a way when Mr. Bingley claims such friendship with him? For surely Mr. Bingley is an amiable man."

"A thorough, determined dislike of me—a dislike which I cannot but attribute in some measure to jealousy. Had the late Mr. Darcy liked me less, his son might have borne with me better; but his father's uncommon attachment to me irritated him, I believe, very early in life. He had not a temper to bear the sort of competition in which we stood—the sort of preference which was often given me."

"Upon my word," she exclaimed, "How strange!" cried Elizabeth. "How abominable! I wonder that the very pride of this Mr. Darcy has not made him just to you! If from no better motive, that he should not have been too proud to be dishonest—for dishonesty I must call it."

"Mr. Darcy is quite skilled at presenting to the world one nature but secretly lives another," Mr. Wickham said with sorrow. "You spoke earlier of his high moral character, but when he is at home in Derbyshire, he and his friends live quite another lifestyle."

"Do you... do you mean Mr. Cartwright?" Lizzy whispered in

horror.

Mr. Wickham looked at her in surprise. "Are you acquainted with Mr. Cartwright?"

"He was the former steward of Netherfield, and he is known to the gentry as an honorable man, but the tenants have seen another side of him—an evil side."

Mr. Wickham shook his head in dismay. "I am afraid Mr. Darcy and Mr. Cartwright have many of the same proclivities."

Lizzy gasped and pressed her hand to her mouth. "What of Mr. Bingley?"

Mr. Wickham merely pressed his lips together in disdain and gave her a pointed look. At that moment, Lydia came over and demanded Wickham partner her at the next round of whist. "For my dear Forster takes all before him, and I am becoming quite cross about it!" the young wife exclaimed as her husband smiled at her indulgently.

Lizzy was somewhat relieved to see Wickham go, having much to consider. *Poor Georgiana!* Lizzy thought in dismay. *How can she bear it? Or is she even aware of what her husband and brother are like?* Then another thought crossed her mind. *What of Colonel Fitzwilliam and his brother, Lord Oakley? Surely, they, too, are not so bad as that! Or Colonel Forster? The two colonels are good friends one with one another.*

At this point, Lizzy's head began to swim. She looked around the room in search of her sisters, but every person she saw wore Becky's terrified face.

Just then, Jane's voice broke through the chaos. "Lizzy?" she asked, concerned.

Lizzy shook her head, the memories fading. Looking around, she saw Jane had finished her game of whist and joined Lizzy at her empty table.

"What is the matter, Lizzy?" Jane persisted.

Shaking her head, Lizzy whispered, "Not now, Jane. Later."

Jane nodded understandingly but remained close to her sister. For some minutes, the two ladies sat silently together while Lizzy regained her composure.

Once the anguish that had arisen from the sudden onslaught of those horrible memories faded, Lizzy was able to examine the conversation with Mr. Wickham with a clearer mind. Closing her eyes, she repeated the words over in her head.

Till I can forget his father, I can never defy or expose him.

Lizzy's eyes popped open, remembering Wickham's contradictory words and behavior. *If he has prevaricated about this, what else might be false?* she wondered. *After all, would I not have seen something in Mr. Darcy's behavior that would indicate such depravities in the two weeks I was at Netherfield? Further, it does not reconcile with his apologies to me about Jane.*

Lizzy spent the remainder of the card party watching Mr. Wickham, searching for any indications he was of a deceitful nature. Such concentration led to her forming a headache by the end of the evening, and she was relieved when the carriage was called for.

The journey back to Longbourn was largely silent, save for the eloquence with which Mr. Collins related his enjoyment of the card party. An occasional comment from Mary was all that he required to continue the conversation until they had reached the house.

Once inside, Mary bid her fiancé a good night, and the four sisters climbed the stairs. Lizzy immediately went to her bedroom, planning to ready for bed and then spend much of the night in solitary contemplation. Instead, however, her sisters came into her bedroom, dressed in their nightclothes.

"Lizzy, what did Mr. Wickham say to you?" Jane questioned, quiet steel suffusing her voice.

"Mr. Wickham?" Asked a surprised Kitty, "Did he cause you any distress, Lizzy?"

Lizzy spent the next thirty minutes recounting all of her interactions with Mr. Wickham, including his reaction to seeing Mr. Darcy and Mr. Bingley the previous afternoon. When she reached the part where Wickham told her of Darcy's friendship with Mr. Cartwright, Mary looked confused.

"But, Lizzy," said Mary, "I do not understand why Mr. Darcy's friendship with Mr. Cartwright should so distress you. I do not remember much about the man, as I was still a girl when he left, but I do remember that he was quite pleasant whenever he dined at Longbourn."

"That is what everyone thinks," Lizzy said darkly, "but he hides his evils behind a mask of amiability. He is *not* a good man."

"What did he do?" Kitty asked in a hushed whisper.

Lizzy looked at Jane, who said quietly, "Perhaps it is best that they know the full details."

Nodding gravely, Lizzy took a deep breath and proceeded to share her experience with Becky and Mr. Cartwright. She left out Becky's name, of course, merely referring to her as a daughter of one of Netherfield's tenants.

"How *vile*," Mary said emphatically. Kitty nodded silently, unable to respond, her cheeks wet with tears.

"And then he wanted to propose to Jane!" Lizzy exclaimed.

Mary gasped in horror, and Kitty paled. "Is this why you spent so much time in London when you were sixteen?" Mary asked the eldest girl.

Jane affirmed this with a nod and added, "Mr. Cartwright was also the former suitor who importuned me a few weeks ago at Hyde Park in London."

"Oh, I am so grateful to your viscount for his intervention!" Kitty said fervently.

"We are much indebted to Lord Oakley," Mary agreed. "I begin to see why Mr. Wickham's assertions of Mr. Darcy's character and friendship with Mr. Cartwright were so disturbing to you."

"Yes," Lizzy said slowly, "but I am beginning to consider the idea that Mr. Wickham was not entirely truthful."

"But how can such an amiable-looking man tell such lies?" Kitty wailed in dismay.

"As I learned with Mr. Cartwright, appearances can be deceiving. You must learn to look behind the mask that a man wears," Lizzy responded.

"Why do you distrust Mr. Wickham?" Mary asked curiously. "I do not disbelieve your interpretation, but I am curious as to how you determined one to be more trustworthy than the other."

Lizzy hesitated. "I am not entirely certain; there are a few inconsistencies, such as the fact that Mr. Wickham claimed he could never expose his friend in honor of his godfather's memory, then proceeded to share all of Mr. Darcy's supposed sins with me, a stranger whom he had just met."

Her sisters nodded in agreement, and Lizzy continued speaking. "There is also the matter of the fact that Mr. Bingley and Mr. Darcy both reacted so strongly to Mr. Wickham. Mr. Bingley, whom I have always considered to be amiable, had such a look of anger upon his face, even more so than Mr. Darcy's. If Mr. Darcy truly was a villain who gave a false façade of gentility, then he would have met Mr. Wickham with false cheer at seeing an old friend. No, the more I think on this, the more I believe Mr. Wickham to be the one hiding a dissolute character!"

At Lizzy's pronouncement, the room fell silent as her sisters contemplated her words.

After some minutes, Jane finally spoke, "Lizzy, at first I thought there must have been some misunderstanding between the gentlemen, but I am sorry to say that I agree with you. Mr. Wickham is the one who is hiding behind a mask, and you were wise enough to look behind it at the real person."

Mary and Kitty voiced their agreement. "What should we do?" Kitty asked. "Should we tell someone?"

Lizzy shook her head. "No, I do not think that would be wise. We would not wish to make Mr. Wickham desperate. We also have no proof. We will simply need to guard ourselves against Mr. Wickham and his false charm. I shan't be taken in by his lies!"

With that, the girls bade one another a good night and retired to their separate beds.

Chapter 24

It seemed to Georgiana that the sun rose earlier than usual on the day that Viscount Oakley was to arrive at Netherfield. She awoke with the sun and chose to breakfast downstairs, instead of taking her customary cup of chocolate in her chambers.

"Someone is awake early," laughed Fitzwilliam when his young cousin entered the dining room.

"As is someone else!" she teasingly replied.

"Ah, but I am a military man! We are accustomed to such difficulties," he said with a sly wink.

"I admit, I am eager to see Oakley," Georgiana said as she served herself a slice of toast with eggs from the sideboard.

"As am I," Fitzwilliam agreed, "I am hopeful he arrives early, as I am afraid I must leave tomorrow for the barracks."

"What?" Georgiana asked in surprise. "You will not be staying here at Netherfield with us?"

"I'm afraid not, my dear," he said, sorrow in his voice. "A good commander endures hardships with his men. I would lose their respect if I were to stay in a manor house with the comfort of servants when they are spending the winter in tents and rented rooms."

Georgiana nodded. "I will be sorry to see you go. At least you will not be far, however."

"No, and I will call on you here and at Longbourn at every opportunity," he assured her.

"You mean, you will call on Miss Catherine at Longbourn?" she corrected with a smile.

Fitzwilliam grinned, which served to render his plain face almost handsome. "I mean to call on *all* the Bennets," he emphasized, "although it would not bother me if Miss Catherine happened to be at home when I called."

Georgiana sat her toast down and gave her cousin and former guardian a stern look. "I like Kitty Bennet; I consider her a friend. I will be very cross if you raise her expectations when all you are looking for is light flirtation."

Fitzwilliam's teasing smile left his face. "I would not do such a thing," he said soberly. "I enjoy spending time with Miss Catherine. I am not at liberty to make an offer of marriage at this time, but I will soon be resigning my commission and taking up the estate my uncle left me. I would like to begin that new step in my life with a wife beside me."

"*Richard,*" Georgiana gasped, "are you planning to ask Kitty to marry you?"

Richard smiled and said, "I am considering the notion. I have not yet made a final decision, but I believe I shall."

"How wonderful!" exclaimed Georgiana, rising from her seat to hug her cousin. "She is a truly delightful girl, and I will be proud to call her family."

"Now, before you jump to matrimony too quickly, I must warn you that I am not in love with her," he said, returning her hug. "However, I have a deep regard and genuine fondness for her. She makes me laugh, and she listens to my stories."

"Ah, I see," Georgiana said with a sly smile. "A girl needs only to employ a few smiles, a few compliments to the army, and you are a lost man!"

Fitzwilliam let out a surprised burst of laughter. "It is not quite that easy to catch me!" he protested.

"Who is trying to catch you?"

Both occupants at the table spun towards the door. "Oakley!" cried Georgiana, and she rushed to throw her arms around him.

"How are you here?"

"Well, there is an incredible animal called a horse…"

"You wretch!" Georgiana giggled as she hit his arm. "How are you come so early? You were not supposed to arrive until this afternoon!"

"As much as I love my sons, riding in the carriage with them became a bit too much for me. I left early this morning to ride ahead of them; they will be coming with the nursemaids on the carriage once they have awoken and departed the inn where we stayed for the night," Oakley explained.

He helped himself to a large plate of bacon, along with some toast, then joined his brother and his cousin at the table. "Now," he repeated, before taking a bite, "who is trying to catch my brother?"

Georgiana smiled and answered, "Catherine Bennet."

"Ah, Jane's youngest unmarried sister," he said nonchalantly before taking another bite.

Georgiana's mouth fell open as Richard started in surprise. "You know the Bennets?" Richard asked as Georgiana exclaimed, "*Jane?!*"

The viscount merely smiled and gestured to his full mouth. After several agonizing seconds of deliberately slow chewing, he finally swallowed and simply said, "Yes, Jane Bennet."

His two breakfast companions looked at him expectantly, while he focused very intently on his plate. After several more moments of silence, Georgiana could not bear the suspense and demanded, "Oakley, how on earth do you know Miss Bennet?"

"Especially well enough to call her by her given name," Richard said suspiciously. "You have—you have not, well—" Richard hesitated, glancing at Georgiana anxiously.

She regarded Richard blankly for a few heartbeats, then understanding dawned on her face. "*No,*" she gasped in horror.

At this, Oakley's head snapped up, all traces of amusement gone from his face. "*Never,*" he growled, fixing his brother with a fierce glare.

Richard sighed in relief. "I really did not think you would take the daughter of a gentleman as a mistress, but you must admit, your behavior is quite perplexing."

"Not to mention the damage that could have occurred to Miss Bennet's reputation had either of my sisters-by-marriage overheard any of this conversation," Georgiana added with a set-down.

Oakley sighed. "You both make excellent points. I should not have indulged myself at your expense when a young woman's reputation could have been so easily marred."

"Do you intend to explain the situation, then?" Georgiana asked impatiently.

Oakley spent the next quarter of an hour relating his relationship with Jane Bennet. At the very end of the conversation, Darcy returned from his morning ride. After embracing his cousin, Oakley began the tale over again.

Darcy's brow was furrowed in concern. "I believe I am acquainted with Mr. Cartwright," he said at the end of Oakley's tale.

"What?!" exclaimed the viscount.

"If it is the same man, then he has a property somewhat near mine in Derbyshire. I must admit, I am not very surprised to hear that he behaved in a less than gentlemanlike manner. I am sorry to hear, however, that Miss Bennet was so importuned," Darcy said.

He then proceeded to share his experience at Cartwright's ball, finishing by declaring that he would no longer have any association with such a disreputable man.

"I find it interesting that you are courting Miss Bennet on such little acquaintance," Darcy mused, "Why such haste?"

"I am lonely, and she is kind to my children," the viscount answered simply.

Knowing his cousin's history with his first wife, Darcy nodded in reply. The three were silent, then Georgiana declared, "I cannot wait to see Mrs. Bennet's reaction when she hears the news!"

Richard burst into laughter as Oakley looked at his young cousin, perplexed. "How do you know that she does not know already?"

"Because the Bennet girls would have told me."

"How do you know Mrs. Bennet simply has not told them?"

Georgiana looked at Richard, who was laughing so hard he could barely breathe, tears streaming down his face. She, too, dissolved into giggles.

Darcy merely looked at them, then turned to the viscount with a sardonic grin. "You shall find out soon enough."

The merriment ended with the entrance of Miss Bingley and Mrs. Hurst, who quickly took over the conversation in an attempt to ingratiate themselves to the viscount. He donned an aloof manner and rebutted their questions with curt one-word answers.

Desperate to turn the conversation from its current miserable state, Georgiana turned to her husband, who had entered the room shortly after his sisters. "Dearest, what do you think about hosting a ball to welcome my cousin to the neighborhood?"

"I think a ball is just the thing!" Charles cried with delight.

"Do you think a ball would be well-received in such a... quaint location?" Miss Bingley asked with a pained smile. "I would advise you, before you determine on it, to consult the wishes of the present party; I am much mistaken if there are not some among us to whom a ball would be rather a punishment than a pleasure."

"When our mother was alive, she hosted balls at Pemberley quite frequently," said Darcy, "and Derbyshire is far more removed from London society than Hertfordshire is. I think a ball to be an excellent choice."

With this lack of support from the party to whom she had indicated with her inquiry, Miss Bingley graciously—albeit reluctantly—withdrew her protest by falling silent.

"I will call on Longbourn today to consult on the best day for the ball," Georgiana declared.

Her brother and both cousins eagerly announced that they would join her. Miss Bingley sniffed and stated that she must send to Town for her best ball gowns, for she had "not thought them necessary in a such a wild place as this."

The ladies excused themselves to prepare for the day. A short while later, Georgiana departed for Longbourn, escorted by her husband and her three male relations.

Upon arriving, they were announced, and they could hear immediate shrieks from the area of the drawing room, though they could not make out the words. Oakley widened his eyes in alarm, and Georgiana whispered conspiratorially, "Mrs. Bennet."

Oakley did not have time to react to this indictment of Jane's mother's poor behavior; they were quickly ushered into the room by the housekeeper and announced to the room at large.

Mrs. Bennet and four daughters stood and curtsied as introductions were made. The moment Mrs. Bennet met "his lordship, Viscount Oakley," she began a steady stream of warm effusions. Oakley just stared while Jane slowly lowered her gaze to her lap, blushing.

Finally, as Mrs. Bennet took a pause for breath, Lizzy interjected, "Since it is such a fine day, we had been discussing a walk. Would you care to join us?"

"Yes," everyone responded at once.

Mrs. Bennet looked around the room, blinking in surprise at the chorus of eager voices. "Well, I shan't keep you young people from your exercise."

House slippers were exchanged for boots, and the entire company, save Mary, went out of doors. Oakley quickly led Jane to one side of the garden, while Darcy and Lizzy went to another corner to continue a lively debate about a book they had both read with divergent opinions.

Colonel Fitzwilliam initiated conversation with Kitty. Georgiana, in a desire to play matchmaker, pulled Bingley away from the conversation by pretending to solicit his opinion of a plant in the garden.

"I am sorry, my dear, but I have no idea what type of plant this is," Bingley said, examining the shrub she had indicated.

Georgiana laughed. "It's a *neottia ovata,* but that is not the real reason I called you over. I wanted to give Richard some time with Kitty."

"Ah," Charles said, waggling his eyebrows at her, "you are in collusion with Mrs. Bennet!"

Georgiana laughingly protested this accusation, but he continued, "No, no, there is no denying it. You are becoming a matchmaker in your old married state."

"I am not so very old," she declared hotly.

Bingley gazed at her warmly, his eyes moving from her face, down her body, and back up again. "No, my dear, you are not."

Georgiana blushed under his gaze, her stomach fluttering nervously. He took her hand and pressed the back of it to his lips in a gentle kiss. Their eyes remained locked, and he leaned closer, parting his lips to whisper.

A bark of laughter from Darcy from across the garden startled the married couple, and they jumped apart, looking around and blushing. Darcy had thrown back his head, laughing at something Lizzy had said in their debate.

"I have never before seen my brother so happy. Tis a beautiful sight," Georgiana said feelingly.

"Yes, it is," murmured Bingley, but his eyes remained on his wife.

Darcy's laughter over Lizzy's accusation that he had chosen an opposing viewpoint just so he could debate with her had interrupted more than just the Bingleys' conversation. The other two couples began moving towards them, and soon all eight were conversing together in the garden.

"Have you chosen a date for your ball, Mrs. Bingley?" Jane asked. With Oakley at her side, she was quite confident in the presence of her former suitor's wife, displaying none of the awkwardness she had initially felt when the Netherfield party arrived that morning.

"The twenty-sixth of November," Georgiana said, "and I hope you shall all come."

Assurances of their attendance were made, and each young man solicited the first set from the focus of his attentions, before turning to the others and requesting a place on their dance cards as well.

That having settled, Oakley excused himself from the group, saying he had a matter to discuss with Mr. Bennet inside. Jane offered to show him to her father's study so the housekeeper would not need to disturb Mrs. Bennet with the news of the guest's request.

Kitty and Lizzy watched Jane lead the gentleman away with a soft smile. Georgiana gave a girlish squeal and said, "He told us this morning that he is courting your sister. I could not be more happy for her!"

"Is he a good man?" Lizzy asked bluntly.

Darcy bristled slightly. "He is one of the best men of my acquaintance."

Lizzy raised her eyebrows at him and said, "Forgive the impertinence, but the question was kindly meant. I had an encounter many years ago with a man who hides his wickedness behind an amiable face. A woman gives up much when she marries and puts herself completely in the power of her husband."

Bingley blushed at this statement, and Georgiana said, "My husband may have acted poorly in the past, but he was never wicked!"

Lizzy stared blankly at her for a minute, then laughed lightly. "Oh! No, my dear friend, I did not mean your husband!"

Kitty began to laugh, too. "She meant Mr. Cartwright!"

Lizzy hushed her sister, but Darcy latched onto the name. "The same man who assaulted your sister in Hyde Park?"

"Yes," Kitty answered. "He used to live here in Meryton years ago. He wanted to marry Jane, but Lizzy saved her."

"How did she know his character?" Richard asked.

"She saw him with a young tenant's daughter," Kitty said.

"*Kitty!*" Lizzy exclaimed in dismay, having found her voice. "I shared that with you in *confidence*."

Kitty immediately closed her mouth and looked at the ground, blushing. "I'm sorry, Lizzy," she said in a subdued tone.

"I suppose there is no help for it now," Lizzy said. She then proceeded to relate the incident she had witnessed between Mr. Cartwright and Becky.

"My goodness," Darcy exclaimed. "I knew I did not like the man even before we heard of what occurred in Hyde Park. Now I feel ashamed at having ever entered his home."

Lizzy shot Darcy a sharp look. "I had understood the man to be a close friend of yours."

Bingley shook his head. "We once attended a ball at his home when he first came to Derbyshire, but other than that, Darcy rarely has dealings with him. Other than rescuing his servants, of course."

Darcy colored slightly and steered the conversation away from his supposed virtues, "Who claimed I was friends with the blackguard?"

Now it was Lizzy's turn to blush faintly. "Mr. Wickham."

Georgiana gave a slight gasp, her hand tightening on her husband's arm. "What else did he tell you?" she asked in a tremulous voice.

"Nothing that was the truth, clearly," Lizzy said. "I had already determined his story about a denied inheritance to be a falsehood, but I was not entirely certain about his claim that you were friends with Mr. Cartwright."

Darcy looked at her in surprise. "You did not believe what he said about the living at Kympton?"

"How did you know he spoke about Kympton?" Kitty asked curiously.

Richard rolled his eyes. "Because that is the story he tells everyone."

"No, I did not believe him. At the beginning I was unsure, but he contradicted himself early in his explanation," Lizzy explained.

Georgiana sighed slightly, relieved, and all eyes turned to her.

"Perhaps we should return home," her husband suggested. "You look a bit faint, and it is almost time for lunch."

Shaking her head, Georgiana responded, "Not until I have told my friends the truth about Wickham."

Darcy began to argue, but she gave him a sharp look. "This is *my* story to tell, Brother, and I will share it with whom I wish."

She spent the next quarter of an hour relating her encounter with Wickham at Ramsgate and the truth of how her marriage came to be. By the end of the conversation, Kitty was in tears. Lizzy embraced her friend and said, "Thank you for trusting us. You have been incredibly brave in the sharing of your story."

Georgiana began to sob into her friend's arms. "I was so worried you would despise me."

Kitty left the colonel's side and wrapped her arms around the embracing pair. "Never," she assured her friend in an emphatic whisper.

As Darcy surveyed the scene, witnessing the Misses Bennet comfort his cherished sister, he could no longer deny the incontrovertible truth. He loved Elizabeth Bennet.

Warmth filled his chest at the admission. He looked at his cousin to see Richard gazing at three girls with a soft smile on his face. Bingley's eyes were suspiciously red.

The tender moment was interrupted by a loud squeal from within the house. The Netherfield party jumped and looked at the house in alarm.

Lizzy began to laugh. "Oh, Mamma," she said fondly. "It appears Papa has given his acceptance and has informed our mother."

"We had best go in and congratulate them," Georgiana said, wiping at her face. Bingley handed her his handkerchief. When she returned it to him, he pulled her close and wrapped her in his arms, enveloping her in a brief, tender embrace.

Kissing her hair, he murmured, "My brave girl."

As the group entered the house, they could hear Mrs. Bennet's raptures more clearly. Congratulations were issued from all sides. It was in the midst of this chaos that Lydia arrived for a visit.

"Oh, Lydia! Can you imagine? Jane is being courted by a viscount!" Mrs. Bennet exclaimed

A sour expression darkened Lydia's face. It lightened somewhat, however, when Charles issued her an invitation to the ball at Netherfield.

"Are *all* the officers invited?" Lydia asked.

The gentlemen exchanged concerned looks. Bingley quickly whispered to Georgiana, who nodded at him.

"Yes," Bingley answered, "Although I may be calling on your husband to issue the invitation in person."

"What a jolly good time we shall all have! The officers are such fine dancers!" Lydia said excitedly. "Mamma, I shall need a new gown!"

"Oh yes, my love, all of my girls must dress their best!" Here, Mrs. Bennet faltered, remembering her husband's reaction the last time she had attempted to purchase new gowns for Lydia. The look of delight on Lydia's face washed away any concerns she had, however.

As the conversation turned to lace and sleeve lengths, the Netherfield party took the opportunity to bid their farewells.

The days leading up to the ball were filled with calls made and returned between the occupants of Netherfield and Longbourn. Discussions about gowns, decorations, food, and more were the topic of notes that flew back and forth between the two estates, and the footmen had formed a well-trodden path that short-cut several minutes from their journey.

Bingley paid a call on Colonel Forster, during which he formally invited the militia. He gave strong hints regarding his concern over Wickham's attendance, considering "Wickham's ill-concealed contempt for my wife and brother." Colonel Forster assured Bingley he would ensure that the man be assigned duty the night of the ball and therefore unable to attend.

At last, the day arrived. Poor Sarah—the lady's maid for all of the Bennet girls—spent the entire day pulling corset strings, mending shoe roses, and putting pins in hair. When at last Mrs. Bennet deemed her daughters ready, the six Bennet residents boarded the carriage and headed toward Netherfield.

Darcy thought he had prepared himself for seeing Elizabeth, but as she entered the front doors at Netherfield, he stopped breathing. She was stunning. Her hair had been pinned up in elaborate twists and knots, intertwined with flowers, with her graceful neck on display. Her ball gown was trimmed with a deep blue ribbon that brought out the color in her eyes. It clung to her curves, flowing down her form in a way that made his hands ache to touch her.

He stared at her for several seconds until Richard elbowed him in the ribs. Startled, Darcy turned to rebuke him but then realized he had been ignoring Mrs. Long, who was next in line to greet him.

"My apologies, madam," he said, executing a deep bow. "I fear my attention was arrested elsewhere. Do forgive my discourtesy."

She gave him a knowing smile and said, "That is quite all right young man. Everyone proclaims Jane to be the jewel of Hertfordshire, but that little Lizzy Bennet is quite the beauty herself."

"That she is," he said in a strangled voice, embarrassed that his emotions were so clearly on display.

The line continued to move, until—at long last—she reached him.

"Miss Elizabeth," Darcy greeted, bowing over her hand and pressing her knuckles to his lips in a tender kiss. She gasped at the unexpectedly intimate gesture. He rose, piercing eyes staring into hers. Retaining ownership of her hand, he whispered to her: "You are stunning."

Lizzy blushed deeply as she curtsied in return. "Thank you, sir." Quickly regaining her equilibrium, she teased, "Handsome enough to stand up with you for the first two dances?"

Darcy leaned in toward her, pulling lightly on her hand that he might draw her closer as well. "Oh, you tempt me," he whispered enticingly, compelling the blush to creep from her face toward the neckline of her gown.

Straightening, he donned an impassive expression to greet Mary

Bennet, who gave him a severe look. "I hope whatever you said to my sister to cause her to blush so was done with honorable intentions," she said in a stern voice.

Darcy's eyebrows rose. "Indeed they are. I would ask her to marry me tonight if I thought she would accept," he admitted, then cursed himself for his loose tongue.

Mary graced him with a sudden smile, causing her plain face to transform. "I shall hold you to that, sir," she said archly, "Based on her response to you just now, I think you can expect a favorable reply, should you choose to do so."

She moved on to greet Richard, leaving Darcy to stare after her, jaw agape. He shook his head to clear the stupor, then continued greeting the remainder of the guests.

When the musicians began to play, Darcy looked for Lizzy. Spying her on the other side of the room with her sisters, he made his way across the room to collect her for the first two dances. He extended his hand to hers, relishing the small gasp she emitted when the contact was made.

Darcy led Lizzy to the dance floor and they began to dance, briefly content merely to gaze into one another's eyes. After a few moments, however, Lizzy smiled and said, "Come now, Mr. Darcy, we must have *some* conversation! Perhaps I should say something about the size of room, and you could make some sort of remark on the number of couples."

He smiled, and assured her that whatever she wished him to say should be said.

"Very well. That reply will do for the present. Perhaps by and by I may observe that private balls are much pleasanter than public ones. But now we may be silent."

"Do you talk by rule, then, while you are dancing?" Darcy smiled down at her.

"Sometimes. One must speak a little, you know. It would look odd to be entirely silent for half an hour together; and yet for the advantage of some, conversation ought to be so arranged, as that they may have the trouble of saying as little as possible."

"Are you consulting your own feelings in the present case, or do you imagine that you are gratifying mine?"

"Both," replied Elizabeth archly; "for I have always seen a great similarity in the turn of our minds. We are each of an unsocial, taciturn disposition, unwilling to speak, unless we expect to say something that will amaze the whole room, and be handed down to posterity with all the éclat of a proverb."

Darcy let out a bark of laughter. Lizzy smiled in satisfaction at having finally broken through his stern façade to the man she had discovered him to be these past weeks.

"Marry me," he blurted out.

At these words, Lizzy tripped over her feet and stumbled into him. "Oh!" she cried in pain.

"Miss Elizabeth!" Darcy exclaimed, catching her before she fell to the ground. As he escorted her from the dance floor, helping her hobble to a chair, he cursed himself for being such a cad.

"You there, fetch some ice! At once, man!" he cried to a passing footman.

"No, no!" Lizzy countermanded. Darcy looked at her in confusion. "It is nothing, really," she whispered to him, "but I wished to continue our conversation without the distraction of dancing."

Understanding dawned in Darcy's eyes. The footman looked between the two of them, unsure as to whose orders he should obey. At Darcy's shrug, the servant continued on his way.

"Are you much hurt?" Darcy asked with concern as she bent over to massage at her ankle. "Perhaps we should get that ice after all."

"No, I am quite all right," she insisted. "Your words merely took me by surprise, and I misstepped. But there is no injury."

Lizzy looked around and saw her sisters and mother headed toward her, worry on their faces. "There is no time to speak at length, but my answer is—" she hesitated, weighing her answer carefully, then concluded in a rush, "I will consent to a courtship to last no shorter than six months."

Darcy had no time to respond, as they were soon surrounded by her family, asking after her. Lizzy reassured them all, going so far as to stand on her feet and bounce slightly without wincing.

"How could you be so clumsy, child?" Mrs. Bennet exclaimed in dismay.

"My apologies, Mrs. Bennet," Mr. Darcy interjected, "but I am the one at fault. I began to turn the wrong way, which forced Miss Elizabeth off-balance. It was only her quickness of foot that prevented both of us from tumbling to the ground."

"Oh yes, my Lizzy has always been an excellent dancer," Mrs. Bennet assured him, ignorant to the contradiction.

"In fact, Miss Elizabeth, I am very sorry that we were unable to finish the dance," Darcy said as the music came to an end. "Perhaps I might request the honor of the supper set to make up for it?"

Lizzy smiled sadly at him and said, "I am afraid, sir, that my entire dance card is filled."

Darcy's face fell, "I understand, Miss Elizabeth. A woman as excellent a dancer as yourself would naturally have all the sets spoken for."

"You could, however, ask one of the other young ladies for your open sets," she suggested, "So often in Meryton many women sit down without a partner due to the shortage of gentlemen."

"An excellent idea," Darcy responded, eager to please.

The music began the next set, and Darcy bowed before going in search of his sister. In between sets with the women from Netherfield and Longbourn, he sought out as many wallflowers as he could. He had never before noticed the transformation that overcame a young woman's countenance when she was asked to dance.

The evening drew to a close. *This has been the most enjoyable ball I have ever attended*, Darcy thought with surprise. *I can see why some enjoy the pastime so.*

Mrs. Bennet cleverly arranged for their carriage to be the last to arrive. They stood talking in the foyer, waiting for the servants to bring their conveyance around, no one noticing that the host and hostess were already absent. As the clip-clop of horse hooves came into hearing, Darcy bowed over Lizzy's hand, placing a lingering kiss on the back of it, the sensation of which did not leave her until after she arrived at Longbourn and had drifted off into blissful slumber.

Chapter 25

Lizzy awoke suddenly to the clamor of loud voices. *What is going on?* she wondered.

Glancing at the clock, she saw with surprise that it was already ten in the morning. *I never sleep so late!* she thought.

The memories of the night before flooded her mind: Darcy's face when he first saw her arrive, his voice as he said she tempted him, and—

He asked me to marry him! She sat straight up in bed and hugged her pillow to her chest, a wide smile spreading across her face. It faded slightly as she recalled telling him that she would only allow him to court her. *But I must be certain before I make such a decision,* she told herself firmly. *I must love him as much as he seems to love me, and I must know that his character is one to be trusted. He seems to have improved much about himself over the course of our acquaintance, and I need to be certain that the change is permanent.*

Another bellow caused her to wince, and she quickly dressed and descended the stairs. She entered the parlor to find Lydia shouting at their father with the rest of the family observing from where they stood at the side of the room.

"Mamma said I could have a new dress! You cannot refuse to pay!" Lydia screamed at her father, stomping her feet and clenching her fists tightly at her sides.

Lizzy joined her sisters and asked, "What on earth is happening?"

Mary rolled her eyes and Kitty said, "Lydia ordered a new dress for the ball. She put it on Papa's account, but he will not pay for it, as she is now married. Her husband says the funds will have to come from her pin money, which she already spent for this quarter. The dress was very expensive and will use up her entire allowance and then some."

Jane had meanwhile ventured across the room that she might try to calm Lydia, but her attempts were rebuffed.

"Where on earth is her husband?" Lizzy asked as Lydia turned an alarming shade of red and burst into mournful wails.

"You *must* pay for it, Papa! Mamma, tell him!" she shrieked.

"Mr. Bennet, perhaps—" began her mother.

"No, Mrs. Bennet," he said in an uncharacteristically firm voice. "Lydia chose to be married, and on that day she left behind the name of Bennet and is now a Forster. If a Bennet is to pay for her dress, then it shall come from *your* pin money, Mrs. Bennet."

Lydia immediately ceased crying and looked at her mother hopefully. "Mamma, that is an excellent idea! After all, you were the one who said I needed a new dress so I could look my best for the ball."

Mrs. Bennet hesitated and looked at her husband, who gazed resolutely back at her. The onlookers watched as a war of priorities waged across her face. The entire room waited breathlessly.

Finally, her shoulders sagged and she said, "I am sorry, Lydia, but I cannot. I have used all of my pin money for this quarter, and I have plans to use next quarter's allotment to replace some things in the mistress's quarters."

If the Bennet family thought they had seen the worst of Lydia's behavior, they were severely mistaken. Lydia's face turned purple with rage; she opened her mouth and unleashed an ear-piercing keen that continued ceaselessly. Mary and Kitty covered their ears, while Mrs. Bennet swooned on her chair. Jane and Mr. Bennet froze in shock.

Lizzy was the only one who remained undisturbed by the chaos. She marched over to a vase, removed the flowers, and proceeded to dump the entire contents of water over Lydia's head.

Lydia fell suddenly silent, water dripping down her face and into her dress. She stared at her sister in shock while the others looked on. After a few seconds, she parted her lips again, but Lizzy slapped her across the mouth.

"Don't," Lizzy ordered in a harsh voice. "Do not *dare* to open your mouth, Lydia Forster, or I shall slap you again!"

Lydia, who had never once had a hand raised to her in anger in her life, went as still as a statue. Her eyes filled an emotion she had never before experienced: fear.

Lizzy crossed her arms and glared at her youngest sister. "Now that you have stopped caterwauling like a fishwife, perhaps you will listen to some sense."

She steered Lydia over to a chair and pushed down on her sister's shoulders, forcing Lydia to take a seat. Towering over the rebellious girl, she said fiercely, "You are a *married* woman. You made your choice to be married at this age when you intentionally compromised Colonel Forster. It is not Papa's responsibility to provide you, nor is it Mamma's responsibility to give up her things for you. If you wanted your parents to continue to give you ribbons and gowns, then you should not have gotten married at such a young age!"

The entire Bennet family stared in shocked awe as Lizzy spent the next ten minutes taking her sister to task. She ended with, "So help me, Lydia, if you ever again behave in such an appalling way, I will tell Colonel Forster to remove your pin money entirely! And you can bet he will listen to me, because no man of his station wants to be married to such a hoyden!"

With that, Lizzy turned her back on her sister, took a seat, and said, "Now, shall we all have some tea? I am sorry to say that I missed breakfast."

Slowly, the room returned to life. Everyone began to move about and quietly converse—everyone save Lydia, that is. The girl—who had never received a cross word before in her life—sat alone, hiccupping, with her hair dripping onto the upholstery as she watched her family resume their business around her.

The conversation quickly turned to Mary and her upcoming marriage. The wedding date was now less than a month away, and the Gardiners would be arriving in a fortnight. There was much still to do, Mrs. Bennet insisted, and now that the ball had passed, their attention could be focused entirely on the wedding.

While Mrs. Bennet dictated a letter—written by Jane, who had the best penmanship—to her sister Gardiner with instructions on the best warehouses for the items needed, Lizzy looked at Mr. Bennet.

"Papa," she said, "may I speak with you privately?"

Mr. Bennet nodded and beckoned her to follow him to his study. Once he had closed the door and settled into his chair behind his desk, he looked at her and let out a chuckle. "Bravo, my dear," he said. "I do not think I have been quite so entertained by a scene in all my life."

"Father!" Lizzy exclaimed in frustration.

He waved a hand at her. "Yes, well, what do we live for if not to make sport of our loved ones and be made sport of in our turn?"

Lizzy bit her tongue, reminding herself that it would not do to disrespect her father. The following conversation would go much better if he were in a light mood.

"Papa," she began hesitantly, "I have a matter of considerable import that I wish to discuss with you."

"Ah, has someone finally asked for your hand?" he quipped. She blushed, and the smile faded from his face. "Lizzy?" he urged curiously.

"Mr. Darcy asked me to marry him last night at the ball. I have told him he may court me for at least six months, after which time I may make a decision about marriage."

Mr. Bennet's eyebrows raised far above his eyes. "Mr. Darcy? The tall, proud one?"

"Indeed, you are mistaken!" she cried.

"What, he is not tall?" he asked with a twinkle in his eye.

Lizzy let out a reluctant laugh and said, "Oh, Papa. Yes, he is the tall one. But he has no improper pride, at least not that I can see. He is a kind man."

"I do not doubt he could keep you in fine clothes and carriages. Indeed, he is the sort of man to whom I would not dare to refuse anything. But this would mean nothing if you really liked him."

"I do like him," she admitted. "I cannot say I love him, and I did not even like him at the first, but I can now appreciate the good qualities I have seen."

"Well, then, I guess I had better grant him an interview when he calls," Mr. Bennet said with a sigh. "I am glad to have you for at least another half year. I do not know what I would do without your sense, Lizzy. Who else will pour water on Lydia's head when she misbehaves?"

Their laughter carried into the parlor, where Lydia still sat, unmoving and uncharacteristically subdued, save for her hiccups. It was the only the sound of Lizzy's footsteps returning down the hallway that spurred her into action. She quietly slipped from the room, with no one taking notice of her departure, as they were all absorbed in discussions of Mary's wedding and Jane's courtship.

At the same time Lydia was receiving a good scolding, the residents of Netherfield Park were finally beginning to rise from their slumber. Georgiana let out a yawn and stretched her arms above her head, which rested still on the pillow. Opening her eyes, she blinked twice at the unfamiliar bedframe.

She sat up in bed, the sheets falling to her waist, revealing bare skin. She looked around and saw Charles, her husband, snoring softly next to her.

At the sight of his face, memories from the night before came flooding back into her mind.

Charles stayed by her side the entire ball, standing up with her three times, even though it was frowned upon in polite society to dance with one's wife. The final dance was a waltz, which caused a stir of whispers amongst the guests. Charles pulled her out into the dance, where she was held tightly. This was the closest she had ever been to man other than the occasional familial hug from her brother and cousins.

The waltz was no innocent hug.

No words were spoken as they danced on the nearly empty floor. Sparks flew between them, and Georgiana thought she would burst into flames at the heat from his body pressing into hers.

At the conclusion of the dance, he escorted her out of the ballroom and up the stairs to their rooms. His eyes were dark, burning into hers, and he whispered, "Georgiana, I am going to kiss you now. But once I start, I will not want to stop. If you are not ready for this, you need to tell me now."

In response, she stood up on her toes and pressed her lips against his, and they stumbled into his bedroom, the door closing behind them.

Georgiana jumped as she felt Charles's lips on her bare shoulder. "Good morning, my dearest," he said tenderly.

She blushed and pulled the sheets up about her shoulders, then laughed at herself. He had seen much more of her the night before, but it felt different in the light of day.

Tension eased from his face at her laugh. "No regrets?" he asked, looking intently at her.

She gave him a warm smile and let the sheet drop. "None," she responded.

~∞~∞~∞~

The weeks leading up to the Gardiners' visit and Mary's wedding were filled with the various activities of several couples that were each involved at different stages in their relationships.

Mr. Collins and Mary—the engaged couple—spent much of their time with Mrs. Bennet and Mrs. Gardiner to finalize the plans for the wedding.

Bingley and Georgiana—the married couple—were coming to

know one another on a level they had not experienced before. Although they had been married for over eighteen months, it was as if they had just wed the week before and were on their honeymoon. Longing looks and secret touches filled their days, and passion filled their nights.

Jane spent much of her time in the nursery. Lord Oakley's three sons were somewhat younger than the Gardiner children, but old enough to enjoy spending time with the other children. There were frequent visits back and forth between the two households, and the nurses were becoming fast friends with one another. Jane took advantage of this time to learn more about Oakley, his situation, and his character. Their courtship was well on its way to becoming an engagement.

Darcy and Lizzy were at the beginning of their courtship, coming to know one another through conversation about the books they had read and their experiences on their respective estates. In some ways, Lizzy thought, it was a bit like performing an interview for a housekeeper or steward, only with love playing an important part of the equation.

Colonel Fitzwilliam spent much time with Kitty. Her lively personality—which in many ways resembled Lydia's, absent the younger girl's immaturity and self-obsession—was as a balm of Gilead to his soldier's heart. Much like his friend Colonel Forster, Colonel Fitzwilliam was interested in a life partner who could help him forget the horrors of war that he had experienced. He could imagine spending his life with Kitty once she was a little older, but for now he was content to enjoy her good company.

During these weeks at the end of November, Miss Bingley—being the only unattached person in the group—convinced her sister, Mrs. Hurst, that they would do better at their own house in town. Mr. Hurst was prevailed upon to end the lease of the current occupant, and the three settled into their own household. Miss Bingley's dowry was of great interest to several fortune hunters, one of whom was successful in wooing the tradesman's daughter. In short order, his title of baron convinced her that she should leave behind the name of Bingley in exchange for being granted the title of Lady.

Miss Bingley's engagement prompted Mr. Bingley to travel between London and Hertfordshire multiple times to fill out the settlement papers. The wedding date was set for four months hence, in the early spring at the end of the Season. This would require Georgiana and Mr. Bingley to reside in London for at least a month to see her off.

Similarly, Mr. Darcy would be required to return to Derbyshire at that time to oversee the preparations for the spring planting. Though his departure was not scheduled to occur for nearly three months, he requested—and was granted—permission to correspond with Lizzy as they sought to further their acquaintance.

Netherfield would be left open, however, for the Viscount and his sons to remain. The boys had become extremely fond of Jane, and Oakley did not want to separate them. Georgiana assured her cousin that he would be welcome to stay at Netherfield while she was at the wedding of her sister-in-law. Since Colonel Fitzwilliam would be remaining in Meryton with the militia until after Easter, when they would travel to Brighton, it made the most sense for Oakley to remain near his brother and the woman he was courting.

Lydia Forster rarely called at Longbourn during these weeks leading up to the December wedding. When she did, it was only in the company of her husband. She was uncharacteristically quiet throughout these visits, content to watch the happenings from a chair in the corner. Lizzy's actions with the water vase had, for the moment at least, terrified Lydia into good behavior. Lizzy was uncertain if these changes were permanent, but she chose to take advantage of the calm while it lasted.

What the Bennet family did not know was that Lydia had returned to the barracks that day, soaking wet, to complain to her husband of her mistreatment. Instead of commiserating with her and calling out her father for not protecting her, as she had imagined he would on her long walk from Longbourn, he had laughed at her and said it was only what she deserved.

This response settled into Lydia's brain and heart in a way that no other correction ever had. Coupled with Lizzy's treatment, it sent Lydia into a sort of shock. Instead of shouting or stamping her foot, as her husband expected, she collapsed onto her bed and dissolved into a fit of tears that lasted several hours. Forster, initially inclined to allow her to cry, eventually became genuinely concerned and coaxed her into sitting up and speaking with him.

What followed was the first serious conversation in which the married couple had ever engaged. Lydia, for the first time in her young life, finally saw herself the way that many others saw her: as vain, idle, and foolish—a silly chit everyone disparaged. Colonel Forster was encouraged by this display of self-contemplation, and he helped her see what she could do to improve herself without losing her *joie de vivre*. Lydia would never rise to the level of her sisters, but neither would she be the laughingstock that she had been before.

Similarly, with Wickham's perfidy being made known to Colonel Forster, the scoundrel was rarely granted enough free time to create his usual chaos. When he was not participating in training or following orders from his superior officer, he could be found attempting to charm merchants out of their wares and daughters out of their petticoats. He was successful at neither, as the Bennets had "accidentally" spoken of his true character in front of their aunt Phillips, who had circulated the gossip throughout the town in less than a day.

With the people most like to cause problems thus dealt with, Mary's wedding day finally arrived free of drama. It was a relief for Mrs. Bennet to bid farewell to a daughter who would one day take her place as mistress of Longbourn. Having a daughter so comfortably settled did much to calm the poor woman's nerves. She cried great tears of relief and gratitude throughout the entire ceremony.

At the wedding breakfast, Mary grasped Lizzy's hands and said,

"Will you come to me in the spring? I would very much like to have a sister with me who will not be intimidated by the great Lady Catherine de Bourgh."

Lizzy began to laugh, but she sobered quickly when she recognized the genuine panic in her sister's eyes. "Of course, Mary. I will always be here for you when you need me."

The Gardiners also invited Lizzy to travel with them that summer to the Lake District. Mr. Bennet, having just given his approval for his favorite daughter's trip to Kent, protested at the injustice of her abandonment twice in a year to go pleasure seeking. Lizzy could tell by the twinkle in his eye, however, that he planned to give his permission after he had finished deriving as much amusement as possible from the situation.

As Mary and Mr. Collins waved their farewells and rode the carriage away from Longbourn, a feeling of optimism and peace prevailed over everyone's hopes for the new year.

Chapter 26

March 1812

Shortly after the wedding, Mr. Darcy travelled to Derbyshire, and Mrs. and Mrs. Bingley went to London. With no greater events than these in the Longbourn family, and otherwise diversified by little beyond the walks to Meryton, sometimes dirty and sometimes cold, did January and February pass away.

Viscount Oakley spent most of those days at Longbourn, as there was no mistress to host Jane at Netherfield. He brought his sons with him for every visit, and they were rapidly become a close family. Lizzy had exerted herself to speak to the servants and had not heard one negative piece of information about Oakley from those who were beneath him. As she also observed the manner in which he disciplined his children—which was made necessary by the mere fact that young children are continually learning how to not misbehave—she had sketched his character to be one of comfortable fairness. In short, Lizzy approved of his match with Jane.

Colonel Fitzwilliam called at Longbourn with his brother the viscount when his duties would permit him. On the days he did not call, the Forsters would visit in his place, as the two colonels shared their duties. Lizzy was much pleased to see her youngest sister's lively behavior tempered with some small amount of maturity.

March was soon to take Lizzy to Hunsford. She had not at first thought very seriously of going thither; but Mary, she soon found, was depending on the plan, and she gradually learned to consider it herself with greater pleasure as well as greater certainty. The only pain was in leaving her father, who would certainly miss her, and who—when it came to the point—so little liked her going, that he told her to write to him, and almost promised to answer her letter.

At last March arrived, and Lizzy began her travels. Originally, Kitty and Mr. Bennet were to accompany her. However, Kitty expressed a desire to stay at home (probably due to Colonel Fitzwilliam's regular letters, but she would not admit that). Jane, too, rejected the notion of travel in order to stay near her suitor and his children. Oakley explained that he would gladly visit Rosings so they could be in close proximity, but his aunt Lady Catherine abhorred the noise of small children, and he would not subject his sons to such chastisements from her ladyship until the boys had grown a bit more.

Mrs. Bennet insisted on staying to help Jane with her courtship. "For how else will she induce the viscount to propose without my assistance in telling her what she ought to do?" she defended.

It was therefore agreed that Mr. Bennet would send a manservant to travel with Lizzy, as he did not trust his wife to not cause difficulties if he were away for weeks on end.

Thus, Lizzy headed toward Kent, with a stop in London at the Gardiners' along the way. It was a journey of only twenty-four miles, and they began it so early as to be in Gracechurch Street by noon. Upon their arrival, she saw her young cousins with their faces eagerly pressed against the nursery window, looking out for their beloved cousin. All was joy and kindness. The day passed most pleasantly away; the morning in bustle and shopping, and the evening at one of the theatres.

The Gardiners issued again their invitation to take Lizzy to the north in the summer. "We have not determined how far it shall carry us," said Mrs. Gardiner, "but, perhaps, to the Lakes. I am sorry, however, that you would miss out on the opportunity to see Jane's courtship progress."

No scheme could have been more agreeable to Lizzy, and her acceptance of the invitation was most ready and grateful. "Oh, my dear,

dear aunt," she rapturously cried, "What delight! What felicity! What are young men to rocks and mountains? No, I have come to know Lord Oakley as much as I can, and I am content to leave him to Jane."

Every object in the next day's journey was new and interesting to Elizabeth; and her spirits were in a state of enjoyment. When the carriage left the high road for the lane to Hunsford, she was continuously in search of the Parsonage, and every turning expected to bring it in view. The palings of Rosings Park were their boundary on one side. Lizzy smiled at the recollection of all that she had heard of its inhabitants.

At length, the Parsonage was discernible. The garden sloping to the road, the house standing in it, the green pales, and the laurel hedge, everything declared they were arriving. Mr. Collins and Mary appeared at the door, hand in hand, and the carriage stopped at the small gate which led by a short gravel walk to the house. In a moment she was out of the chaise, rejoicing at the sight of her beloved sister. Mrs. Collins welcomed Lizzy with the liveliest pleasure, and Lizzy herself was more and more satisfied with coming when she found herself so affectionately received.

She saw instantly that her cousin's manners were somewhat altered by his marriage; his formal civility was just what it had been, and he detained her some minutes at the gate to hear and satisfy his enquiries after all her family. They were then, with no other delay than his pointing out the neatness of the entrance, taken into the house; and as soon as they were in the parlor, he began to welcome them a second time, but when Mrs. Collins laid her hand on his arm, he fell silent and gave her a smile.

Mary rang for tea, and the two sisters began a conversation about how life was for her in Hunsford. Although she and Mary had corresponded regularly, there was always something novel to share in person as opposed to in a letter.

Mary's first letters to Lizzy had been received with a good deal of eagerness; there could not but be curiosity to know how she would speak of her new home, how she would like Lady Catherine, and how happy she would dare pronounce herself to be; though, when the letters were read, Lizzy felt that Mary had expressed herself on every point exactly as she might have foreseen. She had written cheerfully, seemed surrounded with comforts, and mentioned nothing which she could not praise. The house, furniture, neighborhood, and roads were all to her taste, and Lady Catherine's behavior was most friendly and obliging. It was Mr. Collins' picture of Hunsford and Rosings rationally softened; and Lizzy perceived that she must wait for her own visit there to know the rest.

Now that she was reunited with her sister, she was eager to see for herself how Mary got on with Lady Catherine.

"Lady Catherine is a very respectable, sensible woman indeed," Mary said. "And a most attentive neighbor. I have learned much from her instructions on how to run my household."

"Surely you do not need much instruction?" Lizzy queried in astonishment. "You are the daughter of a gentleman, after all, and Longbourn is a larger household than this parsonage, with more servants. No offense is here intended, of course, Mr. Collins."

Mr. Collins assured her that no offense was received. "And please call me William. We are much closer family members now than we were before!" he said with a beaming smile.

Lizzy was much comforted by his ease and kindness. She gave him leave to call her Elizabeth or Lizzy, whichever he preferred.

"But as to your question, it is precisely because Hunsford is smaller that I appreciate Lady Catherine's insights. She took an active interest in how the last vicar's wife ran the household, and she has shared many of those learnings with me," Mary explained.

The tea things arrived, putting a pause on the conversation. After the maid left, Mary continued. "We have a large household at Longbourn, so the quantities of the cuts of meat and other items are very different. The first week I almost allowed an entire roast to become an inedible because I had ordered too much. The following week, I ordered too little, and we ate nothing but biscuits and potatoes for a few days."

Mary laughed at herself, and Lizzy joined in. Mr. Collins patted his wife's hand fondly. "With fewer servants, the routines and chore allotments are very different as well. I can no longer have all of the washing completed in one day and in that same day also have the rooms dusted. In Longbourn, these chores were done by separate servants, but not here."

Lizzy nodded her understanding. "I am looking forward to meeting the lady," she told her sister. "I have heard much of her from Georgiana and Mr. Darcy."

At this, Mr. Collins shifted uncomfortably in his seat. "Ahem, well—" he began somewhat awkwardly.

Mary interjected, "Allow me to explain the situation, my dear."

Mr. Collins nodded at his wife in relief.

"You see," Mary began, "Lady Catherine is unaware of your friendship with her niece and nephews."

Lizzy raised her eyebrows in surprise. "Indeed?" she questioned.

Mary grimaced. "It is only that Lady Catherine likes to keep the distinction of rank preserved. While she has had very useful advice, she also has very strong opinions."

"I am afraid I do not quite follow," Lizzy responded in confusion.

"Lady Catherine wants Mr. Darcy to marry her daughter," Mr. Collins blurted out.

Lizzy let out a sharp bark of laughter. "She does not know that he is courting me?" she asked incredulously.

Mary shook her head. "No, although Miss de Bourgh is aware of it. She has specifically asked us to not inform her mother of the courtship until Darcy is able to come here to do so in person."

Lizzy's eyes widened slightly. "Do you know when he will be coming? For he has said nothing to me in his letters."

Mary hesitated slightly, then said, "Miss de Bourgh may have more information than I have. I did not want to pry; it was clear she was uncomfortable speaking of it to us."

Lizzy's curiosity was now almost unbearable. "What kind of girl is Miss de Bourgh? When can I expect to meet her?"

"I do not know her well," Mary admitted. "She has called on us a time or two as she drives by in her phaeton. William," she said, turning to her husband, "how would you describe her ladyship's daughter?"

"Oh, she is a rose in the flower garden of England!" Mr. Collins cried. At Mary's raised eyebrow, he moderated his voice and continued, "When I first came to Hunsford, she stopped several times to ensure that I had everything I needed to take care of the parish. At times, the tenants and villagers are in need. Lady Catherine does not always condescend to give aid, but Miss de Bourgh will always follow with help of some kind."

"She is quite a little creature," Mary said, "thin and small. At first, I thought her demeanor to be sickly and cross. It was only after the first several visits that I was able to recognize that her expressions stem from physical pain and not emotion."

Mr. Collins nodded his agreement with exaggerated movements. "I know not what ails her, but she has her own personal physician who provides her with special treatments multiple times per week."

"The poor thing," Lizzy said with feeling. "How difficult that must be."

"I believe she will want to call on you, Lizzy, and speak with you herself about Mr. Darcy," Mary informed her.

"I would be more than happy to make her acquaintance," Lizzy said sincerely.

The evening was spent chiefly in talking over Hertfordshire news and telling again what had already been written; and when it closed, Elizabeth, in the solitude of her chamber, had to meditate upon Mary's degree of contentment, to understand her address in guiding—and composure in bearing with—her husband, and to acknowledge that it was all done very well.

About the middle of the next day, as she was in her room getting ready for a walk, a sudden noise below seemed to speak the whole house in confusion; and, after listening a moment, she heard somebody running up the stairs in a violent hurry and calling loudly after her. She opened the door and met the maid of all work in the landing place, who, breathless with agitation, cried out—

"Oh, Miss Bennet! Pray make haste and come into the dining room, for there is such a sight to be seen! I will not tell you what it is. Make haste and come down this moment."

Lizzy ran down into the dining room, which fronted the lane, in quest of this wonder. It was there through the window that she saw two ladies stopping in a low phaeton at the garden gate.

"And is this all?" cried Lizzy. "I expected at least that the pigs were got into the garden, and here is nothing but Lady Catherine and her daughter."

"No, miss!" exclaimed serving girl, quite shocked at the mistake. "It is not Lady Catherine. The old lady is Mrs. Jenkinson, who lives with them; the other is Miss de Bourgh!"

Mary turned to the house and, upon seeing her sister in the window, waved her down to join them. Lizzy quickly donned her shoes and bonnet, grabbing a cloak to take with her, as the wind was quite fierce.

As Lizzy approached the phaeton, she could see that up close, Miss de Bourgh did indeed have a mien that rivaled Darcy's when he was at his most uncomfortable. In that respect, the family resemblance was quite striking, as was their coloring of dark hair and eyes. Miss de Bourgh, however, was clearly much shorter than her tall cousin; her head only came up to the shoulder of her companion's.

Mary performed the introductions. Almost immediately, Miss de Bourgh turned her attention to Lizzy.

"Miss Bennet," Miss de Bourgh said in a quiet, strained voice. "I have been looking forward to making your acquaintance. Would it be too much trouble to invite you to ride with me for a bit?"

Lizzy and Mary looked at each other, surprised. Hesitantly, Lizzy said, "I thank you for the honor, Miss de Bourgh. I have only just arrived; could we perhaps make arrangements for tomorrow?"

Miss de Bourgh glanced at her companion, who shook her head in refusal. "I am afraid I have a treatment with my doctor tomorrow," she explained, her voice even more strained. "They often leave me weak for several days afterwards. Today is the best of health that I have had in quite some time."

Lizzy looked at her sister, who nodded her approval. "In that case, I would be more than happy to accompany you now."

Miss de Bourgh looked relieved, and Lizzy climbed into the phaeton to settle herself next to Mrs. Jenkinson. It was a bit of a tight fit, but as none of the three ladies was very large, it was manageable. Miss de Bourgh flicked the reins with an expert move of her wrist, and the phaeton began to move away.

"Do not worry," Mrs. Jenkinson called back to Mary, "I will look after both young ladies."

Mary nodded and waved, while Lizzy let out a small giggle.

"What do you find so amusing?" Miss de Bourgh asked curiously.

"Oh, only that my younger sister is now my chaperone. I have always looked out for my sisters, and now society says that she must look out for me!" Lizzy exclaimed with a smile on her face.

Miss de Bourgh gave a slight smile, although her eyes remained creased, "It is interesting, is not, how being in the married state suddenly gives the illusion that one is respectable. Our society allows women very few freedoms if they are unwed, and even less so if they marry someone without care."

Lizzy pondered on that statement as they crossed a small bridge and turned into a park that was lined with trees. Here, Miss de Bourgh stopped the phaeton and continued speaking.

"It is on this subject, Miss Bennet, that I wish to speak with you."

"You wish to speak to me about marriage?" Lizzy asked bewilderedly. She glanced briefly at Mrs. Jenkinson, who smiled at her encouragingly.

Observing the look, Miss de Bourgh said in a reassuring tone, "Mrs. Jenkinson is not only my companion, but my dearest friend. She keeps all my secrets, which is vital in my home. My mother likes to have control of things. Although I have reached my majority, I do not have the strength to resist."

Miss de Bourgh let out a series of small coughs. Quickly, Mrs. Jenkinson fetched a water canister and gave it to her mistress. Upon regaining her breath, Miss de Bourgh pressed on.

"Miss Bennet, I do not have much energy or time for pleasantries. My mother is known for her candor, but I believe I will best her in that today. May I call you Elizabeth?"

"Or Lizzy, if you prefer."

Miss de Bourgh nodded. "Lizzy, then, and I am Anne. This is Ruth. Lizzy, as you can clearly tell, I am unwell. It is not fatal; indeed, I will most likely live for many years yet. However, my life is quite dull due to the strength of my mother's personality and my own frailties. She wishes me to marry my cousin Darcy, as she knows he is a good man and would care for me. However, he needs an heir, which I would most likely not survive, though my poor mother refuses to accept that. I also have very little desire to go to Pemberley, and he would not be happy at Rosings. While it is an extremely eligible match where wealth is concerned, it would make the two of us more miserable than we already are."

Lizzy startled somewhat at this description of Darcy. Anne, noticing her new friend's reaction, hastened to assure her. "Since he has met you, Darcy has been happier than I have seen him in years. Probably since the death of his father. I know he is courting you, but we are keeping that a secret from my mother until such time as you have accepted his hand. Her complaints about the situation would make my life unbearable, and I know she would do all she could to persuade you to reject his suit."

"She would not have much success, I'm afraid," Lizzy said kindly. "I am only resolved to act in that manner, which will, in my own opinion, constitute my happiness, without reference to her, or to any person so wholly unconnected with me."

At this, Anne smiled in satisfaction. It was her first emotion Lizzy had seen that somewhat eased the tension around her eyes and brow. "I am delighted to hear it. I know, Lizzy, that it may be uncomfortable for you, and your sister and her husband, to keep something from their patroness. I ask, however, for my sake, to please not reveal your relationship with my cousin. Simply acknowledge you became acquainted with him through his sister, and that your families were friendly to one another while they were in the neighborhood."

"I see no problems in doing so," Lizzy assured her.

"The next request I have of you may seem a bit unorthodox," Anne said, glancing at Mrs. Jenkinson, who smiled at her and patted Anne's hand, which was still resting on the reins, in a reassuring manner.

Anne opened her mouth to continue speaking, but she was interrupted by another coughing fit. It subsided, only to begin again when she tried once more to continue the conversation.

"Allow me, Anne, to explain," Mrs. Jenkinson urged kindly.

Anne nodded, and Lizzy turned her attention to the companion.

"Anne needs the address of Mr. Wickham, to open a correspondence with him," she said.

"What?" exclaimed Lizzy in astonishment. "Are you quite certain that is something you wish to do? Are you—? Do you know—?" she stammered, unsure of what to reveal.

"Yes, Anne is aware of his behavior towards her cousin in Ramsgate," said Mrs. Jenkinson.

"Then you are aware of his deceitful nature!" cried Lizzy. "What reason could you possibly have for wishing to communicate with the scoundrel?"

"I wish to marry him," Anne said simply.

Lizzy stared at her, dumbfounded. After several speechless moments, she finally croaked, "Why?"

"I must marry. It is the only way that I can have some control over my life. I wish to marry someone who has a pleasing countenance and can be amiable and kind if he so chooses, and his success with Georgiana shows that he is quite capable of making himself agreeable if it suits his interest," Anne clarified.

She then took several slow breaths in an attempt to avoid another coughing fit. She waved her hand at Mrs. Jenkinson to continue.

"You see, Miss Bennet—Lizzy," the elderly woman explained, "Anne has almost no freedoms. She must marry someone who has strength enough to stand at Anne's side against her mother. George Wickham is intelligent, charming, and selfish. Once Anne is married, Lady Catherine will be forced to move to the dower house, as declared in Sir Lewis's will."

"But what is to keep Mr. Wickham from taking advantage of you?" Lizzy asked, concern lacing her voice. "If you cannot stand up to your mother—who by all accounts loves you—then how can you protect yourself against a husband who cares nothing for you?"

"With money," Anne said.

"Anne has been corresponding with some of the most prestigious lawyers in London to draw up a marriage contract that would bind Mr. Wickham completely," Mrs. Jenkinson expounded. "He would receive an allowance to do with what he wished. In turn, he would be required to remain at Rosings ten months each year to keep her company. He would have absolutely no access or power other than to carry out her wishes. Myself, Mr. Darcy, and Colonel Fitzwilliam would have full guardianship over Anne for the remainder of her life. The house would be staffed by those loyal to her, and the housekeeper, butler, and myself would send weekly reports on her wellbeing to her cousins."

Lizzy's mind spun with all of this information. Finally, she asked, "At the risk of sounding indelicate, what would prevent Mr. Wickham from taking over if he outlives you? You have a responsibility to your tenants, and from what I understand about his vices, he would soon run Rosings into the ground."

"My child would inherit," Anne said simply.

Lizzy looked at her friend, confused. "Forgive me if I misunderstood, but I thought you were too ill to carry a child?"

Anne smiled and said, "That is the genius of my plan. I will allow Mr. Wickham to take a mistress. She would reside in our home as a second companion of sorts. I do not doubt that he will have urges; all men do. However, part of the conditions for his allowance is that he remain faithful to this woman. I will not allow him to take advantage of any maids or shopkeepers' daughters. When this woman has children, I pass them off as my own, adopting them in secret through my lawyers."

"And if you pass before your heir reaches their majority, how could you prevent Mr. Wickham from using his powers as the father to take control of their inheritance?"

"Darcy and Fitzwilliam will be named guardians in my will."

Lizzy sat back against the bench of the phaeton, her mind awhirl with all of the information that had been shared with her. "It seems you have given this quite a good deal of thought," she said.

"I have been making plans for this since I was sixteen years old," Anne informed her. "I have very little else to do with my time; I spend most of it in bed, recovering from treatments. I do not want to be alone for my entire life. Once I reached my majority, I hired my own lawyers with Darcy's help. He is fully aware of my plans."

"He knows that you wish to wed Mr. Wickham?" Lizzy asked in amazement.

Anne and Mrs. Jenkinson glanced at one another uneasily.

"Well, he does not know who the man is," Anne said slowly. "However, he knows that whoever is chosen will be a charming fortune hunter."

"Why on earth would you choose a man who has brought such pain to your cousins?" Lizzy asked in dismay.

"That is the only part of the situation that still has me concerned,"

Anne admitted. "However, it was Georgiana's experience with him that showed me he would be the best choice I could make."

"I'm sorry, but I do not understand."

"You see, all throughout his courtship with Georgiana, he treated her with kindness," Anne defended. "He did not assault her, kidnap her, or even mistreat her. She was compromised with a few kisses, but no more than that, even though he had ample opportunity to do so."

Lizzy nodded slowly. "I can see how that would make him more desirable than a stranger."

"Precisely," Anne said.

The three women sat in silence for a few minutes. The ponies, which had been lazily nibbling on the grass, began to shift around, eager to be moving again. The slight shaking of the phaeton pulled the ladies from their thoughts, and Anne moved them into a slow trot.

"I will give you the direction for Mr. Wickham on one condition," Lizzy said, "You must write to Georgiana and gain her permission first before you communicate with him. I will not be party to anything that would cause my friend pain."

Anne sat thoughtfully for a minute, then agreed. "I believe that is a fair offer. I will write to her tomorrow before the doctor comes and send it express."

Lizzy nodded her approval. "I will also be writing to her; I would like to see her assurances for myself."

"Perhaps, instead, I shall recommend she come with Darcy for Easter?" Anne suggested. "We could all speak together then."

"Darcy is coming here?" Lizzy asked in surprise.

"Anne, you weren't supposed to tell her!" Mrs. Jenkinson admonished, "He wanted to surprise her!"

Anne looked sheepishly away. "In my haste to arrange things for myself, I completely forgot."

Lizzy laughed. "Well, it was definitely a surprise! Not to worry, I will not give it away. I will act properly excited and surprised to see him."

Then she sobered and said, "I think you should still write to Georgiana about your plan, in general terms, so that she is not taken by surprise all at once when she gets here."

Anne nodded. "We have a deal, then?"

"Yes," Lizzy said.

As they approached the parsonage, Anne said, "Will you please keep this from Mr. and Mrs. Collins? It is not that I don't trust them," she rushed to say as she saw Lizzy's expression, "but only I want to keep this between as few people as possible. I also do not want them to feel torn between myself and my mother. It would be unfair to ask them to keep something of this magnitude from their patroness when it concerns her own daughter."

Seeing the wisdom in this, Lizzy quickly promised that she would keep it to herself. As she descended from the phaeton, she saw Mary coming out to greet her. Turning back to her new friends, she said, "I will simply tell them you and I were speaking of Mr. Darcy."

Anne smiled in relief and gratitude. Although her eyes still seemed pained, they also shone with a hope that had not been present before.

"I thank you, Lizzy, with all my heart."

Chapter 27

Georgiana Bingley sat at her vanity, brushing her hair as she waited for her husband. It had been a busy day; Caroline had been married and was now the responsibility of her husband. *Finally,* Georgiana thought. *If I had to hear one more discussion about how much lace was appropriate for a wedding gown, I would lose my mind.*

The weeks since they had left Netherfield had been filled only with days to be endured. *At least there have been nights to enjoy,* Georgiana mused. She blushed slightly and looked around guiltily, then laughed at her silliness. Women who enjoyed the attentions of their husbands were uncommon in the *ton,* and love matches were more likely to be ridiculed than praised. However, no one was able to hear her private thoughts. She may think what she wish.

Her entire life, Georgiana had been made to understand that she was to marry to improve her station in life and behave in a way that brought honor to her family name. Instead, she ended up almost eloping with a scoundrel, marrying the son of a tradesman, and behaving in ways with her husband that the members of the *ton* would deem wanton.

At least Charles does not mind my wanton ways. She put her brush down and moved to the bed. He should be coming to her soon, and she liked the time they spent in one another's arms as they discussed the day's events. Some nights it led to more intimate moments, but just as often they were content to hold one another and sleep. There was passion and partnership in equal measure, and she felt herself to be the most fortunate of women.

Her eyes began to close, and she soon fell into slumber, completely oblivious to her husband's tender smile as he entered the room and slid into the bed next to her.

Georgiana awoke late the next morning, somewhat surprised at seeing the sun shining through the drapes. Bingley lay next to her, eyes on her face, fingers stroking her arm.

"I'm sorry I fell asleep so early," she told him. "I had every intention of waiting for you."

He smiled at her and replied, "Quite all right, my dear. I was a little late coming to bed."

He leaned over to kiss her, and she felt an overwhelming nausea. She sat upright and bolted towards her dressing room, barely making it to the chamber pot before losing the contents of her stomach.

Bingley immediately went to the bellpull and rang for her maid. "Are you alright, dearest?" he asked. Then he teased, "Is the thought of kissing me that repulsive?"

Georgiana began to laugh as the embarrassment she felt faded. "There is such a thing as morning breath," she countered, but the thought of said morning breath caused her to again cast up her accounts again.

Bingley frowned and approached her, putting a head on her forehead. "You do not seem feverish," he said. "Perhaps you indulged too much on wedding cake yesterday."

"I didn't eat any cake," Georgiana admitted. "My stomach felt a bit unsettled, and I did not wish to become ill on Caroline's wedding day."

His frown deepened, but before he could respond, Georgiana's lady's maid entered the room. Turning to the servant he said, "Have a footman fetch the doctor. Mrs. Bingley is unwell."

"There is no need for a doctor," protested Georgiana. She made to stand, but she stumbled slightly as the room spun around her.

Bingley quickly caught her before she could collapse to the floor. In one swift movement, he lifted her as though she weighed nothing and carried her to the bed. "I insist," he said firmly.

Somewhat concerned herself, Georgiana nodded in acquiescence. After half an hour, the doctor arrived and quickly removed Mr. Bingley from the room, in spite of his protestations.

"I shall be quite alright," Georgiana assured her husband. Gesturing to her maid, she added, "Hannah will remain with me, and I would like to speak to the doctor privately."

This assertion was the only possible thing that could have moved her worried husband from her sickbed. A quick examination by the doctor proved Georgiana's suspicions were correct: she was most likely with child, due to come in October, based on the last date of her courses.

Georgiana was at once excited and nervous about the prospect of her impending motherhood. Her mother had passed through many failed pregnancies before giving birth to a son, then several more before Georgiana's own birth. The doctor assured her that she seemed to be in perfect health at the moment. He recommended she keep some plain gingersnaps on the bedside table to alleviate the morning sickness, but otherwise he could see no reason that she would not be able to carry a healthy child to term.

The doctor bid farewell and left. The door had not finished closing behind him before Bingley rushed into the room, demanding to know all the doctor had said.

She beckoned him to sit on the bed next to her. He did so, his face pale. She took his hands, placed them on her abdomen, and said, "We are both quite well."

He stared at her blankly for a moment, then gasped in shock. "What—how—when?" he stammered in confusion.

Georgiana laughed and said, "I hope I need not explain 'how' to you!"

Bingley blushed slightly and joined her in laughter.

"As to when," she continued, "we shall have a boy or girl sometime in October."

Bingley lifted their joined hands from her abdomen to his lips. "This is the most wonderful news," he said reverently, his eyes suspiciously bright.

The two spent the rest of the morning in her bedchamber, discussing the information the doctor shared, as well as their hopes, fears, and plans. They determined to remove to Netherfield as soon as may be so they could begin preparing the nursery and interviewing for a wet nurse and nanny. The baby would arrive shortly before the lease would end, so they agreed upon leasing Netherfield another year. This meant there would not be a rush to find an estate to purchase before the baby's arrival.

Their discussion was interrupted when a maid knocked on the door to bring them luncheon. Lying on the tray was the day's post. Bingley sorted through the letters and handed two of them to Georgiana.

"You are quite popular today," he remarked.

Georgiana laughed and said, "I have been hoping to hear from Lizzy and Cousin Anne! I wonder how they are getting on."

Opening Anne's letter first, she began to read what her cousin had to say. As her eyes scanned the words, she gasped and turned pale. Bingley's attention left his own letters, and he instead fixed his concerned gaze on his wife.

She put down Anne's letter and picked up Lizzy's. Upon finishing that letter, she looked at her husband and said, "Anne wants to marry George Wickham. Lizzy writes to beg us to come to Rosings as soon as may be."

Bingley's face changed from concern to horror, "I will send a note to your brother."

"He already plans to leave for Rosings in two days," Georgiana reminded him. "I think we should join him."

Bingley nodded and rang for a servant. He began barking orders as he scribbled a note to Darcy, begging him to come to the Bingley household as soon as possible.

While the Bingleys waited for Darcy to arrive, they began to make arrangements to go to Rosings. Knowing they would be travelling in his carriage rather than their own, as it was more well-sprung, they decided to travel to Rosings, then on to Netherfield. This would necessitate closing the house earlier than they anticipated.

Darcy's arrival prompted a repetition of the wide range of emotions the couple had been experiencing that day.

"I congratulate you both!" Darcy said with feeling after hearing the news about the pregnancy. He embraced his sister and clapped his hand on his brother's shoulder. "This is wonderful!"

At the news from letters, his face contorted in anger. "Could you leave tomorrow instead of in two days?" he asked, eager to be on his way.

Bingley shook his head. "We will need to close the house for a while; we will not be returning until long after the confinement."

"Besides," Georgiana said, "it is not as if we are attempting to prevent an elopement. One more day should not make a difference in Anne's decision."

Darcy capitulated, and the three agreed to depart in the early morning in two days.

~∞~∞~∞~

Two days later found Darcy, Bingley, and Georgiana on their way to Kent. They had left early in the morning and made good progress, in spite of Georgiana's discomfort. She would not brook any delays on her behalf. "After all," she remarked, "if a tenant is able to care for her home while in the family way, then I certainly can handle a few days of travel."

Upon their arrival, they were shown to their rooms to freshen up and rest before dining with Lady Catherine, who quickly made known her dismay at Georgiana's arrival with such little notice.

"A well-bred young woman would not dare to put her hostess at such inconvenience," she said, sniffing at Bingley.

Relations had been strained between Rosings and Pemberley since Lady Catherine had discovered her niece had deigned to marry a tradesman's son. "How could the shades of Pemberley be so polluted?" she had cried in dismay.

The scathing letter of disappointment she sent to Georgiana had fortunately been intercepted by her brother, who had consigned the vitriolic missive to the fire. He had relayed the gist of the message to his sister so that she would not be caught unawares. Bingley had also seen the letter before it was burned, as Darcy had felt it necessary to make him aware of the matter, in order to prevent a second letter making its way into her hands. Georgiana had been in a very delicate emotional state in the months immediately following the hasty marriage, and both gentlemen endeavored to protect her whilst she was still regaining her confidence.

Georgiana, having grown much since that time, merely smiled and replied calmly, "My apologies, Aunt, but I have missed the company of my cousin Anne dearly. When my brother told me he was coming here for Easter, I simply could not stay away."

Lady Catherine nodded her head regally. "Certainly, your attachment to Rosings must have grown in the time you were away. I imagine your new station in life does not provide as many fineries as you experience here."

The niece smiled blissfully at the aunt. With her ladyship's ego properly settled, she turned the conversation toward her daughter Anne's assumed delight in seeing both of her cousins. "One cousin in particular seems quite eager to return and speak with her," Lady Catherine said with a knowing smile at Darcy, whose stern demeanor became even more fearsome.

"There must have been some special reason for you to have your sister accompany you this time, Darcy," she added.

"Yes, there is, indeed," he answered solemnly. "Is Anne not to dine with us this evening?"

Lady Catherine's smile grew even wider at this question. "She wanted to get a proper rest before she greeted you tomorrow."

"I see," Darcy said, disappointment coloring his voice.

"Perhaps it is for the best, Brother," Georgiana said with a light voice. "After all, we have had a long journey, and I am certain that your conversation will go much better if we are all well-rested and in a good mood."

At that statement, Lady Catherine rose from the table to signal an end of the meal. "I, too, shall take this opportunity to retire," she said imperiously "Tomorrow is to be a grand day, and it would not do to face it with fatigue."

The party agreed, and they all retired to their rooms for the night. Darcy, before retiring to bed, wrote a note for Lizzy that bade her come to the house in the morning to attend their conversation with Anne. Trusting the note to the capable hands of his valet, he quickly turned to sleep.

Morning came swiftly to all of the members of the household. In spite of their travels the previous day, Darcy, Bingley, and Georgiana all arose with the sun. Georgiana spent the first hour in her bed, sipping a weak ginger tea, to quell the worst of her morning sickness.

At last, the hour arrived for Lizzy to come from the parsonage. She had spent the last several days in contemplation of this moment. After she wrote her letter to Georgiana, begging for her to come to Rosings, she had done what she could to build a friendship with Anne de Bourgh. It was clear that the young woman was in desperate need of friendship and kindness. Lizzy's introduction to Lady Catherine made it clear why Anne was desperate to escape her mother.

She dressed for her first visit to Rosings with care, as her sister and brother were somewhat ill at ease with the meeting. When she came down, Mr. Collins said, "Do not make yourself uneasy, my dear cousin, about your apparel. Lady Catherine is far from requiring that elegance of dress in us which becomes herself and her daughter. I would advise you merely to put on whatever of your clothes is superior to the rest—there is no occasion for anything more. Lady Catherine will not think the worse of you for being simply dressed. She likes to have the distinction of rank

315

preserved."

Lizzy raised her eyebrows at Mary, her nodded and said, "I have found it best to follow my husband's guidance on what will or will not best please Lady Catherine. While she is not the Almighty," she added with a soft smile at her husband, who grinned sheepishly, "it does improve our situation when my husband's patroness is pleased with us."

Lizzy nodded in understanding. As they walked to Rosings, Mr. Collins began pointing out the elegance of the grounds. A pat on his arm from Mary calmed his excitement, and the remainder of the walk continued with quiet discussion amongst the party.

That first dinner was exceedingly handsome and exactly as magnificent as Mr. Collins would describe it. The party did not supply much conversation. Elizabeth was ready to speak whenever there was an opening, but she was seated between Mary and Anne—the former of whom was engaged in listening to Lady Catherine, and the latter said not a word to her all dinnertime. Mrs. Jenkinson was chiefly employed in watching how little Miss de Bourgh ate, pressing her to try some other dish, and fearing she was indisposed.

When the ladies returned to the drawing room, there was little to be done but to hear Lady Catherine talk, which she did without any intermission till coffee came in, delivering her opinion on every subject in so decisive a manner as proved that she was not used to having her judgement controverted. Her attention regularly turned to Lizzy.

She asked her, at different times, how many sisters she had, whether they were older or younger than herself, whether any of them were likely to be married, whether they were handsome, where they had been educated, what carriage her father kept, and what had been her mother's maiden name? Lizzy felt all the impertinence of her questions but answered them very composedly. Lady Catherine then observed,

"Your father's estate is entailed on Mr. Collins, I think. For your sake," turning to Mary, "I am glad of it; but otherwise I see no occasion for entailing estates from the female line. It was not thought necessary in Sir Lewis de Bourgh's family. Do you play and sing, Miss Bennet?"

"A little."

"Oh! then—some time or other we shall be happy to hear you. Our instrument is a capital one, probably superior to——You shall try it some day. Do your sisters play and sing?"

"One of them does."

"Why did not you all learn? You ought all to have learned. The Misses Webb all play, and their father has not so good an income as yours. Do you draw?"

"No, not at all."

"What, none of you?"

"Not one."

"That is very strange. But I suppose you had no opportunity. Your mother should have taken you to town every spring for the benefit of masters."

"My mother would have had no objection, but my father hates London."

"Has your governess left you?"

"We never had any governess."

"No governess! How was that possible? Five daughters brought up at home without a governess! I never heard of such a thing. Your mother must have been quite a slave to your education."

Elizabeth could hardly help smiling as she assured her that had not been the case.

"Then, who taught you? who attended to you? Without a governess, you must have been neglected."

"Compared with some families, I believe we were; but such of us as wished to learn never wanted the means. We were always encouraged to read, and had all the masters that were necessary. Those who chose to be idle, certainly might."

"Aye, no doubt; but that is what a governess will prevent, and if I had known your mother, I should have advised her most strenuously to engage one. I always say that nothing is to be done in education without steady and regular instruction, and nobody but a governess can give it. It is wonderful how many families I have been the means of supplying in that way. I am always glad to get a young person well placed out. Four nieces of Mrs. Jenkinson are most delightfully situated through my means; and it was but the other day that I recommended another young person, who was merely accidentally mentioned to me, and the family are quite delighted with her. Mrs. Collins, did I tell you of Lady Metcalf's calling yesterday to thank me? She finds Miss Pope a treasure. 'Lady Catherine,' said she, 'you have given me a treasure.' Are any of your other younger sisters out, Miss Bennet, besides Mrs. Collins?"

"Yes, ma'am, all of them; and our youngest sister is also married."

"All! What, all five out at once? Very odd! And you only the second. The younger ones out before the elder ones are married! Your younger sisters must be very young?"

"Yes, my youngest is not sixteen. Perhaps she is full young to be much in company and even married. But really, ma'am, I think it would be very hard upon younger sisters, that they should not have their share of society and amusement, because the elder may not have the means or inclination to marry early. The last-born has as good a right to the pleasures of youth as the first. And to be kept back on such a motive! I think it would not be very likely to promote sisterly affection or delicacy of mind. Mary would not have been able to marry Mr. Collins, and we see how well they get on together!"

"Upon my word," said her ladyship, "you give your opinion very decidedly for so young a person. Pray, what is your age?"

"With three younger sisters grown up," replied Elizabeth, smiling, "and two of them now married, your ladyship can hardly expect me to own it."

Lady Catherine seemed quite astonished at not receiving a direct answer; and Elizabeth suspected herself to be the first creature who had ever dared to trifle with so much dignified impertinence. Mary sent Lizzy a small smirk, while Mr. Collins watched the conversation with his mouth slightly agape.

"You cannot be more than twenty, I am sure, therefore you need not conceal your age."

"I am not one-and-twenty."

Throughout the entire inquisition, Anne remained silent, her head bowed. Lizzy glanced at her new friend with concern, but the young woman did not move or speak the entire time. Once, it appeared she was about to comment, but at the small movement, her mother fixed her with such an oppressive glare that it was all Lizzy could do to keep from gasping.

On the way home, Lizzy asked about Mary's smirk about the conversations. Mary replied that Lady Catherine had asked Mary those same questions on her *first occasion to meet the grand lady as well. It amused Mary to see Lady Catherine respond to Lizzy's impertinent answers, as opposed to her own meek responses to the woman, which were given humbly in deference to her husband's position of dependency on his patroness.*

Lady Catherine's treatment of her daughter inspired Lizzy to do all she could to be a companion for Anne during the daytimes when they took rides on Anne's phaeton. The girls spoke of their hopes and plans for the future, and they became quite entrenched in one another's confidence. Of Mr. Wickham, Lizzy did not dare speak. She was content to wait until Mr. Darcy arrived with Georgiana and Mr. Bingley. They would know better than she how to help Anne gain power over her life without subjecting herself to such a wicked man.

It was with a much lighter heart that Lizzy now climbed the steps to Rosings. Knowing that she would have support in helping Anne was the removal of a weight that she had not known existed until it was gone. A quiet knock at the door was all that was needed for the butler to quickly admit her. The man knew which way the wind blew, so he was more than happy to escort Lizzy to Anne's quarters without Lady Catherine being aware of the visit.

Lizzy had never been in the family wing at Rosings. It was decorated in the same garish style that adorned the rest of the house. She was surprised, therefore, when the door to Anne's private sitting room opened to reveal a room that was decorated simply and tastefully.

Georgiana, Darcy, and Bingley were already seated, though Anne had not yet joined them. Mrs. Jenkinson was also absent, likely helping her charge dress and prepare for the meeting. Georgiana and Lizzy embraced as the gentlemen rose to their feet and executed deep bows. Darcy extended his hand to Lizzy, and she sat next to him on the settee. Georgiana and Bingley shared a small sofa, and an empty chaise lounge presumably awaited its mistress.

Lizzy had no sooner arrived than the door leading from Anne's bedroom to the sitting room opened, and the frail young woman slowly made her way to her guests, her hands gripping tightly the arm of her companion. It took her several moments to seat herself in a comfortable manner, after which Mrs. Jenkinson took up a small chair near Anne.

Anne looked around at her three guests and gave a wry smile, "I am delighted to inform you all that reports of my death have been grossly exaggerated."

The tension in the room eased and they all chuckled in response. After a brief coughing fit, Anne continued, "In truth, I am grateful that you all are here. I have not felt this cared for since before my late father passed."

Georgiana's expression turned to one of sympathy, and she reached out a hand to her cousin. "I am only sorry that I have not come sooner."

Anne waved a hand dismissively. "Worry not; I do not blame you for avoiding my mother, particularly given her temper after receiving news of your marriage."

Georgiana blushed faintly, "I should not have been so selfish."

"All of us have been so," Darcy interjected. "We sought to protect ourselves from discomfort. I can only feel shame at my behavior in leaving you to your mother's mercy. Things must feel desperate indeed if you are considering marriage to Wickham as a way to escape."

"What, no small talk?" Anne asked.

Lizzy let out a small burst of laughter. "Oh, Anne," she said, shaking her head. "You know you despise small talk."

A weak smile graced Anne's lips. "I had to relieve the tension somehow."

Then she sobered, "Please do not attempt to change my mind. I assure you, I am quite determined to have my way on this matter."

"I understand why you want to do this. But please, surely there must be someone else," pleaded Georgiana.

Anne shook her head. "I do not trust anyone else."

"But he cannot be trusted, either!" Darcy exclaimed in frustration.

"I understand what you are saying, Anne," Lizzy said.

Bingley, Darcy, and Georgiana gaped at her in astonishment. "How could you?" whispered Georgiana in dismay.

Darcy's face was fierce. "Why do you align yourself with Wickham on this matter?" He demanded. "Has he promised you something to further his cause? Is that why he was in Hertfordshire?"

Lizzy gasped indignantly. "How dare you, sir?" she responded icily, "This is your opinion of me? This is the estimation with which I am regarded in your view?"

The two stared at one another, eyes locked. Finally, an angry Darcy broke the silence. "And this is all the reply which I am to have the honor of expecting! I might, perhaps, wish to be informed why, with so little endeavor at civility, my question is thus ignored. But it is of small importance."

"I might as well inquire," replied she, "why with so evident a desire of offending and insulting me, you choose to question my integrity! To go so far as to accuse me of being in collusion with one of the most treacherous men of my acquaintance! Was this impeachment not a sound inducement for incivility, if indeed I was uncivil in my response to such?"

Bingley looked between the two combatants. "Perhaps, Miss Bennet," he ventured cautiously, "you could help *me* to understand Miss de Bourgh? I would like to know why she is so intent on Mr. Wickham."

Lizzy graced him with a small smile. "Nota res mala, opima," she said simply.

Darcy gaped at her, while Bingley nodded contemplatively. "Now I see," he said. At his wife's questioning look, he elaborated, "It is an old saying from the sixteenth century, but I cannot recall who first said it. In Latin, it means 'an evil thing is known best.' In simpler words, "It is better to deal with the devil you know than with the devil you know not."

"It was Taverner, in 1539," Darcy said quietly. His face had changed from red to white at Lizzy's words.

The confusion on Georgiana's face cleared. "That does make a bit of sense," she admitted.

"Just because I understand, however, does not mean I think it the best course," Lizzy said quietly. "I never said I agreed with Anne's choice, only that I understood it."

Anne looked sorrowfully at her new friend. "Are you to turn your back on me, as well, Lizzy?"

"My dear Anne, of course not!" Lizzy exclaimed, rising to her feet and crossing over to her friend. Kneeling near the couch where Anne rested, she took her hand and continued, "You have very well-connected cousins. While you personally may not be acquainted with or know about many people, I am more than certain that between your family and friends in Derbyshire, Hertfordshire, Kent, and even the militia, we can find someone who is more worthy of you than a nefarious fortune hunter like Mr. Wickham."

Anne shook her head. "But *I* do not know them. How can you be sure they are not misleading you? At least with Mr. Wickham, I would know how to protect myself."

"Because no one can hide behind a mask forever," Lizzy said. "When you take the time to do research and investigate a person, you find it is quite a simple thing to determine their true character."

Anne hesitated. "I don't know."

Georgiana crossed to kneel by Lizzy at Anne's side. "My dear cousin Anne," she said in a soft voice, "You can trust me. I would never, ever allow you to marry someone who could hurt you."

Anne's eyes filled with tears. "I just did not know how else I could find someone."

Georgiana's own eyes were bright. "There is no need for you to do this alone. You have me, and my brother, and my husband, and our cousin."

"And you have me, too," Lizzy said, "should you ever need me."

Anne heaved a great sigh. "Very well, then. Only it must be soon. I do not have the energy to endure this much longer. The doctor has informed me that I have only two years, perhaps three, left before I am confined to the bed."

"Then we will act with urgency, but with caution," Darcy said.

With his comment, Lizzy rose from the floor. "I will leave you to discuss your various acquaintances," she said. "Anne, I hope I may call on you tomorrow."

Anne nodded. As Lizzy crossed the room to leave, Darcy reached his hand out towards her.

"Lizzy—" he began.

Lizzy turned cold eyes towards him. "Sir, I believe it would be best if you addressed me as Miss Bennet. You are not my father nor my betrothed to address me so informally, and I believe I can say that right now, you are the last man in the world whom I could ever be prevailed upon to marry."

Darcy's heart sank in his chest. He opened his mouth to respond, but no words came. Lizzy turned her back and left the room, suppressing the tears until she had made it out the house and down the path to the parsonage. Only then—when she was out of sight from Rosings—did she allow them to fall unchecked down her cheeks.

Chapter 28

Darcy yearned to go after Lizzy, but he had not made it more than two steps before he heard Anne's raspy voice call his name.

"Let her go," she advised him. "You need to give her some space to process her feelings. It was very badly done to accuse her of being in league with Wickham."

Georgiana looked at him with disappointment "I, too, was hurt when first she said that she understood. But I never imagined she was deceitful!"

Darcy hung his head. "I knew as soon as the words left my mouth what a complete and utter fool I was. I need to apologize, to let her know..."

"You need to allow her to sort through her emotions, first," Bingley told him firmly. The room looked at him in astonishment. "What? I have sisters, and a wife!"

Georgiana laughed lightly and rose to her feet to join her husband. She swayed slightly as she stood, and Bingley was immediately at her side to steady her. "Are you alright, dearest?" he asked in concern.

"Just a little lightheaded, 'tis all. I believe I should eat something."

Anne motioned for Mrs. Jenkinson to ring for tea. Darcy looked at the woman, somewhat surprised to see her still in the room. He had entirely forgotten her presence in the commotion of Anne's announcement and his poor reaction.

When the tea tray arrived, Darcy retook his seat. The company sat in silence as the tea was poured and the servant left the room. Once she was gone, Darcy addressed the group.

"I think I am acquainted with someone who would be a good fit for you, Anne," he informed her. "There is a curate at Kympton who is looking for a living. Mr. Benjamin Reid is the fourth son of a baron, and he is a good young man. The vicar there is still relatively young, having only just been appointed to the position in the last few years. Mr. Reid would not be likely to rise to that position for quite some time, and he is eager to be of use elsewhere."

"A curate would not be willing to have a mistress that could bear me an heir," Anne pointed out.

"Would the child need to be of your husband's blood?" Bingley asked.

Anne pondered the question. "No," she said after a few moments, "but since I had assumed I would be wedding a fortune hunter, a mistress was the logical solution to keep him happy here."

"Why do you ask, Charles?" Georgiana inquired.

"Darcy, do you remember someone mentioning that Cartwright's wife had died in childbirth?"

"You cannot seriously be considering Mr. Cartwright as a husband for Anne!" exclaimed Georgiana in dismay.

"No!" Bingley hastened to assure her. "The son, however, is not Mr. Cartwright's only issue; the boy has a caretaker who has unfortunately found herself in the same condition as the boy's mother once was, due to her master's proclivities. She is an impoverished gentlewoman's daughter. Her name is Alice—perhaps Amelia—Johnson, I believe."

"And how do you know so much about the situation?" Darcy eyed Bingley suspiciously.

Bingley chortled, "Why, from your butler! He has kept an eye on the situation at Cartwright's estate and monitored how the servants are being treated. He has written to me on occasion to help with any that are in need."

"Why would he not come to me?" Darcy asked, the hurt evident in his tone.

"Because he already felt you had done enough for those who had suffered at Cartwright's hands. He did not want to add to your burden when he is so indebted to you for your kindness."

Darcy nodded slowly in understanding. "What do you think, Anne?" he asked, turning to his cousin. "Do you think that you would do well with a curate and a young woman who has been mistreated?"

"It is an agreeable alternative," she admitted. "However, I do not know if I could enjoy a somber man of the cloth as a husband. There has been enough solemnity at Rosings."

"The young man is more like Bingley than myself in character," Darcy assured her. "He is amiable, steady, and kind. He came to Kympton with superlative recommendations from the vicar of his childhood home, and I know his father and elder brothers. They, too, are all good men."

"He would also be of use to the parish here, which is under the domain of Mr. Collins." Georgiana wrinkled her nose when she said his name, causing Anne to let out a bark of laughter that quickly turned to a coughing fit.

"We should let you rest before dinner, Anne," Georgiana was quick to say.

Anne began to shake her head in denial, but a stern look from Mrs. Jenkinson caused the frail young lady to emit a vexed sigh.

"Very well," Anne capitulated "I will spend the afternoon considering the matter. I am inclined to accept the proposal, but it must be resolved quickly, lest Mr. Cartwright cause the young woman further harm."

Darcy nodded. "With your permission, I shall begin to draft letters to send express to Mr. Reid, my butler, and your lawyers. I can ride to London tomorrow to purchase a special license, then go on to Derbyshire to fetch Miss Johnson."

Georgiana looked at him in concern. "What about Lizzy?"

Darcy's face became a stone mask. "I shall write her a letter as well, if you will deliver it for me."

Georgiana opened her mouth to protest, but then thought better of it and sat back in her seat with a sigh. "I am afraid you are correct; there is no time to speak with her today, and you truly must leave immediately on the morrow. All must be arranged with the utmost haste, that our plans may come to fruition before our aunt can discover them."

Darcy nodded. "With luck, I will be able to return in a sennight, and I can speak with her then."

With this, Bingley, Georgiana, and Darcy took their leave, allowing Anne to rest for the remainder of the day. Darcy occupied himself in the study, writing his letters, while Bingley took Georgiana to their rooms in order for her to recover her strength. While she would not like to admit it, the travel had worn her out more thoroughly than she had anticipated.

That evening at dinner, Anne sent word that she was unable to join them. Knowing the tumult that was about to occur in a week, she needed to gather her strength. She sent a note to Darcy, wishing him safe travels on his journey to London. Darcy took that as confirmation that she had determined on Mr. Reid, and he informed his aunt that he would be away for several days.

Lady Catherine protested vociferously, but Darcy reminded her that Georgiana would remain behind, and stated that he was eager to return as soon as possible. He hinted that he needed to retrieve something of great value from Pemberley, as well as important documents from Anne's solicitors. Lady Catherine took this to mean that a betrothal ring and settlement papers were being fetched, and she was content to allow him his business.

As he left the next morning, he passed a sealed envelope to his sister. "Give this to her for me, please," he begged, "I have been an utter fool."

"You have," Georgiana agreed, "But that does not preclude your learning from the experience. You have my word; I will see it directly into her hands."

As she watched her brother ride away, Georgiana offered a silent prayer that all would turn out as it should.

$$\sim\infty\sim\infty\sim\infty\sim$$

"How is your headache, Lizzy?" Mary asked with concern as she brought a tray with afternoon tea into her elder sister's room.

Lizzy smiled wanly, "It is a bit improved. I am sorry you have had to wait on me since yesterday morning."

Mary rolled her eyes. "Honestly, Lizzy, it has only been a day. We all suffer from megrims on occasion. You have taken such good care of all of us; now it is my turn to take care of you."

Setting the tray down beside her sister, Mary added, "You have received a letter from Jane. I hope you will share all her news with me after you have read it!"

"Of course," Lizzy replied.

"Oh, and I almost forgot. Mrs. Bingley called this morning. She was quite sad to hear that you were unwell. She said she would return tomorrow to see how you were faring."

Lizzy winced inwardly. "That was kind of her."

"She also said that her brother would be sorry to hear that you were unwell in his absence, but she hopes you will improve before he returns. You did not tell me that Mr. Darcy was to travel for several weeks."

"I did not know. It must have been a sudden decision," Lizzy said.

Mary frowned slightly in concern but did not press the issue. Pressing a kiss on her sister's brow, she said, "I will leave you to your letter from Jane and return with your dinner. Do you need me to fetch you anything before I leave?"

Lizzy shook her head mutely, forcing the tears to remain at bay until her sister had left the room. Once the door closed behind Mary, though, Lizzy put her face in her hands and began to sob.

After she had returned home from Rosings the day before, Lizzy had spent much of the day in her room, pondering the situation. *I should not have become so offended. I should have stayed and discussed the situation with him. Yes, he chose to believe the worst of me. But have I not often chosen to see the worst in him?*

She had determined that the next morning she would call again at Rosings. However, her tears and a sleepless night had caused a true megrim that had yet to abate. *And now, it is too late; I have driven him away with my rash words.*

Lizzy picked up a piece of toast that Mary had brought. As she ate, she turned her attention to Jane's letter. A smile lit up her face, and she quickly stood up to find Mary. The ensuing pain the sudden movement inspired in her head caused her to immediately sit back down. Instead, she called for her sister.

"What is it, Lizzy? Are you all right?"

"Oh, Mary! Jane is engaged!"

Mary beamed with delight. "The Viscount proposed? How wonderful!"

Lizzy read aloud from the letter, which described the romantic setting and the way Oakley had involved his sons as they asked her to be their new mother.

"Although they are not in love, it is clear that he is fond of Jane and will treat her well," Lizzy remarked when she reached the end.

Mary nodded. "I think you should return to Longbourn, as Jane requested. I will be sorry to lose your company, but Jane will need your help in dealing with our mother."

Lizzy groaned. "Yes, she will be impossible, and Jane will allow her to do whatever she wishes in order to keep the peace."

The girls determined that Lizzy would visit Rosings on the morrow to take her leave, and then she would travel to Longbourn the following day. She spent what was left of the current day packing and readying herself for the journey.

Late the next morning, Lizzy walked to Rosings. She had delayed the visit until close to mealtime, so that she might not be prevailed upon to remain any longer than politeness demanded. She was embarrassed at how harshly she had responded to Darcy's accusations. He should have had faith in her, but she should have taken the time to communicate, rather than responding in anger and leaving without any sort of discussion. They cared about one another too much to allow misunderstandings to separate them without making the effort at resolving them.

He will probably never wish to see me again, she thought sadly as she knocked on the door at Rosings.

The butler showed her to the drawing room, where Anne and Georgiana were sitting with Lady Catherine. As usual, Lady Catherine maintained control of the conversation. She chastised Lizzy for leaving on so short a notice but encouraged the girl to use her noble name in gaining the best accommodations as she travelled. To Lizzy's surprise, Lady Catherine was quite accepting of her nephew's marriage to Jane.

"After all, he has already done his duty by marrying with a noble and producing heirs of good breeding. He can afford to take someone of your sister's status as a second wife."

When at last it came time to depart, Georgiana embraced Lizzy and pressed a folded paper into her hand. "We shall see you soon at Netherfield; we will be returning after we complete our plans here," she added, nodding discreetly toward Anne.

Lizzy curled her fingers around the paper. She dipped a curtsy of farewell to the occupants of the room and left.

I wish I had been afforded the opportunity to ask after her brother, Lizzy thought sadly. *He may, perhaps, come for his cousin's wedding.*

Upon returning to the parsonage, she was dismayed to discover that Mr. Collins was postponing some of his regular duties in order to spend time in saying farewell to his wife's sister before she had to leave. Between his prolonged discourse of many hours and her exhaustion from lack of sleep the night previous, Lizzy could muster no more strength than was necessary that night to regain her room and collapse into her bed. She had not even the vigor with which to change into her nightclothes. The letter would have to wait until she had privacy to read it on her journey.

Lizzy awoke the next morning feeling refreshed and eager to depart so she could turn her attention to her letter. There would be no time to do so before she had to depart. Lady Catherine had graciously offered a carriage to carry Lizzy to Longbourn directly. "After all, the sister of my nephew's betrothed should not have to take the post."

Once she had waved farewell to Mary and Mr. Collins, she settled into the comfortable bench seat and lifted the wax that sealed the letter.

Miss Bennet,

Be not alarmed, madam, on receiving this letter, by the apprehension of its containing any repetition of those sentiments so vehemently expressed this morning—

Lizzy shrank at the formal tone of the letter, which was so unlike the dozens of other letters she had received from him when he was in Derbyshire.

The letter informed her of Anne's intentions to wed Mr. Reid, which eased Lizzy's mind considerably. After an explanation of those plans, Mr. Darcy continued.

With regards to my accusation of you being in league with Mr. Wickham, I can only offer my apologies. In my defense, such a betrayal with this very man has occurred in the past—when Mrs. Young, who came highly recommended, conspired with him to compromise my sister Georgiana. I can still remember the devastation on my dear sister's face.

There were also multiple situations during our shared childhood wherein Mr. Wickham's ease of manner and charm would convince our common acquaintances against me. My own excellent father was one of those men. I still clearly remember the anguish I felt when my father expressed his profound disappointment in me at my request that Wickham attend a different school than myself.

Here the letter continued for some paragraphs, illustrating the numerous times that the adolescent Wickham's word had been trusted over Darcy's, or how Wickham had convinced the children from the village to shun Darcy at every opportunity, which they did with great pleasure. Lizzy wept when she read how his governess told a friend that Darcy's mother had died from the boredom and disappointment of being encumbered by a son who was so the opposite of his pleasant friend.

With so many experiences of multiple people, many of whom I knew well and cared about, choosing his charm over myself, I believe my initial reaction to your statement to be natural and rational. With all my history of being repeatedly rejected in favor of one who was more engaging, it was only logical that you would prefer him to me.

You may wonder why all this was not told you last night; but I was not then master enough of myself to know for what reason I accused you of such perfidy. It was not that I truly thought you to possess a deceitful nature; rather, that idea that your lively manners would cause you to prefer another to myself was the incitement of such a reaction, based upon almost three decades of the same occurring.

I shall endeavor to find some opportunity of putting this letter in your hands in the course of the morning, through my sister, Georgiana.

Based on your words as you left the room, I completely comprehend that you will not wish to see me again. I do request, however, that you continue your friendship with Georgiana and Anne, as they are innocent of any wrongdoing other than their being related to me.

I am certain we will encounter one another from time to time, especially if your eldest sister is to become my cousin. I trust we will be able to meet as common and indifferent acquaintances.

I will only add, God bless you.

The contents of this letter threw Elizabeth into such a flutter of spirits, of which it was difficult to determine whether pleasure or pain bore the greatest share. Pleasure that Darcy had not truly thought her so fickle, yet pain at the anguish he must have experienced as a boy, particularly in his formative years. *How could any parent reject their own child in favor of another?* she wondered, her eyes filling with tears at the image of a young, solemn Fitzwilliam left alone and forgotten.

And now I have done the same, Lizzy thought. *By not taking the time to explain myself, by leaving in a fit of pique, he once again believes that he has been rejected and has therefore closed himself off from me. He said before that his good opinion once lost is lost forever. There will be no redemption from this error. I have lost the only man whom I could truly love.*

Chapter 29

The ride to Longbourn seemed endless, but at last Lizzy arrived home. She met her sister Jane with tears in her eyes, and if others interpreted the tears to be born of joy at her sister's fortunate alliance, Lizzy was content to allow them to think so.

Jane looked well; in fact, Lizzy would go so far as to say that Jane seemed to be even more beautiful than she had ever been before. It was clear in the way that she spoke about her betrothal that Jane was close to falling in love with Viscount Oakley, if she was not already.

While the girls readied themselves for bed, Lizzy revealed everything that had occurred in Kent, from her first meeting with Anne to the letter she read as she rode home to Longbourn. She wept as she described the shame and regret she felt at leaving things the way she had with Darcy, but she had seen no other way. Darcy had left before she could speak with him, as it was urgent that he deploy their plans for Anne's happiness before Lady Catherine could discover the plot. Had she chosen to await his return to Rosings, however, she would forfeit these final weeks of living with her eldest sister before Jane became a wife and mother.

"All I can hope, Jane, is that he will come to your wedding and will be willing to speak with me."

"Could you not write him a letter?"

"Where would I address it? By the time any letter could catch up with him, he will have already returned to Rosings, where the arrival of such a letter would have disastrous effects. We cannot allow Lady Catherine to know of our courtship until Anne is safely married to

Mr. Reid."

Jane looked at her sister tenderly. "Then I shall ask Oakley to write to him, confirming his attendance for the wedding. It is still four weeks away; that is plenty of time for Anne to be safely married and Lady Catherine to be safely settled in the dower house."

"It will be a long four weeks," Lizzy said miserably.

"Then I will need to keep your mind occupied with discussions of lace and ribbons for the wedding!" Jane said with a laugh.

Lizzy threw a pillow at her.

~∞~∞~∞~

Darcy breathed a great sigh of relief as the carriage arrived at Rosings. His travelling companions—Mr. Reid and Miss Amelia Johnson— looked at him curiously. "It has been a long two weeks since I was last here," he explained.

They both smiled at his words, having personally witnessed the monumental exercise Darcy had undertaken to ensure his cousin's happiness.

Darcy had made good time on his journey to London. He had been able to quickly secure the requisite legal papers and special license for the wedding, then he had immediately travelled on to Derbyshire to speak with the prospective groom.

Mr. Reid had been extremely surprised at the proposal, but he was eager to be of assistance. The young man had longed to make a difference in the world by helping others, but he had been limited in his capacity to do so as curate to a young vicar. As the master of a profitable estate, he would have great resources at his disposal to ease the plight of his fellow man.

Mr. Reid's cheerful nature had put Darcy at ease regarding his cousin's welfare for the remaining years of her life, however long that may be. Mr. Reid was not at all troubled over the fact that Miss de Bourgh may yet linger in this life for many years, as he had previously determined that he would be unable to afford a wife or children for at least a decade more. He was more than happy to raise another child as his own. His primary concern was for the welfare of those who were dependent upon the estate. His father had instilled good principles in each of his sons, and he was, in turn, determined to pass those on to another generation, whether that child was his by blood or not.

The subsequent conversation with Miss Johnson had been much more difficult. The young woman was quite timid. Prior to his meeting with Cartwright's former governess, Mrs. Reynolds relayed the brutality Miss Johnson had experienced at the hands of her former charge's father. Her compromise was assuredly not consensual, and she had been fearful of men ever since the experience. It had taken Stevens several hours to coax the young lady into the cart he had procured to take her from Cartwright's estate to Pemberley. Even then, only the kitchen maid's repeated assurances that Stevens was a good man could move the young woman from the nursery. Stevens's heart still clenched at the memory of young Master Cartwright's tears when she left.

Darcy's fists clenched tightly as he remembered the first occasion in which he met Miss Johnson and saw the bruises on her face, an ugly combination of old and fresh alike. She could barely speak in his presence, and only the gentle coaxing of Mrs. Reynolds could move her to nod in agreement when the plan was laid out to her.

Miss Johnson's injuries and timid nature had meant a delay of two days at Pemberley until the doctor determined that she was healed enough to travel without harm to herself or the babe that she carried. The decreased speed at which they had travelled—in order to avoid further injury to Miss Johnson—caused a further delay of two days. When the carriage axle broke and uncommonly heavy rains flooded the road halfway through their journey, Darcy had begun to despair that they might—as Moses' wandering people of old—reach their destination only after a protracted forty-year journey. As the party had been obliged to stay at an inn three nights longer than they anticipated—waiting for the rain to stop and the mud to dry—Darcy had wondered if they might not make better progress following the ancient Jews' example to journey on foot.

Thus, Darcy and his travelling companions arrived at Rosings an entire week later than he had anticipated. Due to all of the setbacks, Darcy had not received any correspondence during the entire journey. He eagerly anticipated meeting his sister to inquire as to how Lizzy had responded to his letter. He even held onto some small hope that he might be granted a moment to speak with Lizzy privately, though he dared not allow himself to dwell long on this minute possibility.

Darcy descended from the carriage and was met by a relieved Bingley and Georgiana. They had received the daily missives he had sent to update them on his delays, so they were not anxious over his safety. They were, however, on edge from all the secrecy and having to placate Lady Catherine over his continued absence without allowing her to become suspicious.

Mr. Reid and Miss Johnson were discreetly shown to their rooms. Darcy refreshed himself, then stealthily made his way to Anne's rooms to meet Georgiana and Bingley. Once there, he conferenced with Anne, Mrs. Jenkinson, and the Bingleys on how to ensure the wedding progressed as smoothly as possible.

At first, Anne expressed little desire to meet Mr. Reid before the ceremony, which was to be held the next day in secrecy. Mrs. Jenkinson, however, persuaded the heiress that such an introduction might ease her anxiety regarding the event. Mr. Reid was therefore summoned to the chambers immediately.

It was apparent from the moment he entered the room that the poor groom was nervous. Introductions were made, and Mr. Reid seated himself on the empty chair next to his intended. After several false starts of inelegant conversation, he and Mr. Bingley began a lengthy discussion regarding the residents near Pemberley and their current situations. The conversation never veered into gossip, which relieved Anne to no small degree, as she felt a disingenuous man would be quick to denigrate or overly praise his fellow man. Mr. Reid, however, spoke matter-of-factly about the common acquaintances he had with Mr. Bingley.

Georgiana and Mrs. Jenkinson endeavored diligently to include Anne in the conversation, and almost before the young woman recognized her own participation, the party had passed more than two hours in comfortable discourse. By the end, Anne and Mr. Reid were both wholly satisfied with the union they were soon to actualize, and they had every hope of their future comfort.

When prevailed upon to also invite Miss Johnson into the small gathering, Darcy reluctantly voiced his doubts as to the wisdom in making such a request. The young woman had, after all, been through quite a trauma and was in sore need of the rest of which she was undoubtedly partaking at that very moment.

Due to the unusual circumstances, Mr. Reid and Miss Johnson had both been placed in rooms in the family wing, but far enough removed from Lady Catherine's chambers that they might escape her notice. Knowing that Miss Johnson was near, Anne asked if she might instead go to that woman's rooms. Having secretly placed a few drops of laudanum in her ladyship's tea that morning as a precaution against Lady Catherine noticing anything amiss—a secret she would never reveal, and one which she intended to repeat that evening—Mrs. Jenkinson spoke in favor of the idea, and she and Georgiana accompanied Anne to visit Miss Johnson.

The gentlemen never did learn what occurred in that room during the hour the ladies spent there, but Bingley held his wife tightly that night as she sobbed for hours.

Though the conversation was distressing for Anne and Georgiana, it did much to soothe the fear that had tormented Miss Johnson's soul. The girls seemed to be genuine, with no falseness or malice about them. Anne promised her that she would always have a home at Rosings as the governess of the child she would bear, who would be adopted by Anne and Mr. Reid—who would become a de Bourgh upon the marriage in order to continue the family name.

At last, Anne, Mr. Reid, and Miss Johnson retired for the evening. Dinner trays were brought to their rooms, as they sought to avoid Lady Catherine's notice. In her still-drugged state, her ladyship was uncharacteristically silent at dinner. As the meal completed, she excused herself for the night and rang for a maid to bring her an early nightcap, which—thanks to Mrs. Jenkinson's modification—put her to sleep until late the next afternoon.

The moment Lady Catherine's door shut behind her ladyship, Darcy turned to Georgiana and launched an agitated inquest "How did you find Lizzy—is she well? Did you give her my letter? How has she seemed since reading it? As I can hardly appear tonight at her bedroom window, I plan to speak with her when I call on Mr. Collins tomorrow morning to present the special license and ask him to perform the ceremony."

"You have not yet arranged for him to perform the marriage?" Bingley interrupted, astonished.

"I have not, as I did not wish him to accidentally let any hint of the matter slip to Lady Catherine," Darcy explained, "Tomorrow, however, Anne will become the mistress of Rosings Park. I cannot foresee him refusing to conduct the wedding. But should he demur, the next parsonage is only a few miles away; the man there is most agreeable, if memory serves me."

He then turned back to his sister and said, "Has she mentioned the letter? Has she inquired after me at all?"

Georgiana hesitated, then said, "The day after you left, she received a letter from her sister, Jane. Oakley finally proposed, and Jane wrote to beg Lizzy's help in managing their mother while they made wedding preparations. I was only able to slip your letter into her hand as she bid her farewells. I am not certain if she even read the letter, though I cannot imagine why she would not."

Darcy deflated, "I had too much idle time during this journey, during which I thought only of her pain at my accusations and the chilling manner with which she took her leave. I owe her my sincerest apologies for misjudging her. Each misfortune that delayed my return was an agonizing torture. I despair that I have allowed too much time to elapse between the offense and the apology in which her affections may have dwindled beyond recovery."

"Do not condemn yourself so fully, old man," Bingley said. "You have each endured your own particular life's experiences that may cause you to expect the worst from others. And when your heart is engaged, it is easy to assume they will break you."

Nodding morosely, Darcy said, "There is nothing to be done for it now. I yearn to ride after her this minute, but I must remain here for several days to oversee the transition. After that, may I accompany you to Netherfield?"

"Of course!" Georgiana exclaimed. "Between Oakley's wedding and the coming baby, I expect to have you as my guest for some months longer."

"I will need to go to Pemberley for the harvest, but I should return before the start of your confinement," he assured her.

"For now, then," said Bingley, "let us first get Anne married, then Oakley. Only then may you focus on Miss Bennet! You will have several weeks between Oakley's wedding and the harvest. That should allow you plenty of time to resolve things with her."

"Do you think they can be resolved?" Darcy asked pitiably,. "I have injured her quite deeply."

"Time heals all wounds," Bingley assured him. "The two of you have strong personalities that tend toward vesuvian eruptions when your emotions are pressed. However, you have also forged an enduring friendship through the lengthy conversations—oftentimes debates— and letters you have exchanged throughout your acquaintance. I believe that to be a great deal more powerful than injuries of a moment. Your relationship with Miss Bennet can certainly be mended."

With that hopeful conclusion, the three retired to their rooms, eager to finally see Anne settled.

The morning that Mr. Reid took Miss de Bourgh's name in matrimony could not have been more perfect had it been ordered to do so. The brilliant sunrise was accompanied by the sweet scent of the morning dew and a light breeze that well complemented the surprisingly cloudless sky.

Mr. Collins was delighted to perform the ceremony. When they heard the news that Miss de Bourgh was to marry a man of the cloth who would treat her kindly, he and his wife were overjoyed. Silly though he was, Mr. Collins had not been unaware of the sorrow in the young lady's eyes, but he and Mrs. Collins had felt powerless to help. Aiding her in this small way did much to alleviate their unnecessary guilt.

Happy was the moment that Anne de Bourgh signed the register, no longer a maiden under her mother's power. Her face was alit in a smile that was brighter than any that had before graced her lips. The euphoria of the moment dimmed slightly, however, when the physical toll of even this small exertion was evidenced by her swooning as they exited the church. Her new husband caught her neatly and helped her to the carriage, conducting her back home without any further trouble.

Upon returning to Rosings, Mr. and Mrs. de Bourgh retired to their chambers immediately, so as to prevent any claims that Lady Catherine may have about the legitimacy of the marriage and its consummation. Other than the couple themselves—and perhaps Mrs. Jenkinson—no one could be certain whether the small amount of blood on the sheet were the result of a true marriage coupling or the prick of a finger. Regardless, the serenity gracing Anne's face several hours later when they came down for dinner was enough to reassure the party that no matter what had—or had not—occurred, Anne was being treated very well by her new husband.

As the newlywed couple entered the drawing room where they

were to gather before dinner, as the party did every evening, they were met by an irritable and somewhat dazed Lady Catherine, who struggled with minor withdrawal effects from the two doses of laudanum from the previous day. She blinked twice at the man alongside her daughter.

"Anne, release that man at once!" she demanded in a piercing voice.

Wincing slightly, Anne said, "Mother, please do not speak so loudly at my husband. It hurts my ears."

"Your *husband?*" The shrill voice increased in intensity and volume on the last word so significantly as to cause *everyone* in the room to wince.

"Yes, Mother," said Anne in a calm, matter-of-fact tone. "May I present to you Mr. Peter Reid de Bourgh. We were married this morning by special license in a beautiful ceremony conducted by Mr. Collins."

She sat down at the settee, smoothed her skirts, and waited for Lady Catherine's response with no more disquiet than if she were waiting for a maid to bring her some tea.

Lady Catherine gaped at her daughter. Her mouth opened several times, but no sound was forthcoming. She looked wildly around the room and fixed her eyes on Darcy, who was striving valiantly not to smile at her bewilderment. "But you are engaged to Fitzwilliam!"

"No, she is not, nor has she ever been," Darcy corrected firmly. "I was privileged to give my cousin away to Mr. Reid—excuse me, Mr. de Bourgh now—this morning."

"No! I forbid it!" declared the woman, rising to her feet with a speed that belied her advanced years, "Anne, you may *not* marry this—this—rakish fortune hunter who is clearly more suited to spending his time in the stables than in the drawing room!"

"Why would I marry him again, Mother? Did you not hear me? We were married this morning."

"Nonsense, Anne! I would certainly have known were the wedding of my own daughter to occur! You have clearly lost your senses. Darcy, send for the doctor."

When Darcy refused to move, she turned toward the door and called for the butler. Returning her attention to her daughter she said, "Even if you were married this morning, it is still the same day. If we act quickly, we can squelch any gossip and have the marriage annulled."

For the first time, Mr. Reid spoke. "I am afraid to inform you that an examination of Anne's bedsheets will reveal that option to be quite impossible."

At these words, Lady Catherine's entire countenance turned purple with rage. *"How dare you?"* she hissed, moving towards him.

The door opened and the butler entered. Lady Catherine repeated her demands for the doctor. Ignoring the irate woman, he instead looked to Anne, who shook her head and dismissed him. Lady Catherine became apoplectic, and Darcy began to wonder if perhaps the doctor would be necessary after all.

Georgiana stifled a giggle, and Lady Catherine whirled around to face her niece. *"You!* I blame you for this madness! Your arts and allurement towards a man of inferior breeding have turned my daughter into a *harlot!"*

Anne and Georgiana gasped in shock as Lady Catherine proceeded to spew such invectives at both girls as one would more like to have heard shouted by two fishwives fighting over the same man than in a noblewoman's drawing room.

"Now see here!" yelled Bingley indignantly, just as Mr. Reid stood and cried, "I *beg* your pardon!"

Moving quickly, Darcy reached his aunt before the other two gentlemen. He grasped her shoulders and began to shake her gently. "Come now, Aunt Catherine!" he pleaded. When she continued to disgorge her vile utterances, he slapped her lightly across the face.

The room fell deadly silent. In the sudden absence of such ca-
cophony, the room fairly rang with disbelief. Lady Catherine looked
at her nephew in dismay, then collapsed on the floor in a great fit of
hysterical sobs.

Darcy motioned for Bingley to ring the bell, and the butler and
housekeeper entered immediately, having been ordered by Anne to
wait outside the door for the duration of the conversation. Two footmen were quickly summoned, and the housekeeper led them as they
carried the wailing matron to her ladyship's rooms, followed by
Darcy. Another footman was dispatched to call for the doctor, while
the housekeeper and Darcy gave his aunt another dose of laudanum.
Within minutes, the woman had fallen deeply asleep in her chambers.

Darcy quickly returned to the drawing room, where he found both
of the other men comforting their respective wives. Mrs. Jenkinson
was also present, placing cool cloths on Anne's forehead. After a few
minutes, Darcy asked, "Do you think my uncle will be surprised to
learn that years ago, a malicious faerie swapped his newborn sister
with a fishwife's daughter?"

His heart sank slightly as everyone stared at him silently, then
Anne began to laugh, the sound tinged with a bit of hysteria. It was
the first time she had laughed genuinely in years, and a warmth filled
Darcy's chest to see her so.

"Oh, Darcy, thank you," she said, reaching out a hand to him.

He crossed the room and took her hand, then kissed it gently.
"What say you to eating in your rooms this evening? I can have Cook
send up a few trays."

"No," said Anne in a firm voice. "This is my wedding dinner, as
we had no traditional wedding breakfast. Cook has prepared all of my
favorite foods, and I want to celebrate."

"I shall be delighted to join you," Georgiana said determinedly,
wiping her face with Bingley's handkerchief.

The party went into the dining room and enjoyed a merry evening
of delicious foods and good wine. Cook surprised everyone with a

beautiful wedding cake that Georgiana had commissioned her to make for the occasion.

At the end of the festivities, Darcy leaned back in his chair and surveyed his sister, his cousin, and their husbands. "I want you all to know," he said huskily, "that our mother would have been very proud of *both* her girls. She looked on you as quite another daughter, Anne, and I have no doubt that she would have supported you in the choices you have made to secure your happiness."

Tears filled their eyes, and Georgiana said, "You have looked after our happiness for so long. It is time now for you to find your own."

"I will. I intend to grovel at her feet until she forgives me. I swear it."

Chapter 30

Unfortunately, the fulfillment of Darcy's promise to secure his own happiness was to be delayed more than he had hoped for. Lady Catherine continued to have fits of rage every time the laudanum wore off. Both Darcy and the doctor were concerned about continuing to dose her with such a habit-forming drug. Darcy had heard enough stories from his cousin about injured soldiers who became addicted to the drug during their recovery and could no longer survive without it. Although he was not fond of his aunt, he could not abandon her to such a fate, nor Anne to manage it alone.

After three days of Lady Catherine's fits of rage refusing to abate in between doses, Darcy wrote to his uncle, begging him to come help his sister. Shortly after sending off the letter by express, Lady Catherine suffered an apoplexy so severe that she collapsed onto the bed and was unresponsive for several hours. When she at last awoke, she was unable to move the left side of her body. Her speech was unintelligible due to the paralysis of half her mouth, and she could not rise from the bed.

This development did little to improve her mood. The doctor was once again summoned, and he determined that she had suffered a stroke of some kind. Her new condition was likely permanent. He forbade any use of laudanum until a specialist could arrive from London.

Fortuitously, both the Earl of Matlock and the London specialist arrived within the same few hours of one another. It was agreed upon by both men that Lady Catherine should be removed to the dower house, where she would be cared for by a team of specialists to assure her well-being. No expense was to be spared in her care.

Anne felt strangely relieved at having her mother removed from Rosings with so little inconvenience to herself. She experienced some guilt over those emotions, but Mrs. Jenkinson and Mr. de Bourgh repeatedly assured her that she was not an unnatural daughter for her feelings. With Lady Catherine gone from the house and with the support of her husband and her companion, everything at Rosings was resolved by the end of the week.

Darcy spent much of that week training his new cousin-by-marriage to run the estate. While Mr. de Bourgh had been trained by his father in estate management, there were some unique circumstances at Rosings that required some special attentions. With the additional efforts of the earl, after a week they felt confident in leaving Rosings to go to Netherfield.

With the Collins family to join their group, everyone except Anne and Mr. de Bourgh caravanned to Hertfordshire, just in time for the following week.

"I think I begin to finally understand your mother, Mrs. Collins," Darcy remarked partway through the journey.

"You do?" Mary asked incredulously.

"Yes. I believe I am beginning to see what she means when she refers to her 'poor nerves'. I do not think I can continue to bear the strain of waiting until I can speak with your sister!"

~∞~∞~∞~

Lizzy's nerves were in a similar state as Darcy's, though she did not yet know of his state.

"Jane, are you *certain* they will be here this afternoon?" she pressed her sister impatiently as they waited in the parlor at Netherfield, having been allowed to enter by the Bingleys' butler in their absence.

"Yes, Lizzy," Jane said, an uncharacteristic touch of annoyance present in her voice.

The girls had been planning the wedding for several weeks, and even Jane's gentle demeanor was beginning to wear thin in the face of her mother's nerves, her own nerves, and Lizzy's nerves. The two sisters had finally contrived to escape the confines of Longbourn and the hysterics of their mother under the guise of meeting the company from Rosings that was due to arrive that day.

Lizzy was torn equally between an earnest desire to see Darcy, and an irresistible compulsion to hide from him. She knew he owed her an apology, and she owed him one as well. She knew they could mend their relationship—if her harsh words had not already driven him from her forever.

She had spent the last several weeks contemplating their attachment and the snarl of events surrounding it. She knew she loved him. She knew she wanted to marry him. She had complete faith in his character as a good and honest man who believed in duty and doing the right thing.

She also now knew just how much sorrow and injury lay hidden behind the mask of stoicism with which he fortified himself. In all of his letters, in all of their conversations, she had only seen glimpses of that trauma. At first, she had been hurt that he had not confided in her when she had told him about the things in her past that had shaped herself.

After thinking on the matter, however, she realized that she could not compare the two. While she had once witnessed something truly horrible, that tragedy had not befallen her directly. Darcy's entire childhood had been filled with unending rejections from the very people who were supposed to care for him and love him during those tender years.

Was it any wonder that he could not yet shed that last mask in her company? Especially if, perhaps, he did not realize he wore it?

We people all wear masks, she reminded herself. *No one is entirely exposed, though some of us have donned more concealments than others, and many have worn some certain shields so long that they have begun to confuse the false face for their real one.*

It was something she had realized on the third week of their separation, when she had chanced to witness her father tenderly kiss her mother on the brow in a private moment. She had lived with them her entire life, yet not once had she seen the two share a moment of true affection.

I do not think I can ever fully unmask anyone, not even a husband, in an entire lifetime. But I think with Darcy, I would like to try.

After what felt like an eternity but was likely only a quarter of an hour, they heard hoofbeats sound against the drive up to the house. Lizzy leapt to her feet and rushed to the front door, Jane following behind at a more appropriate pace.

Oakley was already standing out on the drive, waiting for the carriage to come to a complete stop. He extended his arm to Jane while Lizzy stood to the side, desperately attempting to keep from bouncing anxiously on the balls of her feet. Some amount of fidgeting could be hidden beneath a gown, but Lizzy knew that, were she to allow her nerves to take command of her body, her apprehension would be apparent to all.

The coachman opened the carriage door, and Bingley was the first to exit. He turned to hand down his wife, then Lord Matlock, who was moving somewhat stiffly after a long carriage drive. Oakley moved forward to embrace his father before leading him over to Jane.

"But where is Darcy?" Lizzy blurted out as the door to the carriage was closed and it began to move toward the stables.

Georgiana laughed lightly and said, "He is in the other coach with Mary and Mr. Collins. He wanted to see you at Longbourn, so he rode with them to have the excuse of delivering them first before coming to Netherfield."

"He wanted to see me?" Lizzy asked breathlessly.

"Yes, he did," affirmed Georgiana.

Without a pause, Lizzy did the only thing she could think of. She ran.

"Lizzy!" cried Jane, but Lizzy refused to stop.

Leaving the drive and turning onto the road to Meryton, Lizzy sprinted with all the speed she could muster, then she pushed herself harder. She did not think. She did not stop. She just ran.

Abruptly, a carriage sped round the corner, and Lizzy leaped clumsily from the road to avoid being struck. She lost her balance and sprawled the dirt and greenery beside the road. The coachman pulled hard on the reins, bringing the carriage to a sudden halt. The carriage door flew open, and Darcy jumped down and raced to her.

"Elizabeth Bennet! You could have been killed, you little fool! What were you doing, running in the middle of the road like that?"

This time, as she scrambled to stand, Lizzy looked past the remonstrations and saw the intent behind them: the same love and panic and fear that she had felt when she thought he was gone forever away from her, before she read his letter and understood.

That realization drove her forward and into his arms. He took a step back, thrown slightly off-balance by the sudden weight that had crashed into him.

"Lizzy, what—?"

But whatever words he intended to say were lost, because she had lifted her lips to his, pressing a sweet, fervent kiss upon his mouth.

At first, he was unresponsive, stunned by the unexpected affection. Then his lips were pushing back on hers, his arms moving down to embrace her and pull her body against his. He tilted his head down toward hers and deepened the kiss, showing her without words the love and passion he had kept inside him for so long.

She matched her response to his, fueling his ardor. She expressed her unconditional love and complete acceptance in the intensity of her lips on his, her hands gripping the lapels on his jacket. For a moment, nothing else existed in this world apart from their two bodies, pressed tightly together, and the profound love that they shared.

A horse's whinny sounded faintly through the fog, and the couple broke apart, gasping for breath. Darcy looked around and saw the coachman looking pointedly in another direction, off into the trees. Clearing his throat, Darcy attempted to step back, but Lizzy stepped with him, her firm grasp on his lapels pulling her along.

"No," she said, her grip tightening. "You are finally here, with me, and I am not allowing you to leave again."

Darcy laughed with delighted relief. "You cannot get rid of me so easily," he told her.

She burrowed her face into his chest. "I thought I had lost you. Can you ever forgive me for the cruel words I spoke?"

"But what did you say that I did not deserve? You thought me devoid of any proper feeling, I am sure. The turn of your countenance I shall never forget, when you told me that I was the last man in the world upon whom you could ever be prevailed to marry."

"Oh, do not repeat what I said then!" she cried, her words muffled in his shirt. "I assure you that I have been long most heartily ashamed of it."

Darcy shook his head and cupped one hand beneath her chin. He raised her face until he could look reassuringly into her eyes, then, moving his hand up to stroke his thumb tenderly over her cheek, he pressed a gentle kiss to her brow. "No, dearest, I should repeat it, because it bears repeating. I almost lost you to my lack of faith, my selfish pride, my vanity."

A loud clearing of a throat interrupted the two lovers, and they looked around to see that the coachman was now standing beside the horses.

"Beggin' your pardon, Mr. Darcy, sir, but I needs to be gettin' the horses ta the stable ta rest," the servant said, his discomfort clear on his face.

"Ah, yes," Darcy said, clearing his throat.

Lizzy turned her face to hide a giggle at the man's apparent discomfort. Darcy gave her a look of mock chastisement, then directed the servant to take the carriage ahead to Netherfield without them.

"I will escort Miss Bennet to...?" he looked at Lizzy questioningly.

"Back to Netherfield," she said. "I am afraid I ran out on Jane and your sister without so much as a word of explanation. As soon as I knew you had gone to Longbourn because you wished to see me, I could not wait another moment."

The worry lines on his face smoothed away at her confession, and he gazed down at her so tenderly that her breath caught in her throat. He looked as though she had eased a great burden from his shoulders, and she wanted to kiss him all over again.

"I was afraid you would refuse to see me," he admitted, tilting his head down and pressing his forehead to hers. "I thought I could prevail upon your mother to grant me an audience if you would not allow me to beg your forgiveness."

Lizzy laughed. "You would turn my mother into a traitor?"

"If it meant a chance to be with you for the rest of my life? In a heartbeat."

Lizzy raised her face to his in response. He slid his hand around to caress the back of her neck and pulled her raised her upturned face to again meet his. This kiss, though gentle and brief, was so full of promise and love, it left Darcy every bit as perfectly breathless as their passionate embrace had minutes earlier.

"I love you," she whispered. "Most ardently."

"And I love you," he returned. Pulling back that he might look fully into her eyes, he said, "Lizzy, my feelings will not be repressed. I am desperate to never again be apart from you. I know you asked for a courtship of six months, but I cannot wait. Please, ease my suffering, and be my wife."

"Yes."

"Yes?" he asked incredulously, barely able to believe her answer.

"Yes," she repeated with a smile. "I will marry you."

Darcy pulled her back into him and swung her around. She let out a squeal of surprise, then began to laugh. He placed her back on her feet, extended his arm in invitation, and the two began to walk slowly back toward Netherfield.

As they walked, Darcy mentioned his letter. "Did it—" said he, "Did it soon make you think better of me? Did you, on reading it, give any credit to its contents?"

She explained that her anger had eased before she had even read the letter, but the megrim had prevented her from going to him prior to his departure from Rosings. The letter itself had erased any lingering hurt, replacing it with love, compassion, and understanding.

"I thought perhaps I might never see you again, given the ending," she admitted, "I could only console myself with the knowledge that I would be allowed into your presence at least once more, as you would not miss your cousin's wedding to my sister."

"When I wrote that letter," replied Darcy, "I believed myself to be perfectly calm and cool, but I am since convinced that it was written in a dreadful bitterness of spirit. I do not think I shall ever be able to dwell upon it without feeling a measure of abhorrence at my actions."

"The letter shall be burnt," she declared, "and you must learn to adopt some of my philosophy: think only of the past that gives you pleasure."

"I cannot give you credit for any philosophy of the kind. Your retrospections must be so totally void of reproach, that the contentment arising from them is not of philosophy, but rather—what is much better—of innocence. But with me, it is not so. Painful recollections will intrude, which cannot—which ought not—to be repelled. For if I do not learn from my actions of the past, how may I be certain to not repeat them?"

"You shall, for the next time you feel unsure of my love and devotion, I will not walk away or hurl hurtful words at your face. Instead, I shall remain at your side and assure you with the most animated language the violence of my affection."

"Just with language? I had hoped you would, in such a case, use your mouth for something other than words."

Darcy's response was said with such sobriety of expression that

Lizzy halted her steps toward Netherfield and stared incredulously at him for a moment. She then began to laugh as she spied the hint of a smile curling at the edge of his lips.

"Well, you shall have to wait and discover in what manner I might demonstrate my love for you after we are become husband and wife." She shot him an impish grin.

With that tease, she burst into a run toward Netherfield. Darcy remained where he was for a second, taken aback by her sudden actions, then raced after his intended. His legs were much longer than hers, so he caught up with her quickly. He grabbed her by the waist and pulled her to him, enfolding her in his arms as he brought them to a halt.

"Oh, how I love you," he whispered into her hair.

Lizzy turned into him and sighed as she burrowed into his chest. "And I love you," she said.

The two lovers remained in their embrace for several minutes, savoring the solitude. They both knew that once they reached Netherfield, they would have no time alone until after their wedding; society and propriety demanded they have a chaperone at all times.

"When shall we marry?" Lizzy asked as they slowly resumed their walk.

"Would you like to be married with Jane and Oakley?" Darcy ventured hesitantly.

"But their wedding is just a few days away!" Lizzy cried. "There is not even enough time to call the banns!"

Darcy blushed and admitted, "I may have purchased a special license for us when I was purchasing one for Anne and her husband."

Lizzy stared at him in astonishment. "Even after I said such hateful things to you, you still wished to marry me?"

"I knew before you had even quitted Anne's sitting room that I had made a terrible mistake. I had planned to return to Rosings within a week and spend the rest of my life begging you to forgive me. It was my fervent hope that you would grant that forgiveness, and I knew that, should you ever allow me to regain entrance into your affections, I would not give you any time to change your mind."

Too overcome by the ensuing emotional surge within her for speech, Lizzy simply squeezed his arm with the hand she had resting on it. They walked on in silence for a few moments, then they turned up the drive to Netherfield.

Upon entering the house, they were directed by the butler to the drawing room. They were greeted by Jane, Oakley, and the Bingleys, who were all engaged in animated discussion regarding the events that occurred at Rosings with Lady Catherine. Darcy and Lizzy's arrival interrupted the beginning of the story, and Bingley was persuaded to begin again so Lizzy could hear the narrative in its entirety.

At the end of the account, after everyone had laughed over Lady Catherine's express displeasure—except Jane, who could not help but express sympathy for the poor mother whose daughter had married against her wishes—Georgiana looked at Darcy with an expectant gaze.

"Well?" she demanded.

"Well, what?" Darcy asked with affected innocence.

Georgiana rolled her eyes and huffed, crossing her arms in a way that put Lizzy in mind of Lydia prior to her marriage and subsequent improvements.

Lizzy, taking pity on her friend, laughed and said, "We are to be married."

The room erupted into cheers and congratulations. The women all embraced, and the gentlemen shook hands and clapped Darcy on the back.

"Do you know yet when you might be married?" Jane asked with concern. "I am afraid we are taking our wedding trip to the North, and it may be some time before we are able to come back to Hertfordshire, as we must settle the boys at Matlock first. I do not wish to miss your wedding!"

Darcy looked at Lizzy questioningly.

"Well," Lizzy said, "we were hoping, if it would not be too much difficulty, to be married with you in a few days?"

The room erupted into a furor of conversation, and the group spent the next hour discussing plans and offering alternatives. Jane was adamant that she and Lizzy each deserved to have their own wedding day with their share of the attention, as well as Lizzy having time to make a proper wedding gown. Georgiana was just as insistent that Lizzy should marry posthaste, before Darcy could mess things up again. Too blissfully happy to start an argument, Darcy merely rolled his eyes at his sister's remarks.

Finally, the group came to a conclusion that would suit everyone, except perhaps Mrs. Bennet, who would never be satisfied with anything. Darcy and Lizzy exchanged happy glances—they were to be married!

Chapter 31

"A wedding in Derbyshire?" shrieked Mrs. Bennet.

"Yes, Mama," Lizzy said, trying not to wince at her mother's penetrating shrieks. "Mr. Darcy and I intend to marry from Pemberley in a month."

"Why not from Longbourn church, where all your friends can see?"

"Because, Mama, Jane has invited me to stay with her after her marriage. Without a proper wedding trip to Europe thanks to Napoleon, she would like me to accompany her as she takes over her new duties as both mistress and mother."

"Then you should wait and be married after you have seen Jane settled!" her mother pleaded. "Have you no compassion on my nerves? How can I plan a wedding that takes place so far away in the wilds of the north?"

As Mrs. Bennet continued her lamentations, Lizzy's mind began to wander. It travelled to Netherfield, where she knew that Darcy—like herself—was eagerly awaiting the passage of the morning until they could once again keep company—while properly chaperoned, of course.

Darcy had called on her father the previous evening, immediately after the party at Netherfield had come to a consensus as to the location and timing of the wedding. Her father was not surprised by the visit, as he had given his permission for the courtship some months prior. He was surprised, however, by Darcy's genial responses to being teased throughout the interview.

Lizzy had waited until the next morning to share the news of her engagement with her mother, as she had been already quite overcome by the physical and emotional exertions of the day. She had wished for her bed and knew that her mother would not allow her to sleep if she were aware that her daughter was to marry someone with such an income as Darcy's.

"Lizzy? Lizzy!"

"Yes, Mama?" a flustered Lizzy responded as she felt her thoughts ripped back to Longbourn.

"Honestly, child, were you not listening to a word I spoke? We must make immediate plans for travel to London! You should have access to all the best warehouses because your husband is as good as a lord with his ten thousand pounds per year!"

"No, Mama, there will not be time," Lizzy reiterated patiently. "Jane will marry Oakley, and I will accompany them to Matlock, where I will remain until my wedding. After that, we will join Aunt and Uncle Gardiner to tour the Lakes for our wedding trip."

Kitty interjected before her mother could begin to pout, "Mama, I have heard Colonel Fitzwilliam say that his mother purchases all of her clothes from the town nearest Matlock."

"Hmph, well, if the seamstress in Matlock is sufficiently skilled for a countess, then she will be good enough for my daughter, I suppose," Mrs. Bennet sniffed.

"And Mama, if we wait any longer, then Lydia will have already removed to Brighton with her husband and the entire militia. This way, she can travel quickly to Derbyshire for the wedding while the entire company makes the transition," Lizzy reminded her mother.

"Well, I suppose, when you put it that way," Mrs. Bennet huffed in annoyance.

Sighing in relief, Lizzy relaxed against the back of her seat and smiled at Kitty. Since Lizzy's return home, the two had spent much time together—when they weren't helping their mother plan Jane's wedding. Kitty had eagerly anticipated having more time with Lizzy before the younger sister was the only daughter left in the Bennet household. Although Kitty was disappointed her sister was marrying sooner than anticipated, Lizzy had promised that all of her sisters would invite her to visit regularly.

"With Lydia's improvements, you might even be given permission to go to Brighton with her for a time!" Lizzy exclaimed with laughter.

Kitty had laughed with her sister, but the idea had merit. Lydia was still a lively girl, but her marriage had brought a measure of maturity to her character that had not been present prior. The two youngest girls were reforming the friendship that had all but disappeared when Lydia became old enough to demand everything she wanted from her sister.

Once Mrs. Bennet had accepted Lizzy's wedding date and location, she turned her attention back to Jane's wedding. The few days leading up to those nuptials seemed to Lizzy to blur together such that each was indistinguishable from the others. She wished to spend much of this time with her new fiancé, but she knew there would be more opportunities to see him once they had all removed to the north.

The morning of Jane's wedding, the sun was veiled by a blanket of clouds, but these were sufficiently diaphanous as to allay any concerns regarding the fairness of the day. Mrs. Bennet was in raptures over Jane's beauty not being marred by rain or damp grass. Secretly, Jane felt the same relief. She was not marrying for love precisely; but if it was not love, then it was something very close to it, and she wished the wedding celebration to be a festive occasion.

After a busy morning of preparations, the occupants of Netherfield and Longbourn began to gather at the church. As the ceremony commenced, Oakley stood at the front of the church near the parson, with his brother at his side to stand up with him, as well as his young sons.

Lizzy made her way down the aisle towards them, and she spied Darcy sitting in the front row near his cousin. She took her place at the front of the hall and turned toward her intended. As he drank in her appearance, the tender love and unconditional acceptance of everything she was took her breath away. She was hardly able to wrest her attention from his gaze—and even when she did manage to do so, she found her gaze continually drifting back to meet his. She forced herself to watch her closest sister proceed down the aisle and say her vows; even so, Lizzy continued to feel the warmth that ardent stare inspired in her chest and her cheeks.

The parson's words were profound, yet brief. All too quickly, Jane and her husband had shared a kiss and were signing the register. Lizzy moved forward and signed her name as well, stating she was a witness, and gave the pen to Colonel Fitzwilliam. Once that duty was discharged, the colonel escorted Lizzy to where Kitty and Darcy now stood waiting to the side. Partners were quietly exchanged, and they exited the church to find their newly joined families.

Carriages were retrieved and the wedding guests made their way to Netherfield. Georgiana had offered to host the wedding breakfast at the larger estate in order to accommodate more guests, a plan to which Mrs. Bennet happily agreed, especially when Georgiana mentioned that she would greatly rely upon Mrs. Bennet's expertise regarding the seating and floral arrangements.

The wedding breakfast, too, appeared to Lizzy to pass as if in a dream. The guests were lively, the bride exquisitely beautiful. Jane's normally gentle smile had grown into a beam of delight and joy. All too soon, it was time to end the festivities. Plans had been made for Jane and Oakley to head immediately for Matlock, while the remainder of the family would leave the following day with Oakley's sons.

Jane and Lizzy embraced, and Lizzy—after glancing pointedly at Jane's new husband and their carriage, standing ready to convey the couple to their wedding night—gave her older sister a sly wink, causing the new bride to blush. "Lizzy," she scolded slightly, but with a smile.

They all bid the couple farewell, then returned to their homes for the night, eager to depart the next day.

~∞~∞~∞~

As they drove along, Lizzy watched for the first appearance of Pemberley Woods with some apprehension; and when at length they turned in at the lodge, her spirits were in a high flutter.

She had been at Matlock for an entire week now, helping tend to the Oakley boys and get Jane settled in as mistress. Now, with everything proceeding as precisely and as smoothly as clockwork at Matlock, it was time for her to see Pemberley, of which she would soon be mistress.

The park was very large, and contained great variety of ground. They entered at one of its lowest points and drove for some time through a beautiful wood stretching over a wide expanse.

Lizzy's mind was too full for conversation with the maid—who accompanied her for propriety's sake—but she saw and admired every remarkable spot and viewpoint. They gradually ascended for half-a-mile, and then found themselves at the top of a considerable eminence—where the wood ceased—and there it was.

Pemberley House was situated on the opposite side of a valley, into which the road with some abruptness wound. It was a large, handsome stone building, standing well up on rising ground, and backed by a ridge of high woody hills; and in front, a stream of some natural importance was swelled into greater, but without any artificial appearance. Its banks were neither formal nor falsely adorned.

Lizzy was delighted. She had never seen a place for which nature had done more, or where natural beauty had been so little counteracted by an awkward taste. At that moment she felt that to be mistress of Pemberley might be something!

I see now where some of his pride has come from, she admitted. *What it must feel like to have the care of all of this land. He takes pride in his duties, which is a much better pride than feeling himself to be above any appearance of work.*

They descended the hill, crossed the bridge, and drove to the door; and, while examining the nearer aspect of the house, butterflies began again to agitate in her stomach. This was it. She would be introduced to all she encountered here as the future mistress of the house.

The carriage door opened, and Lizzy was delighted to see Darcy there to offer a hand down. She wanted to be demure in their greeting for the benefit of the servants, but she could not help herself. Throwing herself into his arms, she whispered, "This is the most beautiful place I have ever seen."

Darcy laughed, which caused a surprised look to come across the face of an elderly woman, whom Lizzy surmised to be the housekeeper. Lizzy, the future mistress of Pemberley, was quickly introduced to Mrs. Reynolds, and they went inside. Darcy and Lizzy followed the woman into the drawing room, where Georgiana was reclined on a settee, Bingley at her side in a chair. The pregnant woman stirred as if to gain her feet, but Lizzy rushed to say, "Oh, no, Georgiana! Please do not rise on my account! After all, we are to be sisters; I must teach you how it is done, since I have had four already."

Laughing, Georgiana settled back into place. "What do you think of Pemberley?" she asked her friend.

"I was just telling Darcy it is the most beautiful home I have ever encountered. I look forward to the months—if not years—it shall take me to complete my initial exploration of the grounds!"

"Just so long as you take a footman with you," Darcy said with a serious face.

Lizzy made to protest, but he continued: "Because the grounds are so extensive, there are often poachers or wild animals in the woods that make it less safe than Hertfordshire."

Mrs. Reynolds' eyebrows raised minutely at this exchange—the idea of the master explaining himself to anyone!

Lizzy nodded and said, "I understand. Thank you for helping me to understand."

Darcy smiled, relieved, and said, "I promise to find a footman who is an excellent walker."

"That is all I require!" Lizzy said. "Or perhaps even a sturdy maid."

Darcy nodded in acquiescence, then turned to Mrs. Reynolds and said, "I believe we should give the future Mrs. Darcy a tour, should we not?"

Mrs. Reynolds agreed, eager to come to know her new mistress better.

The group spent the better part of three hours going through the house. Georgiana insisted on accompanying them, claiming she had spent the morning conserving her strength in anticipation of watching Lizzy's reactions upon first seeing each of Georgiana's favorite rooms.

The music room was—quite naturally—Georgiana's favorite room of the house. While there were several instruments about the room, such as the harp, the crowning feature was the exquisite piano that Darcy had purchased for his sister shortly after their return from Ramsgate. The gift and its repeated use had done much to soothe the girl's wounded soul.

Lizzy noticed as they toured that many of the decorations appeared to be recent additions. Georgiana explained that her husband and brother had encouraged her to replace many of the outdated furnishings that had been remnants of their mother's styling. The Bingley sisters had contributed many recommendations, Georgiana related to her friend, but those suggestions were not often followed.

At last, they reached the room Darcy most eagerly anticipated showing his betrothed: the library. Lizzy gasped as the double doors swung open to reveal a grand room that reached three stories in height. Rich wooden bookcases with exquisitely carved motifs held thousands upon thousands of books. The towering pillars that held up each case swept up to the high ceilings, where they curved into arches and formed endless loops.

Lizzy entered the room with a reverent awe, slowly turning every which way to see the magnificence surrounding her. "I do not think I shall ever leave this room," she said, prompting a satisfied smile from her husband.

"It has been the work of many generations," he told her.

He led her to a beautiful spiral staircase that wound its way up the towering bookcases, opening into balconies that wrapped around the room, providing easy access to the books without necessitating a tall ladder. She ran her fingers down the intricate carvings in the handrails.

"This is beyond anything I could have ever imagined," she whispered breathlessly.

"I am relieved you like it," he teased, "Is it tolerable enough for you?"

Lizzy laughed and gave him a quick kiss on the cheek and teasingly said, "I suppose it will do."

A hall clock began to chime, and Lizzy gave a small start. "Oh! What is the time?"

Realizing that she was somewhat overdue for her return to Matlock, the two couples made their way to the front door, with Mrs. Reynolds behind them. The elderly housekeeper, having warmed to this new mistress, personally retrieved Lizzy's wrap for her, rather than allowing the footman or maid to do so. The young woman had clearly fallen in love with Master Darcy, whom Mrs. Reynolds had loved as a son since he was four years old. Lizzy grasped the housekeeper's hands and whispered, "Thank you for your years of service. I look forward to coming to know you better."

At last, Oakley's carriage conveyed her from Pemberley towards Matlock. Along the way, she closed her eyes and envisioned the days of bliss ahead with her future husband, a beautiful estate to explore, and an incredible library with new adventures to discover.

Upon her arrival, Lizzy exited the carriage to discover Jane rushing towards her, a harried air about her. "Lizzy! I have been so worried! You were gone so long!"

"Really, Jane, I am only a few minutes later than I anticipated."

Jane threw herself into Lizzy's arms. The young woman had been followed outside by her husband, whose face was grim.

"Jane, have you been crying?" Lizzy asked in concern. She looked up, giving Oakley a hard stare. "*Why*, pray tell, is my sister so upset?"

Oakley returned her gaze steadily. "We have just received an express from Longbourn," he said grimly.

Lizzy looked at Jane in horror. "What has happened?"

"Oh Lizzy, we have just received the most dreadful news about Kitty!"

Chapter 32

Lizzy paled. "What happened to Kitty?"

"Now, dearest, it is not as bad as you are making it sound," Oakley said soothingly to Jane, calmly patting her back. He looked at Lizzy and said, "It appears as though Mr. Wickham discovered my brother's attachment to your sister. In an effort to exact revenge for what he deems his unfair treatment, he cornered her at a supper party and attempted to persuade Kitty to elope with him."

Lizzy's eyebrows knit in confusion. "Kitty would *never*—" she began.

"No, of course not," Oakley assured her. "However, after Kitty made it clear that she was uninterested, he went a bit mad. As she was walking home from Meryton the next day, he attempted to force her into a hired hack. Fortunately, a nearby tenant heard Kitty's maid crying for help. He intervened, and Mr. Wickham is dead."

Lizzy gasped in horror. "And Kitty?" she asked fearfully.

"Unharmed," Oakley said reassuringly. "And apparently now engaged to my brother."

"What?" Lizzy exclaimed in confusion.

Jane sniffed disdainfully and said, "Apparently Mrs. Long saw the beginning of the encounter and thought Kitty was willingly entering the hack with Mr. Wickham. She immediately went to Meryton to spread the tale of their elopement."

"Well, that is one way to get revenge for Lydia's marriage to Colonel Forster," Lizzy said grimly.

"Fortunately, Colonel Fitzwilliam heard the story almost immediately and swiftly shut it down, claiming it to be impossible because

Kitty was engaged to him," Oakley said soberly.

Lizzy bit her lip and sighed. "While I am grateful to your brother for his honorable behavior, I am disappointed that Kitty is being forced into a marriage."

Jane shook her head. "Apparently Kitty had been planning to go to Brighton with Lydia in order to stay closer to the Colonel. She truly likes him, Lizzy."

"I know she does, Jane. I simply wish the choice had not been forced upon her."

"Be assured that my brother will take good care of your sister and treat her respectfully, or he will answer to me," Oakley promised.

"Oh, I am not concerned about that!" Lizzy said, embarrassed her words had been taken in such a way. "I simply mean that it is difficult as women to have so few choices in life. I simply wish Kitty would have had the liberty to accept an offer of marriage herself and not have it thrust upon her."

Oakley nodded and replied, "I believe my brother was planning to return to Meryton after the regiment's summer in Brighton in order to ask your sister to marry him. He was planning on asking for permission to court her while they were at the seaside."

Lizzy smiled at him gratefully. "I must admit, that does alleviate my mind somewhat."

"Poor Kitty!" Jane said sadly. "To have experienced something to dreadful by such a wicked man. Perhaps there was some kind of misunderstanding?"

Lizzy began to laugh. "No, Jane, I am afraid that for all your goodness, you will never be able to find any in Mr. Wickham. I, for one, am glad he is dead, as it is clear he would never cease his vendetta against Darcy and his loved ones."

Jane looked at her sister in mild shock, but Oakley nodded his head approvingly. "I plan to send a solicitor to Meryton in order to represent the farmer on the chance that the death is called into question. With as few friends as Wickham had, however, and so much evidence of his prior evils, I highly doubt anyone will raise a fuss."

"That is very good of you, husband," Jane said, finally leaving Lizzy's arms and giving Oakley a kiss on his cheek.

"I have your example to guide me," he said, smiling down at her.

Lizzy blushed, abashed to be intruding on such a private moment. The corners of her lips twitched upward at the empathy she suddenly felt Darcy's coachman. She cleared her throat and asked, "Shall we all go inside? Jane, I do believe we have some fashion plates to look at!"

At this interruption, Jane turned her attention back to her sister, ushering her inside the home and into the mistress's private sitting room. Soon, the terror that had been instilled in Jane by the express was washed away with the joy of helping select items for her sister's wedding trousseau.

The following weeks leading up to Darcy and Lizzy's wedding were filled with visits between Pemberley and Matlock. The days passed agonizingly slowly for Darcy, but to Lizzy, it seemed as though there would never be enough time to complete everything she needed to accomplish prior to the happy event. Between visits to the modiste, meetings with Georgiana about Pemberley, and supporting Jane in her new role, Lizzy had little time for her betrothed.

The day before the wedding finally arrived. Mr. and Mrs. Bennet had come to Matlock, bringing with them Kitty and Colonel Fitzwilliam. The newly engaged couple had plans to wed at the end of the summer when he retired from his duties.

Lydia and Mary also attended, bringing along their respective husbands. Lizzy was once again awestruck at the improvements in her youngest sister's behavior. Her liveliness was still undeniably present, but she no longer contrived to make herself the focus of attention at every gathering. She even spoke of having made over her dress for the wedding instead of purchasing a new one!

Mr. Collins, too, was much improved. He still tended toward obsequious humility, but he had become adept at curbing his exuberances after one or two sentences, as opposed to waxing so verbose as he had in the past. He brought along the regrets of Mr. and Mrs. de Bourgh, but as Mrs. de Bourgh was now in the family way, the doctor had insisted she remain at rest in the family wing, with only Mrs. Jenkinson and Miss Johnson to attend her, along with Mrs. Collins from time to time.

"It is most fortunate that she was able to fall with child so quickly into her marriage!" he declared. "What a wonderful olive branch to offer her mother, who has been interminably disconsolate at being relegated to solitude in the dower house."

Mary merely lifted an eyebrow at this statement, giving Lizzy a conspiratorial smile.

As they all gathered together in the large dining room at Matlock, Lizzy looked about the space at her beloved family. It had grown so much over the prior year, and the new additions had grown just as dear to her as her own sisters.

After dining, they did not participate in the typical separating of the sexes. Instead, they all migrated as one to the large parlor, where they spoke until late into the night. Finally, Mrs. Bennet declared that Lizzy must get to bed, "Else she will wake with such bags under her eyes that Mr. Darcy will refuse to marry her!"

Everyone laughed at that statement, especially Darcy, who kissed Lizzy on the head and declared that he would marry her no matter what. Even so, the Pemberley group returned to their home, and the guests and residents of Matlock retired to their beds.

Sleep was not to visit the bride-to-be erelong, however. Lizzy's four sisters crowded into her bedroom with her, the way they had when they were younger. The girls, now women, were determined to make the most of their time together. "After all," Lydia declared, "Only the Lord knows how long it will be before we are again able to visit together all at the same time!"

Lydia then proceeded to give Lizzy advice for her wedding night, which set the rest of the room to blushing fiercely. When pressed, however, Jane and Mary admitted that much of what Lydia said was accurate. "And do not believe a word Mama has said on the subject!" Lydia declared in conclusion.

Finally, just as the sun began to make its appearance over the Peaks in the distance, the five sisters fell asleep together, arms and legs a jumbled mess atop Lizzy's bed. The maid who entered some hours later to stoke the fire smiled at the sight of such obvious sisterly love.

Mrs. Bennet came in shortly after to wake the girls, clucking and fussing over the state of Lizzy's hair and the scarceness of lace on her wedding gown. "If only I had taken you to London! You would never have had to settle for such plain dress," she lamented.

Lizzy merely smiled placidly at her mother, unwilling to provoke the squall Mrs. Bennet would certainly unleash, should she reveal that it was Lizzy herself who designed every part of the dress. Lizzy was particularly fond of the delicate touches of lace that accentuated— rather than overwhelmed—the elegant design.

At last, Mrs. Bennet proclaimed Lizzy to be ready. She ushered the other girls out, then spent a few minutes giving Lizzy a lecture of her duties for that night. Lizzy smothered a nervous giggle and nodded her head in the right places, all the while thinking of what Lydia had said was the most important advice point: "If you like when he kisses you, then just let the kisses take you where you need to go. It is clear he adores you, Lizzy, so he will be kind."

Since Jane and Mary had both fervently corroborated this assertion, Lizzy felt it was safe to trust Lydia over their mother in this instance.

Lizzy's attention was pulled back to the present when her mother patted her cheek and said, "You are a good girl, Lizzy. You have made a far more splendid match than I dared hope."

With that backwards compliment, Mrs. Bennet's eyes filled with tears, and she motioned for Lizzy to leave the room.

Lizzy descended the staircase to where her father waited to escort her to the church near Pemberley. The rest of the family entered their carriages, while her father held her back a moment. He looked at his favorite daughter and said gruffly, "Do not think that I do not know everything you have done for your sisters over the years."

Lizzy looked at him in surprise, and he waved his finger at her. "I may be indolent, but I am not a fool. You have done what I did not: you have taken care of your sisters, even helping them to find relationships in which they enjoy mutual respect with their husbands. And now you are to marry a man who can match your intellect and passion, who loves you, and you love him. I could not have parted with you, my Lizzy, to anyone less worthy."

She blinked back tears as his voice choked on the last words. She gave her father a hug and said, "My home will always be open to you, Papa. Thank you for the freedom you gave me with my sisters and for supporting my education."

Father and daughter climbed into the carriage, and off they went to the church. Darcy looked relieved as she entered the building and walked with her father down the aisle to him. Their gazes held through the entire ceremony, not even breaking contact when Mrs. Bennet emitted a heaving sob before her husband put his arm comfortingly around her.

The vows were spoken, rings were exchanged, the communion was taken, and the clergyman recited the scriptures he had chosen for the occasion. Darcy would never be able to remember what the clergyman actually read; all he could see was the beauty of the woman before him, who was giving her name and herself into his keeping. It was the utmost sign of devotion that she could give him, and he knew he was secure in her love.

For her part, Lizzy could recite every word that was uttered; it had been written indelibly in her memory, along with every reaction and emotion that she could read in Darcy's eyes. For those moments, all of the masks were peeled away, and she could see nothing but love, devotion, and acceptance displayed behind them. Whatever may come, whatever they would face, they would face it together as one unit, each utterly dedicated to their partner.

Cheers rang out as Mr. and Mrs. Darcy exited the chapel after signing the register. Darcy's smile was so wide, he thought his face might break open, but he found himself unable to care. Lizzy laughed for joy. As they settled into the carriage to take them to Pemberley— now *their* home—they gripped one another's hands tightly.

The wedding breakfast was all Mrs. Bennet could have dreamed: serving exotic delicacies in the finest ballroom in Derbyshire. The room was filled with gaiety and merrymaking in celebration of the fervent love of the couple.

Eventually, the partygoers bid their farewells. With the exception of the Bingleys, everyone made their way to Matlock House. Georgiana had attempted to remove themselves as well so Mr. and Mrs. Darcy could have their privacy, but Darcy insisted she remain in her childhood home for the sake of her baby. Bingley finally acquiesced on his wife's behalf, and the two of them disappeared into their rooms posthaste, Georgiana claiming fatigue due to engaging in all the festivities while in her condition.

Lizzy and Darcy were alone at last, and they advanced slowly up the stairs of their home, hands clasped and eyes locked. They had been waiting for this moment—to be together without chaperones or in company—since she had run to him from Netherfield on that day when they shared their first kiss. They stood outside the door to their rooms, staring intently at one another, hardly daring to believe that this was real.

Darcy looked earnestly down at his wife, wondering how he could bear to part from her while they readied for bed. Lizzy looked back up at him, chewing on her lower lip uncertainly. Then her eyes brightened, and she declared, "Well, husband, I did promise to show you how much I ardently love you after we were married. You shall have to wait only one further half an hour to find out!"

She stood on tiptoe, pressed her lips briefly to his, then dashed into her rooms, closing the door behind her.

Darcy stood somewhat stunned, then a grin spread across his face. He turned and went into his rooms, calling for his valet.

Lizzy heard those calls and smiled to herself. She had been so nervous until she recalled Lydia's advice: think only of how she felt when he kissed her. That had brought to mind the memory of their day together the last time they were alone, and she knew exactly how to ease her insecurity.

Looking around her new room, Lizzy admired the beautiful wall coverings and soft rugs. It had clearly been decorated tastefully. Although of an older style, the furnishings were in excellent shape. Her lady's maid soon entered from the dressing room and said, "Mrs. Darcy, your bath is ready for you."

Lizzy allowed herself a few luxurious minutes of soaking in the scented water before leaving the tub. She had been gifted several beautiful dressing gowns from Jane as part of her trousseau, and she was eager to see herself in one of them. The maid deftly dressed her in one, then Lizzy dismissed her for the night.

Observing herself in the full-length mirror, Lizzy let out a soft gasp. The nightgown was a deep plum color made entirely of a fine, delicate lace that rendered the garment translucent. The dressing gown layered over it was of the same diaphanous material in a slightly lighter shade. The combined effect of the two colors complemented her features in ways that none of the pale colors of a debutante could.

When she heard the door open behind her, Lizzy turned to face Darcy as he entered the room. His breath caught as he saw his new wife dressed in such a way that he had only dared imagine in his dreams. He slowly crossed the room to her, and reverently lifted a hand to gently stroke her cheek.

"You are so beautiful," he whispered as he brushed his hand deliberately down the curve of her neck to caress her shoulder.

Lizzy's eyes, full of love and promise, looked into his. At that moment, every mask each had worn in their lives fell away. The remainder of the night was spent baring themselves to one another, exposing their bodies and souls in ways they had never done before. Their love transcended time and space, and they became one in mind, body, and soul. The bed formed a mask of its own out of the drapes that hung around it, protecting their sacred union from the intrusion of the world.

The next morning, as the sun rose over the Derbyshire hills, Lizzy looked at her sleeping husband. *Thank you, God, for helping me see behind his mask.*

She then snuggled into him, certain of their future and the enduring love between them.

Epilogue

The reader may be glad to learn that all turned out happily ever after for the new Mr. and Mrs. Darcy. This does not mean they did not have disagreements or misunderstandings. In fact, it was quite the opposite: there were many occasions during which Darcy retreated behind his mask or Lizzy took offense at a poorly worded statement.

It was happy, however, because—in spite of those spats—they never again doubted the love the other person held for them. They returned to one another again and again, reconciling and forgiving, their love growing stronger each time.

Lizzy birthed five children over the years: three sons followed by two daughters. The eldest son inherited Pemberley, while the remaining sons followed in the footsteps of their uncles—one in the army and the other in the church. The example that all five children learned from their parents led them to search behind the masks of those they encountered. Each of the five eventually made a successful love match.

Jane and Oakley settled at Matlock. A few years after their marriage, Lord Matlock passed away, and Oakley became the new earl. Their marriage brought a daughter and a son into the world, in addition to the sons from Oakley's first marriage. Although theirs was not a marriage rooted in love initially, the bond they formed grew to be stronger than most love matches could hope to attain.

Mary and Mr. Collins spent ten years at the Hunsford parsonage before Mr. Bennet fell ill and called them to his bedside. In that decade, Mary gave birth to two sons and a daughter, much to Mrs. Bennet's relief. After Mr. Bennet passed and Mary became the Mistress of Long-bourn, Mrs. Bennet decided to spend her remaining years in the house of her sister, Mrs. Phillips, whose husband had passed away the year prior. The two women could often be seen out on visits, boasting of the excellent matches that Mrs. Bennet's daughters had achieved. Mr. Collins, as master of Longbourn, became a fair landlord, and his wife's dedication to the management of the estate increased its income significantly. Mr. Collins maintained throughout their entire marriage that the most intelligent thing he ever did was listen to his wife's opinions on all matters. Mary only ever smiled at this, pointedly abstaining from any denial.

It was with some relief to the tenants that Mr. de Bourgh replaced Mr. Collins at Hunsford. Although Mr. Collins was a good man, not vicious or cruel, he was unable to provide a strong support for the parish. There had been many changes at Rosings in that decade—most notably the death of Lady Catherine one month before the birth of her grandson—with Mr. Collins only capable of providing middling guidance and care to his flock through such events.

Miss Johnson gave birth to a beautiful boy, who was named Jonathon—ostensibly in honor of one of Anne's grandfathers. Anne and Mr. de Bourgh raised Johnny until he was four years old, at which time Anne passed away, having suffered from what would later be determined to have been anemia and fibromyalgia.

Anne's passing was rapidly followed by astounding news from Derbyshire. Mr. Cartwright had gambled away his entire fortune and had been caught in an attempt to seduce the daughter of one of his creditors. As this creditor was particularly unsavory, Mr. Cartwright's overtures led to the loss of his life. His son was rendered an orphan and was to be sent to the nearest poorhouse. Darcy, upon learning the news, sent an express to Mr. de Bourgh. Young Master Cartwright was biologically Johnny's half-brother, after all. Miss Johnson expressed such a strong desire to see the boy she had raised as his caretaker some years earlier, and Mr. de Bourgh was inclined to agree.

Within three years of the young boy joining the family Rosings, the similarities between the boys had become so apparent that the servants nearly forgot they had not been born of the same mother. The servants were further delighted when Mr. de Bourgh and Miss Johnson—having grown very fond of one another's company in their time together at Rosings—were married. Anne was frequently spoken of in a cherished manner, that Johnny would never forget who had provided him the life he so enjoyed.

Kitty and Colonel Fitzwilliam were indeed married, and no one even remembered that theirs was a forced engagement. The couple were deeply in love, but due to Kitty's somewhat weakened health from her childhood encounter with influenza, she was able to give birth to one child. Their daughter was the apple of their eye, so it was fortunate she took after her Aunt Jane in sweetness of disposition, or else she would have been quite the spoiled child.

Lydia and Colonel Forster never did have any children. At first, Lydia did not mind, as she was enjoying the freedoms of being the wife to a military man and following the drum. When Colonel Forster was killed in battle, Lydia chose to return to Hertfordshire and live with her parents. She could not settle down, however, and eventually moved between the houses of her sisters, helping her nieces with their needlework and telling her nephews stories of the battles she had seen. She often joked that she had no need of children of her own, for she was content to have let her sisters do all the work for her. In the end, she passed away from an ailment of some kind that she had contracted overseas but that had lain dormant for several years. Her death was mourned by many.

Bingley and Georgiana eventually purchased Netherfield. They spent half of their time there, and the other half of their time at Pemberley, which was just as much a home to them as their own. In turn, Netherfield's doors were permanently open to the members of the Bennet family who lived in the north, and they resided there when they visited their mother and their sister Mary at least once per year.

Miss Stewart, Georgiana's kind friend in Ramsgate, never married. She enjoyed her freedom and adventures too much to do so. Instead, she sailed for Canada to seek out new adventures. She would occasionally send a letter to Georgiana, who always responded immediately.

Lizzy remained grateful every single day for Becky, whom she never saw again. She often wondered what happened to her, even going so far as to hire an investigator toward the end of her life. He soon returned with the report that Becky had given birth to only one baby, which did not survive. Becky herself was soon married to a tenant farmer and cared for his three motherless children. By all accounts, the farmer was very kind to her, and she eventually died peacefully in comfort and security.

Lizzy and Darcy lived blissfully together until their fortieth wedding anniversary. Lizzy fell ill with a bad cold after being caught in the rain, and she succumbed quickly to pneumonia. Their children would often say that after losing their mother, their father seemed to have lost the will to live. He became less active, turning the estate over to his eldest son, and was content to watch his grandchildren play and tell them stories of their grandmother as he faded away. One morning, he simply did not awake, having finally succumbed to his pervasive mournfulness. He was laid to rest at the side of his beloved Elizabeth, to whom he would be forever grateful for taking the time to look behind his many masks.

THANK YOU

Thank you for reading A LOOK BEHIND THE MASK, a Jane Austen variation by Tiffany Thomas.

Join Tiffany's mailing list to learn about upcoming releases, deals, and more on her website.

www.authortiffanythomas.com

Made in the USA
Columbia, SC
16 February 2022